SCANDALOUS
LIES

Also by Nigel May:

ADDICTED

TRINITY

SCANDALOUS
LIES

Nigel May

Bookouture

Published by Bookouture

An imprint of StoryFire Ltd.
23 Sussex Road, Ickenham, UB10 8PN
United Kingdom

www.bookouture.com
Copyright © Nigel May 2015

Nigel May has asserted his right to be identified
as the author of this work.

ISBN: 978-1-910751-26-8
EBOOK ISBN: 978-1-910751-25-1

ACKNOWLEDGMENTS

All of my scandalous love to a whole host of people. My lifetime of love to the super-special Louise Porte - not only a fantastic person and best friend but also the fastest speed reader I know. To Georgina Burnett for the stormy behind the scenes weather report. Sleaze and scandal to Martin Boucher for your great taste and undying support and to Matt Keyte for every single RT. Huge thanks to Jo Foster and Clair Perkins for telling me what's what week in week out. To Leann Chivers "Mrs T" for scandal-dipped nights out. Peace, love and words of kindness to Devon Buchanon. Maestro Wayne Brookes – wow! - a million diamond-dipped thank you's as ever. Synchronised thanks to the wondrous dancefloor inspiration from the amazing Heather Parsons and Ian Waite. Shamrock-shaped kisses to Genevieve Ni Reamoinn and Peter Vollebregt for the hugs and hysterics. Scandal, so it is! To the "Vodka Corner" girls – you know who you are! To Victoria Fox for scandalous delights between the sheets and to Carly Cook for demon edits and sharing the salacious shoulder-padded love.

An explosion of gratitude to my new family at Bookouture. You have made me a very happy, grateful, gleeful author. To the legendary Oliver Rhodes, Claire Bord (Viva la bonk!) and the dynamic Kim Nash for welcoming me to the fold and to my fellow Bookouture authors and the fabulous bloggers for letting a new boy crash the party.

Eternal love to Alan "…Sir!" Roberts for listening to endless hours of ideas for my glamorous, scandal-laden plotlines when he'd doubtless rather be watching Food Network or playing with the furry boys.

To BGA, with love

PROLOGUE
Hell's Canyon, California

Daytime

The heat was intense: the sun still burning lava-bright in a one-colour tapestry of the purest idyllic blue despite the late hour of the afternoon; clouds non-existent as a monotonous heat continued to blur the lines where horizon introduced itself to sky. The ground, shouting a natural desire to be quenched by the waters of the heavily depleted river nearby had its request left unanswered as its skin began to crack, an aging process no imminent meteorological surgery was likely to repair. Shriveled plants, those that had survived the brutal heat of one of the fiercest summers on record so far, were only moments from oblivion, a death that would be a welcome one to their moisture-searching veins. Any furry inhabitant that had once scurried across the canyon floor was either long gone in a hunt for food, or showed the idiocy of their tardiness by now remaining as no more than a skeleton. Mother Nature was a bitch and despite the beauty of the canyon and the surrounding area for most of the year, at that precise moment the globe of raging white embellished above the canyon was a dangerous one. A lethal one. Nothing could survive.

Unless, of course, you were currently opening the heavy, curved door of a floor to ceiling fridge freezer combo within the confines of your air-conditioned RV and reaching for a chilled bottle of Moët & Chandon Bi Cuvée Dry Imperial, one of six housed within the confines of the chiller. At a cost of nearly a grand each these were diamond-dipped bubbles, fizz that could extinguish even the most barbarous sunshine. In that case, then survival was easy.

'A sneaky peek to put you in the mood?' asked Foster Hampton, pushing his blonde surfer-dude curls – pure Bondi Beach even though it was British blood that ran through his veins – away from his eye line as he reached for the bottle. The whirl of chilled air from within the fridge enveloped his naked skin as he stood, bottle in hand and faced his lover, lying on the double bed on the other side of the road vehicle.

'You should turn back around and show me that peachy backside of yours again. I was enjoying the view from over here,' answered Mitzi Bidgood. 'It's something I will never tire of. It should be added to every British female tourist's itinerary for a road trip across America. Mount Rushmore, Dollywood, Golden Gate Bridge and Foster Hampton's bubble butt. A pink, glowing spectacle of an ass. A wicked wonder of the world. The tourist board could make a fortune in ticket sales. Not that I'm keen to share it with any passing Yank though, to be honest. That rump is mine, all mine. The view from this angle is totally appetising,' remarked Mitzi, pointing towards the sizable pendulum of meat currently rising to attention between Foster's legs. 'And what, to answer your question, makes you think for one orgasmic moment that I am not already in the mood?'

Foster smiled as Mitzi spread her naked legs and dipped the finger she'd been pointing at his cock into the fleshy, wet folds of her pussy. The weapon between Foster's legs rose to its full length, blood flooding through it with anticipatory desire.

'Now, pop that cork, pour me something beautiful and bring that body of yours into this bed right away. Mitzi needs some loving after that long drive today. I assume we have all night?'

'We are going nowhere until dawn,' Foster replied as he poured the champagne, a flow of frothy bubbles rising to the rim and cascading down the body and stem of the glass and onto the tiles below his feet. 'I did not drive the entire length of this canyon in this monstrosity to just turn around and head back out again. There aren't many cars that can make it this far, so we might as well make the most of our surroundings and the fact that we're the only ones around for miles. Not that I'm going out in this heat. The dashboard thermometer says it's about 113 degrees Fahrenheit. That's way too hot, even for a beach-loving boy like me.'

It was true, the road they had taken to reach the secluded spot at the far end of the canyon was impassible by most vehicles. It was only top of the range RVs like the one Foster and his girlfriend of three years, Mitzi, had hired for their month-long USA vacation that were able to cope. The camper was outwardly perfectly equipped to deal with even the rockiest of terrains and its lavish interior was equally custom built for sheer luxury while travelling with its satellite system, surround sound, DVD player, huge TV and wireless internet. On the few occasions they had used the internet during the previous three weeks of their journey it had only been to check emails from their lives back home in the UK. As a professional dancer on one of her home country's top TV shows, Mitzi needed to find out what the next season of the hot show held for her when she returned in just over a week's time. The rumour mill was circling with the notion that Mitzi's celebrity partner for the next six months would be a fellow reality TV star from *Surf N Turf*, the same show which had seen Foster rise to fame four years ago. The show, about a group of Cornish surfers who also ran their own landscape gardening business, had been a huge hit and Foster had been the breakout star, securing a spot as Mitzi's dancing partner after only one season on *Surf*. Viewers loved his relationship with Mitzi, which quickly spilled from the ballroom into the bedroom. Their Barbie and Ken blonde perfection meant that when the two of them lifted the glitter ball trophy aloft at the end of the series, the offers came flooding in for them both. Sponsorship deals, lucrative cruise tours to showcase their dancing prowess and a massive pay increase for Mitzi to stay on the show, saw both their kudos and their bank balances snowball. Foster's latest project, a documentary in which he would put his gardening skills to the test to turn a downtrodden Cornish council estate into a thriving oasis of green shrubbery and happiness, was due to commence on his return to Britain.

But for now, all that was on the cards for the next few hours was a nerve-tingling, gymnastic symphony of love-making, something their sporty, supple dancer's bodies allowed them to indulge in as often as possible and in positions most sexual partners could only dream of.

'I'll show you what's hot,' moaned Mitzi deliriously as she moved her finger faster, her body arching with pleasure as crests of desire snapped through her inner core, spreading from the heat between her legs. 'Shift that six-pack of yours over here now and ride me like a Texas rodeo athlete.'

Foster didn't need asking twice. Moving to the bed, he poured the rest of his own glass of champagne into his mouth and handed the other to Mitzi. As she placed the glass to her lips, Foster pushed his face deep into the open layers of joy between her legs. The feel of her wetness thrilled him, encouraging him deeper. It was only once his mouth was completely enveloped by the flower of her pussy that he allowed his lips to open and the icy champagne to flow from his mouth into the sexual cavity of her vagina, swirling around his tongue and Mitzi's finger as it did so. She let out a squeal of joy and dropped her now virtually empty glass onto the sheets alongside her. The remaining droplets of champagne dribbled onto the material underneath her body.

Foster looped his tongue around Mitzi's finger and felt an increase in the ferocity of her excitement as she moved it faster and more pressingly inside her. The fusion of the sweet champagne and her own natural womanly flavour washed across Foster's tongue as her finger rubbed against his taste buds. Mitzi's breathing became more urgent. Beads of sweat formed on her forehead and she felt them run down her face and weave down between her round, cherry-peaked breasts. Only Foster could turn her on so quickly, his love-making as pleasing now as it had been when they had first given in to temptation years before. If there was another skill that Foster could add to the many that he already possessed, it was his cunnilingual technique. She wriggled with pleasure as his tongue seemed to reach places that her finger could not.

She felt the three-day old stubble on his chin graze over her tender flesh and a hunger gnawed within her. It was a hunger that only one action could assuage. She let out a whimper, a gasp as the roughness of his feasting centred on her clitoris and reached her hands down to move his head away.

A smiling Foster looked up at her from between her legs, his face shiny with sweat and Mitzi's juices.

'Why don't you fuck me,' she stated. It wasn't a question.

Foster flicked his tongue along the thin line of hair decorating her pussy, circled it around her belly button and feather-kissed his way up to her breasts, taking her to the edge of bliss. He maneuvered himself into position and, as he bit down onto one of Mitzi's erect nipples, allowed his erection to plough into her. Firm, long and proud, his dexterous crescent of flesh caused her to bite down of her bottom lip as he thrust into her.

She could feel her euphoria rising. No lover had ever made her feel like Foster. There had been many, but he was unique.

A scream escaped her lips but volume control was unnecessary. Who would hear her? Only the man causing her to ride the waves of joy in the same skilled way he rode those on the ocean. She was ecstatic for him to hear her appreciation. But no more words came as she pressed her mouth onto his and kissed him deeply. A knowing look from deep within his eyes, one of trust and shared love, told her what was to follow. Mitzi's eyes blurred, her vision smudging as she felt him unleash his liquid into her and her own orgasm climb to its perfect peak. She wrapped her arms tightly around him, attempting to coax him even deeper. He kept his cock, still semi-stiff in his post denouement delirium, inside her. Foster and Mitzi were still in the same position, united in their love, half an hour later.

Nighttime

'This has been the best holiday ever, Foster. Both sexually and otherwise,' giggled Mitzi, somewhat tipsy from the third glass of champagne she'd drunk, accompanying the Caesar salad Foster had prepared her for dinner. 'I mean it. The places we've seen have been amazing and it's wonderful to just spend so much time together without cameras and press interviews and people screaming for autographs. Just to be you and me, us, together. Doing whatever we want, whenever we want. I have loved it so much, and I love you so much.'

'I'll have to make you drink champagne more often,' said Foster, 'if it makes you this mushy. You weren't such a softie when you were barking dance moves at me when we first met, were you? Are you becoming softer with age?' He winked playfully.

'You were my professional partner then and I was doing my job. Now my job is to let you know how much I love you. Do we have to go back home?'

'Not for another week or so, there are plenty of adventures to come yet. It's not over till the gorgeous lady starts dancing, and that's not until we reach UK shores again.'

'Actually, I was thinking of putting on a bit of a show for you now. I love this song!' said Mitzi, rising to her feet from their table outside their RV. It was late evening and the air was finally cool enough to be outside, where they had eaten. The sky had moved from blue to almost black, only a moon and a dotting of stars illuminating the air. She ran inside the camper van, and moved to the sound system which had been playing some of their favourite tunes all evening. It was Beyoncé's 'Drunk in Love' that had just started. Turning up the volume, Mitzi sashayed back to the doorway of the camper van and let her body sway seductively to the beat. Silhouetted by the light coming from behind her in the RV, her actions were a perfect mix of flirty and dirty. The beat of the song throbbed as she moved, her timing perfect.

Just as Foster could feel his cock rising to attention again in his sweatpants, a sudden flash of light further across the canyon startled him away from Mitzi's gyrating. Staring out into the darkness he could see a flicker of bright orange. What was it?

'Stop the music will you, Mitz. What is that over there?'

Mitzi paused the music and silence fell around them. Joining Foster, Mitzi too gazed out into the night.

'It's a fire?' There was questioning in her tone, but there was no doubt.

'But I didn't know there was anybody else out here,' said Foster. 'Maybe the sun started it earlier. We should take a look. It could be blocking the road out of here. And you never know, it may have been some dirty old men watching us through the RV windows earlier. We put on quite a show.' The thought didn't displease Mitzi, she was a showgirl after all. And their afternoon sex session had certainly been a spectacle to behold.

Foster was sure that he could hear something in the air. The sound of music. Was the champagne playing tricks on him? He didn't think so.

'Shall we go take a look?' he asked.

'Why not?' giggled Mitzi, 'maybe it's another hot young couple out here just like us. And maybe they're just as adventurous as us ... and just as horny.' She gave Foster's ass a playful squeeze as they ventured off towards the bright orange glow.

The sky was pitch black yet the air seemed clear as they stumbled, a little giddy on bubbles, in the direction of the light. Mitzi kept losing her balance slightly on the pebbles and loose rocks beneath her feet. Foster took her hand to steady her. 'We can't have you twisting an ankle before dance season, can we?'

Mitzi found the whole situation borderline erotic. She and the man she loved, miles from anywhere, in the pitch blackness of the Californian wilderness. Alone and wild.

Except they weren't alone.

Narrowing their eyes to try and scan the glow, the couple blinked until the crackle of orange came into focus. What they saw made Foster gasp. If Mitzi's gasp earlier during their love-making had been one of total rapture, Foster's was the complete antithesis.

'What the fuck …?' His words petered out.

'What is it, Foster, what's going on?' It didn't look like they were going to run into an amorous couple interested in a bit of fireside alfresco shagging. As she focused, a chill ran through Mitzi's body and she let out a slight shiver.

'Holy shit.'

Dancing around the fire, which they had obviously built themselves, to a heavy tribal musical beat, were a series of figures. They were all dressed in head to toe outfits obscuring their faces. They wore heavy robes, maybe made of hessian, almost monk-like in appearance, topped with wide hoods. There must have been about six of them. As the flames flickered higher, one of the figures stripped off the hood and untied the robe, allowing it to fall to the floor. It revealed a naked woman, Mitzi guessed about the same age as her, mid-twenties. She possessed full, round breasts and a small dark triangle of hair between her legs.

'What the fuck is going on?' Mitzi whispered, reconsidering the alfresco sex theory. Maybe they were just about to witness some kind of outdoor dogging scene with a difference. Mitzi always thought dogging was a load of dirty old men whacking off in a lorry park with some rough old housewife. Maybe the Yanks did it with glamour and lit by a naked flame.

The sound of the beat became louder and more frantic in the air. Foster and Mitzi could see that the other figures surrounding the young woman had stopped, but all bar one of them remained with their hoods in place. The one who revealed his face was a man of about fifty with what looked like a head of salt and pepper hair. It was hard to discern his features exactly as the flickering of the firelight distorted the air.

From one of the sleeves of his robe he pulled out a long, wide-bladed knife. The blade caught the firelight and reflected shards of colour shot into the air.

All of the other figures around the fire held their hands aloft. The music stopped almost instantly. Silence filled the air. 'What's happening, Foster? This is beginning to freak me out,' stammered Mitzi. The atmosphere had turned from daring to deadly.

Foster was unsure what to say.

Then it happened.

The man holding the knife drew it aloft and brought it swiftly across the woman's throat. Even from their somewhat distant position, Foster and Mitzi could see the spurt of deep crimson blood that flowed from her neck as the female clutched her hands to her throat before she fell to the floor. Disbelief and fear stuck in their own throats, threatening to choke them.

For a moment, time stood still, nothing daring to move. Then the full horror of what the couple had just seen hit them. Before she could stop herself, Mitzi screamed. A loud, terrified, blood-curdling scream. 'They've killed her.' It was all she could shout. Her voice pierced the air. Sensible it wasn't, but the noise had escaped from her lips before any semblance of rationality could form.

Once again, for a second, it seemed like all movement halted, nobody sure what their next action should be. Then as Mitzi and Foster watched on in horror, the figures turned to face the direction of the scream.

Moving away from the fireside and the body on the floor, the figures began to run in their direction.

'Fuck, they've heard us, they're coming this way. Foster, we need to get out of here now.'

Foster and Mitzi raced towards the camper van, the sound of footsteps and shouts coming from a mass of directions behind them. They needed to get back to the RV and away from the canyon. Neither was in any fit state to drive, both over the limit, but fear and abject terror spurred them into sobriety. This was a race to survive.

Mitzi could feel her heart burning within her chest as she fumbled her way towards the van. The flip flops she was wearing slid beneath her feet on the loose canyon floor. As one fell off, she jettisoned the other, leaving her barefoot.

Foster ran beside her, his panting just about audible alongside her own. A cacophony of voices sounded behind them. They seemed to be getting closer.

The light of their camper van, guiding them to hopeful safety, didn't seem to be getting any nearer. They hadn't walked for more than a few minutes towards the fire, had they? Maybe it was further than they realised.

Mitzi was suddenly aware that the sound of Foster's breathing behind her had disappeared. Where was he? She called his name, her voice dry with fear. There was no answer. She didn't dare stop and look back. She kept running towards the light. She'd soon be there, soon. Maybe Foster was there already, he was stronger than her.

A voice sounded behind her. Was it Foster? She couldn't tell above the sound of her own heartbeat. Turning to glance, her ankle twisted beneath her as another loose rock slid beneath her toes. She fell to the ground. As she did so, she bit down onto her tongue as the force of the canyon bottom slammed into her face. The coppery taste of blood filled her mouth.

She had to keep going. The light was brighter, she was nearly there.

Dizzy from her fall, she tried to stand up and keep running. She felt wobbly; there was a stabbing pain in her leg. Had she broken something? For a second all she could think about was her dancing career. The bright lights of the dance floor filled her head. Would she ever see it again? Would she ever escape the darkness?

Still on her hands and knees as she tried to stand back up, Mitzi felt the brushing of hessian against her skin before hands gripped either side of her neck. She didn't even have time to scream before a different kind of darkness took her.

The next morning as the sun rose over Hell's Canyon and remorselessly beat down onto the arid land, there was no sign of life again. No animals scurrying, no lush green vegetation thriving, and no sign of the RV or the two famous Brits who had been there the night before.

CHAPTER 1

'So, I'm afraid yet again it looks like the British summer is set to be besieged with rain and heavy thunder storms. Hopefully I'll have better news for you tomorrow. I'll see you then. Meanwhile it's back to Kate, who's on the sofa with Charlie for the showbiz news.'

As the camera cut away from her, weather presenter Georgia Bellamy let the painted-on smile fall from her face quicker than one of the heavy summer raindrops she'd just been talking about. It was her last bulletin of the morning and thankfully she no longer had to inform the viewers of *Rise and Shine* what they would undoubtedly already know if they'd ventured outside or indeed merely looked out of their windows at any point over the last week. The weather was wet again, the sky full of dark ominous clouds and it was all horribly typical for the UK's last few days of a so-called summer.

Georgia had rapidly become the country's favourite 'climatic crumpet' or 'barascopic beauty' depending on which newspaper's website you logged onto. This was thanks to her model-esque looks; she had a shoulder length, jet black retro bob and huge Kohl-rimmed 'bush baby' eyes. Today she was finding it hard to live up to her usual effervescent, bubbly persona. Despite her meteoric rise up the celebrity ladder and the fact that she was gaining more column inches in glossy gossip magazines than a penthouse suite full of young royals of late, her mood was decidedly basement-low. In fact it was darker than the clouds she'd been pointing to all morning on her green-screen map.

The reason for her funk was justified though. Her best friend, dancer Mitzi Bidgood, was still missing. Three weeks into a month long vacation with her reality-star boyfriend Foster Hampton in the States, the pair of them had simply vanished into thin air. Now, three weeks after that, what had once been the lead story on every UK news channel and edge-to-edge front page news was being relegated to 'and finally, still no news on the disappearance of Foster Hampton and Mitzi Bidgood', behind vacuous stories of glamour models having yet another baby with yet another father and former doped-up car crash actresses trying their hand at serious West End theatre glory.

Returning to her dressing room and slumping down into the butter-soft nut brown leather chair in front of the mirror that ran along the entirety of one wall, Georgia couldn't help but imagine the worst. The TV show Mitzi worked on had immediately issued a statement after the disappearance saying that the show would carry on without her, her celebrity partner sadly shelved for the moment, and that they hoped good news would become apparent soon. But the show must go on, and didn't Georgia just know it. Mitzi and Foster were becoming yesterday's news and Georgia's hopes of ever seeing her BFF again were fading fast.

It was the lack of finality that was crippling her. Were they dead? More than likely. Georgia was no stranger to heartache and losing those that she loved. But no bodies meant no funerals and that meant no closing the chapter on her grief. Every day was becoming a horrible wannabe-upbeat-but-failing routine of 'maybe today is the day that news will break'. Then nothing. The police in America seemed to have given up. There was camera footage of the couple's RV as it sailed though some sleepy backwater town in California, and after that, a big slice of nothing.

Georgia stared at the passport booth photo strip of her and Mitzi laughing together that she'd stuck onto her mirror frame. The early days of their soul-mate friendship. In her mind, Georgia figured that if she had a constant reminder of Mitzi in front of her it would keep the flame of hope burning bright. Tears began to pool at the edge of Georgia's eyes as she gazed at the photo strip, a touch creased and dog-eared at the corners. No surprise really, the photo had been taken about two months after the girls had first met, and that must have been six or seven years ago now. It was still one of her favourites, even after the thousands of photos they must have had taken together since, normally drunk and sporting smiles as wide as Oxford Street in some chi-chi London drinkerie with a tequila slammer in one hand and a boyfriend or unsuspecting male in the other. Both of them had always made the delete button on their iPhone Camera Roll their first port of call the morning after to delete any incriminating evidence, praying that one of their gang hadn't already uploaded some boob-out or knicker-flashing moment onto Facebook or Instagram for the world to see. As a tear rolled down her cheek, Georgia cast her mind back to their first encounter …

'Your eyes are insane! They're bigger than my face. They're fucking gorgeously high fashion.'

They were the first words Mitzi Bidgood ever said to Georgia Bellamy. Georgia had liked her immediately. She'd had a lifetime of people talking about her eyes. They were large. It was a Bellamy family trait. At school they'd been deemed odd; freaky, weird and googly by some of her mean girl classmates, but as Georgia

grew older and into her looks, she had learnt the art of make-up
from her mother. Sophia was a beautiful woman steeped in classic, vintage Bianca Jagger cool chic. Striking in an Italian *Vogue*
kind of way, she was a head-turner, adored by Georgia's father,
Devon, and by every man she met. And when Sophia skillfully
worked her make-up bag, it was cosmetic nirvana. There was no
doubting that Georgia was her mother's daughter.

'Er … thanks,' fumbled Georgia, trying to smile, acknowledge the girl next to her and still follow the rather athletic gyra-
tions of the woman leading the Zumba class. 'Although I'm not
sure the sweaty leotard look is particularly big on *Top Model* this
season but cheers.' She looked over at the girl. Taut body, about
the same age as her, eighteen she would guess, but whereas
Georgia was definitely feeling the burn and perspiring in places
she didn't even know she had, the young woman lunging and
whooping alongside her was a vision of sweat-free femininity. In
fact she looked like she was barely out of breath.

'I'm Georgia, nice to meet you.' She leapt up to clap as she
spoke, following the instructor's movements.

'Mitzi.' A quick turn and swivel.

'You make this look very easy,' puffed Georgia. 'I've got a
stitch big enough to patchwork an entire quilt right now.'

'I normally teach it,' said Mitzi, smiling. 'Zumba that is, not
patchwork! I give lessons here three times a week. The room I
use was needed tonight for some swanky business presentation
so I told my group to join this one for the night.' A quick shim-
my to the left and a final holler as the routine came to an end.

Mitzi reached over to shake Georgia's hand as the music
died and a sweep of applause circled the hall they were in. 'You
should join us. I'm a bit more hi-octane than this group and
you'd love the girls. We have a lot of fun.'

I swear her hands aren't even clammy, thought Georgia as they shook. *And was she actually wearing make-up? There was definitely eye-shadow and powder on show. How the hell ...?* Georgia's face would have ended up looking like a painting that had been left out in the rain if she'd worn any make-up. 'I may well do that, cheers.'

Indeed she did. She was fascinated by Mitzi and the two young women hit it off immediately, sharing a love of dance music like Rihanna, Shakira and Kanye West as well as a love for fashion and beauty. Georgia joined Mitzi's Zumba group the following week and often they would meet up both before and afterwards for coffee or cocktails depending on the hour and pore over celebrity magazines discussing their shared interests. Often they would be joined by the other girls in the Zumba group and suddenly it would be past midnight and they would all be crying with laughter in some salsa lounge or champagne bar discussing their dreams; whether it be a lusting for the bright lights of Hollywood or a far more worthy charity trek to some mud-baked corner of Africa. Mitzi dreamt of being a professional dancer. She had competed in, and had huge success with, dancing competitions around the country since she was five years of age and now that ballroom and Latin dancing were bigger and more popular than ever before, maybe the time would be right. Waltzes were no longer just the domain of grandparents at wedding receptions. Georgia dreamt of making her parents proud of her career, but, as yet, was not sure what to choose. She could guarantee it wouldn't be the field of medical science (her father, Devon, had earned millions from that area and she was steering very clear). Her interest in molecular structure stopped at admiring the cheekbones of Jared Leto. Maybe her looks could help her secure a job in TV. She was intelligent, well-spoken and loved the glamorous world of celebrity. Perhaps TV would be perfect.

Georgia adored spending time with Mitzi. Her friendship was infectious. She had such get up and go. Such a zest for life. She was an inspiration. In between her Zumba sessions at the luxury health spa the women frequented, Mitzi would head off to London for auditions, plan outfits for competitions and make sure she was seen at as many chic parties as possible. The word 'networking' was Mitzi's middle name.

Mitzi's Zumba group was a wondrous melting pot of social movers and shakers. They all had money – the health spa was not cheap, it was only affordable to those with big figure bank accounts – and they were all connected. Actresses, models, debutantes, singers.

It was those connections that eventually bagged Georgia her break into television about eighteen months later. One of the girls in the group was the younger sister of a TV executive who was looking to recruit for a new chatty breakfast news show. It needed to be fun, entertaining and the people on it needed to be total visions. Georgia, with a huge amount of cajoling from Mitzi, managed to badger her way into an audition and much to her surprise, she was offered a job as a weather girl. Something she had never thought about before. The thought terrified her. Mitzi thought it was incredible. A fact she couldn't wait to tell Georgia as they toasted her new-found success over a jug of mojito.

'You can learn on the job, and anyway the programme doesn't start for a few months, so they'll train you up. This is so cool, we're both going to be on TV. I've just been offered a job on that telly dancing competition as one of the professional group dancers. I am officially going to be fox-trotting my way up that ladder. And some of the celebs they've had on there have been gorgeous. Did you see the former rugby star on this series? Just to-die-for …'

Mitzi's words slammed into Georgia's brain as she stared at the photo. *To-die-for.* The horrible irony. Mitzi was right. The breakfast show had given Georgia the training she needed. She was the pretty face of UK weather. The shape of Cool Britannia with the news about the soaring temperatures. It was a job that she loved. And now the UK loved her. She owed everything to Mitzi. There wasn't a moment that thoughts of her best friend didn't fill Georgia's mind as she smiled her way through the weather report from various outside broadcasts around London's postcodes. One day she'd be reporting among a flurry of pigeons in Trafalgar Square, then motoring Bond-like down the Thames on a speed boat trying to report on a potential rain shower as she herself was sprayed with the fine mist of the UK's most famous river. Then it would be off to report from the sixties cool of Carnaby Street or a Notting Hill street party with Pearly Kings and Queens by her side. Georgia loved it and she never stopped being grateful to Mitzi.

Mitzi had climbed up the ladder on her show too, spending just one season as a backing group dancer. Her flare on the dance floor secured her a role as a regular partnered professional straight away. She always got the cute ones, indeed she was immediately partnered with a beautifully chiseled former football star. Good for a few months of loving. Then came her next season and her meeting with Foster. Their rhythms had synchronised in more ways than one. He'd been to-die-for …

Georgia let out a sob as she considered the fate of her best friend and her lover. What had happened to them? Somebody had to know.

Her misery was interrupted by a knock at her dressing room door. It was already open so there was no need for her to move. She turned and smiled, immediately a scarf of warmth wrapping itself around her.

There he was, Charlie Cooper, her ray of sunshine. Her friend, her lover, her soul-mate and as of six weeks ago, her fiancé. Mitzi had been elated to hear their news just before she had disappeared, already plotting ideas for hen parties and bridal colour schemes. Mitzi adored Charlie, she always had. He was the roving showbiz reporter on *Rise and Shine*. If a star was travelling from New York to Venice to get married or being arrested for a DUI or confessing to their inner demons, then Charlie was the man to be there. His ice white smile, wholesome everybody's-best-friend demeanor and David Gandy model looks had earned him a legion of fans and admirers of both sexes. It was something he played on both personally and professionally. Celebrities loved talking to him. He was safe. And if it came with a wink and a cheeky flirt along the way then where was the harm in that?

'Oh babe, I know it's not getting any better, maybe there will be some news today.' Charlie knew how fruitless his words probably were. He entered into the room and circled his arms around Georgia protectively. 'The truth will out, it always does.'

Georgia loved listening to him speak, his accent still softly twanged with his USA roots. Even though he'd been in the UK for the best part of a decade – thanks to the monopoly of Ryan Seacrest, his chances of becoming the must-have American host were minimal, hence the move to the UK – his frequent trips back home to see his family and for TV work made sure his accent never wavered. Georgia found it both comforting and totally sexy. It was deep and spiced with a hint of danger. The delicious thin line between best mate and bad boy. Her perfect type.

'You think? I can't bear it, Charlie. People are forgetting about Mitzi and Foster. It's all so unexplained. I can't let her memory just fade away. I can't ...'

Squeezing his arms a little tighter, Charlie bent down and kissed Georgia on the side of her face. The touch of his skin and the presence of his strength made the misery inside her fade away. Just for a second, but it was all she needed. At that very moment, all was right with her life. A world in perfect harmony. Not a cloud in the sky. If only it could always stay that way. If only.

CHAPTER 2

'So you're telling me *Surf N Turf* won't take me back and now I'm out of work thanks to Mitzi vanishing into thin air? For fuck's sake, I need money to live on, especially now I've rented up here. A cup of coffee and a sarnie in this city costs me more than a three course dinner back home.'

The *here* in question was Chelsea, London, not a million miles away from the central London office of Aaron Rose's go-getting new agent. The one who had relentlessly chased him to sign with her when he was working on *Surf N Turf* back in Cornwall. The one who had promised him a bollock-grabber of a deal that she would reveal to him once he'd left the show and moved himself to the big smoke so that he could be near to the media action. The one who was now finding him highly nauseating.

'Get a grip, Aaron, will you? This is all a touch drama queen,' snapped Rachel Jerome, adjusting her two-piece Forever Unique ensemble. It was a bit dressy for daywear but she had back to back meetings today and then was straight out to the Reality Awards later, for which it would be the perfect red carpet look. Rachel, one of London's most notorious agents, was supposedly going with new client Aaron Rose on her arm, but if he was going to be decidedly stroppy and arsey about things just a few weeks after signing with her then, quite frankly, he could take a running jump. She'd take one of the lads from the new man band she'd managed to blag onto *Britain's Got Talent*. As thick as shit and as intellectually stimulating as a night out with a colouring book, nevertheless his Ninja Turtle abs and cock with a girth like an observatory telescope would be company enough for Rachel between the sheets come the end of the night.

'Rachel, you made me leave *Surf N Turf*, telling me you have this amazing offer for me to do the dance show, tear me away from Cornwall to rent a flat in a place I don't even like very much and now you're telling me the dance producers have canned me because of Mitzi Bidgood being abducted by aliens or whatever the fuck has happened? This is not what you promised?'

'I know, darling. Shit happens. Look, you were getting too cosy in *Surf N Turf* anyway and the show is on its way out. Maybe one more season and a kit-off calendar deal was all they could offer so disembarking that sinking ship now was a good move. It's a shame about the dancing but how was I to know that they would not partner you with someone else? I think they wanted you to follow in Foster's footsteps by partnering Mitzi to see what happened. Now she's ... er ... no more,' Rachel wasn't really sure how to phrase it, '... I suppose the offer had to be revoked. I'll try for some compo, darling, but I don't hold out much hope.'

In fact Rachel knew there was no hope. The show's producers had only taken Aaron on in the hope that a spark of romance would ignite between him and Mitzi, even if they had to orchestrate it themselves, in order to gain 'love triangle' press for the show. Rachel had sworn to them that Aaron was already besotted with Mitzi having once met her at a film premiere and that hopefully their union would see them both kicking their legs high and Mitzi spreading hers wide. Total lies, but welcome to the world of agenting.

'I don't want to always be in Foster's shadow!' sniped Aaron. 'I was his replacement on *Surf* in the first place. I never worked with him but always had the press comparing us, and we couldn't be more different.'

Totally true. With his tree trunk build, rugged bearded face and layering of thick dark body hair from the dip of his neck down to the delights of his boxer shorts, Aaron was the antipode of Foster's living doll look. Aaron was Desperate Dan post modelling school.

'Well, word reaches me that Foster was up for some gardening show transforming some godforsaken scrub land on an estate in the back end of East Bumfuck or wherever so if it does turn out that he's met his maker I could try and squeeze you in there. I'm not sure where it is, but a job's a job, darling, no matter where you have to go.' For Rachel, apart from much-needed jaunts to the South of France or a sun-drenched week in the Maldives, all necessary life actually halted, dead-end, at the borders of the WC1 postcode.

'I've just told you, I don't simply want to follow in his footsteps or take his cast-offs. I need some kind of money coming in, and I need it now.'

Rachel had heard enough. She had promised the world so maybe she should see what she could do but she'd had her fill of moaning from Aaron for one day. There had to be some work for him somewhere. It was just a case of finding out where. But right now, she had other fish to fry, and not some little tiddler. She needed to phone her escort for the night. She'd not been able to think about anything else for the last five minutes. Whatever her dumb, young wannabe had planned for tonight he needed to drop it quicker than she'd be forcing him to drop to his knees and service her. Time for action.

'Right, Aaron darling, you'll have to go. I have the Reality Awards tonight and there's a lot of deals to be done. I'll be sure to throw your name into the mix for as many shows as possible.

And not one that's associated with Foster, okay? Now, if you'll excuse me ...'

'But I thought I was coming to the Awards with you?' quizzed Aaron.

'Did you, darling? You must have misunderstood. Now, I'll phone you tomorrow for a catch-up and I'm sure I'll have some news for you. Why don't you go to the gym and keep that body of yours in good shape? There's a lot more TV out there where you can show off those muscles of yours without any need for Lycra or body glitter. Oh, and if you're worried about money, I have some free passes for the gym around the corner. Give it a whirl. You'll probably find half the cast of *EastEnders* and *Downton Abbey* in there anyway. There are more initial contacts made in those showers than any amount of begging emails. Go and work your rustic charm and don't be afraid to drop your towel in the right direction if need be.' She grabbed the passes from her desk, thrust them into Aaron's hand and opened the door for his departure.

For a man whose major decisions in life up until recently were which colour wetsuit to wear for surfing and which hardy perennial to choose for a customer's border, Aaron Rose felt mightily bamboozled by his new agent's hard-hitting London ways. He wasn't sure he'd made the right move in signing with her. If an agent like Rachel thought she could treat him like a stupid glove puppet and shove her hand up his ass to work him whenever she pleased then she had another think coming. As he descended the stairs from Rachel's office and headed off down the far-too-busy-for-his-liking streets of inner London, he stared at the gym card. Maybe a work out was a good idea.

At her desk, Rachel had another kind of work out on her mind. She made the first of two phone calls. One to her toy boy for the night. Who said a well-preserved forty-five-year-old couldn't shag a twenty-one-year-old hunk once in a while? Especially one with no choice.

The second one was to a gay magazine. She could book Aaron a fitness feature for a few quid. Those magazines would take any old half-baked celebrity with a decent pair of pecs who looked good in a pair of tight shorts. She'd tell Aaron tomorrow, forgetting to mention that Foster had done countless similar features in the past, of course. There were certain things some clients just never needed to know.

CHAPTER 3

The top of the moussaka was black. And hard. And totally ined-ible. How had Victoria Palmer-Roberts let this happen again? Hard and unappetising. Hadn't that become the story of her life? The story of her marriage, lately? She feared it had.

She'd spent hours studying the recipe, making sure that her combination of aubergine, potato, minced meat, herbs and spices were all spot on. Making sure that it would be a treat that her financial advisor husband, Scott, would relish with glee after another busy day sorting out the finances of the rich and fa-mous. And then there were the twins, six-year-old Lexi and Leo. They loved Mummy's moussaka. Well, they did when it was the normal colour and actually recognisable as food. The only thing it looked good for now would be to drop on one of the many molehills that seemed to be springing up with alarming regu-larity in the garden of their two-million-pound West London family home. If a knife and fork couldn't crack the surface of the supposed culinary joy, then what chance would a nearly blind, small furry critter have?

Victoria pulled open one of the kitchen drawers and drew out a delivery pizza menu. Scott would not be pleased – Lexi and Leo were supposed to be on a balanced diet, watching their weight, making sure they didn't put on a few extra pounds like their mum seemed to have done lately. A fact that Scott seemed completely at ease with mentioning in not so glorious detail to her both over the dinner table and in the marital bed. He'd freak when a pizza delivery guy turned up with a stack of twelve inch Hawaiians and a calorie-laden Quattro Stagioni, but judging by the charcoal offering in front of her, it was that or starve. Tonight was going to be another night of arguments, she could see it now. Weren't they all?

She should send the live-in nanny, Chloe, on a cookery course. One of those ones run by a TV celebrity chef. That would make Scott sit up and take notice. Then Victoria would have more time to look after herself instead of catering for the family all the time. While Chloe played with the kids and sorted out school duties and organised visits to London Zoo or the Natural History Museum, Victoria seemed to be the one keeping the house clean, making up beds, tidying toys and shopping for food. Chloe was good cop, she was bad cop. Chloe was thin cop, young cop, smiley cop, fresh-faced cop, bloody drop dead gorgeous cop … Victoria was worn-out, knackered, frumpy old miserable cop. Ironic since, at twenty-two years of age, Chloe, their third nanny to date, was actually only six years younger than Victoria. She'd had a body like Chloe's at twenty-two, she'd made time to go to Zumba, to sweat it out with the girls in the sauna, to swim as much as she could and then treat herself to a little something sexy from Miu Miu or Dior. And then she became pregnant, lost her figure and lost her confidence. Even though she adored her twins, Lexi and Leo's arrival had seemed to signal the end of any youthful exuberance she'd once had, whether she liked it or not. Maybe Victoria was the one who needed to get away, to recharge her batteries.

How had this happened? It never used to be this way.

Victoria Wentworth was born in New Orleans, but away from the colour and the jazz-filled madness of America's 'Big Easy' and the voodoo-spiced streets of the French Quarter. She was born in the Garden District, an area so rich and decadent that not even Hurricane Katrina dared to flood it when it struck in 2005. Whereas virtually all of the rest of the city was blitzed by the ferocity of the Hurricane, the Garden District, with its beautifully spaced out houses, surrounded by pillars, limitless blankets of green and corn-stalk fences was a charmed area inhabited by charmed people. People who could smile at the tourists walking past their palatial houses, but who, unless they chose to, would never have to talk to them. The area had always been one of beauty, elegance and tradition. Proper home values with good decent, honest, home-loving people. A wonderfully tasteful slice of American pie.

Originally created in the early nineteenth century, it was a place where new American residents of NOLA could live so as not to mingle with 'those of European descent' primarily living in the French Quarter at the riotous core of the city. Americans who had gained their hard-earned dollars from respected trades like cotton, shipping, insurance and sugar, who could afford to commission architects to create tiered houses in magnificent styles; Victorian, Greek Revival and Italianate.

Victoria's great grandparents had moved there at the start of the twentieth century. Her parents set up home there in the late 1960s and it was expected that one day Victoria and her husband to be would do exactly the same and settle safely within the confines of an area where traffic was minimal, wildlife ran free and houses possessed a charm to rival *Gone with the Wind*.

Victoria loved it there, excelling in school, perfecting her languages like French and Spanish and thriving at sports like softball, track volleyball, golf and swimming. With rose-kissed skin and long blonde hair she was the essence of all-American girl. She had braces at an early age to straighten any rogue gnashers, learnt ballet and horse-riding as necessary skills, and was the perfect pupil, earning the ultimate accolade of becoming Prom Queen at the age of sixteen. One of her finest memories would always be sitting upon her Prom Queen throne, looking at a sea of genuinely happy friends and peers staring up at her, all thrilled for her popularity.

But despite a sign just around the corner from her Garden District house stating, 'On This Site In 1897 Nothing Happened' – the ridiculousness of which used to make Victoria and her friends laugh – suddenly something did. Her parents, persuaded by one of their neighbours that it was the in-thing for smart US families to do, decided to send Victoria away to England to finish her education. She was to spend a few terms at the much-famed Farmington Grange, a place of education for young ladies, especially from families around the world with enough zeroes on the end of their bank account balances to make sure that the extortionate term fees were met. Just before her seventeenth birthday Victoria Wentworth was driven to Louis Armstrong airport in New Orleans with three trunks full of her belongings and waved off by her parents to start a new life in the UK.

Farmington Grange was a place that Victoria enjoyed. If anything, it made her even more confident than she already was. It was full of cliques, there were bitchy girls, there were spoilt brats, there were girls who weren't just born with a silver spoon in their mouths, they were rich enough to have the whole canteen of cutlery, but Victoria managed to fit in. Not attaching herself to any one group in particular she made friends with a selection of different girls. Back home in New Orleans, she had been used to a group of friends whose main ambition in life was to marry a son of a family friend, one with a good dependable job with major career prospects, probably already guaranteed through a family business, and become the model wife and mother. 'Stand by Your Man' as the song says. The expectation was for them to pop out a few children, see them on their path to Prom Queen or soccer team captain and then ad lib to fade as they waited for the onslaught of grey hairs and face lifts.

But Farmington was different – girls aspired to be someone, to make a difference, with or without a man by their side. Girls dream of theatrical acting, of being lawyers, of working in the armed forces, professions that the wives of her Garden District existence might not have considered. There was an excitement about the future that Victoria relished.

When she left a year later she was determined to make a difference and use her skills, especially as a linguist, to forge her way in life. Charity work in Africa? Relief work in the Far East? Volunteer projects in South America? Had she not met Scott Palmer-Roberts, the dashingly handsome son of the owner of one of the UK's most successful financial corporations, she might well have done just that.

But the moment she laid eyes on Scott – his dark curly locks and pistachio green eyes an irresistible combination – all thoughts of any new career aspirations fluttered off on the wings of love. In their place returned the inbuilt, once latent now potent desire to be the perfect wife with the perfect life. And that suited Scott and his family down to the ground. While Scott's career rocketed, courtesy of his blood ties, Victoria became the dutiful trophy fiancée, engaged at nineteen, perfect arm candy wife at twenty and the mother of twins by the age of twenty-two. She may have been living in London, but apart from the geography of her residential time zone, she could have been back in the picturesque serenity of the Garden District leading the perfect life. Nights out with the girls seemed to cease and be replaced with black tie financial boreathons that were both swanky and, more often than not, totally wanky.

For a while the role of the apple pie mother and wife suited her needs. Trips back to New Orleans with her beautiful double babies in a double buggy with matching scallop-edged trims to see her doting parents and her insanely jealous friends were wonderful. Victoria had found her prince, produced two bundles of joy and lived happily ever after. So what if it happened to be away from everybody she'd grown up with and in a foreign land? The end of the rainbow could be anywhere, couldn't it?

But then the trips back home seemed to become less and less frequent. Scott was always saying that something had to be done at work, or that it wasn't good for the children to be constantly travelling at such a young age. Victoria became homesick. Her husband was at work sixteen hours a day, her children were suddenly being looked after by a live-in nanny, and she found herself bored, unable to pop around the corner to see her parents and friends. Sure, she had managed to keep a few friends from her Farmington days, more down to their efforts than hers, if she were honest. There was best friend and her maid of honour Evie Merchant, whose career as an actress was really beginning to soar, plus others who were studying hard in the hope of becoming lawyers, doctors, politicians or fashion designers. Occasionally, schedules permitting, they would visit Victoria. For a few hours they would laugh and joke, reminiscing about their schooldays together over a slice of cake and coffee. But then they'd be gone, back to their exciting lives leaving Victoria to load the dishwasher and eat the rest of the cake. Why couldn't everything in life be as joyful as a slice of rich, crumbly, cream-filled cake? Scott didn't approve of anything too sweet and sugary. He didn't approve of her weight gain. Why was he with her? Thank God he didn't know about her taking anti-depressants to try and mask her unhappiness. If she could apply the same dedication to getting her life back into shape that she did to hiding her tablets away from those around her then everything would be peachy. She was a master at that.

But she needed them. They helped her deal with the fact she was becoming resentful of her friends and their seemingly perfect lives. She tried not to be, but something rotting away inside eroded at her. It was then that her confidence started to crumble.

Walking from the kitchen to the bottom of the stairs, Victoria shouted up at the children who were playing upstairs. 'Leo, Lexi ... it'll be delivery pizza for tea, okay?' A few seconds later Leo stuck his head over the banister on the landing a floor up and shouted down, 'Cool, Mum. Does that mean we're not eating whatever's burnt the house down? We can smell it up here.' How many times had she heard that lately? Far too many.

Back in the kitchen, looking down at the blackened moussaka, Victoria moved to the bin in order to tip the food away. Leo was right, it did smell. As she went to scrape the moussaka into the rubbish, she looked at her wedding ring. The clarity of the huge diamond that sat atop her finger was a complete contrast to the black surface of the food. Not wanting to sully it with the ashy topping of the meal, she placed the moussaka back on the work surface and twisted the ring off her finger to place in her pocket.

She had so much to be grateful for. A beautiful pair of children, a nanny to share her workload, a husband who earned good money and maintained a roof over their heads. It was all she'd ever wanted, wasn't it? So why was Victoria staring at her ringless finger and thinking it looked better that way?

CHAPTER 4

Pulling his body upwards on the jail gym chin-up bar, Jack Christie looked at the muscle definition on his arms. He'd never been in better shape. And it wasn't just his arms. Letting himself drop to the concrete floor he looked into the gym mirror and surveyed his body. Apart from a pair of sweat pants and some sneakers, he was naked. His body was no longer that of a scrawny teenager, he was now a mountain of masculinity. Thick veins ran the full length of either bicep. His chest, covered with a smooth coating of fine dirty blonde hair, stood proud and defined. One pec was completely covered in a tribal tattoo, starting at the nipple and spreading outwards and up onto his shoulder. Another tattoo, a jackdaw, his nickname, sat on his stomach, rising and falling with the movement of his deeply sculptured six-pack. Another covering of hair reached out from under and around his navel and across the hardness of his belly. He possessed a body he had worked on for a long time.

'You're invincible, man,' he cried to himself. He raised his fist to his chest and beat it, Tarzan-style. A grin spread across his face, revealing a remarkably good set of teeth, considering the knocks they'd taken over the years. One, off to the side of his mouth, was gold in colour.

'You reckon so?' The voice came from the doorway of the gym. It was gruff and sneering in tone.

'Any day of the fucking week,' barked Jack. 'I'm in better shape than anybody. Now excuse me, I'm getting out of here.'

He pushed past the man, smiling as he did so. He was right. He was getting out of there. The place he'd spent the last five years for unlawful entry with intention to steal. He'd been stupid and got himself caught. It had always been his problem. A little bit too cocky for his own good. He should have just broken into the house, one of the rich ones in the suburbs of London, and stolen money, cash that couldn't be traced. That was the agreement as ever. But no, he'd seen a really smart silver bird brooch just sitting there on a dressing table. It looked like a jackdaw, just like the one he had tattooed on his stomach. Just like his nickname. Unable to resist he'd pocketed it for himself. A foolish nineteen-year-old, he'd pinned it to his hat the following week and worn it out to go clubbing. That just so happened to be the night the police had nicked him for speeding. When you're a raggedy-arsed teenager, wearing something as distinctive as a silver jackdaw breeds suspicion. A police search revealed that the item had been reported as stolen.

Jack was sentenced to five years, but that was nearly all in the past. As he walked back to his jail cell, sweat still dripping down his chest, he loved what his stay in prison had done for him. It had made him grow up. Not in terms of maturity, but physicality and strength.

Back in his cell, he picked up a marker pen and scored another line on his wall. He'd been doing it for the last month. Another line down, another cross on a five bar gate. Only seven more and he'd be out of there for good. He'd done his time. He'd entered prison as a boy but he'd be leaving a man. The jackdaw was about to fly free and the thought turned him on.

CHAPTER 5

'Do you want the good news or the bad news?'

'Do I have a choice?' asked Georgia. 'Because if so, I'd like the good news followed by some more good news, topped off with a side serving of some fantastic news, please. That's about all I can handle at the moment. I need to live in a fairy tale bubble right now, and everything in the Sunday papers is just doom and gloom. Where's my Disney ending?'

'Well, Princess, seeing as that's what you are to me, let me be your knight in shining armour, your Prince Eric, your Aladdin … whisk you away on a magic carpet.'

If there was one thing that Charlie could always be relied on to do it was to bring a smile to Georgia's face. He'd already done so that Sunday morning with a sensual and tender bout of love-making. It had almost become tradition on their weekends. After a week of ridiculously early mornings working on *Rise and Shine*, both Charlie and Georgia lived for their days off together. Friday night would be curry night, maybe a bar with friends in Shoreditch or a trip up the Shard for cocktails. Saturday would be a trip to Borough Market, to stock their fridges with cheeses, breads and dips from across the globe. Snacking was one of those bad habits that both of them had picked up from working on live TV and if they were going to snack, well, surely a decent knob of bread and a lump of crumbly cheese was better than a choccy bar and a bag of cheese and onion.

Not that either of them really had to watch their weight. Both were blessed with athletic genes and fast metabolisms, meaning that good food was often on the menu. Saturday nights would often find them savouring the delights of pollock balls in lobster sauce or some such culinary masterpiece at their favourite London eaterie, The Duck & Waffle on the fortieth floor of the Heron Tower, where the spectacular views across the capital matched the quality of the food.

Sunday mornings would always begin with sex. As would Saturdays if they were honest, but Sundays had become a tradition. Not in a 'once a week before a catch up on the week's Sky Planner' kind of way. Far from it. Georgia and Charlie had a healthy sex life right throughout the week with stolen passionate moments taken wherever possible, but Sunday morning seemed to be the one moment that always seemed to be stress-free, away from work, away from deadlines, away from any discussion about weather and safely wrapped up in the warmth and comfort of each other's companionship and love. Elton John sang 'Saturday Night's Alright For Fighting', well Georgia and Charlie knew that Sunday morning was always alright for loving.

'So, come on then, break it to me,' smiled Georgia, lifting her head off Charlie's naked chest. They were still duvet-daying at Charlie's Old Street flat. Georgia loved it there. It was clean, modern and fresh, Art Deco in design and perfectly positioned for London life. She adored the melting pot of people who lived in the area; artists who had managed to convince showy galleries that their few blobs of paint and a gilded-frame were hundred thousand pound masterpieces and techy bods, playing the new rock stars in an age of computer innovation. And of course it was rammed with media types. You couldn't pass a deli without bumping into a young hot shot TV producer or an on-trend club DJ. And Georgia and Charlie fitted right in.

They would either spend the weekends there or at Georgia's Grade II listed character cottage in Wimbledon Village. It was away from London madness, a bolt hole from the insanity of their lives, and a place where they could watch the wisteria grow and birds wash themselves in their courtyard bird bath, as they listened to Dusty Springfield, Adele or Coldplay.

'Well, good news first.'

Georgia pulled the duvet and wrapped it around her chest, her interest piqued. 'Go on.'

'You like curries, right?'

'We've cracked enough poppadums together to know the answer to that one …'

'Work have asked me to go to India to interview one of the celebrity chefs from the TV. He's just started courses out there for rich tourists and apparently a few celebrities have already signed up for his tuition, so work thought it might be a good idea for me to spend a few days learning how to beef up my bhajis and vamp up my vindaloo. The course is in Agra, very close to the Taj Mahal, so if you fancy coming along and can swing a few days off, then I thought it would be the perfect opportunity for you to unwind. It's only a couple of days work, but we could tack a bit of sightseeing on the end. What do you say?'

'You had me at "curry",' squealed Georgia. 'I've always wanted to go to India. Dad says it's one of the most spiritual places he's ever been and a colourful assault on the senses. He says he was a much more grounded person after coming back from there. When do we go?'

'If you clear it with work, then we'll leave on Thursday. Can one of the other weather girls step in?' Charlie raised an eyebrow hopefully.

'I'll make sure they can. It's just what I need. I can't switch off from thinking about Mitzi and Foster. There's hardly anything in the papers about them today. It's only been a few weeks but interest is seriously dwindling. Why isn't anybody doing anything? People shouldn't just disappear.' Georgia picked up the papers surrounding them – another Sunday tradition; having physical copies to flick through in bed as opposed to poring over websites – and threw them to the floor.

'People are forgetting already. I can't bear the thought of Mitzi and Foster just being another couple of missing person statistics.'

'Something will turn up eventually, it has to,' offered Charlie. He wasn't sure he believed his own words but he prayed that both Foster and Mitzi were alive. Mitzi had been the one who had welcomed him into their inner circle of friendship when he'd first met Georgia. He could still hear her say, 'You make my girl happy, you make me happy. You shit on her then I will give your sorry Yankee ass a good kicking quicker than you can say "LA" matey,' as if it were yesterday. He loved her because she loved Georgia. As did he. Which spared him any potential kicking.

Georgia sighed. 'Anyway, I am loving your good news, so what is the bad?'

'We won't be alone in India.'

'No, aren't there about a billion or so other people in that country?' replied Georgia, her sarcasm somewhat heavy.

'My mum will be with us. In fact it she was the one who told me about the course, so she is kind of the reason we would be going anyway. She's signed up for it as she loves the chef. Apparently his shows are shown on one of the cooking channels over in the States and she is completely besotted with him. She wanted to take the camera for her own TV show but the big bosses said no. She reckons if she can do a reccy and convince them that it will make fabulous telly then she'll be able to go back again. You know mother.'

Indeed Georgia did. She was a tour-de-force and not always the easiest person to be around, but if she could survive the odd stay with Charlie's mother in the madness of her home city, Los Angeles, then she could survive a few days with her in the calm, spice-scented air of India, couldn't she?

'Does the thought of your mother always do that to you?' indicated Georgia, pointing to the tenting at Charlie's crotch underneath the duvet. 'Please tell me you haven't developed some weird Oedipus Complex.'

'Christ, no,' laughed Charlie. 'But those do.' He cupped his hands around Georgia's breasts that had become exposed as the duvet had dropped while they were talking about Charlie's mother. He bent down and kissed one of her nipples, biting down on it slightly with his teeth. It rose beautifully to attention, as did Georgia's other as Charlie brushed it with his fingertips. A ripple of desire filtered through Georgia's body.

He reached for her hand underneath the duvet and clasped it around his long, hard member. Charlie was well-endowed, possessing both length and girth.

She ran her hand up and down his shaft and then cupped her hands around his balls. She moved them gently and slowly across her palm, tugging at them slightly.

'Well, what do you know, there's a couple of gulab jamuns down here that need eating,' she grinned, making reference to her favourite Indian dessert. She swooped down and placed her head between her lover's thighs, at first working her tongue along the entire length of his cock, before licking a figure-of-eight across Charlie's balls, planting feather-light kisses and expert flicks of her tongue as she did so. His cock strained at her touch, engorged with lust.

Staring up at Charlie from between his legs with her mesmerising eyes, Georgia noted from that angle he did indeed look a little like the Disney version of Aladdin, his hair swept back and richly luxuriant. Very Princely indeed.

'Enjoy your starters? I think it's time for the main course, don't you?' She straddled his body and let his cock slide into her.

All thoughts of Charlie's mum had disappeared from her mind. Which was no bad thing. Oh yes, she knew his mother.

As did the world …

CHAPTER 6

Charlie's mum was none other than Nova Chevalier, the brash, loud-mouthed star of *Champagne Super Nova*, a reality TV sensation in America. In an age where *Real Wives* this and *A-List* that were making stars of the most unlikely of people – look at *Honey Boo Boo's* Mama June for example – it seemed that it had only been a matter of time before Nova had turned into a bona fide celebrity. And right now, Nova was riding a wave of Stateside success that was keeping her up with the likes of the *Keeping Ups*. And after all that she'd been through in life, Nova was determined to enjoy every madcap, bizarre moment. Hell, didn't she deserve it? She thought so.

Nova's real name was Nina Cooper, and she had always been quite a phenomenon in her own little way. A 'freak unique', some would say, given that she came from the most ordinary of backgrounds. A fact she never forgot.

Growing up in West Hills, Los Angeles, Nina was a pretty girl, famed for her long blonde hair and petite pouty lips. She would walk to school with her Penelope Pitstop rucksack glued to her back, full of her books for class.

She was a good pupil and popular with teachers. As she grew older, she became just as popular with the local boys.

Nina had always been a dreamer, loving to watch celebrities on TV or read about them in her comic magazines. She loved seeing who was dating whom, reading about where her faves hung out. One day that would be her, she had no doubt.

It didn't take Nina too long into her teens to work out that she was able to wrap boys right around her brightly nail-painted finger. In fact she was only a few days past her thirteenth birthday when she first let a boy slide his hand up her T-shirt and feel her small forming buds in order to gain a few extra dollars to buy more comics. She'd been savvy enough to realise that as soon as her breasts started to distend the front of her clothes thanks to the onslaught of puberty, boys in the area were literally walking around with their mouths hanging open and their tongues hanging out. And the dollars also came in handy for buying cinema tickets and posters of her favourite movie stars. The craggily handsome Harrison Ford – how she marvelled over his swagger and physique in *Raiders Of The Lost Ark* – or the drop dead gorgeous Mel Gibson in the *Mad Max* films. Dirty, dangerous and dynamic – what a trinity. She also used the extra money on make-up to make herself look a little bit older than she actually was, painting her nails and adding a touch of powder to her cheeks or a slick of colour to her eyes and lips. Getting turned away from the Cineplex for being underage was not an option.

No, Nina knew how to work the boys and dreamt of success outside of West Hills. It was a good area, full of lovely people, but Nina wanted the red carpet glamour she'd seen on TV.

Her parents, good Christian members of the local LA churchgoers, were respectable enough. Pleasant people with decent jobs, putting food on the table. But only child Nina was bored by talk of Harvest Festivals and Nativities. Boys were her outlet.

As Nina's breasts grew, so did her popularity. The two things seemed to be in direct correlation with each other. Larger breasts meant more hands up T-shirts, which meant more money. It was like a cashpoint in reverse. Instead of making a withdrawal, boys would come to Nina, press a few of her 'buttons' and then make a financial deposit into the fund that Nina was accruing in order to escape West Hills. Call it her very own business acumen. She never doubted that she could make her life count and the destination for the action had to be Hollywood, home to the stars.

At the age of seventeen, with enough money in her pocket to enjoy a taxi ride to the streets of Hollywood and immerse herself, albeit illegally, in the bars she'd longed to visit and the glitzy cocktails she'd longed to taste, she ventured to the bright lights.

That was the night she lost her virginity. A pumped up college jock in his early twenties showered her with compliments, supplied her with the cocktails she'd craved and then fucked her up against the wall of a diner in a Hollywood back street. Even though there was absolutely nothing glamorous or movie-star about the act, Nina felt that she had become a woman.

She had no idea at the time that maybe it was allowed to last longer than just a few urgent thrusts, that there was such a thing as foreplay or indeed that maybe contraception might have been a good idea, as would gaining the lad's name and telephone number.

A few weeks later, after Nina had taken herself off to the doctors because she kept being sick, it was confirmed that she was pregnant. Seventeen and up the duff with God-fearing parents. When she told her folks she had literally expected them to string her up from the nearest tree. They didn't, but they were heartbroken. But they stood by her. Eight months later, baby Charlie was born.

For fifteen years, Nina put her life on hold. Her son was her everything. Money was tight but she managed. When Charlie was fifteen his grandfather died from a heart attack while watching him perform in a soccer match at school. Charlie was there to witness the last gasps of breath from the man that had always been a dad to him, as the only fatherly influence he had experienced in his life.

Nina watched as her son became more and more depressed about the passing of his grandfather. The man he used to discuss sports and girls with was suddenly no more.

Nina made a decision. She would try to find love, to introduce another man into Charlie's life. There had been offers over the years, even a few relationships along the way, but none of them had satisfied Nina. It wasn't that they weren't perfectly loving and honourable men, they were, but they just weren't perfect for Nina.

Then one day, while flicking through one of the local newspapers, she found it. An advertisement from an 'older gentleman, seeking a female companion to share his life'. There was no address, just a telephone number. It might as well have read 0800-ESCAPE, because that's what Nina saw in the ad. She rang, she met, she fell in love. Yes, he was indeed older, forty years her senior in fact, but he was kind, he was loving and he was obviously rich as he lived in one of Nina's favourite areas of Los Angeles, Bel-Air.

At the age of thirty-two, Nina and a teenage Charlie moved out of the house she had spent her life in and moved to an area she had always dreamed of. People called her a gold-digger, they called her a whore, but Nina didn't care. Her new man, seventy-two-year-old Goldman Cavill, was a gentle soul with not a malicious bone in his body. So he preferred younger women, where was the harm in that? Nina genuinely loved him, despite what others suggested. He gave her love, a lifestyle she had longed for and provided Charlie with another man in his life. He'd been used to having an older gentleman around in the form of his granddad so he was less freaked out by Goldman's age than any-one.

Just before Goldman's seventy-third birthday, he and Nina were married. It was his second marriage, Nina's first. It was a fact she was proud of as she surveyed the land surrounding their Bel-Air home. She had catered for her son and found love in the most unlikely, yet heavenly of places. And fuck anyone who didn't like it. If it made Charlie happy, and it did, then she was rock solid in her opinion that she was a good mother.

Goldman died, leaving everything to Nina (who had now changed her name to Nova as she thought it sounded more be-guiling) six years later. Charlie was twenty-one. For the second time in his life, he had felt like he was losing a father figure.

Goldman had no children from his first marriage, and his previous wife had died while they were together, so there was nobody to contest Goldman's will. He had found love too and all that he had he was happy to bequeath. Overnight, Nova was suddenly one of the richest widows in LA. She had come so far and even though she would never forget her origins, she was determined to enjoy her new mad, money-drenched world. She and Charlie more than deserved it.

Her first action with her own money was to buy outright her former house in West Hills, so that her mother could live there for the rest of her days worry-free. She'd offered to buy something much more grandiose but her mother, now in her seventies too, had refused. She wanted to be near her friends, her church, her faith.

With riches like Nova's came notoriety and it wasn't long un-til a succession of hopeful suitors came sniffing around. Around forty, widowed, hugely pretty and uber-rich, what wasn't to like?

Nova was happy to go on dates, and with her second pur-chase with her own money, a rather supersized pair of breasts, all of a sudden she was taking herself back twenty-five years as handsome millionaires, media moguls and Lothario nightclub owners tried to seduce her and jam their hands up her rather stretched Rodeo Drive blouses. But Nova had always been a smart cookie. She could see those who were out to deceive and those who could see further than her cantaloupe breasts.

She had countless offers of marriage but turned them all down. Until she met Jacob Chevalier. Jacob was a hugely successful, some said ruthless, celebrity manager, with houses in LA, New York, London and Rio. The one thing he was not after was Nova's money. He had more than enough of his own due to the way he worked Hollywood. He was able to offer her something that she'd always craved. Something that would be the cherry on the top of her already decadently iced world. Fame. Plus it was clear to her that he loved her.

They married and Nova Chevalier was born. Under Jacob's guidance, *Champagne Super Nova* was hatched, a TV show where rich Bel-Air glamourpuss Nova Chevalier let viewers into her fabulous home and they accompanied her across America and across time zones as she lived life to the max. Whether she was whale-watching in Alaska or learning to hula dance in Maui, you could guarantee that Nova would always be there, champagne in hand.

It was pure madness and Nova adored every giddy moment of it. And ratings were Kardashian-huge.

CHAPTER 7

'So you're working with Ryan Gosling and Channing Tatum. Please tell me the movie is called *Threesome* or *Ménage À Trois?*' said Victoria, passing over a slice of something rather large and creamy to her guest, who had arrived, somewhat impromptu, about an hour earlier.

'I know, it's too exciting for words, Vic. But no, it's a period drama so it's all corsets and petticoats I'm afraid. We start filming tomorrow in London so I thought I'd pop in to see you. It's been an age, far too long since I've seen you and I miss you! You're always telling me you're busy with Scott and the kids, so I thought I would turn up on the off-chance and surprise you.'

It had been ages. And indeed it was a surprise. But Victoria had wished she'd known she was coming. She could have prepared and done her hair, found a more flattering outfit to wear and slipped on the suck-em-in pants to try and flatten her slightly domed belly. The last time Victoria had seen her friend – her very glamorous and super thin friend, actress Evie Merchant – it had been not long after the twins had been born. Around about the time when Victoria's insecurities had begun to surface. About the time she'd been unsuccessfully trying to shift all of the baby weight.

Evie had been one of Farmington's rising stars and one of the nicest people she had ever met. Nothing was ever too much trouble. She was sweet, sincere and genuine and when it came to acting, she was in a field of her own even back then. One of those people who has everything, but you actually don't hate them for it. Well, Victoria didn't. She loved her and the feeling was mutual.

Everybody knew that one day Evie would make it. Now she had, with awards, accolades and celebrity lovers under her belt. Victoria had followed her career with a keen eye, even keeping scrapbooks filled with cuttings from newspapers and magazines about Evie's successes. The women had often spoken on the phone, Evie phoning her from film sets around the world or from hotels before some glitzy awards ceremony, but moments together were a rarity. Evie had suggested they meet up many times but somehow Victoria would always find an excuse. At first she had been genuinely busy, but after the children had been born and the weight had begun to pile on Victoria had been somewhat embarrassed to see her glamourous friend. She was hanging out with size zero megastars while Victoria was experiencing zero confidence. Evie wasn't the only friend she'd let slip through her fingers. At least Evie hadn't given up on her. She was grateful for her tenacity. Indeed if Evie had rung today instead of just turning up then doubtless Victoria knew she would have made an excuse to put her off. Insecurity mixed with apathy and an anti-depressant chaser were not the most social of combinations. At least the pills seemed to mask what she saw in herself when she looked in the mirror.

'Oh, I love a period drama. Give me anything with a Jane Austen twist or a touch of the Colin Firths in a white frilled shirt and a lah-de-dah accent and I'm in heaven. It's just so British. When's it out? I'll have to see it.' Despite feeling a tad self-conscious about her change in body shape since she'd last seen Evie, Victoria had to admit that it was great to see her old friend. She had missed her more than she cared to admit. She missed the old days full stop. Missed the girls.

'Sometime next year, or the year after I suspect, these things take forever,' said Evie.

'At least you have something to look forward to. The most exciting thing in my life is choosing what aroma to have for my bathroom pump-action soap.' She shifted awkwardly in her seat, her brain trying to calculate just exactly how many dress sizes she had gone up by since last seeing her probably size-zero friend.

'But you have a beautiful home, and two amazing children, you know how envious of you I am when I see those two?' It was true, Evie may have been one of the world's most sought after actresses but deep inside some of the things that she truly craved from life were the simple joys that she could see Victoria possessed. Out of all of Evie's friends, Victoria seemed to be the one in her eyes who had really hit the jackpot. A stable relationship with a good man, a pair of rosy-cheeked children and a home that she could actually live in as opposed to spending her life in yet another soulless hotel room living out of a fleet of suitcases. Fame and glamour were not all they were cracked up to be.

'Where are Leo and Lexi by the way? I bet they've shot up since I last saw them. It was just before their christening. I am so sorry I missed that. Filming schedules can be a bitch. Another thing I've missed out on.'

The christening. That was probably the last time Victoria had actually invited Evie to be with them. Probably the last time she had seen Mitzi too. Mitzi had tried for a while afterwards to keep in touch but there are only so many no's a friend can take before assuming they should be taking the hint. As Victoria's pounds and insecurity increased, so did her desire to hide behind the doors of her family home. A place where nobody could see and potentially comment on the excess inches.

'What day is it? Monday? Then it's school till four, then swimming practice till five and maybe craft club for Lexi if she fancies after that. Chloe the nanny will be sorting them out. Those children have a better social life than I do. Mind you, that's not exactly hard. I think the last time I actually went out and enjoyed myself you were still contemplating your first movie break.'

Evie was spotting more than a degree of sadness in Victoria's tone. Putting her cake back on the table before a dollop of cream fell from it and landed onto her Hermione de Paula shift dress, she was quick to try and fathom out what was wrong with her friend.

'Care to spill?'

'What do you mean?'

'Come on Victoria, I may not have seen you for a while but I've known you long enough to not beat around the bush and you know how much I care for you. Something's up. Where's the fun-time girl who used to be there on the nights out? The happy smiley bride I saw walk down the aisle?'

Maybe it was time to open up. 'I don't know, Evie. I know I have so much to be grateful for but I just feel that life is passing me by. The kids are happy with the nanny, Scott is always at work, my friends, yourself included, seem to be doing incredibly well and I just feel that I am surplus to requirements in my own life. I can't even concentrate on things anymore. I keep burning the food, and eating any that I can lay my hands on as you can see.' She gestured to her own body, her first reference to her obvious weight gain. 'The other day I ran a bath for Lexi and nearly flooded the place and if I had a penny for every time I've gone upstairs to fetch something and then forgotten what it is when I climb up there, then I'd have more money than most Swiss bank accounts. I just feel smothered by my own mundane, hum-drum blurry existence. Does that sound awfully selfish? If it wasn't for the pills I'm taking and the odd glass of Merlot I really don't know what I'd do.'

Evie wasn't sure if it sounded selfish or not, but she was visibly shocked by her friend's admission. 'You're taking pills? What are they? Anti-depressants? Have you talked to Scott?'

'He doesn't know about the pills. He'd disapprove as he does of everything. I don't blame him. I think not talking to him is a major part of my slump. He's so busy working that we hardly ever seem to spend quality time together. Plus he seems to fly off the handle pretty easily if things aren't quite as he'd planned. I had to order pizza in for the kids the other night as I'd burnt yet another meal and he went berserk, saying that pizza was not good enough for *his* kids. Not ours, but his. I know he has a stressful job but honestly, I feel like I need to walk on eggshells with him most of the time. I know he's a fantastic father, and a great provider but I am beginning to think that he's bored with me. And who can blame him? Would you want to sleep with ... *this*?' Again she gestured to her body.

'There is nothing wrong with your body, Victoria. This isn't Hollywood, you don't have to be as thin as a breadstick to be accepted. Or to be sexy and fabulous. But how are things in the ... er ... that department?' caged Evie, circling her fingers at Victoria's lap.

'Non-existent of late.'

'Oh ...' Evie mulled over Victoria's answer for a few seconds. 'Do you think there's another woman?'

It wasn't the first time Victoria had considered the notion, but she was fairly sure that there wasn't. 'Unless he's shagging somebody at his work, which is unlikely as I've seen his secretary. Let's just say she's all tweed jackets, tight hair buns and the wrong side of forty-five.'

'What about the nanny?'

Again Evie's words were not something Victoria hadn't mulled over already. 'She spends eighty per cent of her day with the kids and the rest sleeping in her room. I know he's not sneaking in there in the middle of the night as I am hardly sleeping right now, must be the pills, and when I do, it's so light I wake up at the slightest noise. I guess I have just become boring to him. I guess I'm bored by myself too.'

'Well then Vic, you need to shape up and fucking do something about it. "I'm bored" is a stupid thing to say. You have so much not to be bored by. Both within these four walls and the whole world out there. And you're in a privileged position to be able to see all of it should you choose. I know you go between here and the States but really you've seen naught per cent of what's on offer. You have an amazing mind, I know that from our time together at Farmington. Your mind is endless and goes on for forever. Our chats after our girly nights out were some of the most stimulating, amusing and inspiring I've ever had. I miss those days, believe it or not. The pleasantries of Hollywood life can be hugely vacuous. You just need to help your mind work out what to do to make things better. Without being cruel, honey, you have no right to say you're bored. Your life is pretty amazing.'

'That's me told.' Victoria could feel her cheeks rouge with embarrassment.

'Not at all, I just want you to be happy. And if that means taking some time out for yourself then so be it. Why not try and book some time away? Just you and Scott?'

'What about the kids?'

'You've just said that they're perfectly happy with the nanny.'

'I don't think Scott will do it, he's always so busy and the business needs him.'

'The wheels of the financial world will not fall off just because you two choose to spend a few days away together. Do something different, something you'd both enjoy. Reignite the flames of passion.'

The thought pleased Victoria, causing her to smile, something she felt she hadn't done in a while.

'And if he says no?'

'His loss,' stated Evie. 'Do something for you. It sounds like you've lost your mojo and you need to find it PDQ.'

'I guess I am lucky.' There was still a streak of insecurity running through her mind.

'Luckier than poor Mitzi,' said Evie. 'I can't believe our drinking partner and Zumba teacher has just disappeared from view. One minute she's enjoying a holiday with her man and the next … no sign. Surely that puts things into perspective? It's horrendous. I haven't seen her for years. We lost touch sadly, as you do, but I used to love our little gang. Mitzi was always right at the centre of everything.'

Victoria nodded and had to admit that it did put things into perspective. When she'd first heard about Mitzi and Foster's disappearance she had been shocked to the core. Weeks on, like the world at large, she had let her own life cloud any continuing concern. Life goes on, even if it's a treadmill one. 'Do you think poor Mitzi's dead?'

'I hope not. She was always the life and soul. But if it was a film I wouldn't be betting on a Hollywood ending. She and Foster have not been seen for weeks.'

For a moment the two women sat in silence, contemplating poor Mitzi's fate. Looking at her watch, it was Evie who broke the silence.

'Listen Vic, I have to go, I need to go over some lines for tomorrow. Are you going to be alright? I'm really worried about you. I've never seen you like this before. And I mean what's going on in your brain, not with your body. You do know you can phone me whenever you need. If I'm on set then I'll ring back and be round as soon as I can. And you should try and stop the anti-depressants. They may mask the symptoms, but they're not taking away what obviously needs to be sorted.'

As Victoria showed Evie to the front door and kissed her on both cheeks, she actually felt a little more upbeat than she had in a while. Evie's pep talk had done her good. It felt good to have a friend who cared. She would work out what to do to lift her air of malaise. She owed it to her husband, her children and mostly to herself.

Parking herself back in front of the cake in the front room she picked up a slice and flicked on the television with the remote control. Staring back at her was the very handsome Charlie Cooper with an advert for *Rise and Shine.*

I'm sure he dates that weather girl, Georgia, she thought to herself. *She used to be in our Zumba group as well. Those were good days. Fun times.* Thin times. She couldn't join one of those groups now though. All that jiggling flesh. She'd be horrified at what she might see in the gym mirror. She'd spoken to Georgia back then a few times, even been on the odd night out. Nice girl. It was a small world. In fact she was pretty sure that Mitzi and Georgia were best friends. *Poor girl must be out of her mind with worry.*

Eating a large mouthful of cake – one slice wouldn't hurt would it? – Victoria listened to the beauty on the TV. 'Join me, Charlie Cooper next week when we report on the latest celebrity chef cooking course that looks set to take India by storm. I'll be live in Agra speaking to the chef himself and seeing which of the rich and famous are signing up to be taught by the man they call The Curry Master in order to spice up their lives.'

Victoria sat transfixed as a picture of the celebrity chef popped up on screen. She liked his shows.

A few days in India on a cookery course in order to spice up your life. It was just what she needed. Grabbing her iPad, she googled his name and found his official website. Sure enough, there were the details about the course. There was still availability for the one starting in just a few short days' time. The price was astronomical but it included London to Delhi flights, transfers to Agra and a five star hotel.

Within a matter of minutes she had booked two places, one for her and one for Scott. It was just what *they* needed. Chloe could sort the twins out. She and Scott would be putting the spice back into their partnership in more ways than one.

Now all she had to do was organise quick turnaround Indian visas. There was no time to waste. But maybe just another slice of cake first. That cream was delicious.

CHAPTER 8

Rachel Jerome had her fingers crossed as she spoke to her client on the phone. 'Apols, darling, but the dancing show have made it quite clear they won't be needing you, Aaron. Not this season anyway. But good news from *Untamed* magazine, they definitely want you for a double page spread and a cover. A fabulous fitness, top off style shoot so I'm hoping you put that free gym pass to good use. They're paying a glorious three hundred pounds plus expenses, but seeing as it's in London it'll only be a couple of tube fares, sweetness. I'll send through the dates as soon as I have them, bye.'

As she put down the phone, she uncrossed her fingers. She was praying that Aaron wouldn't kick off mid-conversation. Thankfully he hadn't. Not that she knew why. She hadn't even phoned the dance show as she didn't want to rock the boat for potential future bookings. If they thought of her as bothersome they might never book another one of her acts at all, and she had high hopes that her singing stallion escort from the other night might be American Smoothing his way onto the next series. At least if her current train of thought came to fruition.

Rachel also thought Aaron would kick off about the money for the magazine shoot. He'd been receiving a couple of grand an episode for *Surf N Turf* so he should easily hope to match that for photo shoots, but maybe she'd been overestimating his value and pumping up his media worth in her own mind. Surely she wasn't losing her touch? No, these things happen. But a client's a client and maybe his time would come. But for now she'd file his number back into her system in a folder marked LOW PRIORITY. For a client there was no worse fate.

Aaron had lost his temper. Hugely. But only once he'd hung up. He'd picked up a glass and thrown it against the wall of his new flat. It was only a cheap glass, that was all he could afford with the rent he was paying, but he'd have smashed it had it been the finest crystal. It was the satisfaction of the action, not the class of the glass that spoke volumes. He'd clear up later. He needed a drink.

He walked to the Smeg fridge in his flat and reached for a beer. Shit, he'd finished the last one the night before. Fuck, he'd have to go and buy some more. But who wants to sit in a flat on their own drinking beer of an evening? If he'd been back home in Cornwall he would have phoned a mate and headed to the pub, or flicked through his little black book full of telephone numbers. Being in *Surf N Turf* had worked wonders for his sex life and it wasn't just old rose bushes he'd been deflowering on a regular basis. Girls had been lining up to sample his bedding technique or lay their hands on his surfing body. Aaron was an animal in the sack, persistent and seemingly tireless with his stamina. He was always happy enough to 'perform a 180' – a term used in surfing to describe the angle of spin of a surfer's board. To Aaron it was alternating his cock between a woman's willing mouth and hungry pussy. And when another conquest had asked him to perform a 'backdoor' in the sack – a surfing term for entering a barrel from behind the peak of a breaking wave – he was more than happy to oblige and ride that wave to completion.

Slamming the door of his flat behind him he marched off in search of a decent bar. He'd not really explored that much since his arrival in Chelsea but even he knew that there seemed to be a pub or a cocktail bar on every corner. Despite his inner country bumpkin, Aaron couldn't help but be impressed by the wealth of boutiques, hotels and bars that seemed to gloriously stare down at him around every turn. It was no wonder the Bohemian artists of the nineteenth century and the floppy-mop-haired music stars of the sixties had chosen to live there. As he passed bars like Raines Law Room, Rye House, The Tippler and the famed restaurant The Bluebird on King's Road – places he'd read about in his online guide to Chelsea – he could see their attraction but he could feel the expense he'd have to cough up free flowing from every affluent doorway.

His mind kept telling him that Chelsea wasn't for rustic folk like him and that he still longed for a decent boozer with a spit 'n' sawdust feel, a rich amber pint of beer and a good bag of pork scratchings. He wasn't sure if he'd ever find it. Maybe Rachel was right to judge him as she obviously did – the man who apparently put the clot into Cornish clotted cream. Christ, that sanctimonious bitch had made him crave a decent drink.

It didn't take him long to find what he needed. The sign outside the bar listed a catalogue of different wines, spirits and cocktails, but more importantly had a long list of beers. It seemed like the perfect place to lose a few hours. A bit posey and maybe out of his league but what the heck, as long as the beer was good then that was all that was required.

Sitting himself at the bar, he ran his hand through his beard, contemplated the list of beers, found one he'd heard of before and ordered a pint.

A pub was the first thing Jack Christie thought about as he stepped out of the prison that had been his home for the last five years. A pint of ice cold beer had been one of the many things he'd missed while doing time. The only thing ice cold inside had been the showers. Every morning, surrounded by his fellow inmates he'd have to stand there freezing his bollocks off while the sadistic fucking guards stood there watching. Mind you, they weren't the only ones. As Jack's level of physical fitness and body mass had increased so had the stares of some of the other inmates towards his naked body in the shower. At first, he'd been freaked out by their glances. How fucking gay could you be? Just because he had a decent body and a sizable cock on him, it didn't mean he was free rein for any passing lag who blurred the lines between hetero and homo to try and suck him off. But five years was a long time, and after a while, the desire to feel a pair of lips around his erection was too great to resist. If alone in his cell or in the showers and one of the other jailbirds was happy to service him, then Jack was more than happy to lie back and imagine he was popping his seed into the mouth of one of the wank rag girls he had pinned to his wall instead of some hairy-arsed deviant who'd been banged away for too long. As long as he was taking and not giving, then it didn't count, did it?

No, a good woman and the feeling of a moist piece of snatch around his cock was another fancy high on his freedom wish-list. Maybe he could find that in the same place as an ice cold beer.

The woman who sat herself down next to Aaron at the stainless steel super reflective bar was petite in size, probably reaching up to Aaron's chest if they'd been stood alongside each other. Her hair was red, almost terracotta in colour, and ran down, poker straight past her shoulders. He guessed her age at about thirty. Similar to his. She wore a huge pair of sunglasses, unnecessary given the fact she was now inside a relatively dark bar save for the ultra-thin neon strip lighting running across the back of the bar and around the walls. As she placed her bags to the floor – she'd obviously been shopping and judging by the ribbon-tied tissue paper parcels piled up within each of the bags, it was apparent that she'd spent a small fortune – she slid her sunglasses onto her head revealing a small but beautifully dark brown pair of eyes. In horticulture terms they were the shade of conkers and doubtless just as appealing to the male species. She was a fine looking woman, a fact that didn't escape Aaron as he failed to take his eyes off her and downed his much-needed pint.

It was something the woman couldn't help noticing too and as she positioned herself up onto the plush barstool next to Aaron she turned and acknowledged his attention with a small smile and nod. Aaron smiled back, hoping that she hadn't noticed the bulge rising within his boxer shorts. He adjusted his position slightly to face his crotch away from her.

She ordered a large glass of Sancerre and took a hefty gulp of it as soon as it arrived. As she lifted her glass to her lips, Aaron noticed a band of gold on her wedding finger. He felt his cock subside. Oh well, another non-starter unless she was playing away from home. Still, he was in the mood to chat and providing she hadn't seen his appreciative boner he figured he had nothing to lose by breaking the ice.

'Thirsty work, shopping, then?'

'Very much so, but a lot of fun. I enjoy it.' Was there a richness of accent in her voice? It was invitingly exotic but he couldn't place it. She smiled, a green light to continue as far as he was concerned.

'What have you been buying? Looks posh.'

A stain of red seemed to colour her cheeks as he looked down at her bags. Her skin possessed a polar white innocence that suggested she was naturally very fair, but the summer had given her a subtle bronzing, although not enough to hide her flush.

'You don't recognise the bags?' She curled her lips into a tiny smile.

'Actually no, I've only just moved into the area, so I'm kind of the new man in town. A stranger to these parts. Let me see …' He looked down at the bags and read the names aloud. 'Rigby & Peller, Intimissimi, Coco De Mer … no, I don't know any of them.'

Was the woman smiling at him or about him? With amusement or disbelief? He wasn't sure.

'You're forgiven, I've been buying underwear. It's good for the soul.'

'And for the husband, I bet.'

The woman laughed. It seemed genuine. At least he hadn't offended her. 'You can ask him yourself, this is him now.' She pointed over Aaron's shoulder towards the bar entrance where a man, a good deal older than her, Aaron guessed, was striding towards them.

'Hello, darling. Been busy, I see,' said the man.

Aaron wasn't sure if he meant the shopping or her close proximity to himself. It was true, there were a lot of empty chairs in the bar and she had chosen to sit next to him. *Still got it*, Aaron thought to himself with an inner smile.

The woman peered down at her shopping. 'Of course, I have to look nice for you, don't I? I think you'll appreciate the effort I've gone to. Anyway, shall we go?' She took another large gulp of wine from her glass and drained it clean. She made to step down from the bar stool.

'There's no hurry,' said the man. 'I found a parking meter for an hour so we can stay for another drink if you like. And besides, you haven't introduced me to your friend here.' He looked at Aaron quizzically. A little too quizzically for Aaron's liking. He'd obviously seen them chatting when he came in. *Jealous type*, mused Aaron. *Mind you, with a looker like that for a wife, who could blame him?*

Aaron held out his hand and introduced himself. 'Name's Aaron Rose. Never been here before and maybe at these prices I won't again.'

'Devon Bellamy.' The pair shook hands. 'I see you've met my wife.' There was a distinct blanketing of sarcasm in his tone. Jealousy, a hint of a threat or an acknowledgement that his wife was indeed drop dead gorgeous? Aaron couldn't be sure.

'Well, to be honest, no, I knew she was married, but I don't even know her name.' He held out his hand to her.

She took his hand. It felt tiny within his, like a fledgling being placed into the mouth of a crocodile. He was almost afraid to shake it, through fear of crushing it. 'Tanya.'

He turned his attention back to Devon. He was a good looking man, late forties, a grey but full head of hair, virtually line free skin. He was as smooth as Aaron was hairy. Aaron would have described him as suave, almost borderline posh, definitely dapper and a snappy dresser for a man of his age. He looked sharp. Every detail thought about. His crisp, open-neck shirt and dark blue Levi's suited him. On many people his age it would have screamed mid-life-crisis.

'Tanya was just explaining to me about the shops she'd been to,' proffered Aaron. 'Not that I know them. I don't think they exist where I'm from. Must be a London thing.'

'And where might that be?' asked Devon. Any trace of hostility in his voice had definitely diluted.

'Cornwall, I was working on a TV show there about surfing and gardening and moved to London for my big break, but so far it's been a big fat zero. No work, no money, so I came here to drown my sorrows.'

Why was Aaron telling him all this? He didn't need his sympathy. He guessed it just felt good to talk. He could hardly tell Rachel what a crap job he thought she was doing, could he? Having a shit agent was one thing, not having one at all was quite another.

'I've never heard of it.' Slightly mocking in tone? Aaron wasn't sure. 'I suspect Tanya has, though. She loves shows like that, being so young and impressionable. Always has her head buried in a trashy magazine featuring that type of thing. Can I buy you another beer? Tanya, what will you have?'

Tanya felt her cheeks colour as she pointed towards her empty glass and said, 'Same again'.

Was the man belittling his wife? Aaron felt a little awkward but a free drink was a free drink and he wasn't exactly in the position to look a gift horse in the mouth. 'Thanks, that would be awesome.'

Having bought the drinks, the three of them moved to a table at the side of the bar. Devon wiped its surface with a napkin before they sat down.

'So you do a bit of gardening then, Aaron?' enquired Devon.

'Er, yeah, the show I worked on was about a team of landscape gardeners. We used to surf in our spare time, the perfect thing to do on the Cornish coast. It was called *Surf N Turf*. The show has been pretty big to be honest, but I secured an agent who thought it was time I left and moved up here. So far, bad idea.'

'As I said, I haven't heard of it,' said Devon. 'Have you, Tanya?'

She shook her head, seemingly less chatty and slightly fearful now that her husband was here.

'So are you looking for work?'

'Hell I am, sure.'

'A gardening project? We live near Hampstead Village, north London. It's an affluent area and we have a good home with a sizable garden, but I need it overhauling. Some of the areas are not looking as orderly as I'd like. I'm away from home a lot with work and Tanya's not exactly green-fingered. It's a decent project but we'd obviously allow you to do your TV thing if that's what you're trying to achieve as long as you kept us prioritised. Plus we'd pay the going rate and my wife can look after you and give you anything you need.'

Aaron loved the idea of Tanya giving him just what he desired, but found it a little odd that Devon seemed almost to be offering his wife to him. 'Is it a one-man job? Because I'm flying solo right now.'

'Why don't you tell us?' He reached into his pocket and pulled out a business card. 'This is our address and telephone number. Ring us when you're free and we can arrange a time for you to take a look and we can take it from there.'

'Sounds perfect. I don't know what to say.'

'Well, hopefully you'll say yes. I need the garden sorted. Now come on, Tanya, we had better make a move, one minute over the meter time allowance and the bastards around here tow you off straight away.'

Devon and Tanya emptied their glasses and moved towards the door.

'Great to meet you both. I'll be ringing you as soon as possible,' said Aaron.

In fact, judging from the smile and suggestive wink that Tanya flipped him as she left the bar behind her husband, shopping in hand, Aaron thought that it might be even sooner than that.

His cock twitched back into action as he watched her glide out of the bar. It only subsided when he caught sight of Devon staring straight back at him through the front window. He wasn't smiling. Something told Aaron that Devon didn't smile a lot.

CHAPTER 9

Opening her eyes made no difference. It was two shades of black. An eerie darkness that wrapped around her. The silence was deafening. Attempting to move was futile. Pain and restraints blocked that capability. Movement that had once been so free, so fluid, was now impossible.

The floor below her was hard and cold. Was it wet? She couldn't tell. If it was, then maybe it was of her own making. Thoughts inside her brain wrapped around each other like bindweed, as brutal and painful as barbed wire. Thoughts of past, present and future spliced together, smothered with uncertainty. What was this? How had it come to be?

Was that a noise coming from somewhere? Voices …

CHAPTER 10

Georgia stared at the plaque on her Wimbledon Village bedroom wall. It was a quote from one of her favourite books; 'I've learned that waiting is the most difficult bit, and I want to get used to the feeling, knowing that you're with me, even when you're not by my side.' It made her think of Mitzi. How could it not? Everything did. Every minute she had to wait – the minutes that turned to hours, the hours that turned to days – a little piece of her strength and hope that her friend was still alive seemed to be chipped away. But she willed herself to remain hopeful because it was all she could do. She'd spoken to Mitzi's mother as much as she could. She didn't really know Mitzi's mum that well and she suspected that her countless phone calls searching for any hopeful scrap of news were becoming an annoyance to her. Each 'how are you coping?' conversation had become a carbon copy of the last and indeed the one before that. Mitzi was an only child and her father had died years before. Her mum, a women in her early sixties and frail before her time, had tried all she could think of to find her daughter, but to no avail. Georgia's bombarding of mutual friends on Facebook and Twitter for any information or clues had offered a wealth of well-wishers but nothing concrete. Everyone who knew Mitzi prayed for her safe return, as did those Georgia had contacted connected to Foster, but nobody could deliver any clues as to what had happened. The young lovers had simply vanished and somehow the world kept turning. And it was a world that Georgia wanted to halt so that she could momentarily forget about the horror of what might be.

Which is why the idea of a few adventure-full days in India were stirring her senses into the first sense of vague normality she had felt in weeks.

Work had been totally understanding about her need for a few days off and had actively encouraged her to join Charlie for the trip. She had no intention of partaking in the cookery course but the idea of a few days doing nothing more challenging than reaching for a streak of factor twenty to smooth over her skin as she contemplated a swim in the pool or another cocktail from the bar was her idea of an idyllic Indian experience. Guilt streaked through her that she was enjoying herself while the mystery of Mitzi continued but she had to believe that the authorities were far more skilled in tracing any clues than she could ever be.

As Georgia piled her clothes – a combination of cooling silks and crisp, loose cottons – into her suitcase, she couldn't wait to escape the UK. The constant 2.45am alarm calls for work and her worry over Mitzi's disappearance were beginning to turn her brain into a maelstrom of panic and pent-up anxiety. At least a change of scenery, especially one with an architectural legacy of majestic monuments at every turn, was guaranteed to alter her mindset a little. Shutting her case and snapping the padlock into place, Georgia picked up her phone and rang the number of her local cab firm.

Within twenty minutes she was in a taxi and ready to head towards the airport to meet Charlie. She wound her window down and allowed the late summer breeze to caress her face as the taxi sped off.

Watching her Wimbledon Village cottage vanish from sight, she then closed her eyes and tried to envisage the colourful, sense-awakening delights that awaited her five thousand miles away.

She truly couldn't wait.

There was no colour, no delight, nothing to sense apart from the dry, split, painful feel of her own lips. She tried to swallow, attempting to force some form of moisture into her throat. The binding clamped between her teeth made any attempt both fruitless and feeble. There was a stench in the air. Soiled and rotten.

She could still feel the burn inside her chest from when she had run away from what she had seen. The horror of the blood, it's deep, deadly, finality evident to her even from a distance. Every muscle inside her stretched to the max as she tried to escape the barbarity of that night. The night that everything had changed. The night that would live with her for forever. Stay with her for her entire life.

But what life? What was left of it? All she could do was wait. Wait for an end … whatever that may be.

If Victoria had to read the *Hello* feature detailing the busty, dumpy ex-pop star and her 'joy' at finally finding Mr Right in the shape of her fifth husband one more time she was liable to scream. Not only did she know that the gobby blonde was having the best sex of her life, that her kids (all by different fathers) were already calling Hubby Number Five 'Daddy' and that she planned to reform the group she had once mimed her way through to try and have another crack at chart glory, she also knew that she was likely to deck the low-rent Z-lister should she ever meet her. 'Odious' had a new dictionary definition. And seeing as Victoria was sitting in the VIP Lounge at London's Heathrow waiting for Scott to join her, there was actually a slim possibility. The article did state that the talent vacuum (unless you considered diet yo-yoing and releasing fitness DVDs a true talent) was considering India as a honeymoon destination, although she wasn't sure as 'the kids prefer spaghetti hoops on toast to curry and all those hot dishes would shoot through her like a bullet from a smoking gun as she was strictly a meat and potato pie kind of girl'.

At least the speedy evacuation of her holiday fare would help with the dieting, contemplated Victoria as she flicked the pages to stop herself from reading the article again. If it hadn't been for a juicy Victoria Fox eBook, a behind-the-scenes magazine feature on Evie's last film in her *Hello* magazine and her supply of anti-depressants, then the last three and half hours of waiting for Scott would have been unbearable.

Where was he? Last time she had spoken to him he was ready to leave the office and head to the airport. She'd not heard from him since and every time she rang his mobile, it went directly to the messaging service.

Still, the flight wasn't for another hour and a quarter so there was still time. She'd just have to wait.

Throwing the magazine down onto the glass table, Victoria contemplated her next move. Scott had reluctantly agreed to the trip, not that he had been given a huge amount of choice considering she'd served him with a fait accompli, in the form of a set of tickets, an Indian itinerary and a severely depleted bank account.

Chloe had been given her orders that she was to be nanny twenty-four/seven for the next few days, something that the kids had revelled in when Victoria had told them. The next few days were to be a chance for her and Scott to rekindle the embers of whatever heat their marriage still housed.

But there would be no rekindling without a husband to re-kindle with. Where was he?

Victoria scanned the lounge. She recognised a couple of faces. A young actor from one of the TV soaps and a Loose Woman seemed to be chatting cozily a few tables away, obviously aided by the two glasses of fizz they were clinking together with a flirtatious regularity. *I wonder if they're on my plane,* pondered Victoria. *Could make for amusing in-flight entertainment.* Thankfully there was no sign of the woman from the magazine and her brood of hoops-loving offspring.

Maybe a glass of something bubbly would be a good idea while she waited for Scott to arrive. A quick trip to the executive lounge bar later, Victoria returned with the requisite champagne in hand. She eased herself back into the comfort of her lounge chair and picked up another magazine, which thankfully somebody had deposited while she had been ordering her drink. She glanced over the headlines emblazoned across the cover. 'MY TATTOO TRAUMA BY TALENT SHOW TV TOTTY'. *Where would magazines be without a bit of alliteration?* smiled Victoria, the comforting glow of the champagne washing through her. 'SOAP STAR MONTANA PHOENIX'S LATEST FAMILY NIGHTMARE!' Oh, Victoria liked her, she'd been at school with her daughter. That could be a juicy read. 'NOVA'S BOTCHED BOTOX FEARS!' Nova Chevalier, the US's latest reality star discussing her worries about 'growing old gracefully'. *Ironic,* thought Victoria, *seeing as she's had more plastic inserted into her than a cashpoint.* Victoria found herself reaching for the magazine in order to pass the time.

Twenty minutes later, her flight to India now announced as boarding and her knowledge of Spongebob tummy-tucks and buttock implants somewhat enhanced by her time reading, Victoria's phone sounded.

It was a text message from Scott. 'Vic, we have to cancel. Am needed by major client at the office. Can't let him down, he brings in millions. Sorry. Will make it up to you. Forgive me xx'

So that was it, no more India. Money wasted – not that finances mattered – and her dreams of a few cardamom-scented romantic days in the land of the *Kama Sutra* smashed into pieces. And to add insult to injury, by text message.

The screen of Victoria's phone flashed another message, a battery warning that her phone needed charging. She read the words, but the message that suddenly weaved through her thoughts was completely different. Say her phone had died, say she hadn't read Scott's text, say she'd just assumed he'd been delayed and was on the next flight out to Delhi. Say, say, say ...

Without any further contemplation, Victoria switched off her phone, drained the last few drops from her champagne glass, grabbed the magazine – she had soap stars to read about – and marched determinedly towards the departure gate. She should have been thinking about Scott, but instead found herself imagining what she would look like with a buttock implant. The notion amused her. She was still smiling as she watched the runway disappear beneath her from her first class seat on the plane, another glass of champers in hand.

'Now, you see, Jacob, that man would look fabulous on TV. Bel-Air has never seen the likes,' cooed Nova Chevalier as she waltzed into the lobby of the Wyndham Grand Hotel in Agra, India. 'Did you see his red turban and that cute little outfit, and that bushy little mutton-chop beard of his. He's like some fabulous Dickensian character, just with darker skin of course. And he's very skilled at bringing in the luggage too. He was balancing those cases like a seal in the circus. Seriously, we need him on

Super Nova. Why the bigwigs aren't here is beyond me. You need to convince them that *Nova Goes to Bollywood* would make an unmissable episode. Me, stirring some goat curry in a beautiful figure-hugging sari with a pretend ring through my nose would be a ratings grabber. Now, give the darling man some poopies, or whatever this currency is called, and we'll settle into our suite, angel. And pass me my electric fan will you, Jacob, I am borderline clammy over here. It's hotter than hell, and I can't be sweating in front of fans. We are syndicated here, aren't we? And take photos of everything. If it's Indian, snap it.'

And with that, a deliriously happy and playfully giddy Nova Chevalier and her husband-slash-manager-slash-dogsbody, Jacob, arrived in India. Ready to try out the cookery course, ready to await the arrival of Nova's beloved son, Charlie, and his girlfriend Georgia, and ready to convince the telly execs back in LA that sending Nova back to India for a future episode of TV's most talked about reality show would be an idea hotter than the rays of the midday sun currently baking the Agra skyline.

CHAPTER 11

Jack by name and Jack by nature, Jack Christie was definitely a Jack the Lad. Freedom had never felt better. His balls unloaded, he walked down the street away from last night's lay's flat and felt the warming rays of the sun against his skin. He considered his options.

He could head to the nearest station and catch a train to his mother's house. He hadn't even told her he was out and to be honest he doubted very much if she would care. She'd pretty much disowned Jack the moment he'd been put away and hadn't visited him in the entire time he'd been inside. She was deeply religious and had always hoped that she and her vicar husband had raised Jack to a lifetime of righteousness. Their hopes had been dashed with his first conviction, and despite their love of a 'higher power', they had never actually seen the light as far as Jack was concerned and been able to turn the other cheek. Not that Jack cared. The thought of returning home to a house full of crucifixes and 'thou shalt not …' verses decorating every surface was about as appealing as a full body wax. And probably more painful.

No, it was time to reestablish a few contacts of old. He needed money and excitement and those were definitely two things that would not be readily forthcoming if he returned to the unwelcoming bosom of the family home. He needed to get his life back on track, and he knew exactly where to go.

CHAPTER 12

'This is what I call five star luxury,' sighed Georgia, as she let her naked feet sway from side to side in the Wyndham's swimming pool. The cooling waters were the perfect complement to the feeling of heat kissing her shoulders from the Indian sunshine as she perched on the edge of the pool.

'I tell you the viewers will freaking love it. Take some photos, darling Jacob.' It was Nova's words that cut through the serenity of the air. 'Didn't I tell you this was the perfect idea for a family reunion, Charlie? Could life be any more glamorous?'

Despite the barking of her orders, Georgia had to admit that it was good to see Nova and Jacob again. She may be larger than life, but she always raised a smile. Didn't they say that you should always surround yourself with people who are going to lift you higher? Nova always did that. And with thoughts of Mitzi and Foster still filling her mind, Georgia needed every distraction she could find. Nova was a tonic for sure. Jacob might not have agreed as he quit the slumber and comfort of his canopied poolside chair and grabbed his camera for more photography duties. He must have already taken about a hundred photos since their arrival at the hotel a few hours earlier.

'No, indeed mother, this place is pretty special,' agreed Charlie, smoothing a layer of sun tan lotion onto his chest and arms. 'This hotel is the perfect setting for the course. I can't believe you're doing it. I seem to remember your speciality in the kitchen when I was growing up was corned beef hash and eggs. Not exactly exotic.'

'Your mother likes to travel, Charlie,' said Jacob, his camera clicking as he spoke. 'I think it was the lure of the location and not the urge to beef up her culinary skills that brought us here. Now, how about a family portrait? Charlie, Georgia ... in with your mother, please?'

'As long as this is not used to promote your blessed pro-gramme,' stated Charlie, moving into position alongside his mum. 'I'm tickled pink by your success but I want nothing to do with that show, okay?'

'Oh, you're *tickled pink*, are you? How very Mary Poppins, darling. You are too British for your own good,' mocked Nova, her accent clipped and pinched. 'A spoonful of sugar for my son.'

Charlie had always distanced himself from his mother's show. Not that he wasn't proud of her, he was. Immensely. But he wanted his own career to be about his skill as a reporter and not merely the nepotistic link that he was Nova's only son. He had made it a rule that neither he, nor Georgia, would feature in her mother's televisual adventures. It was an arrangement that both he and Georgia were adamant they would stick to.

'Anyway,' stated Nova. 'You should be thrilled I heard about this course, it's managed to blag you a free working trip that you could bring dear Georgia on. We all love a freebie even if we could afford to splash out for it anyway. That's the madness of the world we live in. Jacob and I could pay for everything but quite often we pay for nothing. It's fabulous! Now, come and sit down next to me, darling girl.' She patted the seat alongside her and motioned for Georgia to join her. 'I need to ask you some questions, Georgia, woman-to-woman.'

Georgia, knowing that opposition was futile, settled herself alongside Nova.

'Why don't you go and grab us some cocktails, Jacob? I see the bar is open.' Nova flicked her fingers dismissively – a reality TV diva tendency she had picked up without realising – and pointed Jacob towards the submerged pool bar at the centre of the hotel pool. The gesture from anybody else would have incensed Jacob, dented his masculine pride, but Nova was her own woman, and if Jacob knew two things in life it was that his wife loved him deeply and that her actions, although sometimes seemingly rude, were always served up from a heart of pure adoration. There were moments when Nova played a caricature of herself, but Jacob knew her well enough to see beyond that. Underneath any adopted TV mannerisms she was definitely more gratitude than attitude. And he knew how to play her to both his own advantage and hers. Nova was a breeze after some of the players he'd dealt with over the years. A man like Jacob Chevalier had climbed the Hollywood ladders of business by playing the right tune to charm many a snake along the way.

'And you Charlie, be a sweetie and fetch Georgia and me a list of treatments from the health spa would you?'

Charlie headed off as instructed, mouthing 'good luck' to Georgia as he did so and blowing her a kiss. Georgia couldn't help but smile, an inner glow melting her heart as only Charlie could.

The two men in her life dispatched at her wishes, Nova turned to Georgia, making sure that her son was out of earshot. 'Isn't Charlie divine? He's always been such a good lad, as you well know. Now, what are your thoughts on getting married? Has he even hinted at setting a date as yet?'

Marriage. Nova's number one topic of conversation.

'No, not at the moment, Nova,' grinned Georgia. The thought pleased her immensely but she was aware they hadn't discussed the actual wedding yet. 'Charlie and I are really happy as we are. A long engagement suits us just fine. If anything changes then you'll be the first to know.' Georgia had lost count of the number of times she had indulged in the same, identikit conversation with Nova.

'Well, you're not getting any younger and neither is Charlie, Georgia. Just saying. You think you have all the time in the world and then, boom, your body clock has ticked past its sell by date and then there's no-one to carry on the Chevalier name.'

'Cooper,' said Georgia. 'I'd be Georgia Cooper.'

'Of course, darling, of course. But a Chevalier wedding would work wonders for the ratings. Kanye and Kim anyone? Are you sure you can't persuade Charlie to be in our little show?'

Oh yes, you could always rely on Nova to be a tonic, that was for sure, and for a while all thoughts of Mitzi disappeared from her mind.

Victoria's mind was full of Mitzi as she made her way across the terraced lawns of the Wyndham and headed towards the pool area. Mitzi had always been such a ball of energy at the Zumba classes. It was tragic to think that maybe that energy was no more. Her thoughts drifted to days gone by …

'And reach for it, girls, stretch up and feel that burn. And again from the top. To the left … and one, two, three, clap!' Mitzi's voice was popping like a cork as she excitedly gave out orders to the young women gathered in front of her. 'C'mon Vic, you are working it, lady …'

Victoria, out of breath but loving the fizziness of physicality running through her, smiled at Mitzi from her place in the front row of the fitness group as she spoke to her. Mitzi knew how to make her savour every last moment of the Zumba lessons. It was forty-five minutes of high energy hip-swaying, booty-gyrating action and Victoria loved it.

'You know I am, Mitzi!' shouted Victoria, allowing herself to holler as loudly as her frenzied breathing would allow. She turned to the woman at her side, Evie, and smiled at their enthusiasm. There were about twenty women in the group, of all ages, and she and Evie were always placed front row, centre stage. They let out a whoop as they spun around and followed Mitzi's choreography. As they did so, they could see those gathered in the rows behind them, all equally bubbling over with Mitzi's infectious excitement as they moved their bodies to the sounds of a beat-laden slab of Christina Aguilera. Many of the women in the group had been on nights out together. There was Mitzi's best friend, Georgia, she'd spoken to her a few times, spinning tip to toe in skintight Nike Pro, a friend of Evie's called Nush from college bumping her Skechers in the air and a whole host of hyped up ladies loving the feeling that Mitzi was giving them. And the exciting thing was that after most lessons you could guarantee that Mitzi would insist that those willing decamped to the local bar. Life was for getting fit, but as Mitzi said, 'you get fit for the fitties'. And by that she meant men.

And men were definitely on the agenda as Victoria, Evie, Mitzi, Nush and Georgia giggled their way through bottles of Prosecco while flirting with a group of guys frequenting the same bar. Victoria, her inhibitions doused in bubbles, was gyrating her buttocks, rock hard post class, into the more than willing groin of a licorice coloured beauty with biceps wider than her waist and a smile that outshone the Aurora Borealis. And from what she could feel it wasn't just his biceps that were impressive in size. Evie and her friend Nush watched on, grinning their approval. Mitzi and Georgia, both downing Sambuca at the bar, squealed as they watched Victoria in action, carefree and enjoying every moment of her suitor's admiration.

Victoria snogged the man, loving the feel of his lips against hers, her kisses deep and urgent. For a moment she forgot completely that there were people around her, able to watch her every move. Blame the drink, she didn't care. She was having the time of her life. It was moments like this that made her grateful that her parents had all but deported her from New Orleans to start school at Farmington Grange. It was there she'd met some of the best friends she'd ever known.

It was a drunken Mitzi who pulled Victoria and the chisel-jawed beauty apart. Not because she objected, far from it, she had something to say. 'And the prize for best bloke pulling of the evening goes to …' She let out a makeshift fanfare with her lips. '…Victoria Wentworth!' As Evie, Georgia and Nush applauded Victoria, Mitzi reached down into her Michael Kors bag and pulled out a tiny silver trophy.

'I meant to give this to Zumba mover of the night, but I forgot,' slurred Mitzi. 'So, Victoria, you receive it, honey, for fabulous drunken services to womankind in snogging beauties like him.' She pointed at the man, somewhat embarrassed to find himself suddenly the centre of so much female attention, and handed the trophy over to a beaming Victoria.

She still had it somewhere. Probably in a box underneath her and Scott's bed. How come she still had that, but had managed to let herself lose contact with Mitzi? When she had met Scott all Zumba lessons and girly nights out seemed to dwindle, despite Mitzi and Evie's constant asking. Victoria had shifted from hedonism to homemaker at a rate of nought to sixty in as many seconds. From trophy winner to trophy wife.

Despite thoughts of Mitzi, Victoria's mind was already de-stressing since her arrival in India. If she had any reason for suspicion about Scott she consciously pushed it to one side and wouldn't let it shadow her brain. If she couldn't be here to rebuild bridges with Scott, then she would try to rebuild them with her former self. Maybe it was the romantic air of India but she was determined to feel good about herself and her relationship again.

Her mind snapped back to reality as she nearly bumped full-pelt into the virtually naked torso of a very handsome man. Actually, make that drop dead gorgeous. He was wearing Havaianas and a pair of snug-fitting swimming trunks that obviously housed something that could make even the most innocent of women raise an inquisitive eyebrow. His dark hair was slicked back onto his head and his skin gave off the healthy, glossy glow of a man who obviously looked after himself.

She could feel a flush of colour stain her cheeks. She immediately thought of her own body shape and size. Thank God for the loose fitting kaftan-like creation she has chosen to head poolside in. In a rare moment of lust, though, all thoughts of her own extra body inches were replaced by a contemplation of what the man was housing in his bathers. She inwardly smiled at the thought, more than a ripple of desire taking her by surprise.

'I am so sorry, I wasn't looking where I was going. I think I had the sun in my eyes,' he said.

A touch perplexed, Victoria remained silent for a moment, staring deep into the man's face. Didn't she know him from somewhere? Suddenly aware of how awkward she must have seemed, Victoria began to speak.

'No worries, I was miles away too. I was just taking all of this in.' She gestured to her surroundings.

'It's amazing, isn't it? Are you here for the cookery course?' Charlie couldn't help but inwardly smile too. It was obvious the women fancied him. It was still good to know that he could turn a good-looking lady's head. Especially when she bumped into him while he was wearing the most minimal of outfits. *Does any man ever tire of that?* mused Charlie. He thought not. Red blood was red blood and it was always good to advertise.

'Er … yes, I am. Thought I'd give it a try. I'm fed up of burning everything back at home. Needed an extra bit of help, love the chef, thought it would give me a certain culinary flair?' Victoria was rambling.

'Are you here from the States?' I'm detecting an accent,' said the man. 'Me too. Although I live in the UK now. My name's Charlie Cooper.'

'Of course, you're the man from the morning TV show. You were the one who told me about this course in the first place. On the TV I mean, not in person. We've never met, but I've seen you a lot.' Recognition may have fallen into place, but she was still rambling. 'And yes, I'm from the States, New Orleans, but I live in London now, which is why I know you …' Her words filtered away, she was not quite sure what to say next.

'And you are?' Charlie held out his hand to shake hers.

'Oh sorry, I'm Victoria Palmer-Roberts. Nice to meet you.'

'You too, doubtless I'll see you on the course. Or poolside if you're heading that way. I'm just going to the spa for a list of treatments for my mother and girlfriend. They're plotting what to have. Have you tried the spa yet?'

Victoria didn't answer. She hadn't actually heard the question as she'd stopped concentrating when he'd mentioned the word 'girlfriend'. Of course he was taken. And she knew who by, of course. Georgia. She hadn't seen her for years, and now she was mere metres away. For a whisper of a moment she felt guilty that she had been having the most wanton inner desires about Georgia's man but she quickly surpressed it. She didn't really know Georgia, did she? Not like she knew Evie and Mitzi. And if she wasn't mistaken, there was a glint of danger in Charlie's eye that suggested that he was not as wholesome as he was handsome. Was that her imagination? Something told her otherwise. For the moment, it wasn't just that her husband was physically thousands of miles away, but any thoughts of him were, too.

Realising that an answer wasn't forthcoming about the treatments, a bemused yet pumped up Charlie said goodbye and swaggered off towards the spa.

Victoria smiled, waved her hand and carried on towards the pool. She'd say hi to Georgia. It would be good to see her again, wouldn't it? Her skin prickled slightly as she started to walk. Was it the sun causing that or was that a slick of jealousy she was suddenly experiencing? Victoria wasn't sure.

Georgia recognised Victoria straight away. The American girl who used to be part of Mitzi's Zumba group and had shared a few nights out with the girls.

'Oh my God, now you're a blast from the past. It's Victoria, isn't it?'

Victoria was amazed she could remember her name and instantly warmed to Georgia. Even though they had shared evenings together they had never been close and Victoria couldn't help but feel that her appearance had changed drastically since the two women had last crossed paths.

'Yes, and you're Georgia. Nice to see you again. Especially somewhere as beautiful as this. I think the last time was probably on drunken nights out way back when with Mitzi and Evie.' The two women hugged and as they did, in some small way bonded, without words, over their connection to Mitzi. Two satellites, disconnected in their own worlds, but that had both once circled the same moon.

For the next ten minutes the women talked about their lives, Victoria filling Georgia in on her marriage to Scott and her children, and Georgia talking about Charlie. Georgia introduced Victoria to Jacob and Nova. Victoria instantly recognised her and couldn't stop herself from mentioning that she'd been reading about her on the flight over.

Charlie rejoined the group. 'I see you've all met,' he commented. Both Georgia and Victoria's eyes fell on him in appreciation as he reached the pool.

'It's amazing, I used to be the same Zumba group as Victoria a few years ago,' laughed Georgia. 'We were both taught by ...' Her voice faded away before she completed the sentence, almost afraid to mention the common link between them.

'Mitzi,' said Victoria. A moment of hush seemed to fall across the group before Victoria spoke again.

'Isn't the latest news just awful? I was just reading about it on my iPad. I was praying the outcome would be different.'

All heads turned quizzically towards her.

'The latest news? What do you mean?' asked Georgia, feeling a shiver down her spine.

Victoria reached for her iPad and flicked to the article she'd been reading back in her room. She handed it over.

Fear gripped Georgia as she read the headline. 'DEAD BODY FOUND IN CANYON COULD BE THAT OF MISSING BRIT TOURIST.'

CHAPTER 13

As a businessman, Jacob Chevalier could be harder to manipulate than the back row of a rugby scrum and just as tough. He could be a softie for the right woman, and there had certainly been many of those over the years, but when it came to dealings inside the boardroom, Jacob came from the school of thought that equated ruthless and decisive with invincible. And he knew what worked. He had built his empire on a foundation of fear, respect and taking risks. If these risks occasionally caused a ripple of insecurity deep in his soul, this would definitely be hidden, fathoms beneath the surface. In his world, a crack of weakness could only grow and destroy.

Men feared him, women adored him and he loved it that way. It gave him power. Strength. Like that of his heroes; Don King, Aristotle Onassis, Don Arden. Promotors, agents, billionaires, tycoons ... men who succeeded in life. Players who could see what was good for them. Men who could spot the act to make the next million and see the opportunity to unite with someone who would be their perfect partner. And do everything it took to keep them on top. To Jacob, he and Nova were invincible. Even if at times she could drive him completely round the bend. If she merely worked for him then she would have been fired by now. End of. No questions. But when he met Nova, not only did he see someone who could snowball his bank account with six-figure zeroes TV appeal, but also someone who could work his heart to perfection. He fell in love. Sometimes even the hardest of shells could house the softest of centres.

CHAPTER 14

Since his agent hadn't rung him since his *Untamed* magazine shoot, Aaron was more than keen to take Devon and Tanya up on their offer of gardening work. He felt much more at home felling trees and planting foxgloves than he did getting his kit off and prancing around in tight shorts and boxing gloves at the magazine shoot.

As he walked into the garden at their huge London home, Aaron couldn't help but take a sharp intake of breath at the expanse of green that lay before his eyes. This was the gardening equivalent of winning an Oscar.

'So you'll take the job?' questioned Devon as he, Aaron and Tanya walked around the garden.

'Absolutely. You've got some seriously tasty trees here. Stuff's a bit overgrown in places and there are flowers that need reviving or repositioning but I can have this place looking ship-shape in a matter of weeks. If you're happy with my price, then I'm happy to start as soon as possible.' Aaron beamed from underneath his beard.

Devon looked at the quote again written on the sheet of paper held in his hands. 'I have no issues paying this at all,' he said. 'It's a case of when can you start? I want rid of anything overgrown as soon as possible. Some smart orderly flower beds and rows of trees would be perfect.'

'You've got it. Do you have tools here? I can have mine sent up from Cornwall in the next couple of days but if you have some here right now then I could start straight away. The sun is out so I might as well make the most of it.'

'They're all lined up in the shed at the far end of the garden.' Devon gestured towards a large outhouse in the distance. 'There's a tractor mower in there too and some overalls and gloves if you need to get changed. If you want to get washed up or use the bathroom there's one in the studio alongside the main house. My first wife used to paint in there so it's pretty much a self-contained unit. You can treat it as your own.'

'Right then, I'll get started,' said Aaron.

'Good,' replied Devon. 'And I'm sure Tanya can bring you some drinks, can't you, Tanya? I'm sure you'll soon work up a sweat in this weather. You'll sort that, Tanya? I am sure you'll enjoy it.' It was more of an order than a question and laced with suggestion.

'With pleasure. I'll go and prepare something,' she replied.

Shaking Devon's hand and sealing the deal, Aaron watched as the husband and wife walked back towards the house. Tanya looked good from behind too, her shapely ass filling her skinny leg jeans to perfection. Rolling up his sleeves and heading to the shed, Aaron knew that he was going to enjoy this job. Both the money and the view. Even if he did find Devon more than just a tad creepy.

Devon walked into his study and sat himself down at his desk. He stared at the vibrant piece of artwork hanging on the far wall of his office. It was a delicious riot of colours. The opposite of how he lived his life. Slashes of paint fused together in a Jackson Pollock style. He stared at the name written in paint at the bottom right hand corner. Sophia Bellamy, his dear departed first wife. Six feet under but always present and alive through her paintings. She had been a true talent. So gifted in so many ways. A good and beautiful wife, a doting and caring mother. Sophia had brought so much to the family home.

But then it had all gone wrong. All of that hadn't been enough to keep her happy. Devon had not been able to keep her satisfied. As a husband he had failed. The order of things had been broken. Not as it should be. Something was out of place.

That was when the demons had started inside his mind. The doubts, the insecurities, the worms of anger that seemed to spread some kind of plague within his body. Despite his best efforts to bring her back to where he wanted her in his heart, Devon could feel his wife slipping from him. No amount of expensive jewels or bottles of her favourite scent could guide her back into his arms. The something that was out of place was well and truly shattered. He returned home one day to find her wardrobe empty, her car gone and a note on the dresser stating that she had decided to leave. Her reason – the love between them had died. The real reason – she had found love with another man.

She wasn't coming back, she never would. She couldn't. Death was so final. And anyway, he had Tanya now.

Devon felt his anger rise within his core. He stared at the painting. The slash of green, the colour of his jealousy. The slash of black, the colour of his soul. The slash of red, the colour of her betrayal. The colour of sin. The colour of blood.

CHAPTER 15

'This is fucking good stuff, Andy. Where's it from? It's better than a lot of the shit we used to push back in the day. Some of that was like bags of washing powder.' Placing the rolled twenty pound note to his nose, Jack Christie bent over the table and snorted the fat white line of powder. He felt the numbing of his teeth, the taste of it at the back of his throat and within a few minutes the sheer buzz of the coke within his system had taken hold.

The Andy in question was Andy North, the man Jack had first hooked up with when he left his parents' home and ran away to London at the age of seventeen. They'd met each other in a seedy dive of a bar in London's East End. Jack, fresh off the train and already a petty criminal with convictions for breaking and entering, was keen to see what the capital could offer. With no more than a couple of hundred quid in his pocket, nicked from his mother's emergency cash tin – like the silly bitch really didn't think he'd seen her stashing cash away in her secret tin behind a row of recipe books in the family kitchen – Jack was ready to live a little. With an attitude of 'never let your fear decide your future', Jack headed straight into the roughest looking watering hole he could find, marched to the bar and ordered a pint. Under age? Bollocks to that.

Andy, a local East End lad, was about five years older than Jack. He'd been in the pub with a couple of mates and Jack could see from afar that he was definitely an epicentre of action.

People gravitated towards him. To a seventeen-year-old like Jack, Andy seemed the pinnacle of cool. And if Jack wasn't mistaken, he was definitely dealing some kind of drugs. He clearly had a good thing going on.

Jack had never tried drugs before. Growing up in his parents 'house of God' did not lend itself to an opportunity to experiment with narcotics. The church wine was about as exciting as it got under the roof of his mum and dad. Fuelled by the beer and the desire to sample London life, Jack had half-swaggered, half-staggered over to Andy and asked if he could buy some coke. A bold move that could have resulted in a broken nose as opposed to a coke-filled one, but Andy had liked the kid's bravado.

They'd talked, hit it off and Andy had treated Jack to his first ride on the white powder highway. At the end of the night, at kicking out time, Jack had been so wankered that Andy ended up letting him crash at his place on the sofa. With all of his money spent and no job prospects, Jack was hardly likely to book himself into a hotel or try to find a deposit for rental on a flat. Jack never left Andy's.

Andy earned his cash from breaking into people's houses and using the cash to buy drugs to supply. Jack knew he had found a kindred spirit and Andy seemed happy to play big brother and teach his new apprentice. They made a good team. They made mistakes, but they made them together.

The two of them had an unwritten bond. They had survived, only just, but they had survived, until Jack's stupid little mistake with the silver brooch. Wearing it out to go clubbing, and getting nicked for speeding in the wee small hours of the morning was a school boy error. But at the age of nineteen, just two years after first rocking up in London, Jack was sent down.

The police had grilled him as to whether he worked alone or with somebody else. Jack took the full hit. It was his fault, after all. Andy's flat was searched but the men had always been savvy. Nothing they nicked was left on the property and Andy had disposed of all drugs the moment Jack was arrested.

It was the same property the two men were now snorting coke at.

'I could never work with anyone else when you were put away,' said Andy, sniffing between words. 'It didn't feel right. You did the smart thing, not taking me down with you, but I appreciate it, man.'

'I was the stupid one. I fucked up. But I'm back and I'm ready for action.'

'The team back together? Is that what you're saying?' The wry smile that formed on Andy's lips told Jack that he was not against the idea.

'I'm smarter and I'm stronger. Prison did me good.' In an attempt to prove the point he lifted up his T-shirt a little, revealing his jackdaw tattoo and the hard formation of his stomach muscles. 'I'm not a kid any more, Andy. The Jackdaw has all grown up.'

'I can see that. Those are some serious abs.'

'So …?' Jack's voice was laced with hopeful expectation.

'Fuck man, welcome back.' Andy held out his hand, took Jack's in his and pulled him towards him in a hug of both nostalgic reminiscence and renewed friendship. 'The spare room is full of my shit but it's yours if you want it. Just like the old days.'

Jack's smile was so wide his face could barely contain it. 'Let the adventures begin, man.'

'Well, funny you should say that, I've just got wind of a job that could prove to be a nice little earner.'

CHAPTER 16

Watching her MacBook Air spark into life as she sat in her Indian hotel suite, Georgia had never felt so grateful to have Charlie in her life. After the horrendous news the day before that a dead body had been found in a canyon near where Mitzi and Foster had last been seen alive, Georgia's spirit had felt beyond crushed. She felt helpless and didn't know where to begin. Was the body Mitzi's? The thought was too much to bear.

Georgia had read the article over and over again. It was an early report and details were sketchy to non-existent. A body had been found in a cave by a hiker trekking through the canyon. The hiker had taken shade in the cave as a way of escaping the searing California sunshine. He'd noticed a smell within the cave and followed his nose until he had stumbled across a rotting corpse. It was after the grisly discovery that the authorities were alerted. As yet there was no further news.

Charlie had held her all night. Their first night in India was supposed to have been one of romance and joyous adventure but the news about the body had stemmed any flow of excitement that Georgia might have had over their exotic new surroundings. Not even the five star luxury of their hotel room with its deep, dark wooden furniture and its plush selection of finest woolen rugs seduced Georgia and Charlie to disconnect themselves from their fears about the body. As Georgia lay on the bed, her tears falling onto the soft embroidered bolster pillow underneath her face, it was misery, rather than the softness of the crisp cotton sheets, that blanketed them.

They had kept logging on to the internet all evening in the hope that more details were forthcoming but news was patchy.

Charlie had made some phone calls to his contacts in America and also back to the news desk on *Rise and Shine* to try and find out any extra morsels of information, but the cupboard was bare. After fruitless hours of searching for more news, Georgia had eventually fallen asleep in Charlie's arms, the sanctuary of his warmth comforting her as much as possible. Her dreams had been peppered with images of Mitzi and Foster, fading into the distance as she tried to reach out to them. She had woken up more exhausted than the night before.

Nova and Jacob had dined together at one of the hotel's many restaurants. The news had shocked them both, too. They had not actually realised just how close Georgia was to Mitzi, and through association, Foster. Jacob had tried to console her as best he could, saying that until identification was complete, there was hope that maybe the body was unconnected to the case, but Georgia, grateful though she was, could tell that Jacob didn't believe what he was saying. She could see that he was a man who could never cotton-wool the truth, no matter how hard he tried. It might work on Nova, but Georgia could see right through it.

Nova did the best she could to keep spirits high too, saying that maybe they should all dine together. She had even extended the invitation to Victoria, but she, like Georgia and Charlie, said that she would rather return to her room.

Unusually for Nova, she and Jacob had crawled into bed relatively early. She too found solace and warmth in the arms of her lover, as Jacob held her close to him. Life as Nova was fantastic but having a good man alongside her to share it all made it even more special. She blessed the day he had come into her world. He was such a sensitive soul for one so ruthless in business. He may be feared and hard-hitting when it came to the boardroom ways of media LA but to Nova he was that perfect combination of pussycat and powerhouse. A man's man, someone even the sharpest of ballbreakers could respect for his ruthless business know-how, but someone who had enough love in his heart to fill the San Andreas Fault. He could be firm with her, sometimes even bossy and overly strict, but he was always fair. In the mad world of La La Land TV, he was perfect at grounding her when, as he said, she was becoming 'a touch too Hollywood'. There were moments when his words could be cruel, maybe crueler than she deserved given how she had turned her life around, but for her career, for Charlie, for her dreams, she would forgive him anything.

Victoria had spent her evening ordering room service – a selection of rich Rajasthani Indian desserts – and luxuriating in the jasmine and lavender scent-filled delights of her deliriously deep bathtub.

But sleep evaded her. Her head spun with thoughts of Mitzi, Charlie, Scott. Late into the evening she walked to the hotel village restaurant and watched a puppet show and local dancers. She thought about Charlie. He was a strikingly handsome man, one whose features she could not erase from her mind. Every time she closed her eyes, there he was. Georgia was a lucky woman. She couldn't help but think that maybe she was too lucky.

Not that she wasn't lucky herself, of course. She had Scott. He was good-looking, rich, successful, a great husband. She hoped he found her a good wife, even if there was a little more of her than there used to be. So the sex had dried up a bit – almost to a state of drought – but surely that happened to every married couple after a while, especially when there were children to deal with. Nothing screamed passion killer like a child with whooping cough or a dose of the chicken pox. And then there were her body issues.

But was she making excuses for him? Blaming family life and her own increasing waistline for his lack of interest in the bedroom. It was an easy conclusion to draw. Scott was a man who enjoyed sex. When it did happen, his pleasure was evident. Was he finding it elsewhere? Her own tip-toeing thoughts of possible infidelity had made her realise just how easy it might be for a person to stray. The more she thought about it, the more she considered the possibility that he was having an affair. She and Scott had spoken when she returned to her room. She needed to hear him, to help give her some kind of clarity in her own mind about their situation. It was good to hear his voice even if he had seemed a little distracted.

'How is India?' he asked.

'Hot, humid, rather beautiful and full of people I've seen from the TV.'

'Like who?' enquired Scott. 'Hang on, darling, just wait one moment, Leo wants his dessert. Chloe's made them oatmeal brownies.'

She could hear the children laughing in the background as Scott gave their son his brownies. *How very healthy*, she reflected, *brownie points indeed for Chloe*. Victoria had been serving them trifles and sponge puddings of late. She could hear Lexi in the background too, 'Chloe, you make the best brownies, so crumbly and yummy.' It had deflated Victoria's spirit somewhat. So Chloe was joining them for dinner. Should she be jealous? She guessed not, but was unable to banish the worry that leaked into her brain.

Scott returned to the phone. 'So, who is there?'

'Nova Chevalier and her husband, Jacob. She is like a carica-ture of all things Los Angeles and rather fabulous to be around. Quite brashy and trashy. She's from *Champagne Super Nova*.'

'Oh, okay … Lexi, mind your orange juice, and don't spill it, darling. Chloe, can you grab a napkin?' So, she was definitely at the table. She normally ate in her room.

Victoria continued with her conversation. 'And her son is Charlie Cooper from the news show in the morning and he's here with his weather girl girlfriend, Georgia. Evie and I used to be in a Zumba class with her. Taught by Mitzi, the dancer who has gone missing in America. It looks like they've found her body, poor girl.'

'Really? Wow.' Scott started to laugh. Given the news Vic-toria had just delivered, this immediately irked her. 'Lexi has spilt juice all over her brownie. That will make for an interesting flavour. I'd better go, darling. Have a good time and enjoy the course. The kids send their love.'

'Can I speak to them?' But it was too late. Scott had already hung up.

It had not been the most satisfactory of conversations and as Victoria replayed it in her mind she couldn't help but worry about the way her marriage seemed to be potentially crumbling apart like one of Chloe's blessed oatmeal brownies.

But as she drifted off to sleep later that night, her mind stew-ing thanks to a cocktail of another anti-depressant coupled with the nausea that she might have to prepare herself for the fact that her husband was indeed finding solace between the legs of another woman, it wasn't Scott's face that filled her thoughts, it was Charlie's.

The following morning Georgia typed the words 'body found in canyon' into the search line of her MacBook, rubbed her eyes with tiredness and waited with dread to see what the search yielded. Unsurprisingly, there had been no mention of the discovery of the body on the Indian news channels because Mitzi and Foster were unknowns outside of the UK.

Georgia was on her own and would be for most of the day as Charlie was working on the cookery course, filming interviews. Nova, Jacob and Victoria were all taking part too. The day was hers to do with as she pleased, but all she could think about was Mitzi.

The search results immediately confirmed her fears. The body had been identified. But the headlines revealed that it wasn't Mitzi. It was Foster.

Every online newspaper in the UK seemed to be leading with the same story. 'Reality Star Foster Hampton's Body Found In Canyon Cave.'

Tears began to fall again as Georgia read the reports. Foster's decomposing body had been found and identified. The cause of death was a massive blow to the head and the case was now being treated as a murder investigation. The suggestion was that his body had been moved to the cave in a remote part of the canyon in order to try and hide it. As yet, an ongoing extensive search of the area had not revealed any further bodies or a murder weapon. The disappearance of Foster's girlfriend, dancer Mitzi Bidgood, was still being treated as highly suspicious and the search would escalate and increase now that foul play was suspected.

Georgia switched off her MacBook and rushed to the bathroom to wipe her eyes. The news made her feel bilious. Poor Foster. But at least there was still a glimmer of hope. Until they found Mitzi's body as well, Georgia had to believe that her best friend was still alive. And nothing would stop her until she knew the truth.

CHAPTER 17

'Why am I here? I don't want to die. Maybe if I'd run a little faster, or tried to reason then I wouldn't be staring death in the face.' The thoughts pinballed through her head as she twisted her mind back to that night. The face staring down at her. That demonic look in the eyes. The face of her own doom. Why hadn't she managed to escape? She dug her nails into her palms, annoyed at her own weakness.

She could still hear the sound of the stumble alongside her, the deadening of breath as body hit floor. At school she'd always been the first to finish the race on sports day. What the fuck had happened to her now? Was it panic and blind fear that had slowed her down? Sent her to this vacuum of a grave?

She attempted to inhale as deep a breath as possible as the rope was removed from her mouth. Her throat scorched as she felt the air, acrid with odour, hit her windpipe. Her mouth, rusty with misuse, tried to let out a cough. Was she alone? Was there a familiar figure alongside her? She couldn't tell.

The first human contact in what seemed like an eternity had come from a hand as it ripped at the binding gagging her mouth. There was no way she could see who the hand belonged to in the darkness of her surroundings. Her own hands and feet were still tied.

'We need to clean you up? Get you ready.' The voice. Maybe there was an inkling of recognition but her fatigue wouldn't let her decide. A hand grabbed at her hair, pulling her roughly upwards and *a water-soaked cloth passed over her face. She tried to suck some of the moisture from it as it moved across her lips.*

A few tiny drops seeped down her throat, not enough to satisfy, but enough to gift her a moment's clarity. One thought crashed into her mind. Ready for what?

CHAPTER 18

'Well, don't you have the magic touch when it comes to my bush?'

Aaron raised his eyebrows and smiled. There was no doubting Tanya's double entendre even if it was smeared in her heavy accent.

'Yes, it just needed some tender love and care,' smirked Aaron. 'Don't they all?'

'No, you are doing a great job, that abelia hasn't looked so good in months. All pink and healthy. But then it has never had such expert hands on it. You've done so much in such a short space of time.'

Aaron had only been working on the garden for a few days but already he was loving seeing the transformation. Trees that had been overgrown and forgotten were cut back and shaped, ready for a new lease of life. Shrubs and bushes that had been parched and left to slide into extinction had been resuscitated back into colour and vitality. And it felt good to have the sun on his back. A shirtless one that he was quite happy to show off in front of Tanya. Aaron was in great shape and manual labour in the garden had a fantastic knack of moulding even the most forgotten of muscles into glorious high definition. And judging by the way that Tanya had been making regular trips down the garden to see his shirtless torso, bringing him drinks and snacks with increasing regularity, especially while her husband was at work, he guessed she was a fairly bored housewife. His favourite kind.

Her latest trip down to him was with a much needed beer and a sandwich. Not that Aaron was overly sure about what he was eating. He was a BLT kind of guy and this wasn't his usual palate.

'Cheers for the beer, it's much needed. And the sarnie. What is it?'

Tanya looked confused? 'The what?'

'The sarnie ... sorry, the sandwich. What's in it? It's tasty. I like it.'

'Kielbasa and Russian cheese.'

'I'm none the wiser.'

'Kielbasa is a Polish sausage. It's one of my favourites and the cheese is a flavour-full one from Russia.'

'Smart. Beats egg and cress!' he smiled. 'So, is that where you're from? Poland? I love your accent.'

'I'm Russian. The Polish sausage just happens to be something I love to eat, but the cheese is from my homeland.'

'Tanya's not a very Russian name, is it?'

'Oh yes it is. I was born Tatiana, but is it shortened to Tanya. It is said to mean I am illustrious, open to anything and born to travel.'

'Well you certainly made it to the UK. What brought you here?'

'Love. I met Devon when he was working in Russia. He was there working on his science projects.'

'So from Russia to all of this?' Aaron nodded towards the house and gardens surrounding them and swigged his beer.

'This doesn't even compare with my life in Russia. I am the daughter of a Russian oligarch. My house in Russia was three times the size of this. My family were very popular but after the collapse of the Soviet Union the rich people were blamed for a lot, and became very unpopular with the Russian public.'

'How come?'

'They blamed us for all of the turmoil that the collapse caused. It was said that Russian oligarchs were as popular with the average Russian as a man idly burning bundles of fifty pound notes outside an orphanage. So when I met Devon I was glad to leave. I can go back there whenever I want but my life here has many attractions.' She paused and stared directly into Aaron's eyes before adding, 'Many.'

Draining the last of the beer and finishing the rest of his sandwich, Aaron couldn't help but comment. 'Beautiful and rich. I wish I could find a few women like you in this country.' He was hoping it would be the green light he assumed Tanya was after. To his surprise, his words seemed to have the opposite effect.

She took the bottle from his hand and smiled. Without saying a word, she wandered back towards the house, leaving Aaron and the erection that was beginning to grow within his trousers hanging. Should he follow? He wasn't sure. Maybe messages were a little bit more mixed in Russia. Adjusting his cock to a more comfortable position, he walked towards the shed in search of tools for his next job.

Aaron was still in the shed about ten minutes later when the door opened and Tanya stood there, her form outlined by the sun shining down on her from behind. She was wearing the tightest shorts, a vest top and a pair of sandals. She had changed outfits since their conversation minutes earlier when she'd been wearing a loose fitting T-shirt and a pair of jeans. In one hand she held a long, tubular object.

Without saying a word she entered into the shed and pulled the door shut behind her. There was still enough light to see her clearly as she walked to a bench table on the far side of the shed and sat herself upon it. Placing the object beside her on the table she lifted her lower body, unfastened her shorts and slid them down her legs and threw them to the floor along with her sandals. In a second her vest top came off too leaving her naked.

Aaron had already began to remove his trousers, his cock hurting from being contained underneath the fabric of his clothes. In a matter of seconds he was also naked, his thick chest hair glistening with sweat and streaks of dirt from the garden smudged across his skin. His cock stood hard and proud.

He moved towards her and placed his lips on hers, almost biting down on them in his urgency to satisfy his lust. He'd been waiting for this ever since he'd first met her in the bar in Chelsea. He looped his tongue around Tanya's, enjoying the sensation of her skin against hers. She reached up and grabbed his face with both hands, running her fingers through his hair and beard.

Tanya forced his head down to her breasts. She had small round breasts with large, sensitive nipples. They rose to attention as his lips met them. He nibbled them gently, letting his teeth bite lightly down upon them. He then stroked the lustrous hair of his beard across them. Tanya let out a squeal, lost in her enjoyment. She could often orgasm just through the teasing of her nipples alone, but today she needed more. She had a plan for Aaron.

Aaron returned to greedily sucking on Tanya's risen buds, but again Tanya maneuvered his head further down her body. As Aaron kneeled on the floor before her, she positioned his face in front of her vagina. The scent of it stiffened Aaron's cock further.

The light covering of hair on her pussy was the same delicious red as the hair on her head.

Tanya placed her hands between her legs and pulled back the outer lips of her pussy, exposing the sweet, dewy delights of the walls within. Holding her lips open with one hand, she grabbed Aaron's hair with the other and just as he was about to bury his tongue within her dampness, ordered him to stop. He knew he was not to argue. The flower between her legs lay just out of reach of his tongue.

'You wait,' purred Tanya, her accent even more seductive than Aaron had imagined it would be during sex.

She reached over and picked up the object lying beside her spread-eagled legs on the shed work bench.

'You say you've never tasted Kielbasa before. Well, now you taste it my way. You look but you don't touch.'

'Fucking hell.' It was all Aaron could say. He cock was ready to burst as he stared deep into the tissuey folds of her vagina.

Tanya picked up the sausage and began to rub its length against the outer lips of her pussy. The scent of the sausage, mingled with her own natural odour hit Aaron's nostrils. It was a heady, horny mix.

Parting her legs, Tanya began to slide the Kielbasa inside her. The moisture of her pussy meant that she could move it freely deep within her, the sausage sliding back and forth. She let it rest a good few inches inside her, moaning with ecstasy at the ripples of euphoria it caused to wash over her.

Aaron watched, his eagerness to fuck Tanya growing ever stronger, his cock ever harder. He was contemplating standing up and ploughing his manhood deep within her there and then, but instead looked on as Tanya withdrew the Polish sausage from her pussy and rubbed it across Aaron's beard and lips.

'Now eat it,' she barked, pushing the sausage into his mouth.

The smell was intoxicating. Aaron licked the meat, lapping at the juices coated on it before biting down. It had tasted good in the sandwich but this was something else.

Tanya flipped the sausage over so that the non-bitten end was closest to her pussy again. She inserted it back into her triangle of desire and pushed it as far as it would go. When it was almost fully inserted she moved her hands away and spoke.

'Now, eat it like that.'

Aaron didn't need asking twice. He buried his head deep between Tanya's legs, allowing his tongue to explore around her pussy and at the food within it. As gently as he could he bit down into the sausage again, making sure not to bite into her tender flesh. She let out a cry as he did so.

Aaron removed his face from her heat and spat the sausage to one side. There was only one thing he wanted to feast on now and that was the juices spreading between Tanya's legs. Burying his head inside her again, he gripped his teeth around the sausage and pulled it from within her. She quivered as the meat slid out of her. Again he spat it to one side and reassumed his feast, zoning in and sucking on her clitoris and flicking his tongue across it. He worked his cock with his other hand, aching to climax. A slick of precum glossed across the head of his shaft, eager to explore further.

Rising to his feet, Aaron grabbed Tanya's hips with his hands and slid her forward on the work surface. The wood grazed her backside as he repositioned her but the feeling was one of pleasure not pain. Lining the top of his cock up against her pussy, he could wait no longer and drove his full length into her. She rocked back and forth, determined to draw every inch into her as deeply as possible.

Tanya grabbed Aaron's shoulders and pulled him towards her. The hair on his chest rubbed against her breasts. It was a different sensation to the smoothness of her own husband's body. It reminded her of some of the bear-like men she had been fucked by back in her home country.

Aaron's movements became stronger, deeper, faster and harder. Sweat poured down his body and mingled with Tanya's as he felt his orgasm rise.

Tanya began to shudder as her own vigorous release heightened. Wrapping her legs tightly around Aaron's firm buttocks she clamped onto him determined that he should fire his seed as deep within her as possible. A few seconds later it happened. A river of hot liquid burst into her as her own orgasm reached its heavenly peak.

Basking in what had just happened for a few moments longer they let their bodies stay locked together.

It was Tanya who spoke first.

'I had better go back to the house. Devon will be home later.'

'That was incredible,' smiled Aaron. 'And very tasty ...'

He slid his now semi-flaccid cock from inside her with a satisfying post-coital, sweaty-bodied slurp and looked at the half eaten sausage on the floor. 'I'm always up for tasting new delights.'

Tanya leapt down off the bench and gathered her clothes. 'I'm glad you enjoyed it. Now you had better get on with the gardening.'

'Yes, ma'am,' said Aaron. 'What shall I do with the food?'

'Oh give it to the foxes, they'll enjoy it,' said Tanya. Still naked, her clothes bunched in her hands, she opened the shed door and ran back towards the house. Her backside was as pink and as glowing as the abelia bush Aaron has been tending to earlier.

Foxes? Now, Tanya was one fox Aaron would certainly look forward to feeding again. And the sooner the better.

CHAPTER 19

The hard stone floor still pressed against her face. There was nothing refreshing about its temperature. Strands of hair clung to her forehead and down across her eyes. Was it blood that stuck them there? She couldn't tell.

A circle of brightness suddenly exploded in front of her. Was it a light? Through eyes that still felt half closed with both pain and lack of use she tried to focus. The contrast between its glow and the envelope of black she had been experiencing just a few seconds before was severe enough to cause pinpricks of pain that stabbed at the corner of her eyes as she looked into the glow. Something in the back of her mind told her to try and gather any information she could about what she was seeing, any clue to link to the night that had caused all of this. A clue as to what had caused the pain and hurt that tore through her body. A clue as to where things might end.

'Why are you doing this?' Her voice, encased with feebleness. No answer was given.

A camera, a tripod, a figure behind the lens. It was still too dim to work out whether it was male or female. Or maybe she was just too weak. Just trying to keep her eyes open seemed one of the most difficult things she had ever had to do. They were heavy, weary, and ready to give up.

A voice sounded. 'So, this is what I need you to say.' But she never heard it. Her eyes had closed once more and darkness had taken her again.

CHAPTER 20

There is nothing to prepare for that moment when your eyes focus on India's Taj Mahal, the most famous white marble mausoleum in the world, for the first time.

Which is why Georgia was very grateful that Charlie had persuaded her to spend a few extra hours in India before heading to the airport for their flight home. As she basked in the glory of the soft curves of the Taj's domes and the rigid uniformity of its minarets, just for a while all thoughts of life and the horrors it held outside the confines of the Taj gardens, with its raised walkways and reflecting pool, were erased.

'It truly is amazing,' said Georgia, linking her arm through Charlie's as they sat themselves down in front of the building.

'And I adore the story behind it. A true tale of love between a man and a woman. So romantic.' Charlie gave Georgia's hand a squeeze and leant into her to nuzzle lightly against her neck.

'So who built it?' Georgia had read the information back at the hotel but with all her worries about Mitzi dominating her thoughts, any excess information just hadn't been able to settle.

'It's a completely bewitching tale. It was built by Shah Jahan, a Prince, for one of his many wives. I think he had three. Her name was Mumtaz Mahal and he first fell in love with her when they were both of a young age, in their teens I think. He saw her in the street selling opulent silks and spellbindingly beautiful glass beads and immediately declared his adoration for her. I believe she was just slightly older than him but their age didn't matter as they were in love.'

Georgia couldn't help but smile as she began to listen to Charlie. If there was one thing Charlie loved to do, it was storytelling. She guessed it was why he did the job he did. He was definitely a weaver of words and as easy on the ear as he was on the eye.

'So, Prince Shah Jahan was her toy boy, eh?' smirked Georgia.

'Shah Jahan went back to his father after meeting the girl and said that he wanted to marry her. For many years life was good, and the couple were pretty much inseparable. Shah Jahan had other wives but Mumtaz was always his favourite.'

Georgia raised her eyebrows at the thought as Charlie continued.

'But when Mumtaz was giving birth to their fourteenth child, there were complications and unfortunately she died, leaving Shah Jahan bereft. While she was on her deathbed, her husband promised her that he would never marry again and that he would build her the most incredible monument and the world's richest mausoleum over her grave. Which is how the Taj Mahal came to be.'

'That is some tombstone and some story,' remarked Georgia. 'Teenage lovers, multiple wives, more children than Brad and Angelina and the most incredible final curtain. I'm surprised Hollywood hasn't reworked it a million times over,' she said, pulling Charlie close to her. Despite the warmth of the Indian day the talk of death and lost love chilled her slightly. She didn't need to search to know why.

'I'm sure they have,' said Charlie, sensing her mood and wrapping his arm around her. 'And if they haven't then doubtless Bollywood will have turned it into a song and dance number.'

It was talk of Bollywood and life back home in America that occupied Nova and Jacob as they too wandered around the grounds of the magnificent Taj.

'I definitely think an Indian theme to one of the episodes of *Super Nova* is a must, Jacob, if not a whole series. There's enough scope here to work with. This place is just incredible. It's like something from Vegas but much older of course. This is something I never dreamt I'd be able to see when I was growing up in West Hills. I thought the closest I'd get to India is ordering from a takeaway menu. I love it here! All this talk of princes and princesses would be a massive hit with the viewers, as they love a bit of romance.'

Despite loving Nova's fizzing exuberance about the project, Jacob knew that it would all come down to the dollar. He'd spent enough time schmoozing, wining and dining TV types to know that it was money that talked. And he knew how to play the bankrollers.

'Didn't we stay in the Taj Mahal in Atlantic City? Donald Trump's place? That was a ritzy hotel, even if the clientele were all about three hundred years of age with skin stretched tighter than a kite. We were the most natural looking people there and I know that's ironic given these,' said Nova, shaking her breasts to emphasise the point.

'Can you *not* jiggle those around in here, Nova? Have some respect, woman, will you?' Jacob, despite being a breast man all the way when it came to sex, knew that there was a time and a place for showing off her assets and this was not it. 'And is that the spoilt Hollywood diva I'm spotting rising to the ugly surface again? If I remember rightly you actually had a great time at that hotel playing blackjack and roulette with some totally charming people who were genuinely excited to meet you – a star from the TV. Not that different from how you'd have felt about Harrison Ford or one of your favourites back in the day. You're no different to anyone else, you know. You're just luckier, that's all.'

'Calm it, Jacob. No need to be tetchy. I know I'm very lucky, thank you. And yes, those people were lovely.' Nova felt she had been scolded like a schoolgirl. 'I just get carried away from time to time. I never thought it would happen to me.'

'Well, it has and you deserve it, but why do you have to be so crass? This is one of the most beautifully poetic and serene places ever and you jiggling those around in front of a few hundred Indian families is not going to exactly gain you the column inches you want is it? R-E-S-P-E-C-T darling.'

'Crass? I'm the star of the most successful TV sensation since *Breaking Bad*, Jacob. I'm the biggest thing from Bel-Air since the Fresh Prince. Crass is in my job description, dear Jacob, it's what people expect.' There was a streak of joviality in Nova's voice, but she did mean what she said.

'But not here. This is a million miles away from our life of chaos and media madness back in Bel-Air.'

'Fair enough, I'll let people stare at the Taj's domes and not mine, then, shall I? They have been around a lot longer. How come they manage to keep the building so clean?'

'Well, a bit like you, Nova, it undergoes regular beauty routines. Every few years a mudpack treatment is applied to the marble as it starts to yellow with air pollution. A thing of beauty needs its upkeep whether it be the most majestic building on earth or the most flawless woman in Los Angeles.'

Jacob reached out and placed his hand under Nova's chin and raised it to admire her beauty. Despite any faults she had and those moments when she temporarily forgot her roots, Jacob worshipped her. 'And it is also said that washing in the rivers around here is supposed to wash away any sins that a person may possess.'

But Nova wasn't listening. Something had grabbed her attention. 'That's it,' she cried. 'That's how you win the bigwigs over. That seat over there ...' She pointed to a bench situated directly in front of the Taj Mahal. 'That's the one Princess Di sat on to make the world fall at her feet. I need to do the same. All demure and vulnerable in front of that slab of magnificence. I'm sure Oprah did it too. Come on Jacob, grab your camera. The producers will just lap this one up, it's so historical and royal, and that's two things our show lacks. We need a sense of history. Plus the nearest we get to anything vaguely regal on our show is when Perez Hilton rocks up to one of my parties.'

'And back to crass,' whispered Jacob to himself as Nova pushed her way towards the bench.

CHAPTER 21

'It's just at the top of the street, last house on the right, just by the corner.'

Victoria couldn't wait to get home. It had only been a few days but she missed the twins like crazy. Her time in India had been wonderful, and judging by the HEAVY LUGGAGE labels now adorning her suitcase as a result of all the packed spices and recipe books she had purchased through the cookery course jammed inside, her reignited love of cuisine preparation was something she was keen to share with her husband and family.

It was a balmy late afternoon, and her taxi back from Heathrow was just about fifty yards from her house when she spotted Scott, the twins and Chloe walking along the pavement towards home. It was a bright day and she guessed they'd been out together, maybe to the local park. Judging from the packed picnic bag that swung from Chloe's right hand, they had obviously made a day of it. Was that a rolled blanket Victoria could spot sticking out of the top, and some bottles? Was one of them a wine bottle? Victoria couldn't tell but it certainly didn't look like something the twins would have been drinking. Chloe held Leo's hand. This irked Victoria even more than the possibility that Chloe had been out drinking wine with her husband. All of the suspicions she had been feeling about Scott during her stay in India surfaced again. She had tried to bury them but they rose like the undead once more.

What day was it? Victoria has lost track during her stay in India. It was Monday. Why wasn't Scott at work? He never took days off. He'd cancelled India because he was so busy. Victoria could feel her annoyance increasing.

The four of them seemed to be laughing. Whatever they had been doing, they had obviously enjoyed it. Leo and Chloe let their arms swing together in unison. Scott, surprisingly dressed down in a casual Fred Perry shirt and a pair of shorts was positively throwing his head back in gleeful mirth and Lexi stared up adoringly at her father.

Victoria tried to cast her mind back to the last time they had all been out together as a family. She was unable to do so. It must have been when the twins were very young. She had a vague recollection of feeding the ducks on a Sunday afternoon, but Leo and Lexi hadn't long been out of a pushchair at that point. Plus she seemed to recall that she and Scott had argued. There was no air of disharmony in the idyllic scene of joy she was gazing at now through the taxi window.

'You can stop here,' said Victoria. The taxi pulled into the kerb opposite the house. Scott and the kids hadn't spotted her arrival.

Victoria paid the driver and climbed out of the back of the taxi, lugging her heavy case behind her. She could have called across for Scott to come and help her. She could have announced her return to the twins. But something inside kept her silent. What was it?

Unable to stop herself, Victoria just stood on the opposite side of the street and watched Scott, Chloe and the kids as they strolled towards the front gate of Victoria's marital home.

Now in the open, she could hear that they were all singing. A jolly chorus of 'Ring A Ring O' Roses' filled the air. It had never been a favourite of Victoria's and this performance was not increasing its appeal. As they reached the chorus of 'Atishoo, Atishoo, we all fall down,' both Leo and Lexi dipped to the floor, causing laughter to burst forth from both Scott and the nanny.

Victoria started to pull her case across the road, all the while watching her family, the people she loved; the three people she shared her life with but who were suddenly unrecognisable alongside Chloe. It was like watching a party that she hadn't been invited to.

What happened next caused Victoria to stop in her tracks. The group finished singing as they approached the gate, and Scott lifted his hand up and placed it at the back of Chloe's neck. Just at the nape where her hair met her skin. It was an odd gesture and seemed somehow intimate. He left it there just a little longer than was necessary. Not that it seemed necessary at all.

Victoria stood paralysed, dread creeping over her. A car sped round the corner. It was too fast to stop. A screech of brakes came too late as the car ploughed into her. She just had time to see Scott and the twins beginning to turn their heads towards her and to hear the noise of the brakes before everything around her went to black.

Atishoo, atishoo … it was Victoria's turn to fall down.

CHAPTER 22

Aaron had always been very black and white in his views. A country man with a simple outlook on life. He believed that you should treat every stressful situation that life throws your way just as a dog would. If you couldn't eat it, hump it or simply piss all over it then you should just walk away, no matter what the cost.

But it was the cost that was bothering him. Since he had started working at Devon's and Tanya's he had seen a huge chunk of absolutely nothing materialise into his bank account. And cash had started to run a little dry. In fact it was borderline desert. Devon was not being as quick to settle bills and pay receipts as he'd promised, which surprised Aaron as Devon had struck him as being incredibly anal and efficient in all areas of his life. He wouldn't have just forgotten, surely? Aaron was beginning to feel that the word MUG had been permanently tattooed on his mud-smeared forehead.

He had tried to approach Devon and found him frosty, to say the least. In fact some of his icy glances could have killed off even the hardiest of perennials. Aaron was tempted to down tools but he didn't want to risk losing the gig. Plus the fact that he'd never signed a contract meant that, for all the outside world knew, Aaron could have merely been doing the work as a favour. Not that the rent and upkeep on an SW10 London postcode leant itself to favours. Bills needed cash, rent needed paying.

And it wasn't easy to walk away from some of the most mind-shatteringly horny sex he'd ever had. Ever since his first food-based encounter with Devon's wife, the two of them had fucked wherever they could. The woman was insatiable.

Tanya was an easy lay in more ways than one. She was more than ready to have her way with Aaron whenever possible, allowing him to do things that most women would more than likely give an amber-to-red-light to. Upon her request, actually make that *command*, he'd bound her with rope from the shed and forced her to her knees as he face-fucked her, stuffing his hard prick into her mouth so deeply that he only allowed her to breath comfortably once his torrent of seed had been unleashed into her throat.

He'd taken her from behind as he bent her over the tractor mower he used to cut the lawn. It was again an act she'd instigated. Turning up to where Aaron was working wearing the shortest of skirts and no knickers, Tanya had then bent herself ninety degrees over the mower as she switched off the engine and parted the fleshy joys of her own sexual dynamo, inviting Aaron in. A passionate plunge into sexual fulfillment followed.

On another occasion, as Aaron coppiced one of the large oaks at the bottom of the lawns, running a chainsaw through one of the thicker, unwanted branches, he had been almost surprised into falling as Tanya, naked apart from a pair of trainers, had appeared behind him in the tree, holding a blanket. Spreading it as best as she could in a dip housed within the inner sanctum of the tree she lay back, no words necessary, spread her legs and inserted her fingers into her evident wetness, bringing herself to orgasm in front of him. After Aaron had shed his own clothes quicker than the shedding of the leaves in autumn, he entered her and rocked her to a second.

Tanya seemed to thrive on the danger, the thrill, the fetish. In some cases the downright awkward. There was a love of the unusual. Vanilla was not her taste. She was a deep, dark, dangerous flavour. And Aaron was permanently ready to relish.

Sex with Tanya was also easy as Devon seemed to spend a good ten to twelve hours a day at work. And while the cat was away, Aaron was more than happy to taste the cream on offer.

If only the cash from Devon was as easily available. It was something that he was keen to bring up with Tanya after another one of their bouts of animalistic fucking. The pair of them had just shared a shower in the bathroom of the studio alongside the main house. Devon was yet again at work and a bored Tanya had joined Aaron as she spotted him heading to the studio after a particularly dirty day of gardening. The late British summer had finally seemed to break for the afternoon and a down pouring of rain had left Aaron muddy, soaked and in need of dry clothes for his journey back to Chelsea. Just the mere sight of him looking so filthy turned Tanya on. She had stripped bare and joined him underneath the power jets.

As he pulled on his dry clothes afterwards, he broached the subject of cash.

'I need some kind of money from you and Devon. I keep asking but your husband keeps making excuses and saying it will always be tomorrow. Well tomorrow never comes, Tanya. I can't keep doing this for free. You have money, I don't.'

The news seemed to surprise Tanya. A look of consternation spread across her face.

'Really, he hasn't paid you a thing?'

'Not a bean.' The phrasing seemed lost on the Russian. 'Not a penny,' he corrected.

'Can you wait a few minutes?'

'Of course. But what are you …' Aaron's words stopped as a naked Tanya ran out of the studio and back towards the house.

She returned to the studio about five minutes later, still naked, but sporting a look of devilish mischief. He body was dotted with raindrops from the fall that continued outside.

'So, you want paying?' smiled Tanya.

'I do.'

'Then come and find it. I have your money.' As she said it, she walked across the studio and lay herself on the floor across a raised area at the far end of the building. It was where Devon's first wife, the late Sophia, had always painted as it received the most light in the room.

It was obvious to Aaron that she wasn't carrying any money in her hands, which were empty. Within a few seconds he had joined her on the floor and inserted his fingers into the melt-pot of mischief between her legs. It wasn't just the raindrops that were causing wetness. As he let his digits slide deep within her, Tanya let out a gasp of total satisfaction.

Aaron let out a gasp too as his fingers came across a package within her pussy. He teased his fingers around it, applying a little force to his search, adding a sense of role-play.

'Now, what have we here?' He pulled the package out. It was a small, clear, plastic bag, sealed at one end. He could see a roll of notes inside. Despite the juices on his fingers, he pulled open the bag and took the notes from it.

'A thousand pounds do for starters?' asked Tanya.

Aaron didn't answer. He merely nodded and buried his face back between Tanya's legs.

As he headed home a little later, the grand safely housed in his trouser pocket, Aaron had a smile on his face and the taste of Tanya's sex still upon his lips. Working for the Bellamys was one situation he did not want to walk away from. Especially now that it was paying in all areas.

CHAPTER 23

The day that Sophia Hopper had married Devon Bellamy was one of the happiest of their lives. A simple ceremony, just a few family and friends sharing the intimacy of two people deeply in love. Devon, the stylish geek, knowledgeable and friendly, the person people would turn to for advice and opinions on their life laundry. His new wife, Sophia, the fashionably elegant and Carnaby Street-cool art gallery worker who possessed a sexuality and beauty that perfectly straddled the camps between Hollywood vamp and English Rose innocence. It was a match made in heaven.

For many years their union was an idyllic one. Devon's career flourished, his scientific flare and ground-breaking ideas putting him in demand all over Europe and indeed even further afield. He was a man on the up and Sophia, also content in her art-inspired world, was happy to support him all the way.

Not long into the marriage, Sophia fell pregnant and nine months later, Georgia was born; the perfect mini-Sophia with huge eyes that doting parents could swim in. Sophia found herself at home, a full-time mother, a job she also adored.

As the years advanced, so did Devon's career, bringing him awards, accolades and huge financial benefit. His skill, go-getting ways and thirst for advances within his field saw the family of three move from a fairly humble suburban apartment to a massive house in North London where Sophia could once again indulge in a creativity she had always possessed from her art gallery days. Rooms were converted, a specialist art studio built, areas decorated in a variety of styles. Sophia turned a huge space into a family home and it was one that became a hub for socialising. The Bellamys were the epicenter of entertainment.

When they weren't entertaining, Sophia abandoned herself to her painting. She savoured the richness of colours, the feel of the paint against the bristles of her brush, even against her skin as Sophia used her body as a human brush. Now that she had her own studio she let her imagination go wild with her art. She could lose herself for hours inside her artistic sanctuary.

The body painting was something she had always experimented with. The idea had first come to her when she was finger-painting with Georgia and the children in her daughter's school class. She loved the freedom of having the paint daubed onto her skin as opposed to the brush. Often, in the solitude of her own studio, she would coat her hands or arms in a myriad of colours and squash them against a canvas, revelling in the results.

Then one day, while watching *All Of Me*, a documentary about one of her all-time style icons, the Hollywood model Farrah Fawcett of *Charlie's Angels* fame, she discovered that she was not alone. Farrah would paint her breasts, her buttocks, anywhere on her body and roll across wide stretches of paper to great effect. The result was slapdash but beyond liberating, and having seen it, Sophia was determined to try it. It became her signature style and occupied her for many hours, even days, while Devon was working abroad and Georgia was at boarding school.

It was her love of art that caused the destruction of her marriage to Devon. Word of Sophia's outlandish masterpieces spread and she entertained an eclectic set of people, many from the art world, at the family home, often while Devon was still away. Despite his genius mind, Devon couldn't help but feel excluded from his wife's new, multicoloured world. A world of creation, glamour and art into which he simply didn't seem to fit. At the soirees he did attend his best efforts to make conversation with those gathered appeared to fall on deaf ears. Ears that cared nothing for what he had to say. For a man of such great talent in his own field, Devon felt crushed by their lack of interest. Did it make him a lesser person because his world was science not sculpture, petri dishes not paints? To a man laced with pride, vulnerability and a fear of failure it did.

When millionaire gallery owner Nicolas Belvoir was introduced to Devon's wife at one of these gatherings, the art-obsessed Sophia immediately felt a connection. A thunderbolt moment. It was a bond that highlighted the deep disconnection she now seemed to feel for her ordered, fastidious scientist husband, Devon. She and Nicolas would discuss everything from their shared love of Francis Bacon and Salvador Dali to more obscure tastes like Keith Haring. Unable to stop it, she and Nicolas fell in love and the canvas of their new-found joy became the tapestry of torment for Devon. And despite the expertise of his brain when it came to saving lives with molecules and medics, it seemed that the know-how of saving matters of the heart evaded him.

On his return home one day he found the note. Sophia had left him to go and live with Nicolas. His heart broke, and a piece of his vulnerable soul died forever.

Georgia took the news badly. To see her mother and father apart was something that she had never considered. At twenty, she was old enough to understand but the physicality of seeing them separately, of witnessing her father's unhappiness and her mother's need for pleasure combined with a heavy sense of guilt was, at times, too much to bear. To realise that her perfect mother and perfect father were no longer perfect for each other was difficult to comprehend.

But nothing prepared Georgia for what came next.

Sometimes, even to this day, in the middle of the night, the horror of that phone call would still echo in her mind. A deadly tolling shooting through her senses. Devon telling her that her mother and Nicolas had been found dead at their home. Sophia's throat had been slit, and her chest housed a bullet wound. Both brutal, either fatal. Telltale bruises across her body suggested a struggle. Nicolas had been discovered in the same room, his brains blown out by the very gun that had pumped into Sophia's chest. It was virtually still in his hand.

The police ruled that Nicolas had killed himself after rampaging through the house and shooting his girlfriend. There was no suggestion of robbery or any other suspicious circumstances. No motive was given. People blamed it on artistic temperament. Like Sophia's creative style, their relationship was seemingly vivid, bold and dramatic. Like Sophia's canvasses, their bodies were splashed with colour.

Georgia had lost a mother, Devon had lost a true love. A woman to share his world with. Until he met Tanya.

CHAPTER 24

'You look shattered, Dad.'

Georgia was worried about Devon. In a life where not many things had remained consistent for Georgia, her father had always been her rock, the man that she could turn to and rely on for true unadulterated love. He knew her better than anyone and she him.

But something was wrong. He never looked anything less than immaculate normally. Nails would be buffed, shirts would be spotless and hair would be groomed. But something wasn't right. There was almost a crazed look in his eyes and on top of her ever-growing angst about Mitzi it was the last thing she needed right now. 'Are you working too hard? You look …' She searched for the right word. '… haunted.' She reached out to touch his leg. A simple action but one soaked in tenderness and caring.

Devon did indeed look beyond tired. He'd been working long hours and his normally radiant, healthy skin had definitely slid from vitality into shades of grey.

There was a tightness in his reply, a brusqueness that Georgia didn't associate with their everyday loving father/daughter conversations. 'If I don't work, Georgia, then many a scientific revelation would remain unearthed. Plus Tanya has an addiction to shopping that needs constant watering.'

Devon was indeed one of the most respected men in his chosen field of scientific advancement. If only his personal life could always follow suit.

'Where is Tanya, by the way?'

Georgia and her father were sitting in the front room in the Bellamy family home that Georgia had grown up in and which Devon now shared with Tanya. 'She's shopping. Doubtless buying some more clothes, draping herself needlessly in the latest fashions despite having fifty similar items in various hues already. Pointless exercise.'

Georgia had never seen her father so vexed. And especially when it came to fashion. Devon had always prided himself on being a very stylish individual, housing a wardrobe with designs from Antony Price, Ralph Lauren and Tom Ford through to Armani and Paul Smith. And he loved those around him to be equally as stylish. One look inside his wardrobes would reveal suits lined up in order from black tie through to white linen, cufflinks neatly placed in symmetrical rows and shoes in collections of tan, black, brown. All expensive, all impeccable. He knew fashion as well as he did science and surely there weren't that many people who could say the same. Brains like Professor Brian Cox or Stephen Hawking were hardly famed for their love of Oswald Boateng were they?

'Something's wrong, Dad. You never slate Tanya's fashion sense, even if some of it is a little dubious in my humble opinion,' snipped Georgia. 'Has the Russian diamond lost her sparkle?'

The look on Devon's face made it clear that she had both hit a nerve and that her father didn't want to talk. But it was obvious that something was troubling him. For a few moments there was an awkward silence.

Georgia had never hidden the fact that Tanya was not exactly her favourite woman on earth. The two of them had always been civil but not exactly seen eye to eye. It was no surprise. Georgia had never really got over the death of her own mother, Sophia, and there was a part of her that harboured a canker of dislike for Tanya and what she potentially represented. In Georgia's mind she couldn't help but feel that Tanya was an unworthy, and somewhat ungrateful, replacement for the hole left in her father's heart when Sophia had died. Everything about her father's marriage to Tanya had whispered 'gold digger' to Georgia. The whole way that Devon's second wife had entered into her father's life had irked Georgia greatly. She couldn't help but compare her to her own mother and that was fatal.

It had all been so quick. Sophia had only been a few short years gone and suddenly there it was. The announcement. Georgia, still in her early twenties and trying to find her own way in the world as a woman, summoned to the family home to meet Devon's new bride, the daughter of a Russian oligarch. Tanya, a woman who at twenty-three, was virtually the same age as Georgia herself, give or take a few months.

Her father's new wife. That she could accept. But her new mother? That would never happen. Something sat uneasily and acceptance had never come. There was a mutual mistrust. On what grounds, Georgia didn't know. But something seemed as duplicitous as a wartime spy. It was a seed of doubt that had never germinated, but had never died either.

'I should go. I have an early start in the morning back on the TV and I need an early night.'

Georgia rose to leave. She had been at her father's for over an hour and they had discussed the loss of Foster, Mitzi's continued disappearance and Georgia's recent visit to India, but it was clear that for now, Devon had reached his fill on talking.

He remained seated and silent, staring out of the window as Georgia kissed him on either cheek. She followed his gaze. 'The garden looks amazing by the way, very neat and tidy, just how you like it. Someone's working wonders on it. I'll let myself out.'

It was the garden that Devon was staring at. It was looking good. Aaron was working wonders, he had to admit. The boxed-off borders and right-angled plots were just as he'd hoped. If only that was where it ended.

His suspicions had been confirmed. He'd been holding off payment, enjoying the piece of control he felt he had over the gardener. Aaron needed money and that had to come from Devon, which made him the one with the power; the devil who held all the cards – the flexible, cash-laden ones. Yes, he could fire Aaron, but where was the fun in that? Not paying him and making him dangle on a thread like some meathead marionette was much more of a power trip. Firing the bastard would be too easy. Thinking he could fuck Tanya and get away with it. Devon would prove him wrong.

He'd seen it with his own eyes. Tanya running naked from the studio the night before, entering his office and taking a wad of cash from the safe. Bagging it and inserting it inside herself and then returning to the studio. She'd not seen her husband. Why would she have? He had been deliberately hidden. Silent as he watched her. That's why he'd returned home early from work. He'd suspected it; known it would happen when he'd first seen them together in the bar in Chelsea. He'd recognised the signs. The idle flirtation, the sashay as she walked. History repeating itself. Wife number two, betrayal number two. The order of things breaking down once again. Control slipping from him. Aaron might not be the first and he probably wouldn't be the last, but nobody had what he had with Tanya. No-one had his power. Devon would never be second best again. And besides, his love for Tanya was unique. This time it couldn't go wrong. He had control.

He'd watched from afar as Aaron worked his wife, the bobbing of his head between Tanya's legs. Why wasn't he enough for her? Why had she strayed? And what was he going to do about it? Their sex life together had been wonderful. Adventurous and exciting. Dangerous, on occasion. Maybe a touch sporadic of late but he wouldn't lose another wife to another man. He'd do what he needed to do. Start planning. Work out the best solution for the experiment at hand. Betrayal. Once bitten twice shy. But never ignored.

CHAPTER 25

'EVIE MERCHANT INVITES YOU TO A BLACK-TIE CHARITY PARTY ...'

The invitation was on ice white card, edged with gold leaf. The typeface bold, clear and unfussy. It was designer without being showy, an understated sense of grandeur without the brash, flashy nature that often attached itself to Hollywood success.

It contained just the facts. The London venue, one of the capital's finest. Food would be a buffet from around the world. Entertainment would be provided by legendary names. Dancing until carriages at 2am. The reason? To raise as much money as possible for Evie's chosen charities. The date would be in just a few short weeks, timed perfectly so that Evie had wrapped on her latest movie and to make sure it didn't clash with any major awards ceremonies. The dress code was to be black-tie Hollywood, guests were to dress to impress.

It suited Evie perfectly and, as she had always preferred, she was handling the sending out of the invitations herself. She could have left it to agents and publicists but where was the personal touch in that? It felt right for her to do it herself. Why wouldn't she? In a world where she was given a needless assistant for virtually every simple task, it was a pleasure to actually use her own brain to do something creative. And besides, Evie wanted to make sure that she was the one cherry picking her guests.

Because behind the party invitation was another purpose. To raise money and to keep the awareness heightened for the search for Mitzi Bidgood. A girl with so much to live for, yet seemingly her life hung in the balance. Since Foster's death there had still been no news and as hope faded, so it seemed did news coverage and public interest. If Evie could do something, anything to keep Mitzi's spirit alive then she was determined to do so. She had been thinking about it ever since her meeting with Victoria. Remembering the nights out she had spent with Mitzi. They had been fun, carefree times. So, Mitzi hadn't been one of her direct, closest friends. So both she and Victoria had lost contact with Mitzi. So what? Isn't that sometimes what happened in life? But if Evie could use her celebrity for something good instead of just another day of walking a red carpet and smiling inanely at a camera answering questions from some stick-thin fashionista about what heels she was wearing then it would be worth it. In a world where shallow was *de rigeur* maybe this event could be something tangible that would keep public interest high. Plus she felt in her heart that this is what she should do. Sitting in her London home, Evie placed one of the invitations in an envelope and sealed the flap. She was just about to handwrite the front – another necessary personal touch – when her telephone rang.

She picked it up.

'Hello, is that Evie?'

'Yes, who's speaking?

'It's Scott, Victoria's husband. Listen, I'm afraid there's been an accident. Victoria's in hospital. She's been asking for you.'

Evie listened as Scott relayed the details. She could feel herself tearing up. Another young woman with so much to live for and yet once again, a life hung in the balance.

Hanging up the phone, she grabbed her coat and headed to the door, leaving the envelope unwritten.

CHAPTER 26

The alarm sounded at 2.45am as it did every working morning for Georgia. It was the first of six alarms pre-programmed onto her phone at regular snooze intervals just in case she nodded off. Something that this morning she would have been more than happy to do as she was dreaming about a rather sexual encounter with Adam Levine.

'God damned you alarm, that was hot,' she cursed, pressing the button on her phone to silence it. 'And sorry Charlie, but there's no such thing as cheating in your sub-conscious.'

Not that Charlie was there with her. Despite working on the same programme, it was rare they would sleep together on a night before work. It would only take one of them to be restless or wake the other and they would both be looking like a Shar Pei come 'lights camera action'.

Georgia grabbed a coffee and jumped into the shower. This was always the moment that would suddenly spark her into action, the heat of the jets against her skin bringing her to life. Life pre *Rise and Shine* had meant getting home at this hour from some Soho nightspot, but with TV weather girl fame came responsibility and hideously early nights.

Her phone sounded twice as Georgia slipped on an off-the-shoulder sweater and a pair of Levi's jeans. No make-up or designer dress required as she would change at the studio. The first message was from her regular driver, Todd, confirming that he would be at hers to pick her up at 3.30am. The second was from Charlie.

'You awake and ready for action? See you by the coffee machine. Mine's an Americano.'

She smiled. It was all part of their morning ritual. Before she liaised with the duty forecaster who worked with the Met Office or dialled into the morning weather conference, she would meet Charlie by the drinks machine. He would pay for her skinny latte and she would return the compliment with his Americano. They would sneak a coffee-tinged kiss, and then go their separate ways until the morning's live show had finished at 9ish. If anyone thought the world of isobars and occluded fronts was glamorous then they needed to think again. Georgia loved her job but some days the sheer boredom of it enveloped her.

Today was one of them. Her mind was far from able to concentrate on the job in hand. Luckily for her the weather was one of those easy days full of a little wind and light showers so she could coast through the forecasts with a painted on smile and a figure hugging contrast colour dress from Henry Holland.

It was becoming clear to Georgia that she needed to have some time away from the studio. No matter where she looked now, all she could see were reminders of Mitzi. A feather in the street would remind her of a garment Mitzi once danced in, a tune on the radio would do the same. She had found herself thinking about her friend mid forecast that morning. At one point she could feel tears pricking the corners of her eyes as she was supposed to be bringing the news of the day's weather to the nation.

Foster's funeral was taking place that day in Cornwall too. It was strictly a family affair. She hadn't really known Foster that well, but sent flowers from both her and Charlie. They had enjoyed a few days and nights out as a foursome but normally it would just be her and Mitzi. Mitzi's mother was invited to the funeral but given her frailty she had decided not to go. Travel in her condition was next to impossible. It was a confession that she'd shared with Georgia on the phone when they had spoken after Georgia had finished that morning's broadcasts. There was a despair in Mitzi's mother's voice that cut into Georgia's heart like a sabre. It was beyond sorrow. Mitzi's mum was alone, frail and unable to do anything about it. 'If I could, I would board a plane and fly to America and search under every last stone until I find my daughter and bring her home ... dead or alive.' She had barely been able to finish the sentence before bursting into tears. Georgia's tears had come once she had hung up. The conversation had led her to make a decision, her mind was made up. She herself wasn't frail, she could board a plane, she could try and do something ... anything. She'd been thinking about it for days, but Mitzi's mother had been the catalyst she needed to convince her about her next move. She needed to do something and she needed to do it now. It was a matter that she was keen to discuss with Charlie as soon as they met at her dressing room.

'I've been to see the boss. I have some holidays still owed to me and I'm not concentrating on the job in hand. My mind is elsewhere. In a canyon in California to be exact. I'm going to take some time off. She's said it's okay.'

It was no surprise to Charlie, in fact he'd been expecting it ever since the news about Foster. He wrapped his arms around her as he spoke, eager to share his opinion.

'Do you want to go and stay with Mum and Jacob for a while? You need to try and be close to Mitzi, don't you?'

One word was sufficient. 'Yes'

'I have some interviews and stuff scheduled in for here over the next few days, but maybe I can arrange a few celeb drops in LA for next week and come join you. Failing that I'll take the time off anyway. I need to be there for you, Georgia. I want to be. I loved Mitzi too.'

Georgia could feel a sense of relief spread itself across her shoulders as she left her work studios that day. Nothing had changed, but just the mere thought that she would soon be heading to the same time zone where Mitzi had disappeared, where Mitzi may still be alive, gave her a shadow of hope.

Eight hours later, having packed her case and been driven to the airport by Charlie, Georgia was sky high and heading towards Los Angeles. What to find or do, she had no idea.

CHAPTER 27

'The doctor says that if it hadn't been for your heavy suitcase taking the brunt of the force from the car then you'd more than likely be six feet under right now.'

It didn't bear thinking about, but Victoria couldn't help herself. What if the last image she'd seen had been her husband and twin six-year-olds having a storybook-happy time with the nanny? To think that such a painful scene could have been the image she'd have taken to her grave.

'I guess I have to thank all of those Indian recipe books I'd bought and packed,' smiled Victoria, attempting a minor laugh but restricted by the pain in her broken ribs. 'Who ever thought curry could be so good for your health?'

'I seriously thought you were dead when Scott rang me,' said Evie, who had spent the last forty minutes seated at the bottom of Victoria's hospital bed. 'So, what happened?'

Victoria recounted the story of what she'd seen to Evie. The sweep of shock and disappointment streaked across her friend's face was easy to read. She may have been an actress for a living, able to convey the most complex of emotions with the slightest nuance but in real life, with friends, Evie was unable to hide her true feelings. It was clear to see.

Victoria picked up on it.

'So you think he's cheating on me with the hired help?' There was definitely bitterness in Victoria's voice.

'The fact that Scott chose not to come to India with you after you'd arranged it all is very suspicious. That and the day trip out together is a bit more than a coincidence, don't you think?'

Victoria did. 'So what do I do to make it better?'

'Hire a detective. Either you find out that he really loves you and that Chloe is merely tucking Lexi and Leo in at night, or if he is playing bedroom Buckaroo with the nanny then you chuck her sorry backside out PDQ.'

'A private eye? Has it come to this?' lamented Victoria. But she knew she needed to find out the truth. Evie was right. Maybe it wasn't just the aftermath of the car crash paining her right now. Maybe it was something much closer to home. She punched the sheets on her hospital bed as she weighed up the potential of Scott's infidelity.

CHAPTER 28

Aaron gave a satisfied shudder as the last few heightened bursts of his orgasm left his cock. Tanya's nails dug into his buttocks, pulling them towards her as he unleashed the final few moments of his seed.

He pulled his manhood from within her and rolled over, to lie alongside her on the bed. Tanya, who had raised her legs and placed her feet either side of Aaron's head during their sexual adventure to allow for deeper penetration, brought them down to a more gravity friendly position. Her body was covered in a delicious post-coital film of sweat.

'Is this your bedroom?' asked Aaron, his own body equally wet, the thick hair of his chest clumped together in dark, manly patches.

'No, I only fuck my husband in our bed,' said Tanya. 'This is one of the many spare ones that I don't think Devon ever comes into. I think the only time it's used is if his daughter comes to stay.'

It was the first time Aaron had been in the main house. Since he and Tanya had pretty much exhausted the places they could have sex in the garden – there were only so many times you could twist your body around the trunk of a tree or bend over a work bench and happily put up with splinters in the most intimate of places – they had taken their tryst inside to both the dry and the warm.

'You not a fan of his daughter?' There had been something about the way that Tanya had pronounced the words 'his daughter' that had voiced her dislike.

'We send Christmas cards, but it ends there. I think she sees me as the second wife and that means second best. It's not important to me.'

'I've not seen her at all, does she visit much?'

'Now and again. She's away at the moment though in America. Her best friend disappeared on a holiday with her boyfriend, who has turned up dead. Georgia's headed to LA to try and play detective. Devon told me last night.'

Aaron's ears pricked up. 'Not Mitzi Bidgood?'

'That sounds familiar. You know her?'

'She was the girl I was supposed to be dancing with on the TV. It was her disappearance that ruined my chances. The producers binned me because she was out of the picture too. So, your daughter is best mates with Mitzi?'

'She will never be *my* daughter. We're virtually the same age. She doesn't like me being with her father; that much is clear. I guess I am not what you British people call her *cup of tea*. That is right, yes?'

Aaron nodded.

'And anyway, if your dancing partner hadn't disappeared,' declared Tanya, 'then you'd never have ended up here with me, would you? So everything happens for a reason. Now, enough of this talk, why don't you show me some more of those sexual dance moves of yours?'

Tanya crushed her lips against his and pushed her tongue inside his mouth. Aaron reciprocated hungrily. He could feel his cock stirring back into life. A few seconds later Tanya swooped her head between his legs and greedily took his cock into her mouth, sucking it expertly until it had grown once more to its full length.

Aaron lay back and watched his Russian lover work her magic on his member. The temptation to make dance analogies quickstepped through his mind. She should work his meat *slow, slow, quick, quick, slow* and see if she had enough *ballroom* in her mouth to suck on his sack. He almost spoke but instead just lay back and watched Tanya in action. His words might have been lost in translation anyway, so why ruin the moment?

As Aaron felt the delirious sensation of blood flooding back into his cock once again, Devon was sitting behind his work office desk letting the darkest of thoughts flood through his mind.

'That Russian slut, how could she? After all I've done for her.' His words were unnecessarily whispered seeing as he was alone in his office, his colleagues having left for the day. Devon had not been able to concentrate on his work. One of the many beneficial things about being so well respected was that nobody dared to question the speed at which you worked. Genius was never on a timer.

Devon's brain was full of betrayal, hurt and anger. He had known betrayal was coming. He'd suspected infidelity, wasn't it what always happened to him? He'd seen the clues, spotted the disorder, could sense his loss of control. The redness of Tanya's cheeks when she climbed into bed at night, the telltale faint red lines around her wrists where she had been bound. He recognised them. Hadn't their own love-making been a thing of experimentation and danger not that long ago? But he hadn't indulged in such activity with her for weeks and not at all since Aaron's arrival. It was clear that there were undiscovered lies as yet not known to Devon.

It was such deception that could erode the very tiers of a husband's self-esteem. Dent him. His ego. His pride. His control. When Sophia had cheated on Devon, it had destroyed his outlook on love, tainting his view of future relationships and shattering any feelings of peace and tranquility. But it had been unexpected with Sophia. Hadn't he always known Tanya would cheat on him? She was young and beautiful. But wasn't he the one who had given her everything she desired in life? Now he could change all that if he wished.

Devon reached inside his Pal Zileri suit pocket and pulled out a set of keys. He located the one he required. Small, shiny and silver in colour.

He placed the key in the lock of a tall set of filing cabinets on the far side of his office and opened the top drawer. It was full of case study files, all alphabetised. Neat, tidy, efficient. Inserting his hand into the drawer, he felt around, searching for the object of his quest. It only took a second or two to locate. A smile, his first all day, swept across his face.

Pulling out his hand, he stared at the small gun housed in his palm. The sight of it impressed him every time. Small enough to hold in one hand, but mighty enough to end a life. Total control. An underdog of a weapon.

He'd used it before and been successful, and he knew that he'd use it again. In fact he was certain.

CHAPTER 29

The pain in Victoria's side was unbearable. She swallowed another painkiller with a swig of water from the white plastic beaker on her bedside table. Popping pills was becoming even more of a regularity since her accident. Anti-depressants and painkillers on a loop.

It had not been the best of days. When had been, lately? She was still in hospital and it looked like she would be for another few days yet and the pain from the accident seemed to be getting worse and worse. She had read every magazine the hospital had to offer, ploughed her way through a Jackie Collins, successfully demolished a Sudoku puzzle book and listened to every Radio 4 play she could stay awake for but still she was restless.

The twins had been to see her a few times, but their initial excitement about seeing Mummy in a white gown, connected with tubes and asking if they could see her bruises had turned to a dull fatigue by visit three with the realisation that Mummy wasn't able to play hide and seek or indulge in any such fun. Playtime doctors and nurses this wasn't.

Scott had brought the twins at first, playing the caring, dutiful husband which Victoria hoped he still was. Nothing had been too much trouble. He'd plumped her pillows, tidied the bed and recharged her Kindle. Made sure she was as comfortable as she possibly could be.

All thoughts of hiring a detective to find out if he was having an affair with Chloe disappeared and for a day or two, Evie's suggestion was forgotten.

But then Chloe turned up at visiting time, Lexi in one hand, Leo in the other. She was as pleasant and professional as ever and the kids seemed happy to be with her, but something about her oh-so-sweet ways seemed to grate on Victoria immensely. In fact, the honeyed pleasantries and talk of how she was looking after everything at home while Scott worked so hard, and how Victoria was not to worry and just concentrate on getting better, made Victoria sick to the core. As soon as Chloe and the kids had left, Victoria had phoned the private investigator recommended by Evie and employed his services. She needed to know the truth.

Victoria was contemplating buzzing her bedside alarm for another painkiller when there was a knock at the door.

'Mind if I come in?'

A wave of delight weaved its way across Victoria's face as she spied Charlie Cooper in the doorway. For a moment all pain disappeared as she stared at him. He looked beyond handsome. His sculpted beauty suddenly reminded her that she was looking far from presentable herself, a fact that suddenly seemed to matter. Her hair hadn't been styled in days, her face was make-up free and white hospital gowns were a look that not even Selena Gomez could make sexy. And she was not Victoria's body shape.

'Charlie, how lovely to see you. What a wonderful surprise.' Who needed painkillers when simply staring at a thing of beauty like Charlie could perk up any patient?

'I heard about what happened. I thought I'd pop in with these.' He was carrying enough magazines to keep a recycling plant in business for a year. 'There're some fashion magazines, celebrity ones, interiors. I picked the ones I'd seen lying around at Georgia's flat.' He winked at her. Was it flirtation or mere bravado?

A little stab of jealousy pricked Victoria's heart at the mention of Georgia's name.

'She sends her love, by the way. She's in the States so couldn't come with me today.'

Damn. Victoria had been secretly hoping that Charlie had come to see her alone of his own free will. He pulled up a chair, turned it towards himself and sat down next to the bed. There was an air of cockiness in the way that he straddled his legs over the chair and pulled the seat as close to the bed as possible. Victoria could feel a flush of colour run to her cheeks. Was he green-lighting her?

'Is she working there?' enquired Victoria, trying to keep herself together.

'No, not at all. She wants to be closer to Mitzi, to find out what's being done to try and locate her. Georgia is determined to do what she can. She's staying with my mum and Jacob.'

'Give her my love.'

'I will. So, have you had many visitors?'

'Scott and the kids have been in, so has the nanny. Apart from that it's just been Evie and you. It's a bit too far for my parents to pop in. Hopefully I'll be out of here before they'd even reach New Orleans airport.'

'Evie Merchant?'

'Yes, we were at college together and she was in the same Zumba group as Mitzi. As was your Georgia.' Victoria silently berated herself for adding the word 'your'. Like she wanted reminding. And she hoped that he didn't, either.

'I'm actually interviewing her tomorrow about her latest film. I'm really looking forward to it. I've never met her before.'

'That surprises me, I would have thought a showbiz reporter of your calibre would have met everybody by now.' She was fawning but couldn't help herself. It definitely took her mind off the pain.

'No, she's on my wanted list, along with Cher, Coco Rocha and Shaquille O'Neal.'

'Well, I could have helped with Evie, but it sounds like you already have it covered. As for the others, well, I'm afraid I've actually only heard of Cher. And seeing as she's not been in for a visit I guess I can say we're not bosom buddies.' Victoria allowed herself to laugh, amused by her own joviality, but her joy turned to pain as an incision of discomfort shot into her side, causing her to break into a fit of coughing.

Charlie stood up and moved towards her. 'Woah, that sounds harsh,' he commented. 'You need me to fetch a nurse?' Without realising it, he had taken one of her hands in his. It was an action that didn't go unnoticed by Victoria and she squeezed it gently. For a moment, both her coughing and indeed time itself seemed to stop.

'No, I'm fine,' lied Victoria. 'It's just the pain from my ribs. I'll live. I just won't be doing any paragliding or zip-lining for a while,' she smiled, coughed, smiled.

'Look, I'll leave you be. I just wanted to pop in and say that I was thinking about you, and that if there is anything we can do, then be sure to ring Georgia and me. You girls swapped numbers in India, didn't you? You take care of yourself and make sure that husband and nanny of yours look after you well. Take lots of bed rest.'

Charlie leant in to kiss her goodbye on the cheek. Victoria took advantage of their closeness to enjoy the feel of his five o'clock shadow against her flesh and the smell of his cologne. He smelled as divine as he looked.

As he left she watched him walk out of the room and down the hospital corridor out of view. Even from behind he looked a picture perfect vision of masculinity. God, bed rest? If she was under the sheets with Charlie Cooper, the last thing she'd be doing would be resting.

Victoria snapped out of her daydream, a sharp jolt of heat jabbing into her side again. 'Screw this, I need more painkillers,' she winced, pressing the button for a nurse.

If only Charlie Cooper was available on prescription. She'd gladly take three of him a day to ease the pain.

CHAPTER 30

'Okay, Nova. We need you to jump into the pool again, grab the inflatable crocodile and jiggle around on it in an attempt to swim. If you can stick your ass above the water as you do, so we can get that on camera, too? You need to look like you really want to impress Cain.'

The voice, twisted with a mixture of hope, professionalism and exasperation, belonged to the director of the latest bizarre episode of *Champagne Super Nova*, one in which Nova decides that she would like to learn to swim in the hope of auditioning for a *Baywatch* remake. Props for this episode included the tiniest of leopard print bikinis, barely covering either Nova's breasts or her fulsome backside, an inflatable croc to add a fun element and Cain, the Chris Hemsworth lookalike swimming instructor, also wearing the most crotch-grabbing miniscule piece of fabric the show makers could find to enhance his role as Nova's tutor.

He was no more a swimming instructor than Georgia was. She was watching the action with Jacob, somewhat jet-lagged but sun-kissed beside the family home swimming pool. Or at least as close to the pool as the bank of cameras, producers, directors, assistant producers, runners and Uncle Tom Cobleys blocking her view would allow. Georgia thought she knew TV, but TV LA *Super Nova* style was something else.

This was Take Fourteen of what she assumed would be no more than maybe a forty second clip on the show. They'd been filming it ever since her arrival at the house some four hours earlier. Poor Nova must have been running out of ways to jiggle.

'Is it always like this?' joked Georgia, turning to Jacob. It felt good to be in LA, nearer to where Mitzi might be. Nearer to the truth. She adjusted the loose fitting Zara shirt that draped over her swimsuit as she turned towards Charlie's stepdad.

'This is a good day. Take Fourteen is nothing. If we're not happy with the angle of the shot, how Nova's body looks, how the sun is glinting off swimboy's abs over there then the scene is reshot. The only trouble with today is that Nova jumping into water means having to redo hair and make-up between every take. Heaven forbid the world see Nova with smudged lipstick or a hair out of place. She'd have my balls under one of her six inch heels, and that's the last thing I want. It's the madness of it all, and Nova gets that. I call scenes like this her "caricature" moments. She knows just how to play up to the LA lunacy.'

'I assumed you'd be knocking the shows out as you produce so many. I guess I'm used to live TV and the immediacy of it all. I really didn't think it would be so complex.'

'Imagine what it's like for the Kardashians. At least with Nova being the sole star she is the only one we have to focus on to make sure she looks better than the rest. With the mass of females in their show there has to be a bit of, how shall I say, *friendly rivalry*, to see who obtains the best shot. And I've heard on the grapevine that the guys on that show are just as precious.'

'Are you on your show very often?'

'As little as I can get away with. Nova insists now and again but if it was down to me I'd rather be the enigma husband, like Dolly Parton's. People know he exists but nobody really sees him. But Nova has turned this production into one of the most lucrative global shows ever, so what she wants, she can bloody well have. As long as I agree, of course. I'm boss.'

Georgia liked Jacob. He was old-school, maybe a touch overly honest and brutal with his words at times but he knew that success came from keeping the talent happy. And it was clear that he loved the talent of this particular production to her bikini-covered bones. She made him money, she made him happy.

'How do I look, darling?' It was Nova shouting across the pool at her husband. She gave one of her obligatory boob wiggles as she asked. The leopard print strained against the expanse of taut flesh barely contained below it.

'Fabulous, my angel, fabulous. Like something from an erotic Busby Berkeley musical.'

The reference was lost on Georgia, but clearly not on Nova who squeezed her breasts together at him like a larger-than-life Marilyn. She reminded Georgia of one of those curvaceous Hollywood sirens from days gone by. She was old-school too. No wonder she and Jacob were the perfect lid for the perfect pot.

'And what about you, Georgia? Are you loving this? Isn't Bel-Air just the most?'

Georgia gave the thumbs up, unsure what to say. It felt wrong to admit that she was enjoying the frivolity of it all, a brief respite from the darkness that constantly circled her thoughts concerning Mitzi, but she needed today, because tomorrow would be so, so different. Of that she was sure ...

'This is my future daughter-in-law, everybody, Georgia Bellamy. Devoted girlfriend of my darling Charlie, fresh off the plane from England.' Nova was enjoying holding court. Being the star turn at the circus.

Georgia held her hands up and wiggled her fingers at those gathered as if to acknowledge the fact. Again she was unsure what exactly the most fitting response should be to Nova's exuberance. She noticed a hushed ripple of conversation circle around the pool as she waved.

'Just go with it,' said Jacob, reaching over to squeeze Georgia's knee. 'It's Nova's way of showing her approval. But you get married in your own good time.'

Georgia smiled. Nova may be a broken record but she was still one Georgia enjoyed listening to. And Jacob was the perfect DJ. He knew just how to play her. His way.

Georgia sipped her drink and lay back, enjoying the sunshine. She had to force herself to relax after her flight and today was her only chance. She had decided that tomorrow she would drive to Hell's Canyon, the scene of Mitzi's disappearance and the place where Foster's body had been discovered. There she could hopefully start piecing things together. There wasn't a moment to lose.

Evie was thoroughly enjoying her interview with Charlie Cooper. She had spent a career trying to avoid awkward questions about her past, her leading men, her failed relationships, her celebrity friends, so for once it was wholly refreshing to lose herself in an interview that was all about fun. Light, frothy and not at all hard-hitting. She found Charlie captivating and incredibly easy on the eye. Georgia was a lucky girl. The only air of seriousness came when Evie was having her microphone removed and Charlie mentioned having seen Victoria the day before. The concern was plain to see on Evie's face.

'The poor girl, but she's lucky to be alive. It could have been so much worse. I hear she's due out very soon. It'll be good for her to be at home. Or at least I hope it will.'

Charlie wasn't quite sure what Evie meant but didn't push the matter.

Charlie explained that Georgia had just headed out to America to try and find out the truth behind Mitzi's disappearance and the death of Foster Hampton and that she was staying with his infamous mother.

Evie's face lit up. 'That's right, your mother is Nova Chevalier, isn't she? Victoria mentioned it. I have to admit, her programme is my total guilty pleasure. A couple of my close friends have interviewed her and they say she's fantastic. I can see where you get your Hollywood looks from now.'

Boom! Still got it, mused Charlie. He could feel his chest swelling. He never tired of hearing beautiful ladies complimenting him, and Hollywood A-listers ranked high on the pride factor. He'd be lying if he said it didn't make his head swell too.

'I'm going out to join them in a few days. I want to be there to support Georgia.'

'How lovely. Listen, I hope you don't mind, but can I give you this?' Evie bent down and fished into her Chanel handbag, pulling out a white envelope. 'It's an invitation for a charity event I'm hosting in a few weeks' time. I want to raise money but I also want to keep awareness rolling about Mitzi. Please God she'll be back home safe and sound by then and if she is, she'll be guest of honour. I'm only intending to invite a select few but I'd love it if you, Georgia and even your mum and stepdad came along if they'd like to. I understand if they're busy with the show, but if they can, then great.'

Charlie was genuinely touched and took the invitation with glee. 'Thank you, Miss Merchant. That's amazing and I'm sure Georgia will be thrilled. Anything to keep Mitzi from just becoming another forgotten statistic is an awesome idea. We'll definitely be there.'

'Good stuff,' smiled Evie. 'And please, call me Evie. Miss Merchant sounds like something from *Annie!*'

As Charlie headed back to the *Rise and Shine* studios he couldn't stop smiling. How lovely to meet somebody that you really admired and to find out that she was just as nice, if not nicer, than you'd ever dreamt she'd be. And highly sexy too. He couldn't count the number of times he'd interviewed a celebrity, especially ones as big as Evie, and found their egos to be totally overinflated.

CHAPTER 31

'Surely you can ditch the fucking gardening for a few days, darling. This is a major opportunity and not one that comes around very often, so I suggest you *drop your hoe* for a little while and do as I say.'

Aaron wasn't sure if his agent, Rachel, was talking about the gardening tool or his affair with Tanya.

'Is that what it's called, that thing you use to scrape up the leaves, or is that a rake? I've no bloody idea and I care even less.' Rachel clarified her meaning. And anyway, how would she know about his adventurous love-making with the oligarch's daughter or the scientist's wife, as he thought of Tanya, depending on how guilty he was feeling about the whole thing. Today, it was not at all. If Tanya wasn't gaining sexual satisfaction from Mr *Big Bang Theory* then maybe it was only right that Aaron was the one giving her a big bang worth talking about of her very own.

'So what's the offer? You've obviously dragged me into your office for a reason. I haven't heard from you in weeks. I thought you'd *done a Mitzi* and vanished.' Aaron had lost any semblance of respect for his agent a while back. Whereas not that long ago he would have been all sweetness and light, now he had regular money coming in from the gardening gig he was more than happy to say goodbye to any kind of media jobs. And if that meant saying goodbye to Rachel for good then so be it.

'Less of the cheek, sunshine. And that quip is in very poor taste, especially given what I'm about to tell you.'

Aaron bit his tongue and listened.

'With all the media coverage of Mitzi and Foster, obviously your photo – supplied by me, I may add – has popped up in a lot of news reports and magazines. Despite the lack of money coming in for your services, putting your rugged chops out there has obviously done some good. I've had a phone call about you. One of the Hollywood newspapers ran a piece and they included your mug shot. Well, it seems that with pilot season ready to go in the not too distant future in Los Angeles, a producer over there would like to see you. They're looking for a British action hero for a new show and even though I've told them you're not an actor, they'd like to see you anyway. Apparently this hairy faced masculinity of yours is all the rage right now and they want somebody who is the antithesis of all the pretty boys swanning around Hollywood playing high school kids well into their thirties. I've assured them you have a body to die for as well. I assume you've been keeping in shape?'

'I've been working out, shall we say.' Sex with a hungry Russian beat the treadmill or a vibrating plate any day of the week.

'Can I see? I'm not sending you to Los Angeles with any semblance of a man boob. My agenting name would be dirt.'

Aaron stood up and stripped his shirt off. The look on Rachel's face was one of approval.

'Good, but you might want to think about a bit of manscaping with that.' She motioned to his chest hair. 'I want them to think of you as the next Jason Statham, not the next Chewbacca.'

Suddenly the penny dropped. 'Hang on, you're sending me to LA for an acting audition? I can't act. I'm a surfing gardener, or a gardening surfer. Take your pick.'

'Why don't we let the producers decide, shall we? It's the same production company behind the reality smash *Champagne Super Nova*. Big bucks TV. I think they've had a hand in things like *Empire* and *Devious Maids* as well so they know what they're doing.'

It was all white noise to Aaron. Him an actor? No fucking way.

Rachel could obviously read his fears. 'Look, Jason Statham was a member of Britain's National Diving Squad long before he started beating the crap out of people in Hollywood. And then there's Vinnie Jones. One minute he's grabbing people's bollocks on the football pitch and the next he's sharing the screen with Hugh Jackman. So just head to Hollywood with an open mind. This is a major opportunity. Don't blow it. Now put your sodding shirt back on!' Aaron did as he was told. Maybe Rachel was actually back in his good books again. There may be no money on the table right now, but a gig in Hollywood would soon change all that.

'So when do I go?'

'I've booked you on a flight first thing tomorrow morning. Someone from the production crew will meet you at LAX. You'll be there about five days or so I reckon. I'll email you all the details. Now get out of here and get yourself to a man groomers. Try this one in Islington. I hear it's fabulous.'

Rachel scribbled down a name and address and handed it to Aaron. 'And then get yourself home and packed for LA. And no fucking this up.'

Talking of fucking, I'd better let Tanya know that I'm out of action for the next few days, reasoned Aaron as he left the office. He wasn't sure how she'd take the news.

CHAPTER 32

As Aaron's text popped through to Tanya's phone telling her that he would be disappearing for a short while she was standing with her husband in their bedroom, admiring the dress he had just presented her with.

The Harrods-bought, tissue-wrapped Balmain studded long sleeve mini-dress was a riot of sexy crystallised studs. It oozed evening chic and would not have gleaned much change from two and a half grand. Ignoring her phone on the bedside table, she let her body slide into the dress. It was a work of art and the feeling of it against her skin was a total turn-on. Especially as all she wore underneath were the Coco De Mer panties and open cup bra she had bought on her recent shopping trip to Chelsea.

'Oh my God, Devon. It's divine. How did you know I wanted a Balmain? They were the toast of Paris Fashion Week.'

'I know, you're not the only one with an interest in fashion in this house, you know that.'

It was one of the many things that had actually first attracted her to Devon. His flare was fashion was something that most men his age could only dream of. It wasn't necessarily true that money bought taste. She'd seen that often enough back home in Russia. But luckily for Tanya, Devon had both.

As she stared at him across the bed she could feel a sexual glow creep across her body. Whether it was the thought of Devon or the expensive piece of designer wear caressing her flesh she wasn't sure but she was determined to find out.

Walking around to the far side of the bed, she turned her back to her husband, lifted up her hair and asked him to do up her zip. He dutifully did so. As she faced him again, she placed her hand over the bulge forming in his trousers, a sign of his appreciation of her beauty. She grabbed it between her fingers, balling her hand almost into a fist. He appeared to grow harder, enjoying the thin line between pleasure and pain.

'Now, undo yours.'

Devon didn't need asking twice, sliding down the zip on his trousers and releasing his cock through his flies. It was long and hard.

Tanya immediately compared it to Aaron's in her mind. Aaron's was thicker and hairier, maybe not as long, but definitely with a lot more girth. She ran her hands down her dress as she stared at Devon's cock, the feel of the crystallised studs under her fingertips bringing her sexual nerves to attention. She bent forward and took Devon's cock in her mouth. She shut her eyes, unusually for her, and worked her tongue up and down Devon's shaft. There was a slight saltiness about it. It seemed different, lighter in odour and somehow less masculine than the earthiness she'd been experiencing with Aaron.

Devon placed his hands on either side of Tanya's head and worked her mouth up and down his prick, controlling the speed as he pumped into it. His groan of joy told her that she wouldn't have to endure the taste for too long. Indeed, a few seconds later he shot his cum into her mouth. A hot, thick spurt. It had obviously been a while since he had last climaxed. There was something deeply arousing about the thought of something so animalistic and carnal being performed whilst wearing such an exquisite dress.

Standing up again, she licked her lips and lent in to kiss Devon's. She could still taste his seed. 'Thank you for my dress, darling. I love it.'

'I'm glad, because you'll need to pack it for where we're going,' grinned Devon, slipping his cock back into his trousers.

'Really, we're going somewhere? Where, darling?'

'Milan. I thought a weekend of shopping and clubbing would suit us down to the ground. The gardener won't be around so I thought it'd be the perfect opportunity for us to get away and spend a bit of quality time together. I'd been working long hours lately and you must have been so lonely here with nobody to speak to, so I thought you deserved a treat. I've hired a private jet and it takes off in about four hours' time, so you had better start packing.'

Tanya tried to show as much joy as she could. She loved the idea of going to Milan, a place she had never been and one that was at the summit of fashion. But how could she? All she could think about was that Aaron wouldn't be around. Why? What had happened? Had Devon fired him?

'Now, get packing, and make it sexy.' He unzipped her dress and slapped her playfully on the backside as he left the room.

Tanya slipped the dress from her body and contemplated the weekend ahead. Her phone beeped again, reminding her that she had a message. She picked it up. It was from Aaron. 'Have spoken to Devon and said I can't come round for a few days as have to go to States for potential work. I'll miss you. Think of me while I'm gone. X'

Think of him? Despite trying to do otherwise that was all she'd been doing while fellating her husband. Tanya suddenly realised that maybe Aaron had gotten under her Russian skin a little bit more than she had planned.

Deleting the message, she started her packing. At least Devon didn't know about the affair. If he did, he certainly wouldn't be taking her off to Milan, would he? Or buying her such wondrous dresses.

As she packed she was already counting down the minutes. Not until take-off, but until the next time she could be in Aaron's arms.

It was twenty minutes later, while Tanya was showering, that Devon returned to the bedroom. He walked over to her phone on the bedside table and picked it up. Unlocking it using the code he'd seen his wife type in on countless occasions, he touched on the Messages icon and looked at the most recent one that had come through. As he had suspected when it had first beeped, it was from Aaron.

Devon had watched Tanya when the phone beeped for a second time as he'd left the room. She'd not seen him as he stood, peering around the doorway, watching her face light up with a smile as she read the message. She'd been overjoyed to read his news; that was clear. Surely she couldn't think that Devon had not noticed the look of consternation on her cheating face when he'd mentioned that Aaron wouldn't be around for a few days. He wasn't stupid. Far from it. She thought that he'd fired him. He could read her like a fucking book. His brain wasn't just a scientific one, it was a scheming one too. And there was no doubt about the answer to this equation. Revenge. He was smarter than she could ever be. His plan was working, he would make her realise what she had to lose. No woman would make a fool of him again. Milan would be an experience that Tanya would never forget. He'd make sure of that. As Devon heard the sound of the shower power jets switch off, he placed Tanya's phone back on the table and walked out of the room again. A demonic smile twisted itself across his face.

CHAPTER 33

Quite how it had come to this, Victoria wasn't sure. She had assumed, wrongly it seemed, that being back home in the comfort of her own family bosom would have been just the stimulant she needed for a speedy recovery. But the truth of the matter was that the pain in her side seemed to be getting worse.

She'd heard all of the doctors dishing out their prescriptive placatory pleasantries saying that time would be the best healer and that eventually the pain she was feeling, the pain that seemed to drag at every one of her inner tissues and pull it in a million agonising directions, would simply fade away to nothing. But their words of wisdom were easily drowned in a sea of pain. Even the pain of giving birth to a pair of melon-sized twins hadn't been this bad.

God bless pills. The only thing that seemed to help was the painkillers. Those little white miraculous chalky tablets that she housed in a bottle alongside her bed. They seemed to be the only remedy that could stop Victoria from tensing her body with every slight movement and clenching her muscles in agony. Her frustration was already beyond exacerbation at hearing Leo and Lexi asking why Mummy didn't like to hug any more. How do you explain to a six-year-old that the pain in your side outweighs the wish to hold your children tight? Of course it didn't, but to the two children, her refusal to hug them cut like a knife. They wanted their mummy, and they wanted a fully working one that came with hugs, kisses and the ability to play Twister when required. And for now, that wasn't Victoria.

But for a short while, after the effects of the painkiller had taken hold across her body, there was a feeling of contentment. Relaxation would envelop her, a coating of calm would wrap itself around her aching core and a sense of being a normal twenty-eight-year-old woman yet again would once more caress her. A warm welcome back to life, back to normality – even if it was a painkiller anti-depressant cocktail induced 'normality'.

She found it amazing what an actual pill could do. No more thought of pain, no more thoughts of Scott's possible infidelity, no more thoughts of poor Mitzi. Sleep would take her, a blanket of joyous recuperative sleep, to a field of dreams where all woes were banished. To a place where naughty delights like the possibility of Charlie Cooper filled her head.

Victoria knew she was being foolish but she couldn't stop herself. In the days since her return home she'd had ample opportunity to think about Charlie. Lying in bed, or shuffling around the house while the twins were at school left her hours for contemplation, and it was mostly Charlie who filled her thoughts. Despite knowing it was no more than a silly, imbecilic crush, like the ones she'd had in her youth on James Van Der Beek from *Dawson's Creek* and the boys from Hanson, Victoria couldn't stop herself. She'd even found herself becoming annoyed and, dare she say it, a touch jealous, when Evie had texted to say how wonderful she thought he was. It had to stop. But maybe not just yet. In a world where she was already convinced that her husband didn't fancy her any more, she longed for a bit of romance, albeit within the confines of her own mind for the moment.

She knew it was the pills. And she didn't care. The anti-depressants had been with her for so long now – was it weeks, months

… she'd lost count – that the blurred softness they created over some of the more bitterly jagged areas of her life was becoming a very welcome relief. Adding the painkillers into the mix, suddenly new heights of blurred ecstasy seemed to be achievable. Even the thought that she was potentially watching her family shatter into tiny fragments somehow seemed bearable when the pills took hold. The soft foggy cloud of smudged reality they took her to was a place she welcomed. And she had no intention of stopping her visits there. The pills acted like a magic carpet transporting her away from her woes. From her pain, from her insecurities, from her doubts, from her thoughts of Chloe and Scott.

Victoria had binned the detective she had employed only a few days earlier to find out the truth about her husband's extra-curricular activities. What was the point? She knew the truth. Her worries about Scott and Chloe weren't just the product of an insecure woman's paranoia. Could any woman see her husband touch the nape of another woman's neck and not doubt his fidelity? It was such an intimate gesture. Victoria's doubt wasn't about whether her suspicions were grounded in fact. She didn't need a private detective to tell her that. It was about her own ability to face the truth and deal with it. Whether her own strength and state of mind could cope with it right now. She needed to look to herself first for strength before confronting the weaknesses of others.

After dining on another Chloe-made evening meal, a moussaka that wasn't black, Victoria rose from the table where she and the family were eating and gingerly made her way to the sink to pour herself a glass of water.

'Here, Victoria, let me help you,' offered Scott. It was obvious to him that his wife was in pain.

It was a thoughtful gesture but one that Victoria was determined to turn down. Since the accident, her inability to do much for herself was already damaging her deeply, and she was determined to do as much as she could to get back to normal, and regain some independence.

'No, it's okay, I can manage.' It was clear that she couldn't as she raised her hand to turn on the tap. She took a sharp, loud intake of breath and bent forward as pain lacerated her side. She dropped the glass she was holding and it cracked into two separate pieces in the sink.

'Oh, for fuck's sake!' Her anger was both loud and bitter. Both Lexi and Leo stopped what they were doing at the kitchen table to stare, open-mouthed at their mum. They'd never heard her use a naughty word before, and especially not that one.

Scott ran to her side to help. 'Come on, let me do that for you.' He picked up the two broken pieces of glass and placed them to one side. 'And mind your language in front of the kids, eh?' he whispered. He wasn't angry with her, as he could feel her frustration. 'You go back to bed for some rest. You're trying to do too much. The doctor said you'd experience pain for a while as you have taken quite a battering. Your body's black and blue.'

'Along with being a bit saggy, out of shape and in need of an MOT,' snapped Victoria.

'And self-deprecation isn't going to help, Victoria.' There was a now a *soupçon* of annoyance in Scott's voice. 'You've been through a heck of an ordeal.'

She had, but her failing body was not helping with the feelings of failure that she had already been experiencing prior to the accident. And it certainly wasn't helping her temper. She needed a painkiller. How many had she taken today? She'd lost count. But however many it was, it wasn't enough.

'Go back to bed. You need to rest, you look tired. And you're obviously getting a little narky.' It was a fact, not a criticism. 'Chloe, can you take Victoria back upstairs, please? I'll finish off down here.'

'Of course,' said Chloe, dutifully doing as requested.

As Chloe escorted her from the kitchen, Victoria could hear Lexi asking her father, 'Daddy, why did Mummy say a rude word? We know not to say things like that.'

Victoria cursed herself inwardly. She'd have to control her temper.

'Mummy's just feeling a little unwell and not herself at the moment,' said Scott. 'Now, which of two scamps would like to help their dad load the dishwasher? Any willing volunteers receive lemon and raspberry sorbet for pudding.'

Victoria couldn't see the twins raising their hands but she knew, as Chloe assisted her upstairs, they would be.

Chloe helped Victoria climb into bed.

'Isn't your job description to tuck in the children, not the mother of the house?' smiled Victoria.

'Yes, but I think they're fine with their dad right now. He seems to be coping well,' replied Chloe.

'He does, doesn't he? Do you like working here, Chloe?'

'I love it. The twins are great.'

'What about Scott and me?'

It was a strange question and one that Chloe seemed unsure how to answer.

'Um … you're both great, too. Wonderful to work for. I enjoy my job.' Something told Chloe that the conversation was leading somewhere she didn't want to go. 'Why do you ask?'

'No reason, Chloe. I just wondered. The children really like you and I suppose a good nanny is always a terribly hard thing to find so I just wanted to make sure you're happy here. Especially now you're playing nurse maid too. Doesn't give you much time for anything else, does it?'

'No, I suppose not.'

'Do you have a boyfriend, Chloe?'

'Not right now, no.' Chloe shuffled a little uneasily at the questioning.

'Men can be a real pain, especially if they start to get in the way of your job. I suppose you have to be certain that they're the right one for you.'

Okay, this is all becoming a bit too cryptic for my liking, thought Chloe. She was keen to change the subject.

'Is there anything else I can do for you?'

'Just one thing, can you fetch me a glass of water? I think I'm going to take another painkiller and try to doze a bit.'

'Certainly I can. Hold on two seconds.' She left the room and returned a few moments later with the glass of water. 'Is that all?'

'Just one other thing. Can you ask Scott to phone the doctor for some more painkillers for me? I only have a handful left and this pain is not subsiding.' Victoria was counting out her tablets on her palm as she asked.

'Of course.' Chloe handed Victoria the glass and bid her goodnight. 'If you need anything else then give me a shout.'

'I will.' Victoria watched as Chloe shut the bedroom door behind her. She was chewing over her thoughts about Chloe as she swallowed one of the painkillers.

Pleased to feel the coolness of the cotton bed sheets underneath her, Victoria lay down and closed her eyes. She could feel any clouds of temper vaporising as she drifted into a much needed sleep.

It was dark when Victoria woke up. The pain in her body had returned once more. She automatically reached for the painkillers. She placed one in her hand and grabbed her glass. It was empty.

She looked at the clock. It was just before midnight. She didn't want to shout for Scott as she might wake the twins. Scott had been sleeping in a separate bedroom since Victoria's return from hospital as he didn't want to disturb her sleep with late nights and early mornings. Victoria missed his body alongside hers.

Slipping out from under the sheets, she moved towards the bedroom door. She opened it and headed as quickly as she could, considering the pain in her side, to the nearest bathroom. She left the lights off for fear of waking Leo and Lexi.

It was as she walked back to her room that she heard a noise. A soft whimper. One that chilled her to the core. It was coming from downstairs. She knew what it was even before peering over the landing banister to the living room below. She was horribly aware of what she was about to see. A betrayed woman's instincts.

Victoria stared down to see the naked backside of her husband thrusting as quietly as he could between the open, willing legs of Chloe. Even in the dim light, Victoria could see that Chloe's eyes were shut and the expression on her face showed that she was enjoying the ride.

Her body pained now with a new misery, Victoria simply turned back to her room and tried to eradicate what she'd seen from her thoughts. It just confirmed what she had known all along and had been too tired to face.

Victoria took the painkiller, happy in the knowledge that at least it would blitz some of the aching she was feeling. Then she just lay awake. She was still wide awake as the first rays of light began to seep through the bedroom curtains the next morning.

CHAPTER 34

She'd been told what to say, how much to ask for, what orders to give. The voice, female she thought, had told her that if she did this then maybe her time in this hell would come to an end. An end where nothingness wasn't the final destination. Maybe this was a droplet of hope in a repugnant, fetid sea of desolation.

The slap across her cheek, already numb with pain from lying on the floor, had woken her from darkness yet again. The brightness of the light scored into her brain once more. She had been dragged to a sitting position, the ropes binding her hands used as leverage. She had nothing to fight with, allowing her captor to drag her as they chose. The ropes burnt at her wrists. Did they draw blood? She couldn't tell. She didn't care. Maybe death would be a better option.

The voice in the darkness told her what to say again. Did she understand? She did. She'd do what was required and see what happened after that. Would somebody come for her? There were those who cared. Those closest to her. They wouldn't give up, would they? Even if her own spirit was close to submission.

She spoke the words as instructed into the camera. Her voice was dry and raspy, her tone no more than a croaked whisper. As the light clicked off after her words, the room plunged into darkness once more. A chink of light appeared from a doorway illuminating the room slightly. Was it above her? She wasn't sure. She wasn't sure of anything anymore. She felt her wrists being untied and a plate of food appeared in front of her. A sandwich. Alongside it, a drink.

Her reward for playing ball. Maybe. She placed her hands around the drink and put it to her lips. Water. Lukewarm but water nevertheless. She downed it in one.

'Now eat.' The voice was an order.

She picked up the sandwich and placed it to her mouth. As the silhouette of her captor carried the camera and tripod from the room, the door shut once more and the chink of light vanished, leaving only darkness.

She attempted to swallow the mouthful of sandwich. It seemed alien to her and caused her to retch.

She began to cry. Tears for herself. For her family. For those she'd left behind. Surely somebody would be coming for her. Somebody. Anybody …

CHAPTER 35

Georgia had risen before dawn on her second day in LA and driven the nine-hour journey to Hell's Canyon, Siskiyou County, to the place where Foster's body had been found. She'd borrowed one of Nova and Jacob's bank of cars.

Jacob had told her that the journey would take her most of the day and had even offered to hire a plane for her, but Georgia was adamant that she would drive. The time alone would give her a chance to think. She had no idea where she was really going other than the coordinates she'd set on the car's inbuilt sat nav; she wasn't sure what she was going to do when she arrived there and indeed what she hoped to achieve, but she knew it was something that she had to do.

She had arrived in Hell's Canyon by mid-afternoon. It was the flip-side to what she had been experiencing in LA. Instead of flashy, trashy Hollywood homes and displays of vulgar riches at every turn, life around the area of the Canyon was simple and relaxed. It was rich in greenery as opposed to million-dollar properties. She could immediately see why Mitzi and Foster had chosen to visit. It was light years away from the illuminations of any television dance floor.

Georgia ventured briefly into the Canyon. She needed to experience what her friend had seen. The sun overhead was relentless as she stepped out of her car and surveyed the enormity of the area before her. Georgia loved the sunshine but this was an extremity like no other she had felt before. Her skin immediately cowered as it felt the change of temperature, scared of its brutality and afraid to be away from the comfort of her car's air conditioning. The scene before Georgia was a desolate one. Any greenery that thrived and flourished outside the Canyon itself seemed to stand no chance here. The form of the rocks and the contours of the land shaping almost a bowl of fieriness that was not just red hot, it was almost scarlet. The land was beautiful but arid. Dynamic yet as dangerous as a virus. And despite the beads of sweat already forming on her skin as she looked into the Canyon, the thought that Mitzi had been here just a few short weeks ago warmed her more. It made her feel a few steps nearer to her missing friend.

Georgia's visit to the Canyon was brief. There was nothing she could do there. In an ideal world she would walk the canyon floor and find an as yet undiscovered piece of evidence that the local authorities had been too clueless to notice. Maybe a note hinting at what had really happened, a vital sign that Mitzi was still alive. But this world was far from ideal and any clues would surely have already been unearthed by the police teams who had been working the area since the discovery of Foster's body. She took some photos and uploaded them onto her Facebook, Twitter and Instagram accounts. Maybe something, no matter how seemingly irrelevant, would jog somebody's memory. What else could she do?

Georgia had expected to see posters of Mitzi displayed in the local shops. A 'Have You Seen …?' hope that the search was ongoing. There were none. It was a fact she took up with the police when she visited the local police station.

'Miss, things like this are not good for tourism around here,' the officer at the front desk had told her. 'And believe you me, we've had teams of people searching every hidden part of that

Canyon since the body of that young man was found. If your lady friend was there we would have found her by now.'

'But somebody must have seen something. If you had posters up reminding people of what had happened then maybe it would jog somebody's memory. In all kinds of cases evidence comes to light weeks, months, maybe even years after the crime actually happened. You can't give up.' Georgia's voice was streaked with frustration.

She felt helpless. It was as she left the police station that she felt any last ounce of hope leaving her body. She tried to fight it. She couldn't allow herself to feel this way, she just couldn't.

'Two more days and I'll be there with you.'

It was good to hear Charlie's voice. She needed a splash of something uplifting as her day had been both fruitless and exhausting.

'So, where are you now?' asked Charlie.

'Sipping warm beer in the bar of the hotel I'm staying at. Jacob booked it for me as the thought of driving another nine hours back to Bel-Air after the day I've had was about as appetising as the burger I've just eaten in the restaurant.'

'Not good?'

'It could have been grizzly bear for all I know. No taste whatsoever, but I wasn't really very hungry. I am just about ready to call it a day.'

'You're off to bed. I'm just heading into work. I have to interview some young buck who's just joined the cast of that soap my mother loves, *Peregrine Palace*. I'll book my flight and I should be with you the day after tomorrow. I've missed you.'

'I'll head back to LA in the morning and try to work out what to do next. We can't give up on Mitzi, Charlie, we can't.'

As she hung up the phone, a wave of tiredness washed over Georgia's body. She was just about to stand and leave to go to her room when a young woman approached her.

'Excuse me, were you just talking about somebody called Mitzi?'

The mention of her friend's name on a stranger's lips jolted Georgia back into alertness. 'Yes, I was, who are you?'

'My name's Alice Kilbride, I work on reception here.' The woman was no older than her late teens, with small round glasses perched on her nose, her hair scraped back severely off her face in a tied bun. She was nearly pretty but not quite.

'I wasn't listening to your conversation, honest, but I heard you mention that girl Mitzi. She was the one who disappeared with her friend and now he's turned up dead in the Canyon, isn't she?'

Georgia simply nodded, eager to not interrupt what the girl had to say.

'I met her. She came in here a while back. I remember her name as I thought it was so unusual. Kind of exotic.'

'You met Mitzi?' A burst of excitement exploded within Georgia. Maybe the day wasn't going to be so fruitless after all.

'Yes, it was a few weeks back, just before the disappearances were reported.'

'Was she alone?'

'Yes, or at least I think she was. I didn't see anybody else with her. She was all upset. She wanted to clean up as she'd been crying.'

'Clean up? She could have done that in her camper van, surely? Why did she come in here?'

The girl shrugged. 'I don't know. I didn't see any camper van but then I didn't look. My dad runs the hotel and I just get paid to work here and help people if they have any questions.' There was a simple honesty to the girl's voice.

Georgia was keen to extract as much information as possible. 'Why was she upset?' The thought of her crying scratched at Georgia.

'She said she'd had a fight. I think her lip was bleeding – there was some blood on her face.'

'And there was no sign of Foster? Her boyfriend?'

'No, just her. She used the restroom, cleaned up all the dirt and blood and then asked me how long it would take her to get to Mexico. I told her the border into Tijuana is about ten hours from here. Then she left. She was so pretty and I loved her accent. I didn't really think about her again until the body turned up. When I read that it was her boyfriend, I kind of assumed that maybe she had done it. You know …?' The girl left her words hanging although her meaning was crystal clear.

'Have you told the police all of this?' Georgia knew that she would do so herself even if the girl, as she suspected, hadn't. Her feelings were correct.

'No, my dad didn't really want the hotel linked to a murder case. It's not good for filling rooms. What would I say? She was obviously heading out of town.'

Georgia's mind raced with questions as Alice made her way back to the reception area. *Had Mitzi fled to Mexico? Was she running away or on the run? From her own guilt or from danger? Why was she bleeding? Was the blood on her face in fact hers? Who had she been fighting with?* Another question kept Georgia wide awake as she lay in bed that night. *Was it Mitzi who had killed Foster?* She wouldn't allow herself to believe it.

CHAPTER 36

'Welcome to Los Angeles, Mr. Rose. My name is Addison Downes. It's great to meet you. I'll be your contact here in LA. If there's anything you need then feel free to contact me day or night. And naturally I'll be arranging all of the details for your audition.'

Now this was a life Aaron could get used to. The blonde, who had met him at LAX airport and had manoeuvered him into the back of a waiting limousine, was hotter than a chilli pepper. The dark roots just tinting the top of her glossy LA locks showed that she was not a natural blonde and she wore the merest hint of make-up to enhance what was already a nigh-on-perfect Pamela Anderson pre-surgery beauty. Her nails were long, polished and splashed with the sexiest red Aaron had ever laid his eyes on. Her teeth were as white as her nails were red. Aaron guessed she was in her mid-twenties, maybe a little more. Feeling his loins stir as he melted into the backseat of the car with Addison, Aaron had a feeling he might be phoning her for all sorts of reasons given the chance.

'So what am I actually here for? My agent said you guys saw me and thought I should try out as a pilot or something?'

'Not *as* a pilot, but *for* a pilot. A pilot show. Although I'm sure you'd look hot in a pilot's uniform.' Flirting or just Hollywood banter? A naïve Aaron couldn't tell. 'A lot of the TV networks make pilot TV shows which they hope will be made into future TV series. Not many are actually commissioned but if you manage to find yourself on a successful one then you are made, literally overnight. Major bucks. Look at *Friends*. Had you even heard of Jennifer Aniston before that? No. I was the first in school to go for the Rachel cut. It was the must-have for me as a teenager. She's my shero. And Matt Le Blanc was seriously hot. We're trying to get them both for *Super Nova*. Nova thinks *you're* seriously hot by the way.'

Aaron's head was spinning. 'So I'm wanted for a pilot show?'

'Well, kind of, the producers of *Super Nova* are planning a new action series for the networks. They want it to be really British, plummy accents and the rest, I blame the whole William and Kate phenomenon. Plus James Bond of course. Everybody loves a Brit in Hollywood. Your accent is really cute by the way. Is it Scottish?'

'I'm from Cornwall.'

'That's near Scotland, right?'

Aaron didn't correct her. He was finding Addison's effervescence hugely entertaining, as was the bouncing of her breasts as the limousine sped its way into central LA.

'TV networks want a new action hero, all smart yet oh-so-English so everyone is on the lookout for the right face. They saw yours in a feature about those two British dancers, Foster and Mitzi. That was *so* sad by the way.'

Having lengthened the word *so* to three times its natural length, Addison stopped talking for a second. Genuine empathy or another slice of frothy LA interaction? Again, Aaron couldn't tell.

'They were reading the article and your photo stood out. They liked your look and found your agent.' She slapped Aaron's leg light-heartedly to emphasise the glorious, if somewhat bizarre, chain of events that had led to Aaron's current situation.

'When is the audition? What will I have to do?'

'In three days' time. Well, if it's anything like the ones I've been on, if they like the look of you you're half way there, but to get the part you'll have to read a few lines from the pilot script and maybe strip off a bit too. I understand the action hero won't just be getting action crime-fighting on the streets. He'll be a real ladies' man too. The women will love you.' Addison paused for a second again. 'You're not gay, are you? Mind you, how many in this town have played the All American Guy when really they're an All American Gay?'

'No, I'm all straight,' smiled Aaron. 'So do you act too?' This seemed ironic, seeing as Aaron didn't actually act himself, but it seemed as though that was the last thing anyone was actually considering.

'My main job is working as a production assistant on *Champagne Super Nova*. You must meet Nova while you're here. She could get you on the show. She is a-ma-zing, another shero. But everyone is a wannabe actress in LA, no matter what their profession. Me and my flatmate, Diana, we've both done a few bits and pieces. Mainly straight to DVD flicks where you're either covered in blood, covered in bugs or being eaten by some mutant terror. I think between us we've been up for or bagged every freaky critter flick going - *Zombeavers, Hellyfish, Piranhaconda, Squidosaurus, Crabzilla, Camel Spiders, Big Ass Spider* ... you name it, we've fought it off or been chewed up by it at some point. I'm waiting to hear on a part in *Clampires* right now. Giant blood-sucking clams that pray on hapless swimmers in the shallow waters of Summer Camp City. It'll be a blast. If I scored a part in a *Sharknado* flick I swear I would literally die a happy woman. Tara Reid, another shero.'

'So will I see a script beforehand?' questioned Aaron, still mulling over the thought of a vampiric clam. It was like Addison was speaking a foreign language.

'All in your hotel suite. There're a few scenes for you to learn and information about night-life near your hotel. There are some fabulous bars around there so if you fancy a drink then just give me a buzz.'

A come-on or Tinseltown politesse? Either way it brought a smile to Aaron's face. As the limousine pulled up outside his hotel all thoughts of horticulture, herbaceous borders or rampaging weeds seemed a million miles away. He was ready to taste a slice of fine American Pie.

Addison left Aaron to check in and departed with a cheerleader-cheery wave. She was smokin' hot. He was thinking about the weird world he'd just landed in. The one thing he wasn't thinking about was Tanya.

Tanya had thought of nobody else except Aaron on her entire journey to Milan. The attendant on their private jet, all bearded and welcoming, had reminded her of Aaron. The swarthy Italian chauffeur who had met her and Devon at Milan's Malpensa airport and driven them swiftly to their five star hotel had a masculine, devilish and dangerous air of Aaron about him. Even the trees and greenery of Corso Concordia, surrounding the opulent splendor of the Chateau Monfort Hotel immediately transported her back into the arms of the rugged gardener. It was as if she was being taunted at every Italian corner.

But she was here for Devon, for her husband, for the man who really loved her and despite her wishing she was thousands of miles away in the embrace of another lover, she was determined that he should not get even the merest breeze of a notion that she was being adulterous.

'I was thinking we could go shopping before dinner, Tanya. Maybe pick up a few outfits prêt-à-porter for our evenings together,' suggested Devon, as he splashed a few drops of Clive Christian cologne onto his freshly shaven cheeks in one of the mirrors of their hotel suite. 'I was thinking you could buy some more of that outrageously sexy lingerie you love to wear for me.'

Devon walked towards his wife and wrapped his arms around her from behind as he spoke, allowing his lips to nuzzle gently against Tanya's flesh.

He smelled incredible, the heady exotic tones of the after-shave lighting her senses, acting as an instant aphrodisiac. For a split second she felt turned on by the man next to her. She closed her eyes and turned to him, finding his lips with hers. His kiss was deep and urgent and Tanya could feel his arousal straining under the fabric of his trousers.

She tried to respond to Devon's hands as they travelled up her body, cupping her breasts and finding her nipples between his fingers. They automatically hardened, the mere touch enough to activate her desires. But something was blocking her. Something wasn't allowing Tanya to continue. She pulled away from her husband, removing his hands from her breasts.

'Easy, Devon. There is plenty of time for that.' Sensing his disappointment, Tanya reached down and gave his hard cock a mischievous squeeze. She raised her eyebrows suggestively. 'Later, my lover, later. You are right, we are in Milan and we should shop. Let's put that credit card to work shall we?' She kissed him again to show how much she loved the idea of spending. 'You know how much shopping turns me on.'

She hoped it would, because as it was right now, the only thing in Milan that wasn't reminding her of Aaron was her husband, and unfortunately he would be the one expecting to make love to her later on that night.

CHAPTER 37

Victoria seethed and watched as Chloe kicked the football back towards Leo, his gap-toothed smile lighting up an otherwise grey day as he and the nanny played in the back garden. She was watching them from the window of her bedroom at the back of their family home.

It had been less than twenty-four hours since Victoria had seen her husband ploughing his cock into the nanny while she, the woman who had raised his children and played loyal wife for the best part of a decade, was supposedly sleeping upstairs trying to recuperate from her car accident. This was not the makings of the happy ever after endings she'd been promised on their wedding day.

As yet, Victoria had said nothing. She could feel the venom running through her veins for both Scott and Chloe. No matter how hard she tried to erase the image of the two of them together it was there, embossed on her senses. She hated them both. Chloe, for taking advantage of her husband while his poor wife lay incapacitated, unable to fulfil her marital duties in the bedroom. And Scott, for succumbing to the obvious joys of a younger woman, for being weak and spineless and for not keeping his dick in his pants. Or should she actually lay the blame at her own doorstep for allowing the sexual flame of their marriage to extinguish itself without a fight. The one time Prom Queen had let her crown slip and become a Has Been.

But she would not let her marriage crumble, of that she was certain. There was no way that she would allow Leo and Lexi to become children of a broken home. Her body may be broken and weak but her family would not be. Scott was hers. Nobody else's. This wasn't just about keeping up appearances, this was about what she had wanted on her wedding day. What Scott had wanted too, as they had looked to their future.

Their wedding had been so perfect. Victoria resplendent in her Chanel dress, Scott in his bicep-hugging tux, both of them loving the moment when their friends and family – including Evie as her maid of honour – could see that they would be together forever. That Victoria Wentworth had found the man of her dreams. Because even though her marriage may have pushed all of her professional aspirations to one side there was never a millisecond of doubt in Victoria's veil-clad head that Scott was the man for her.

They'd honeymooned in Barbados, in a beautiful five-bedroomed luxurious Bajan beach house. It was unnecessarily large, but just metres from the clear blue ocean and it sported a 180 degree view of the golden powder-soft sands. They had spent their time watching the turtles lay eggs on the beach, swimming in the calm waters and making love underneath the stars. They had christened every bedroom too. It would have seemed churlish not to. It was a perfect time. Before her insecurities, before her need for pills, before her weight gain, before her husband had strayed …

Before Chloe. Which left Victoria with just one option. She would have to remove her from the family equation. Scott wouldn't like it and neither would the children but there had been nannies before and there would be nannies again. The next one would not find the need to babysit her husband's cock, Victoria would make certain of that. Her own mother had once told her that being a mother was all about discovering strengths that you didn't know you had and dealing with fears that you never knew existed. Her words echoed through Victoria's brain. Despite the lack of strength and the punch bag of pain moving through her own body, she would deal with this nightmare as she saw fit. The fear of her family falling apart had never been on her radar before. Now it was. And despite her inner screams it was a fear she would not surrender to.

Despite having staff to do everything for her, there was one job that Nova would never let anyone else do and that was preparing Charlie's room for when he came to stay. It was her ultimate delight as a mother. Despite all of the fame and the riches, her favourite role in life was still welcoming her only child back to the family home. Even if the house she now shared with Jacob in Bel-Air was a lifetime away from her roots growing up as Nina Cooper in West Hills, wherever she lay her large-brimmed designer Hollywood hat was her home, and she would always turn one room in the house into 'Charlie's room' for any visits. She would decorate it herself, polishing his high-school sports trophies and dusting the framed photos of him and her together over the years. She would take extra special care of one showing a young Charlie with his granddad just before his death and another of Charlie and her first husband, Goldman.

Charlie had phoned his mother to tell her he would be arriving in just over a day's time to join Georgia. Even though she was under no illusions about the fact that he and Georgia would be sharing one of the mansion's king-size bedrooms together, Nova's autopilot mothering insisted that she prepare 'his' room. He and Georgia could share that if need be but the room would still be there for Charlie to savour. A four-walled memory book containing a lifetime of the precious moments they had been through together. Nova smoothed down the silk sheets on his double bed and made sure that every inch was crease-free. She sat his favourite childhood teddy, a rather cloth-eared but much loved cuddly bear called Fred, on top of one of his pillows and vacuumed around the bed until the floor was free of any specks of dust or dirt. Charlie's stays were the only times Nova would ever entertain doing the vacuuming in her own home these days. That was what maids were put on earth for. But for her child, nothing was too much effort. The noise of the vacuum drowned out the slight creak of the bedroom door opening and Jacob walking in. She wasn't aware of him until he wrapped his arms around her. The action startled her.

'Oh Jacob, you scared me, darling. I was just sorting out Charlie's room for him. He'll be here tomorrow. How does it look?' She switched off the vacuum as she spoke.

'I could eat my dinner off that floor, it's so clean. Talking of food, I have just had a call from the networks for *Super Nova*. Ratings for the new episodes are through the roof and they want to throw you a celebration party – champagne, caviar, nibbles, that kind of thing, in Hollywood tomorrow night to say thank you. No filming for the show, as they want you to relax, but a few snaps may make the press the next day I dare say. They want to know if you have any ideas about entertainment. They're keen to book a name.'

'Oh, a party, how fabulous!' Nova clapped her hands together with anticipatory delectation. 'Charlie will be back, so we can make it a double celebration. A welcome home to my one and only son. It's perfect. Now who does he love? Isn't it Cher he adores? Can you try her?'

Jacob curled his lips in thought but didn't answer at first. 'You should vacuum more often. It's spotless in here. The rest of the house looks positively shabby in comparison.'

'Has the sunshine gone to your head and made you wacky, Jacob Chevalier?' sneered Nova. 'We have Juanita for that although I must confess I do seem to be a little more thorough than she is with this blessed machine lately. The other day there were loose strands of material all over our bedroom floor. One of my frocks must be moulting. Can you have words, darling? And do see if Cher is available for tomorrow, but don't let her wear anything too over the top, okay?'

Jacob left the room, a smile fastened across his face at another of Nova's mad Hollywood moments. The sight of Nova with a vacuum always made him laugh. It seemed so out of place. He'd speak to Juanita later.

He flicked on his phone and dialled the network. 'Nova wants Cher.'

Their response made Jacob smile even more as he hung up.

'She's a million dollars per appearance. We'll book a tribute drag queen instead. Nova won't even notice.'

To be honest, with her son back home and in the same room, she probably wouldn't. Jacob smiled at his slick efficiency. Another transaction done and dusted.

As Georgia drove back onto the freeway just on the outskirts of LA, her mind was on her mother. There wasn't a day that went by that she didn't think of how empty the world somehow seemed without her mum, Sophia, in it. Memories of her tragically short existence filled her head. Such vibrancy and a thirst for life, a wanderlust to experience new joys scythed down in its prime.

Georgia cast her mind back to Sophia's funeral. The sun had shone overhead but that had been the only light on an otherwise black day. It was she who had supported her father as he sobbed uncontrollably. His grief was palpable, his loss for the woman who had shared his life for such a long time evident for all to see and hear. Georgia had managed to contain her own flow of tears, her sadness almost too great and overwhelming for crying. It was only when she'd seen Mitzi, the best friend who had supported her during every heart-breaking moment since Sophia's death that she allowed her own tears to tumble.

As the coffin was lowered into the ground and disappeared from view it was as though all physical connection between Sophia and Georgia was suddenly severed. They would never actually touch each other again. On her return home from the funeral, a cacophony of images invaded her thoughts; her mother baking cakes with her, fitting her with an outlandish costume for Halloween to go trick or treating, brushing her hair a hundred strokes and then plaiting it into a ponytail. These were memories of happy, halcyon days that could never be lost. If she closed her eyes, she could almost still feel her mother's touch. Almost.

As she pulled up onto the drive at Nova and Jacob's, it was a feeling that she hoped would never leave her.

CHAPTER 38

The first part of Tanya's night in Milan with Devon had been an enjoyable one. She doubted that there was a woman alive who could rival her when it came to designer clothes and jewellery shopping and if there was one thing that Milan was able to deliver by the catwalk-full it was high end fashions.

Tanya had sashayed from A to Z. From Alberta Ferretti and Bulgari through to Versace and Yves Saint Laurent, she had been unstoppable, the smell of designer leathers and the feel of shiny hot new fabrics as addictive to her as cocaine to a rock star. And Devon had been more than happy to let her run away with her addiction.

After her six-figure shopping spree, the couple quickly changed back at the hotel and headed out to sample Milan's nightlife. Their destination was the Just Cavalli restaurant and club; the signature of Italian cool with its glass walls, animal prints, black lacquered staves and bevelled mirrors. Tanya and Devon had indulged in one of the best meals they had ever tasted, losing themselves in the divine flavours of a plateau of Alaskan king crab and a serving of aphrodisiacal oysters. As the wine flowed and the bill rose, all thoughts of her gardener lover seemed to fade in a haze of fizzy bubbles and heady musical beats coming from the enormous garden and terrace outside the venue. It wasn't long before Tanya found herself in the arms of her husband moving her body across the dance floor to the dynamic rhythms of Jason Derulo, Justin Timberlake and Ariana

Grande. She was lost in an intoxicating mix of dance. Beauty and the beats.

It was approaching 3am by the time they returned to their hotel. Tanya could feel the effect of the evening's drinking causing her to sway as they vacated their taxi and made their way into the lobby and up to their room. Devon protectively held her steady as they walked, much more stable on his feet.

Once inside their room, Tanya removed her clothes and let them fall to the floor as soon as she could, happy to be liberated from their constraints. She was tired, beyond drunk and if she was honest, more than ready for sleep. Seeming to read his wife's thoughts Devon scooped her into his arms and carried her lingerie-clad body to the four poster bed at the centre of the room where he lay her gently against the silky covers. The freshness of the material felt good, enveloping her in an organza bow of comfort. In a matter of a few seconds she drifted into sleep.

The next sensation Tanya felt was a sharp, almost painful digging into her wrists. It took a moment for her to register where she was and what was happening. She tried to move her hand. She couldn't. It was attached by a cord to one of the four bedposts. Her other hand was also tied, the cord again attached around the bed frame.

It wasn't the first time Devon had used the art of bondage for their bedroom activities but something worried Tanya about her current situation. It didn't feel like one of their normal playtimes; a red light was flashing in her mind. As she tried to move she realised with horror that her feet were also bound. She tried to call for Devon, but no voice came, just a muffled cry as she found that her mouth was also gagged. She could see the clock on the far side of the room. It said 4.15am. She must have been asleep for about an hour. The lights were still on but there was no sign of Devon.

Tanya writhed around trying to free herself from her imprisonment. It was in vain; the cords held her in place. Her mouth felt dry as she tried to shout, her lips straining in an effort to form the words.

It was then that Devon appeared, naked and coming out from the bathroom of their suite. In his hand he held a large rubber dildo, something that again they had used in the past as part of their love-making. But the look on his face was not a look of love, far from it. This was the expression of a man on a mission, a man who knew what he intended to do. The thought sent a frisson of abject fear through Tanya's body.

Without saying a word, Devon climbed onto the bed and placed his free hand across the pair of panties Tanya was wearing. With one sharp tug he ripped the knickers away from her body, leaving the lace tattered and torn. As he moved his fingers urgently into her, the feeling Tanya experienced was far from sensual. Despite Devon's evident arousal as his cock sprung into life in front of him, not one of the many nerve endings housed between her legs erupted with horny delight. Instead all she could feel was a sense of abomination as Devon continued to work her pussy. A solitary tear fell from each of her eyes as she tried to understand what Devon was trying to achieve. Until he spoke she was clueless. But no words came.

Taking the dildo, he placed it between her legs and let the head of it rest against the outer lips of her sex. He withdrew his fingers and then slowly but surely inserted the dildo into her. Normally she would find this pleasurable but this was no normal night. She closed her eyes in vain attempting to think of Aaron to see if that helped, but the total fear she felt outweighed any lascivious thoughts she tried to conjure up about the gardener.

Why was Devon doing this to her? He could see that she was not enjoying it. Why was such a kind, gentle caring man behaving in such a way? She expected it of others but not from him.

Devon worked the dildo into her, the lack of moisture between her legs making its passage difficult and awkward, as if ripping tender flesh within. Unable to object, unable to move, she was helpless to put up a fight. She looked deep into Devon's eyes. Was that sadness she could see there too, amongst the anger? Maybe it was. But why? What was he gaining?

She could only watch as Devon pulled the dildo from her and then positioned his own body over hers. His cock, still erect, hovered over her sexual opening. He placed his hands either side of his wife's body and brought his face down until it was just a few inches away from Tanya's. She blinked, causing more tears to tumble from her eyes.

The tears seemed to act as a catalyst. As hers fell, so did his own, suddenly unleashed from within. Long pitiful sobs erupted from his throat and he sat back up, kneeling between her legs. His cock had shrivelled back to its flaccid state, all thoughts of any penetration gone. She had never heard Devon cry like this before. It was a heart-wrenching sound. For a second she felt a moment of pity, but it was quickly eclipsed by the nightmare of the ordeal he had just put her through. She couldn't take her eyes off him. She wouldn't allow herself to, for fear of what might come next.

A still sobbing Devon got off the bed and pulled open the bedside drawer. Tanya turned her head to see what he was doing. She wished she hadn't as her husband removed a gun from inside the drawer and pointed it in her direction.

CHAPTER 39

Victoria had been thinking about Scott and their moments of happiness together. Having upped her dose of anti-depressants to try and cope with the truth about his infidelity with Chloe, Victoria would often find herself lying on her bed, almost stoned on the combination of uppers and painkillers. It was those hazy dreamlike moments under the influence that made her happiest and it was during those moments that she would remember just why she had loved her husband, and despite everything, still did.

She needed to get rid of Chloe. Victoria had chosen her moment. Scott was at work, the twins were at school and she and Chloe were alone. And seeing as her last painkiller was just beginning to wear off, Victoria was in no mood to suffer fools. Especially ones who thought that they could shag her husband behind her back.

The pain in her side was still making it difficult for her to move freely around the house. She placed that morning's opened post that Scott had brought up before leaving for work on the bedside table. One bill, some junk mail and an invitation from Evie to a charity party in a few weeks' time. The thought pleased her. If she was well enough, which she was determined to be, and if Scott and she were back on form then a night out with Evie and her celebrity friends was maybe a perfect band aid for their marriage woes. Not that Scott knew that she had any. And that was how she intended to keep it.

Victoria called down for Chloe to join her. About half a minute later Chloe entered the room and moved to the side of the bed. Her smile was saccharine sweet. She scanned the post on the table, her eyes automatically drawn to the celebrity name on the invitation.

'Did you want something?'

'I need my painkillers. Did you ask Scott to fetch me some from the doctor?'

Chloe seemed confused. 'Oh, did he not tell you? The doctor said that you weren't to have any more and that you should just take ibuprofen from now on.'

Bomb-like, Victoria's fury exploded. 'Ibu-fucking-profen. Is he kidding me? My insides are in agony.'

'I don't know what to say, sorry. He asked yesterday so I assumed he would have told you. It must have slipped his mind. Do you want me to go and see if he's put some in the medicine box?'

It was too much for Victoria and as another bullet of pain shot into her side she let rip. 'The only fucking box he's been putting something into is the skanky one between your legs. I've had it, Chloe, just pack your bags and go.'

'But ... I ... I ...' stammered Chloe, the fact that Victoria knew about her and Scott's guilty secret slashing her like a knife.

'I saw you. The night before last. Downstairs. So don't try to deny it.'

She didn't. 'But what about the children?' asked Chloe. 'I love this job and they really like me.'

'So did I, until you started sucking my husband's cock. Just get out. I'll tell Scott that you had to leave because of a family crisis. You can be gone by this afternoon, can't you?'

Victoria doubled up on the bed as she spoke, her body obviously succumbing to a spasm of agony. The sight of it shocked Chloe.

'Are you okay?' It was a stupid question.

'What does it look like, you dumb whore? I will be when you're gone. Now get the fuck out.'

But Chloe wasn't going down without a fight. She liked her job, loved the children, and over the last few weeks had become incredibly fond of Scott. A rich boss with a sexless wife and a straying length of cock was one of the best gigs she'd had in a long time and she had no intention of giving it up. In fact, she wasn't against the idea of being with Scott long term. He liked her, showed her affection and made her feel special. And she certainly looked a lot better than Victoria did of late. No, she was not going to give all of that up. Scott had feelings for her, she knew it. She just needed more time with him to work out exactly how strong they were. She could feel her brain whir into action. As it did, a potential solution presented itself.

'What about if I manage to get you a continuous supply of painkillers to stop your agony? No questions asked. I'll supply you and you let me keep my job.'

Before she even had a chance to hate herself for saying it, Victoria heard the words come from her lips. 'And my husband?'

'He's off limits. It only happened once and he regretted it straight away. That won't happen again, you have my word.' She was lying, but her poker face gave nothing away.

As another incision of pain slammed into her ribs, Victoria already knew what her decision was. If the only way she could beat the pain was to keep Chloe on the payroll then maybe that would be just what she had to do. For now.

'How soon can you supply me the tablets?'

Chloe looked at her watch. 'Give me a few hours. So if I do this, can I keep my job?'

'For now, yes. But I want some strong fucking painkillers by the end of today. And if I ever catch you even laying so much as a finger on my husband again I swear it won't just be the pain being killed around here. It'll be you too. You hear me?'

She did. As a smiling Chloe left the room she heard the voice of a pitiful wife who was evidently more reliant on a mixture of pills than she realised. And if keeping Victoria high meant Chloe keeping her job and maybe keeping her man then she would maintain a constant supply of the little white miracles. She knew just where to obtain them.

CHAPTER 40

'So the police aren't doing anything about your poor friend?' bemoaned Nova to Georgia as they sat in the much-needed shade of a palm tree on a sunken garden terrace at the Chevalier Bel-Air home.

'Not really, the police around Hell's Canyon say they've reached a dead end. And I spoke to the police here in LA but they seem to have let it slip down their priority list. I'm going out of my mind. I believe Mitzi is out there. I can feel it in my heart and I need to try and work out how to find her.'

'Well, if there's one thing LA is more than good for it's a continual supply of crime,' said Jacob, joining the women and handing them freshly made Manhattans. 'Between the murders, drug crimes and the carjacking, the police do seem to have their hands full.' Georgia found herself slightly annoyed at Jacob's air of almost dismissiveness.

'What about this girl's information about Mitzi heading to Mexico?' asked Nova. 'Surely that changes things?' Georgia had been filling Nova and Jacob in.

'Well, the police in Hell's Canyon said they would talk to Alice, the girl at the hotel, and take a statement from her. And the police here in LA just added the information to the file on Foster and Mitzi and said that it would be considered with their on-going investigation. But to be honest they couldn't have sounded more disinterested if I'd just told them I was trying out a new colour of nail gloss.'

'I've a good mind to phone them up myself and order them to find some results. There must be clues out there,' snapped Nova, her words a tad theatrical.

Jacob was quick to answer. 'You will not. The last thing this show needs is any scandal attached to it, Nova. One scent of anything dodgy and you're off the air.'

Georgia appreciated the gesture but she knew that Nova's hands were tied.

'So, what are you going to do?' It was Jacob who asked.

'Well, Charlie arrives tomorrow and I was thinking we could take a visit to Tijuana. I'll print off some photos of Mitzi and take it from there. Stick them on every street corner if I have to. I was checking Mitzi and Foster's twitter feeds and there are a few photos of their holiday before they disappeared so I'll use those. There's some photos of the big camper van they were using so maybe the border police have records of it being driven into Mexico. To be honest, I don't know what to do. I'm a weather girl, not a hard-faced investigative journalist so this isn't my field of speciality. I just have to do something to keep my hopes afloat. Anything.'

Jacob aired his concerns. 'It's a long shot. There are over a million people in Tijuana and it's famed for its violence. I really don't think you and Charlie should go.'

'Neither do I,' piped Nova, draining the last drops of her Manhattan. 'But I do understand that you'll do whatever you think you can for your friend, even if she might be ...' Nova considered her words before completing her sentence, '... on the run.'

'Of course I've considered that, but it's not even a possibility as far as I can work out. Mitzi adored Foster and they had so much to live for. All couples argue but not enough to end in bloodshed, not those two.' The thought was more than alien to Georgia.

'Do the police suspect her?' asked Jacob.

'Of course, especially after the hotel girl's new information, but until they find Mitzi they're as clueless as we are. They think it's more likely that some passing chancer attacked Foster but they need to find Mitzi, dead or alive, to even try and eliminate her from their list of suspects.'

Nova was determined to lighten the mood a little. 'Well, you and Charlie are going nowhere until after the party tomorrow night for the ratings. It's going to be wonderful and I want to use it as a welcome home to Charlie. We'll have some big names there and we can spend a few hours just being a family without all of this talk of murder and violence. So all thoughts of Mexico will have to wait until then. You need to slow down a bit, Georgia. You're moving about faster than a tropical cyclone and as a weather girl, you know how dangerous they can be.'

Indeed she did. And she knew that the chances of finding any kind of information in Tijuana were slimmer than the wispiest of isobars. But she had to try, even if it meant heading into danger. What was it she had read about Tijuana?

'So close to America, yet so far from God.'

CHAPTER 41

Slipping the ring onto his finger, Jack Christie held up his hand in front of his face and whistled an exclamation of sheer and utter laddish delight. The chunky silver piece was shaped like a bird's head, as close to a jackdaw as possible and was a one-off. The two eyes of the bird were highlighted with deep green emeralds. It was perfect and just as he had commissioned.

Life post prison was turning out to be, as he had said to Andy, 'fan-bleeding-tastic'. The robbery jobs the two men had teamed up on had, so far, gone without a hitch and the bond and understanding between them was growing stronger every day. They worked well together. Just as they always had. And for the villainous birds of a feather the rewards were turning out to be measurable.

Andy had upped his game since reuniting with Jack. Instead of two bit smash and grabs on corner shops and post offices, the pair of them had set their sights higher, targeting homes where cash was definitely there for the taking. And it was cash that enabled both men to reward themselves accordingly. Their taste in clothes had suddenly gone from Superdry to Savile Row and the flat now seemed to house more high end gadgets than a 007 flick.

But the ring was Jack's pride and joy; a symbol of their success, but also a symbol of his own identity. The rich spoils of spoiling somebody else's life. And he loved the way it looked.

Big, bold, unmistakable and unique. He also figured it could cause some serious damage if he punched somebody while wearing it, a thought he was more than looking forward to trying out.

Andy was out, seeing some wannabe girlfriend and doubtless getting his end away so Jack had the night to himself, not that he would be alone for long. A surprise text had proved that earlier in the day. 'Heard you're out. Long time no see. Where are you these days?' It was a welcome blast from the past and one that he intended to act upon. He had replied straight away.

He checked the time on his phone – 7pm – yep, she was due any minute. Right on time, the flat intercom buzzed. Feeling a twitch of anticipatory horniness run through his cock, he answered it.

The voice was just as he remembered it. 'Hi, it's Chloe, can I come in?'

Chloe Alexander was 16 when she first met Jack Christie in the none-too-glamorous surroundings of a London fish and chip shop. But despite the overpowering odour of frying oil in the air and the scattering of chip forks strewn across the floor, as far as Chloe was concerned it was as romantic a meeting place as a gondola ride in Venice or a secret rendezvous at the top of the Empire State Building. Not that Chloe had done either, of course. She'd never actually been outside of London. When you have to play housemaid, cook, cleaner and mum to a younger sister, the chances of grabbing your passport and checking out foreign climes were non-existent. The closest she came to anything vaguely continental was making spaghetti Bolognese, a dish which had become her signature meal ever since she'd been thrust into the role of *woman of the house* at the age of fourteen when her mum had done a runner to move to Glasgow with a pub landlord.

Chloe had been in the chippie buying tea for her sister and waste-of-space dad – maybe the chips could soak up some of the alcohol he'd spent his day guzzling – when Jack had swaggered in. She was immediately smitten. He was thin in the extreme, nothing like the posters of muscled actors and pop stars decorating her bedroom wall at home, but Taylor Lautner and Usher had never breezed into her local fast food joint, hair all tousled in a designer don't-give-a-shit way and cockily asked for the biggest battered sausage they had. Jack was mesmerising and Chloe could not take her eyes off him. And when Jack spotted her gazing his way, he was quick to react, giving a cheeky wink. Chloe felt her face stain red immediately.

She'd waited for him outside the shop, running the risk of her food going cold. She didn't care. Her dad would be too pissed to notice and she could stick her sister's in the microwave. She might never see this boy again and she had to talk to him. He had winked at her after all.

When he did appear, his hand diving into his open bag of sausage and chips as he did so, she couldn't look in his direction and immediately lowered her head to face the floor. The pavement was just as decorated with chip forks as the inside floor of the shop.

Luckily he spoke. 'Some people are dirty fuckers, aren't they? Fancy a chip?' He pushed the bag of chips in Chloe's direction. Her face felt redder than a passing double decker bus but she timidly took a chip from the paper and popped it into her mouth. It was surprisingly hot and she awkwardly chewed on it, trying to deal with the burning inside her mouth and say thanks at the same time.

'Don't scald yourself. Especially your tongue, you might need it later.' Jack laughed and placed his hand under her chin playfully. It was their first contact and immediately a bolt of excitement shot through Chloe's body. He was electric. And Chloe could feel a thousand switches turning on inside her as he spoke, his cheeky words causing her to blush ever deeper. By the time Jack had finished his sausage and chips, aided by Chloe, the pair of them had swapped phone numbers and he'd promised to show her 'a good time that didn't involve any salt and vinegar'. As Chloe walked back home, a plastic bag full of lukewarm food swinging alongside her, she was euphoric. She'd had boys chat her up before, she was a great looking girl, but there was an excitement about Jack Christie that she had never experienced. She felt charged enough to launch a rocket. Not even the sight of her drunken father slumped on their sofa, a line of dribble cascading from his lips when she arrived home could wipe the smile off her face.

Jack became Chloe's first boyfriend. Well, to her, he was. Jack would never say it. He was a free-spirited lad, unable to say any kind of romantic words that would actually tie him to her. Jack the lad was indeed just that and she knew it. She was even prepared to put up with it.

She gave him her virginity, an act that she didn't take lightly. She knew that he was probably shagging other girls behind her back but Jack made her feel special. When they lay in bed together after sex, Jack rolling a cigarette as Chloe gazed adoringly at him, it was, to her, pure romance. She had no desire to tame him. Simply to be by his side from time to time was enough.

She was fully aware of what Jack did for a living. The clues were there. The flat he shared with Andy had lines of white powder chopped out on surfaces and bags of weed laying on the table. Jack hid nothing from her and she respected his honesty.

She couldn't judge him. She knew the world wasn't a perfect place from her own experience. But hadn't she always been taught that if you want the rainbow, you have to put up with the rain? She could forgive any shady dealings he was involved with as long as she could be part of his life; a part that took her away from the hardship of having to deal with a younger sister and a pisshead father at home.

Jack gave her money to help at home, for bills and weekly shops. She never questioned its origins. Jack had swaggered into her life for a reason and in the eighteen months they spent in each other's company Chloe turned from a bashful girl outside the chippie into a young woman who was experiencing things she had only ever seen in movies before. Not all of them were legal, but with Jack by her side, life was the closest thing to heaven she had ever known.

The day that Chloe learnt that Jack had gone down for five years for breaking and entering was one of the worst days of her life. The cheeky, dirty blonde-haired rogue who had opened her eyes to the world was gone. Not for good maybe, but behind bars and away from her side. He missed her eighteenth birthday, a day that he'd promised to make special, by two weeks. She'd ending up celebrating it, if you could call it that, by buying fish and chips for her sister and dad.

'Why didn't you want me to come and see you in prison?' asked Chloe as she sat nervously on the sofa beside Jack. All of the timorous feelings she had experienced outside the chippie all those years ago had flooded back at seeing him again. She hardly recognised him. It was as if someone had pumped him up; his muscles, hitherto unseen by her, inflated to bodybuilder proportions. He had become a man and he looked amazing, even if wearing a completely different outer shell to the one she had last seen him in.

'To do what?' asked Jack, matter of fact. 'To show you that I'd fucked up? To let you see that I'd done wrong? I didn't want anybody to see me like that. And besides, you had your life to carry on with.'

'It all seemed remarkably dull after you went inside. I took your silence as an indication that our time was done. I thought I might have received a visiting order.'

'Nobody did, babe. Nobody.' Jack placed his hand upon her knee as he spoke. There was that electricity again. It shot from her knee in a direct line to the area between her legs. She needed to think straight, she wasn't here to rekindle an old flame. There were more urgent matters that needed attending to.

'I didn't think about you until now. I couldn't. There was too much going on. Too much you could never share with me.' The first sentence was a lie. She had often thought of Jack, more than she yet cared to admit. Was there a crease of disappointment in Jack's face as she'd said that? She wasn't sure there was. Was he still the island of a man he'd always been?

'So why the sudden text? Need some money to buy some booze for your old fella? Thought you'd see if I was up to my old tricks?'

There was a levity in his voice, but his words still scored at Chloe's heart.

'My dad died three and a half years ago, Jack. Choked on his own vomit in front of the TV. My sister had already left home to live with her boyfriend up north. I found Dad. Mum didn't even make it to the funeral. Said she'd be abroad with her bloke. The house was mine and I sold it. My sister has half the money, me the other.'

'I'm sorry.' Jack's words were genuine. 'So, how did you know I was out?'

'Lucky guess, I suppose.' Again a lie, but she didn't want Jack to know that she'd been counting the days.

'So where are you living now?' asked Jack.

Chloe filled Jack in on her life since the death of her father. Finally having nobody to look after or wipe up after, Chloe had looked at her skill set. It wasn't exactly plentiful. She was good at looking after people, able to cook and clean and had no luggage or ties. Becoming a nanny was the obvious answer. When she secured the job with Victoria and Scott she moved in with them. The house money was now almost gone, but what there was of it she intended to dip into to buy Victoria's painkillers. That's if Jack could give her what she wanted.

She explained about Victoria and her need for the pills.

'So what do you need?'

'You tell me, you're the drug dealer. Something to stop this woman's pain. But not too much, eh? I like the idea of her being a little out of action for a while longer yet. I have some plans I need to work on. My job depends upon it.' Chloe couldn't stop thinking about Scott. He was a married man but he still seemed to respect her, which was something she had never really had from Jack. The days with him had been fun and adventurous but not ones that she wished to live through again, that was for sure. She'd been too vulnerable. And certainly not ones that would provide a foundation for a lifetime together. Even if he had blossomed into an incredibly attractive young man, she'd moved on to better, brighter and yes, she was proud to admit it, richer things. She couldn't risk losing Scott from her life. Not when she thought that maybe there was a chance for them to be together. To form a foundation and potentially never be vulnerable again. Dare she think it? For him to love her.

'I may have just what you need right here in the flat. Andy always keeps a stash of as much gear as possible hidden away.'

'So, what's it going to cost me?'

'Well, how about this for starters, Chloe?' He gave the bulge straining underneath the crotch of his jeans a squeeze. 'You're looking good and maybe we can work it into some kind of discount for the drugs.'

As he spoke, he unzipped his trousers and let his erect cock spring forth. He placed one of his hands around it and worked the shaft in his palm. Chloe noticed the large bird ring on his finger as it moved up and down.

Forty minutes later Chloe was walking down the street with a blister pack of strong painkillers in her pocket and the salty sweet taste of bargaining on her lips. Jack had given her a discount for blowing him. It was a price Chloe was more than happy to pay.

CHAPTER 42

Devon and Tanya's private jet came to a halt on the runway as it touched down in London. Neither of them had spoken for the entire journey. Tanya wasn't sure that she ever wanted to speak to Devon again after what had occurred in Milan. She had faced many dangers in her life, especially back in her homeland, but the fear that Devon had put her through in Italy outweighed everything. She placed her fingers to her temple, a small disc of bruise still painful to touch. She looked down at the chaffing on her wrists, the red marks a sore reminder of the moments just hours before when she had thought that her life would be over. Ended by the man she loved, or at least had loved. Did she anymore? Could she?

The tears rolled down Devon's face as he held the gun to Tanya's forehead. His hands shook as he pushed the hard, cold metal of the barrel against the soft, pink, tender flesh of her skin.

Tanya froze, afraid that any excess movement would cause the trigger to explode, spraying her brains in a mucky arc against the silk pillowcases and across the bedhead between two of the four posters. So this was how she would die. At the height of five star luxury at the hand so her own husband. *Why was Devon doing this?* It was as if he was possessed, no longer in control of his own sanity. His calm transformed to carnage before her very eyes.

It was true what they said. When you are staring into the jaws of death your life does indeed flash before your eyes. And Tanya's was a life that contained a collage of images that most people would have no notion of comprehending. Images of her father, her childhood, her orthodox upbringing, the men she had loved and those she hadn't all flooded into her thoughts, the images changing with a high-shutter speed that she was finding it hard to keep up with. Snapshots of her marriage to Devon raced through her brain; the feel of his lips against hers, so tender and loving as they exchanged vows, now seeming somehow meaningless. An image of Aaron, their time together brief, beautiful and burning.

Tanya prepared herself for the end, her fear blanketing her. This was to be lights out, the final curtain on the production of her life. One that would now always to be remembered as a tragedy.

She stared into Devon's eyes, trying to understand the torture that lurked there, the darkness that was polluting him from within. She searched for an answer, something to hold on to as she drew her last breath. For a millisecond there was a glimmer of doubt in his eyes. The hatred replaced by some faint ember of love that still glowed.

She continued to look deep into his soul. Somehow, it worked. Moving the gun away from her forehead, Devon buried it deep into the pillow behind her head and fired it. An eruption of feathers fountained into the air around Tanya's head, some landing on her face, sticking there, glued by the tears that still wetted her cheeks.

She felt another kind of moisture as a flow of warmth pooled between her legs, a pitiful yellowish puddle forming on the sheets where her own distress had caused her to lose control of her bodily functions. After everything it was the ultimate humiliation. The tears came, flowing freely, in relief that maybe she would survive the ordeal, at least physically. They continued to flow as Devon, also still sobbing, untied the gag around her head and the two restraints on her wrists. As a silent Tanya undid those attaching her ankles, she could see a sliver of daylight coming in through the gap in the velvet curtains dressing the room. She wanted to scream, she wanted to grab the gun and force it into Devon's skin, to let him know how she had felt. But watching him, slumped on the floor, naked, tears still flowing down his face, she didn't know what to think. She wanted to hate him, but before she could do that, she needed to understand him. Why had he treated her in such a way?

'Don't you ever let that fucking gardener lay his hands on you again, or I swear next time I'll kill you both. Now start packing, I've arranged for the jet to leave in two hours.' Despite his sobs, Devon's meaning was clear. He'd planned the whole thing. This was his revenge. The trip, the spending spree, the cocktails. Hadn't he drunk, too? Now that Tanya thought about it, maybe not. He had needed to be in control. That would explain why she'd had so much and felt so drunk. No wonder she'd slept while he tied her to the bed. He had mapped out the evening in his mind, mapped out the whole Italian trip. Maybe even mapped out her death. Did he plan to kill her? Had he bottled it or was scaring her so much the plan all along? Tanya didn't know.

CHAPTER 43

The celebratory vocals of Meghan Trainor's *'All About That Bass'* burst out from the speakers.

It was the first time in a long while that Georgia had let her hair down and immersed herself in a classic seemingly carefree piece of 'dance like nobody's watching'. Even if she knew deep down that really she was just putting a brave face on things for the sake of the evening's celebration she was determined to paint on a party smile. And the fact that she was able to dance with Charlie gyrating his snake hips alongside her was the icing on the cake as far as making herself faux-happy for now was concerned. The cake in question being the rather ginormous three-tiered one at the corner of the dance floor with a sugar paste Hollywood sign perched on it and a top-heavy fondant Nova decorating the top layer. The two balls of fondant forming her breasts alone were the size of tennis balls.

Georgia was enjoying the party to celebrate the *Super Nova* ratings and she had to admit that it had been a long while since she had been so star struck by those around her. She'd already spotted about half a dozen singing stars she had downloaded onto her iPod, several TV talent show judges and countless *Real Wives, Drag Race* queens and *Top Models*. It was autograph hunter heaven and a fruity mix of vamp through to camp. Georgia couldn't help thinking that Mitzi would have loved it.

Charlie's arrival eclipsed any shining star though in Georgia's eyes, and he had arrived at the party's venue, directly from the airport, changing into a muscle-hugging tuxedo in the back of a limousine on the way. If he was suffering any jet lag then he certainly wasn't showing any signs of it as he flexed his body across the dance floor.

Planting her lips on his as they vacated the dance floor – she would never tire of kissing him – Georgia and Charlie moved over to a corner of the club where Nova and Jacob were holding court to a group of revellers. Nova squealed with delight as they approached, reaching out her arms for Charlie. She had hardly left him alone all evening.

An eclectic mix of people stood listening to Nova as she announced yet again that Charlie was her 'pride and joy'. A pair of drag queens, between them a shower of cat's-whisker-long false eye lashes, poppy-red lips and ceiling-skimming wigs, hung off Nova's every word, pouting and laughing at what they deemed to be the right moments. Beside them, a couple of fifty plus suited gentlemen, whom Georgia assumed must be network bigwigs, seemed bemused and stunned into silence by the gaiety of the party yet happy to be quaffing bubbles by the flute full and downing nibbles from any passing waiter. Completing the group were two girls that Georgia recognised as being part of the *Super Nova* crew from her day watching filming poolside, and a man she recognised but couldn't immediately place.

Any confusion was short-lived as one of the girls introduced themselves to Charlie and Georgia.

'I'm Addison Downes. I work with your mother as a production assistant. This is Sarah Ellison, second assistant on the show, and this is Aaron Rose from the UK. He's in town for an audition for one of the network shows next season and I think your mother has taken quite a shine to him. As have our friends here,' said Addison, signalling the drag queens. Both raised their already sky-high eyebrows to another stratosphere and flashed sets of the whitest teeth Georgia had ever seen.

Georgia suddenly twigged where she had seen Aaron before. She had seen his photo in the press reports about Mitzi as the man who had been picked to dance with her friend on the television. Plus she kind of knew him from his former TV show back in the UK too.

The group exchanged pleasantries for five or so minutes, Georgia taking the opportunity to enjoy yet another free cocktail and also work out if she liked Aaron, Addison and Sarah. Her first impressions said she did.

When Nova grabbed Charlie and waltzed him towards the dance floor to shake her ample curves to Iggy Azalea, the two drag queens in tow, Georgia found herself alone with Aaron and Addison, as Jacob requested that Sarah join him to talk shop with the two execs. Georgia directed her conversation to Aaron as Addison listened in.

'So, you were due to dance with my friend, Mitzi? The reason I'm here is to try and find out what happened to her. I have to hope that she's still alive.'

'It's all very tragic,' said Aaron, a little unsure about what to say. 'I didn't know her or Foster but what's happened to them is just crazy. Have you uncovered anything?'

'Maybe, but I'm not any closer to actually finding her.' For a second Georgia's voice cracked as she fought to hold back the tears that had begun to form. Her momentary sadness was noted by both Aaron and Addison. Addison reached out and touched Georgia on the arm in an attempt to uplift her spirits.

'Sorry, it must be the drink. I shouldn't touch anything with gin in it, as it's bound to get me maudlin, but when I think about poor Mitzi and the fact that she might be lying somewhere, dead in a ditch …' Georgia knew this was neither the time nor the place but, drink or otherwise, something was prompting her to consider every conceivable outcome to Mitzi's disappearance, including the worst case scenario. She guessed it was meeting Aaron.

Right on cue, a line of tears began to slide its way down her cheeks. Georgia dabbed at them with her hand, causing her eyeliner to smudge. It was Addison who reacted.

'Okay, smudgy eye alert, girlfriend to the rescue. It looks like somebody's taken an inking block to your face. You are coming with me, right now.' Her words fired out with supersonic speed as she linked her arm through Georgia's. 'Restrooms this way. Nova will not want tears at her party. Aaron, you go shake your money-maker on the dance floor with Nova and *les girls* and see if you can bag yourself a spot on *Super Nova*. And tell Charlie that I'm going to fix poor Georgia's makeup. It's time for some girl-on-girl serious restoration work.'

Leaving a confused Aaron to work his way to the dance floor, Addison scuttled Georgia off to the ladies. Once they were inside, she hugged her. 'Are you okay?'

From the outburst of tears that followed it was obvious that Georgia wasn't. Unable to stop herself, Georgia let every pent up emotion she'd been feeling about Mitzi's disappearance pour out to Addison. It felt cathartic to let it spill out to a fellow female, especially one of her own age. Even if it was somebody she'd only met five minutes earlier. In some ways that made it so much easier.

It was half an hour before the women left the ladies' room, Georgia's make up reapplied to its former glory. The sight that greeted them was Nova trying to teach Aaron how to twerk on the dance floor to Nicky Minaj and Charlie being given a lesson in the finer details of how to flounce a catwalk by the two drag queens. Perhaps the drinks were stronger than Georgia realised. Perhaps stronger than anyone did.

CHAPTER 44

She was alone again, the room quiet and soulless. Were her eyes finally becoming accustomed to the darkness? Perhaps they were. She could make out a wall. Her feet remained tied at the ankles. Her hands and mouth had been bound again too, her captor only allowing her a minimal window of opportunity after her 'piece to camera' to eat her food. Mustering as much strength as she could, she shuffled her backside across the floor to try and work out the dimensions of the room she was in. It took no more than three or four shuffles to find herself up against a wall. It was equally as hard and cold as the floor underneath her.

With the little strength that remained in her body given her bound state, she shuffled back to what she assumed was the centre of the room. She could hear the sound of her own breathing becoming more laboured as she did so. There were stone stairs in front of her; that was for sure. She had seen her detainer, still no more distinguishable than a silhouette, using the stairs to exit the room.

The only other thing she could see was a bucket, maybe a metre or so in front of her. She had already witnessed what this was for. Her underwear and clothing were pulled roughly down as she was made to squat over it. It was the ultimate degradation. Despite her captor emptying it, the stench of what had been still coated her nostrils. It was an odour that she suspected she would never forget. One that mingled with the stench of approaching death that crept over the room.

Her mind, more focused than it had been in days, attempted to think about moments that had meant so much to her throughout her life. Nuggets of hope to try and give her strength. The love she had for the man who had disappeared alongside her, where to and why she still had no notion. The rhythmic highs of their bodies, moving as one, both inside the bedroom for their own beautiful pleasure and in other more public arenas for the entertainment of others. Two bodies, two minds, two hearts together. She remembered the moment they had first met, the initial spark that had ignited between them. The skipping of her heartbeat as she first ran her fingers through his hair, across his body. Would she ever feel it again? Hear his voice or those of her closest friends? Was this a prison that she would ever escape?

CHAPTER 45

As the celebration for *Super Nova*'s ratings wound to an end, only a party of five remained, sitting at one of the booths in the club. Charlie sat with his arm around Georgia's shoulder, her head resting against his neck. She was tired and the evening, despite its fun moments, had been a draining one. She needed to head to Mexico, to try and fit together the next piece of the Mitzi puzzle. Every second counted and her inner core was wracked with guilt that she had spent an evening even vaguely enjoying herself while her best friend's existence still remained a mystery. If it hadn't been for Nova's insistence that the party was also a welcome home celebration for Charlie she would have asked that they be excused from attending.

Aaron had enjoyed his evening. The Hollywood madness was all new to him and he was revelling in the delirium of it all. Plus he had to admit that having Addison sitting on one side of him and Sarah, who had only just managed to escape work duties with the execs, on the other was doing wonders for his ego. They were both fine looking women.

Charlie hadn't exactly been oblivious to Addison and Sarah himself, and he knew they'd been checking him out – why wouldn't they? He picked up the last bottle of Cristal on the table, popped the cork and poured it into their glasses.

'One for the road … one for Mitzi?'

Silence fell across the table as they all raised their glasses.

'She'd have rocked tonight,' said Georgia. She could think of nothing she'd rather have less than another glass of champagne but given the toast, it would have seemed wrong to decline. 'She would have been the first on that dance floor and the last off it.'

'And she would have been twerking like a loony, no doubt,' said Charlie.

'I'm sorry I never met her,' stated Aaron. 'I think we would have hit it off.'

'I'm sorry too,' said Sarah, a little awkward at the conversation, as was Addison. They both raised their glasses.

Charlie began to laugh. 'And she would have loved that dreadful Cher impersonator. I think Mum reckons I thought it was the real thing but I'm not that stupid.'

He turned to Georgia. 'Do you remember when Mitzi managed to blag us into that mental after party for some TV show Cher was on. You, me and Mitz. There were loads of celebs there, no Cher sadly, so I was gutted, but Mitzi was determined to dance with as many of them as possible.'

Georgia began to giggle as the memory of that night flooded back. 'She was on a mission. One fuelled by cocktails. Didn't she say she wouldn't go home until she'd managed to bump and grind with at least five soap stars, three boyband members and one actor she'd seen at the cinema.'

'Yep, that's right, and she managed every one!' laughed Charlie. 'She was moving around that dance floor with stealth-like precision. Resistance was futile.'

'Nobody was safe and nobody could say no.' Just the mere thought made Georgia grin from ear to ear.

'And didn't she end up taking one of them home?'

'Well, let's just say that the next time she saw him appearing in a cinematic love scene she was very much *been there done that.*'

'Just one of many nights of Mitzi madness,' said Charlie. He raised his glass again in toast. 'To Mitzi.'

The five of them clinked glasses.

'And here's to hopefully many more,' said Georgia. She tried to make her words as upbeat as possible. From the look of the others' faces she wasn't sure she had managed.

CHAPTER 46

Aaron could feel the beads of sweat running down his back as he pulled the studio door shut behind him. He liked to think of himself as a man. A dude. A daredevil. Someone who would happily bungee jump off a bridge, swim with sharks, hike through snake-infested jungles if need be. And he'd do it all with adrenaline running through his veins as opposed to fear. But the last hour of his life had been one of the scariest he had ever experienced. He had literally felt his knees tremble with terror from the moment the team of people judging him had introduced themselves.

At least a few of them seemed familiar. He recognised most of them from the party two nights ago. Industry players with both the money and the kudos to rocket his career in a whole new direction should they decide that he was right for the part. One of them was Jacob Chevalier, whom Aaron had spent time speaking to at the *Super Nova* bash.

Not that Aaron was still that sure about what the part was. He'd learnt some lines as instructed by Addison, and he felt he'd put as much emotion into them as he could. He was hardly Tom Hardy when it came to perfect delivery and sure, there had been a few stumbles here and there, but at least he could relate to what he was saying. The character was a cheeky UK crime-fighter type who seemed to investigate his cases by interviewing as many scantily clad female suspects and witnesses as possible, pumping them for information in his own irresistible way. Aaron just imagined he was chatting up one of the women at his local pub back in Cornwall. He wasn't sure if it had worked but the other people in the casting room seemed happy. Especially a middle-aged woman sitting to Jacob's left hand side whose sharp intake of appreciative breath when Aaron removed his shirt as instructed was loud enough to reduce the men around her to laugh at her delight. Aaron figured that was a good sign and had winked at her accordingly. The blushing of her skin showed her approval.

But Aaron couldn't have been more pleased when the casting came to an end. Jacob shook his hand, as did the others and said they would be in touch. Who was Aaron to believe otherwise?

'How did it go then?' The voice was Addison's, who was waiting outside the room.

'Terrifying. But good, I think. I remembered my words and flexed my muscles accordingly.' Aaron gave his best comedy strongman pose to demonstrate his physique to Addison.

'Very impressive. Were they smiling at the end? That's always a good sign if they actually smile. If you flunk an audition the faces are normally longer than an Oscars' acceptance speech.'

'They smiled, so maybe I did well. We'll see. But I could murder a beer after putting myself through that.'

'Well then, that's exactly what you shall have,' beamed Addison. 'My instructions are to make sure you get to and from the audition and to make sure that your every whim is catered for. So if you want beer, then a beer it shall be.'

'My every whim, eh?' Aaron smothered his sentence with suggestion, a fact not unnoticed or rebuffed by Addison.

'Yes, "your every whim" were the words said to me. I remember thinking at the time how thorough you have to be in this job. That a good assistant should always be prepared to go above and beyond.'

Aaron curled his lips. Now if that wasn't a green light he must be colour blind.

'Mind if we swing back to the hotel first then, so that I can get changed and showered? I'm a little sweaty after all that fear.'

'Of course …'

Less than thirty minutes later, Aaron found himself naked in his hotel suite shower being soaped up by an equally naked Addison. He couldn't help but think how convenient it was that Los Angeles hotels seemed to have shower cubicles that were big enough for two. Aaron was loving the delights that LA offered. All of them. And as Addison bent herself over in front of him and pulled her pussy lips apart giving him perfect access to her clitoris, he took full advantage and slid his cock into her. Aaron heard his second female gasp of the day. But this was one performance he would never need a script for. He knew the part inside out.

While Addison's squeals of exultation heightened as Aaron rocked her to orgasm, Aaron's phone, discarded onto the bed, beeped, signalling another missed call. It was one of six within the last few hours. One was from Rachel, his agent. The other five were from Tanya.

Victoria feared that her life was spiralling out of control. Painkillers, anti-depressants, cake … every one an enemy, but foes that she couldn't stop. As she looked in the bathroom mirror, the reflection that stared back at her was not her own. Her face seemed lifeless; her skin grey, fine lines appearing deeper than they had been just a few short weeks ago. Her hair, normally sunshine blonde and abundant in TV-ad vitality now just clung to her face, drooping and unloved.

But it was her eyes that scared Victoria the most. The whites of her eyes, once so glacial and pure, now were streaked with tired veins of red. If she had been back home in New Orleans, her parents would have thought she was possessed by some voodoo spirit from the mysterious underbelly of the city.

The mirror began to steam as she stared at her reflection, caused by the water pouring into the bath behind her. An icing of bubbles swirled across the surface. Victoria turned to look at them and for a few seconds she was lost in thought, trying to see shapes in the froth. As soon as the shapes formed, they disappeared again, merging into something else as the bubbles continued their migration.

'Is my bath ready, Mummy?' It was Leo who spoke, naked and excited, peering over at the writhing mass of suds before him.

Turning the taps off Victoria bent down to pick up her son and went to place him in the bath. At the age of six she didn't really need to but after everything that had happened recently a vulnerable Victoria was taking every possible chance to hold her offspring close to her. She couldn't let them slip away.

Her side exploded with pain; one that she had become used to over the last few days but one that still caused her to recoil in agony. She was due another painkiller. She let go of Leo as the pain took hold and the young boy fell from her grasp, one foot dipping into the water and the rest of his body falling outside of the bath. He landed on the floor, the thud of his arrival accompanied by a scream of slasher movie proportions. The volume of his cries even drowned out the stabbing of pain that perforated Victoria's body.

The cries also brought Scott running to the bathroom. 'What the hell has happened?'

Seeing Leo on the floor he immediately bent down to comfort the naked boy. Victoria remained silent and just stared on, horrified by what was happening, unable to move or speak.

'On my God, we need to phone an ambulance, now. Look at Leo's foot.'

Victoria did so. It was poppy red and the skin burnt and angry where it had spent time submerged. Just for a second but enough for blisters to already appear to pinprick the surface of the skin. Leo screamed in agony as his father picked him up and held him in his arms.

'What the fuck happened, Victoria?' He would never normally swear in front of the children but the words fell from his lips without consideration. 'Did you check the temperature of the water? It's boiling hot for Christ's sake. You could have scalded the poor boy to death.'

It was true, she could have. Had it not been for the pang of agony in her side she would have placed Leo's entire body straight into the water. Water that would have given him untold burns. How had she let this happen? Become so out of control? Why was her body letting her down, causing her such pain, causing her to fail as a mother?

'I'll phone an ambulance.' It was Chloe who spoke, standing in the doorway of the bathroom, holding Lexi's hand as the shocked girl looked on.

Victoria watched as Chloe and her daughter moved out of sight; as her husband looked directly at her and hissed, 'What kind of mother are you, for God's sake?' and then left the room, with a still crying and traumatised Leo gripped in his arms.

What kind of mother was she? Fear consumed her as she tried unsuccessfully to answer her own thoughts.

CHAPTER 47

Not many things in life had rattled Jacob over the years. Not being picked first for the school soccer team, not being heralded as 'most likely to succeed' in his high school year book, being the first person shot on a company paintballing day out. The occasions had been few and far between. But there had always been a solution. If he wasn't picked first then he would play harder, even dirtier, to make sure that he was first choice next time. As for the year book doubters, well, his millions had proved them wrong. And paintballing? An accidental trigger happy spray of fire sent after his 'death' in the direction of the person who shot him had made him feel much better. No, there was always a solution.

But unlike many of the partygoers at the *Super Nova* ratings celebration, Jacob's evening had not been totally joyful. In fact, something he had seen, heard and been told had irked him greatly and for once he wasn't that sure how to deal with it. It was a feeling that Jacob wasn't used to and one he did not intend to live with for a second longer than necessary.

'I seriously thought somebody had spiked my drinks at Nova's bash and I was suffering from some kind of post party hallucinogenic freakiness. So I did just see that, then?' Georgia asked Charlie, more than a little confused as she pulled the car into the car park of their Tijuana hotel. 'I did just see a zebra? In Mexico? In the middle of a busy city?'

'You did,' smirked Charlie, his head buried in a guidebook about the city. 'It's not a zebra though, it's a Tijuana zebra, which is actually a painted donkey. Apparently they're popular tourist attractions and have been since the 1940s. The reason for painting the donkey black and white was so that the poor beast could be seen in photographs. As the donkeys were mostly white, on sunny days with old black and white photography the donkey would look like some kind of ghost and that wasn't right. So they were painted to look like zebras. They are also known as zonkeys.'

'Zonkeys?' laughed Georgia as she switched off the ignition. 'You are kidding me?'

'The guidebook Nova gave us says so, it must be true. It's a pity we're not here for some fun as the local waxworks, the Museo De Cera, looks a scream. Maybe we could suggest they add a model of my mother to sit alongside Tom Cruise and Michael Jackson. Well, I think it's Tom Cruise.' Charlie turned the page ninety degrees as if that might help his guesswork.

'Those breasts of hers would take a lot of wax, Charlie. They'd have to melt down the entire Jackson Five to cater for it.' Georgia laughed, a sense of cheekiness and fun washing over her. It felt good and made a welcome change, even if it was swiftly replaced by a cocktail of painful remembrance as Mitzi filled her thoughts again.

The last few days had been really tough for Georgia, feeling close to Mitzi again in some ways yet still a million miles away from any kind of closure or clue about her disappearance. The party in LA had been a great way to try and forget for a few hours but her tearful outburst to Addison only reminded her how much she missed her friend and how she would never be able to find inner peace until she had discovered the truth. No amount of laughter with Charlie or faux happiness about wax museums in South America could take away the pain that boiled within her soul.

As she and Charlie walked into the lobby of their hotel, she hoped that maybe Tijuana would hold the answer. Or at least a vital clue to move her in the right direction.

Aaron was not in the best of moods as he sat himself down in the lobby of his LA hotel and waited for his transfer to the airport. He was loving his time in Los Angeles and was in no rush to leave. But he needed to head back to the reality of his life in the UK and judging from the two phone calls he'd just experienced, it wasn't exactly going to be a bowl of cherries.

The first call had been with Rachel. Was he actually beginning to warm to her? He thought he was. Whether it was the eternal California sunshine that was making him see her in a different light or whether it was the fact she'd sent him to Tinseltown in the first place for the casting, he had actually looked forward to speaking to her. It was a shame that the conversation between them had not been as pleasing as the Hollywood temperatures.

'The network people liked you but they are keen to see a few other talents first before making a decision. I hear on the grapevine they're maybe looking for a more established name but you never know, so keep the faith.' For a newbie to all of the audition process, Rachel's words had been anesthetising to Aaron. Numbed by a lack of news. He had assumed, albeit wrongly, that he would hear straight away as to whether or not he had been successful, and he hadn't really contemplated the possibility that he had not. In his head he had already planned a home in Beverly Hills, seen his face on billboards on Sunset

Strip and bagged himself a star on the Hollywood Walk of Fame. Plus he could imagine the women like Addison that he could have on tap. Easy, breezy, sleazy. He guessed he'd have to wait.

Not that it was all bad news. 'Nova loved you though, and whatever happens she wants to squeeze you in somewhere on her show. Apparently she loved your twerking. Aren't you the dark horse? You shaking your rump made quite the impression.'

'Shall I stay in LA, then?' Aaron would have been more than happy to check back into his hotel room and have his flight cancelled quicker than you could say paparazzi.

'Nothing works that quickly in Hollywood, darling, unless it's a face or tit lift, so no can do. The current series of *Super Nova* is all planned out but you could pop up in next season's. Nova just needs to decide how to work it ... or should I say *twerk* it?'

Rachel laughed at her own joke. Aaron didn't.

'So, what I am coming back to? Have any more offers poured in?' Aaron was enjoying being in demand and was hoping that it was set to continue. It wasn't.

'Nothing concrete, doll. But I will put out the word that Nova loves you and see if that can pull any strings. Anyway, enjoy your flight and as soon as I hear from the US network chaps I'll let you know. Bye.'

She was gone before Aaron could reply.

As soon as Rachel had hung up on him, his phone had sounded again. This time it was Tanya and she was hysterical, her accent stronger than ever. At first Aaron found it hard to comprehend what she was saying. Her words seemed a touch slurred too. Had she been drinking? With the time difference it was more than feasible.

'Tanya, just slow down, will you? What on earth is the matter?'

Through copious sobs Tanya explained to Aaron what had happened in Milan with Devon and the fact that he now knew about their affair. Aaron could feel his own depression about going back to the UK spreading through his body like strangulating weeds as she spoke. The only job he had – and a well-paid one at that – was slipping from his grasp.

Or at least he thought it was.

'Devon says that you are not to touch me again, that he will kill us both. We will have to be careful.'

Aaron was confused. 'Hang on, so you're telling me that your husband knows we've been up to no good and he still wants me to work there. Why?'

'To hurt me more I guess. He thinks that I will give you up, but I won't. He's having cameras installed everywhere but I will find a way. We will.' She paused before adding, 'Won't we?' It was more questioning than she would have liked.

Aaron could feel his anger rising. 'Your husband nearly raped you. It's him you should be giving up. Why are you putting up with that? Leave him.'

'He is my husband, Aaron. I am his wife.' There was a strange finality in Tanya's sentence, as if that were reason enough. As if that made sense. It baffled Aaron, his disgust at the situation mounting.

'Well, you didn't give him much consideration when I was banging you up a tree.'

'You are my lover. He is my husband. I won't lose either. I need you.'

As he hung up on his conversation with Tanya, he weighed his options. If he hadn't needed the money, he would have jacked in the gardening job there and then. Who wanted to work for a loony with a gun? But until something more concrete came along he couldn't. And the thought of more sex with Tanya did please him, as the twitching of his cock proved. He was incredibly fond of her even if he didn't understand why she would want to stay with a maniac like Devon. What was his hold over her? He may have been a real player in his time, a shagger, but something chivalrous within Aaron's core told him that he needed to be there for Tanya. Something wouldn't let him just leave. He had no idea why Devon would even keep him in employment given what he now knew. He wasn't sure he understood his gut reaction not to walk away but he certainly had to listen to it. And he was sure that Devon would never actually use the gun. He was too wet for that.

'Excuse me, you know Mitzi Bidgood, don't you?'

Aaron looked up from his thoughts. He recognised the face of the woman talking to him but couldn't quite place it.

'I don't know her, but I was due to dance with her before she disappeared. Why? Who's asking?'

'I'm Evie Merchant. I knew Mitzi a while ago and can't stop thinking about the circumstances surrounding the death of her boyfriend and her disappearance. It's too tragic for words.'

She'd lost Aaron at the mention of her name. Of course he knew her face, she was only one of the biggest names in the acting world, up there with Jolie and Kidman. And she was talking to him.

Christ, isn't this just another fabulous reason to love this bloody town, thought Aaron, a smile spreading across his face. This did not happen back home in Cornwall. There was nothing about LA he didn't like – the sunshine, the bodies, the bars, the chance meetings. Cornwall did not compare. His short time Stateside had been five star all the way and he was definitely getting a taste for it.

'I knew I recognised you from the news reports. I'm just passing through LA for a couple of days to record some voiceover work before heading back home and well, I just wanted to say hello. Mitzi was a truly lovely person. Totally mad at times which is why I liked her even more. I was always a bit reserved growing up but evenings out with her were always pretty full-on and I loved them.' Evie's words were maybe a bit much for a first meeting with someone who didn't even know Mitzi but her thoughts of days gone by had let her mouth nostalgically run into overdrive.

Aaron wasn't sure what to say. 'Er … everyone I've met connected with her says she was a great girl. Shame to think she might be … you know …' He couldn't complete the sentence. He didn't need to.

The two of them chatted, and Aaron told Evie about why he was in Los Angeles. About the casting and the party. At the mention of the celebration he'd attended for Nova's TV show Evie's eyes lit up. 'Oh, her son just interviewed me back in the UK a few days back. Charming man and his girlfriend is lovely too. She knew Mitzi very well, of course. We were in the same fitness group. Mitzi taught us.'

'It's a ridiculously tiny world,' commented Aaron.

'Listen, I have to go as I'm due in a recording booth a few blocks away in a matter of minutes but I'm having a charity event back in the UK in a few weeks, keeping the Mitzi flag flying as it were, and seeing as you're connected to the whole Mitzi situation you'd be more than welcome to come. Bring a friend too. It's kind of in her honour, whatever happens.'

Evie reached into her bag and pulled out an invitation. Aaron scanned it without reading the words. 'I'd love to. Thank you. That's incredibly nice of you.'

'Have a great trip home.' As Evie began to walk away, Aaron couldn't stop himself from saying, 'Oh, before you go, could I possibly take a quick snap with you? My mum is a big fan.' It was a lie, Aaron's mum was more impressed with the likes of Paul Hollywood than she was with A-List Hollywood but he needed to say something, this was too good an opportunity to waste.

'Of course. No problem.' Evie loved his excitement. It reminded her of her early days in the business.

Two minutes later as Evie departed in a waiting car and his own ride to the airport pulled up outside the hotel, Aaron was sending the selfie of himself and Evie to virtually everyone in his phone book. Including Rachel. She could add Evie Merchant to her list of people that her client Aaron Rose hung out with. He didn't send it to his mum.

Having freshened up after their journey, Georgia and Charlie ventured out into Tijuana. Despite the deluxe splendour of the hotel Nova and Jacob had chosen for them, they decided to head to another hotel on the city's bustling Avenida Revolucion for their evening meal, called Caesar's. Georgia had read about it in Nova's guidebook while Charlie had been showering.

'So why are we going here?' asked Charlie as their cab dropped them off at their destination.

'Well, firstly because there are loads of bars around here and I figured we could hand out some of the flyers I've had made up asking for information about Mitzi. Somebody might have seen her – the age range of people around here and the vibrancy of the nightlife is perfect for Mitzi. I kind of figure that if she is still in this city then this is where she might be.'

'And secondly?'

'I want to try the Caesar salad here, as apparently this hotel is the place where the Caesar salad was first created back in 1924. Seeing as it's one of my all-time favourite dishes it seems stupid not to try the original recipe while we're here. And there's live music too and the waiters are said to be super cute, so what's not to like?'

Charlie grinned at Georgia's touristy glee. It was good to see her happy, despite the sombre reason for their trip into Mexico. 'Super cute, eh? I'll have to watch you, won't I? Not that they could possibly be sexier than me?' He was only half joking. 'Either that or I had better start wearing a poncho and a sombrero to keep you happy.'

It was nearly two hours later that they left the restaurant, having fallen for the glamour of the décor with its shamrock-green mosaic walls and its bright, vibrant lighting. An eclectic mix of people surrounded them as Georgia enjoyed one of the best salads she had ever tasted and Charlie filled himself up on tapas. The place was trendy without a door policy elitism.

With a backpack full of flyers showing Mitzi's photo and a number to ring with any information, they hit the bars. Two hours and about two hundred flyers later, they ended their efforts. Their search had been fruitless. Charlie and Georgia had gone into as many of the Avenida's dance bars as possible in the hope of finding Mitzi or someone who knew of her whereabouts. They had drawn a complete blank in every bar. Nobody had seen Mitzi other than having read about her in newspapers when she had first disappeared.

They considered going into the Zona Norte, adjacent to the Avenida and famed as being Tijuana's Red Light District but given the late hour and the fact that Charlie feared for their safety if they strayed too far away from the main strip, they decided to call it a night and head back to their hotel.

As they were exiting their cab outside their hotel, something in the car park caught Georgia's eye. It was a few hundred feet away but large enough to catch her attention. She was sure it hadn't been there earlier.

She stopped, staring into the semi-darkness, her hand in Charlie's. Her halting caused him to do so, too.

'What is it?' he asked, sensing her intrigue.

'That road vehicle, on the far side of the car park. It looks just like the one that Mitzi and Foster were in.'

Charlie was not convinced. 'It also looks just like a million other road vehicles as well.'

'I know, but all the same, let's take a look.'

They both walked over to the van, talking as they did so. 'The police said it would be impossible to trace whether Mitzi had driven into Mexico through the border in a particular road vehicle. They have hundreds of them come through every day,' said Charlie.

'And I'm sure they could trace anything if they really wanted to. But in a city famed for crime I don't think trying to track down a vanished British dancer ranks high on their priority list behind drug cartels and illegal immigrants. I think it's more the case that they couldn't be arsed.'

'So how do you find out if this camper van is Mitzi's?' asked Charlie as they reached the vehicle.

'That's easy.'

Georgia took her phone from her pocket and pressed her finger on the Photos icon. She enlarged one of the thumbnails she had saved there. It was a photo taken from Mitzi's Twitter account showing her and Foster in front of the camper van. The registration plate was clearly visible. She noted the number in her mind and stared down at the registration of the van parked in front of them.

They were identical.

CHAPTER 48

Devon slid a CD into the state of the art Wave music system placed at the corner of his first wife's painting studio and waited a few moments until the first sombrous tones of Beethoven's *Symphony No.7* burst forth from the speakers. Classical music made his mind tick, spurred his senses into life and brought every fibre of his being into action. It resurrected any dead corner of his heart and soul that had been killed off by hurt, by deceit, by betrayal. And right now he needed resurrection on a Frankenstein-sized scale.

Devon had always performed his best work to a background of Debussy, Holst or others from his vast collection. Ideas seemed to flow as the rhythms of an orchestra engulfed his mind in perfect harmony. His scientific work had benefitted greatly when he had been left alone at his laboratory, the passion of an up-tempo piece or the delicate flutterings of a classical lullaby moulding his thoughts into solutions and breakthroughs. Music was often the spark that would ignite his genius.

But it wasn't an equation or methodical piece of mathematics that needed solving right now, it was the subject of Tanya's infidelity. Devon had been close to the edge in Milan, he had nearly given in to a demonic place deep within him that screamed for revenge. One squeeze of the trigger and the symphony of his love could have been over, once and for all, another climatic finale signalling the end of his second marriage.

But something had stopped him. Love, desire, forgiveness? His overwhelming cloak of anger and hurt? Maybe even madness or his deep vulnerability. Devon wasn't sure, but knew that his life with Tanya was not over yet. She had strayed. Roamed away from him like a feral creature in search of satisfaction. But she could be tamed, taught to obey, of that he was sure. He had the power. The control. The ability to torment. To return the heartache that she was giving to him. All that was needed to keep her by his side.

Devon sat himself down on the studio floor in the exact spot where he had seen Aaron with his bearded face between his wife's legs. The images of her betrayal ran through his mind. How she had tormented him. What was it about this place? Why did the four walls surrounding him breed such treachery? Was it here that Sophia and Nicolas Belvoir had first made love? Was it over the canvases of Sophia's multi-hued creations that the bold brush strokes of desire had initially daubed themselves across his first wife's heart? Was it here that she had hatched the plan to leave him, to vacate the nest of love they had shared together for so long?

Sophia and Nicolas. Tanya and Aaron. Sophia and Tanya. People who had tainted Devon's life, made him doubt everything he believed in. The equation of love. That one and one make two for a lifetime. For always and forever. He'd learned that wasn't true. The hard way.

Devon stood up and moved back towards the sound system. The music didn't suit his mood. He was dealing with an issue that needed the perfect soundtrack and Beethoven was not his man. He picked another CD from the pile stacked next to the player and stared at the cover. *Scheherazade* by Rimsky-Korsakov. It was perfect. He slid it into the machine.

As the music began, Devon considered the similarities between the tale of Scheherazade and his own state of misfortune.

The story said that every day the Persian king, Shahryar, would marry a new virgin, and send the previous day's wife off to be beheaded. This behaviour was due to the king's anger that his very first wife had been unfaithful to him. He could trust no-one and tainted all women with the same loose morals. He had killed a thousand women by the time he was introduced to Scheherazade, the daughter of a high ranking vizier.

Scheherazade was prepared to spend one night with the king and assumed that she would die the next day like all of the women before her. During their night together she started to tell a story, a tale that captivated the king's imagination. As dawn broke the story was unfinished and the king spared her life to allow her to finish on the second night. When she did, she then began to tell him another rich story that transfixed the king. Every day he spared her from beheading. After a thousand and one nights he decided that he should spare her life and make her his true queen. He had fallen in love.

Tanya was Devon's Scheherazade. His love for her controlled so much. But now it appeared that she wanted to share her stories with another and that was something that Devon couldn't allow. To lose control was not an option. He could fire the gardener, force him to leave. But what would that gain? If Tanya wanted to see him then she could do so behind Devon's back easily. There were a million London hotels where the lovers could fuck. He needed to be in control and she belonged to him. Devon loved her, of that there was no doubt, but to stop history repeating itself it needed to be love on his terms, ones that would allow him to quash his inner paralysing doubts and fears. He needed her in his life, and if she left him then others would know that he had failed again; failed to satisfy, to keep hold of what was once his. Lost control. And besides, she needed him more than anyone knew. He knew his wife better than anyone.

But no, what was the saying? Keep your friends close, and your enemies closer. His revenge would be one of torment. That suited the twisted nature of his mind. He would toy with her. If he kept Aaron close, under the watchful eye of the cameras he'd had installed at their home, then he could see what he was doing. He needed him close. He needed him within range. Just in case. Tanya had been warned. Would she risk breaking his heart again? She knew what she had to lose.

Devon rubbed his fingers across the outline of the small gun nestled in his pocket. It was one of a handful he had dotted around the house. He had the ammunition too. It wasn't loaded now but just the sheer fact he had it about his person made him feel stronger, more powerful. It made him feel like the king. It would take seconds to load, to aim, to fire. He knew that, he'd used it before. Devon cast his mind back to the last time ...

Devon had been working late at his laboratories. The hours had flown by and it was 3am before Devon even contemplated returning home. He could feel his eyes beginning to drop, the toll of a nineteen-hour day finally enveloping him. Maybe a few hours' sleep would rejuvenate his brainwaves.

The journey home would take him forty minutes, he could be in bed by 4am and up again at 7am to return to the office.

What was the point? He might as well bed down at his workplace. He'd used the couch in his office on many an occasion and his wife was used to him stopping out until all hours in the name of scientific glory. All he needed to do was clear it with security.

He phoned the desk. There was no answer. That was not a surprise, maybe the guard was doing his rounds. Devon would go and let him know.

What greeted him at the security desk was not what he had expected. The guard on duty was laying on the floor behind his desk, a small puddle of dark red blood pooling from his head. Devon checked for a pulse. He wasn't dead but whoever had hit him had obviously meant to cause some serious damage.

Devon's heart began to race. The laboratory had been targeted before. It was the reason Devon had his gun. Nothing and nobody would come between him and his work. He removed it from the cabinet in his office and waited for the police to arrive.

It was no more than thirty seconds later that he heard a crash from his laboratory. Somebody was there. In *his* workspace.

He tiptoed as quietly as he could from his office towards the lab. Even in the dim light of the early hours he could see a figure, head to toe in black.

Devon could feel his heartbeat thumping within his chest. He would not let this man spoil months of work. Unable to focus fully in the half-light Devon didn't see the table leg as he kicked it, causing it to scrape across the shiny surface of the lab floor. The intruder turned in his direction. He was wearing a balaclava and held a gun in his hand.

He pointed the gun in Devon's direction. Was he going to fire? Devon would never know as he squeezed the trigger on his own gun and watched as the man crumpled to the floor. Devon had killed him. Taken a life. It was like a scientific equation. Something bad equals punishment. Nobody would stop his work.

You kill once, it's much easier to do it again. Devon listened to the final moments of *Scheherazade* and smiled as he pressed the eject button on his sound system. He placed the CD back in its case, put it back in the pile and walked out of the studio. His fingers were still tracing the outline of the gun in his pocket. Yes, he had all the answers, Tanya would learn that.

CHAPTER 49

'Are you sure this is the van, Georgia?'

'There's no doubt about it. Look, the registration is exactly the same as the one on Mitzi's Twitter feed.' Georgia held up the photo on her phone to Charlie to prove her point. 'We've found her.'

'No, Georgia, we've found the van. Mitzi may not be with it.'

Nothing could wipe the hopeful smile off Georgia's face, though. She marched round to the door of the camper van and started to bang on the door. There was no reply. She continued to knock until her knuckles hurt. It was only when Charlie took her balled fist in his own hand and moved it away from the door that she stopped.

'There is nobody inside, Georgia. Maybe they're in the hotel. Let's go and see if Mitzi has checked in.'

Georgia's mind was racing. Mitzi had to be in Tijuana. The girl in Hell's Canyon had mentioned it, and now the appearance of the camper van … it was as if fate was guiding Georgia. But doubts were forming in her mind like black heavy clouds on her weather map.

'But why would she be here, Charlie? Driving this van? If she were alive then surely she would go to the police, let people know she was okay?'

'And if she did have anything to do with Foster's death, then surely she would try to erase any kind of link? She'd have ditched the van as soon as she could. If she wanted to disappear then that would have been the sensible thing to do.'

'So you think she's dead?' It was the first time Charlie had asked directly.

Georgia couldn't say the words. 'I don't think she's a murderer.'

'Then we need to find out who's driving that camper van.'

Aaron watched the lights of London shining brightly through the rain-streaked windows of his tube journey from the airport. Less than twenty-four hours ago he had been nuts-deep in a Los Angeles beauty in a five star hotel and now here he was, tired and tetchy and regretting being back in the UK.

What was there here for him? Sure there was Tanya, but that could never amount to anything, could it? She'd made that pretty clear in her conversation to him on the phone. If she chose to stay with her psycho of a husband then that was her fault. It was just a pity that Devon was the one paying him right now. Not that he had, so far; the money had come from Tanya. 'Thank God for joint bank accounts,' mused Aaron.

No, he would have to suffer the gardening job no matter how awkward the dynamics of the situation might be. Money was obviously going to be tight for a while, which is why he had chosen to ride the grimy delights of the Piccadilly Line back from the airport instead of getting a cab. Now he was back on UK turf he was having to reach into his own pocket and maybe he should start to look after the pennies.

Nova's mode of transportation could not have been more of a contrast to the chewing-gum-covered, fast-food-bag-strewn ride that Aaron was experiencing on the outskirts of London.

Allowing her skin to be kissed by the softest leather interior of her Rolls Royce Phantom Coupé – her favourite car from the collection she and Jacob had amassed – Nova stared out of the window and sighed. It was a sigh of deep, satisfactory jubilation and one that swirled around her with a warm comforting glow. Through the darkened windows she stared out at the streaks of lights flashing past the car as the Roller headed back to Bel-Air, skimming along the freeway with an elegant athleticism.

It was a time to reflect. Nova loved her life and adored being in the spotlight but occasionally it was nice to just sit back and take stock of what she had and where she'd come from. To appreciate it all.

She had so much to thank fate for, especially Jacob. The man who had made her a star. The man who had taken her into a whole new chapter of her life. All she felt was one hundred per cent pure love despite his peccadillos. He could be grumpy and harsh but she needed that, appreciating that it kept her grounded.

They would stay at Jacob's Kensington house on their next visit to London. It was one of her favourite cities on earth, and looking down at the invitation in her hands she knew that she would be there in a matter of weeks. At the request of Evie Merchant.

How incredible was that? Evie had given Nova the invitation over the dinner the two stars had just shared at BOA Steakhouse on Sunset, a meal arranged for them by Charlie. Nova had loved Evie immediately and it seemed that the feeling was pretty much mutual. Despite a virtual two decade age gap, the women had thoroughly enjoyed their evening together discussing the fripperies of LA life. No subject had been off limits, with Nova more than happy to discuss everything from her own plastic surgery – 'I've had a fair bit done but I'm hardly a Donatella, darling, am I?' – through to her former years in West Hills and the details of Charlie's conception.

Fame suited Nova. She loved its trappings. The glamour, the beauty, the travel and the wealth. But none of that came close to the love she had for Charlie. She would give up all of the sparkly bangles, the diamond-covered dresses and the houses around the world with their ridiculous price tags just to have the one thing that she still deemed priceless – her beloved son.

As her driver parked the Rolls Royce on the driveway of her Bel-Air home, Nova checked her phone to see if he had called from Tijuana. He hadn't. A bolt of panic shot through her. All the glamour and riches in the world could never stop a mother from worrying.

Georgia and Charlie's search of the hotel had been fruitless. Charlie had tried the bars and restaurant, flashing Mitzi's photo to see if anyone recognised her. Georgia had been busy at reception showing the same photo to see if Mitzi had checked in or passed through. She had also asked about the road vehicle parked outside. Neither the man nor the woman behind the reception knew anything about it, although they did suggest that it wouldn't definitely belong to someone staying at the hotel as often the car park was used as an overflow for people going into the hotbed of Tijuana.

As they regrouped in reception Charlie was convinced about what they should do.

'We phone the police. We let them deal with the van and let them investigate.' He could see tears of frustration forming at the edges of Georgia's eyes as he spoke. 'We're getting nowhere.' He placed his arm around Georgia and pulled her close. She let her head fall against his shoulder, enjoying the hug.

'Well, even if we're going nowhere, at least I'm going nowhere with you by my side.' Georgia wiped a tear from her face as she looked up at Charlie. There was an air of acceptance about her. She knew Charlie was right.

'Let's phone them and see what they say. We'd better check the van is still there.'

The couple walked outside and in the direction of where the van was still parked.

It was then that Georgia saw her. The figure, in a black hoodie, covering what was obviously a head of rich blonde hair. She was wearing jeans and trainers. She looked athletic, even though her outfit was far from flattering. She was walking towards the van from another part of the car park. From the angle of her approach it was hard to gain a full view of her face but Georgia was certain. It was Mitzi.

She called out. As she did so, the figure in the distance looked in their direction, reacting to her name.

'My God, Charlie, she's alive. It's Mitzi …' stammered Georgia.

Georgia and Charlie started to run towards her, calling Mitzi's name. She started to sprint towards the van.

CHAPTER 50

Victoria was finding it easy to hide her constant need for pain-killers from Scott. She was well practiced with the anti-depressants. With Chloe keeping her in plentiful supply she was popping more pills than any doctor would recommend, but if that kept her pain at bay then that was exactly what she would do. Lost in a world of addiction.

She had some hidden under her mattress, some camouflaged in her vitamins bottle, even some in the layered depths of her jewellery box underneath a mountain of gemstones she'd not seemed to have considered wearing for the longest time. It was simple to not let Scott know about her addiction, especially as they were virtually living separate lives. She wasn't sure he'd care anyway. They had separate rooms, he seemed reluctant to even let the children be in the same room as her, and had had a one-night-fling that she suspected was so much more with the live-in nanny. Why would he?

She wanted to make things right, to erase all the heartache and start again. Deep down she really did. She just wasn't sure she knew how, or indeed if her brain and body would allow her to.

It was the side effects which weren't so easy to hide. She felt constantly sluggish and her mind wandered. Actually it didn't just wander, it migrated time zones with its nomadic ways. She could be sitting at breakfast with Scott and the children and her mind would be contemplating shapes in the wood grain of the kitchen table or trying to pronounce every ingredient on the back of the packaging of her pumpernickel bread, as opposed to hearing what Leo and Lexi had to say. She could lose herself for hours in front of daytime TV watching endless back-to-back cookery shows featuring fat women and camp chefs or find herself engrossed in the whys and wherefores of makeovers performed by stubble-faced men in dungarees. And then there were the times that even though she was sitting in silence, her head was alive; thoughts ricocheting around her brain with a rapidity that would put the speediest of pinball machines to shame. Her eyes would twitch, her fingers fiddle, her brain snowball.

Leo and Lexi had hardly come near her since she had scalded poor Leo's foot. It had been bandaged ever since and Victoria had done her best to apologise for what had happened, but no amount of cuddles and promises of sponge fingers and trifle could regain their trust. Something had changed about their mother and even at their tender age they could feel that she was a ticking time bomb.

It was only when Scott was at work that Victoria could approach Chloe about her needs.

'I want some more painkillers and I want them now.'

Chloe, summoned away from Lexi and Leo, who were back home from school and amusing themselves with dolls and action figures in the playroom upstairs, knew that she couldn't argue, but the welfare of the children had to come first.

'It'll have to wait until Mr Palmer-Roberts comes home, as I need to care for the children.' Chloe couldn't wait for his return. Like most nights lately, she would watch his every move as he interacted with her and the children, his smile as he looked at her. She'd apply an extra slick of lip gloss or a deeper shade of eyeshadow to try and tempt him back into her arms. And it had worked. She could no longer count the times they had had sex on both hands. Maybe not always full sex but enough for her to know that he was interested. That there was hope for the future. Life post Victoria. Not that he'd said as much, but she could tell. He wanted her, she knew that.

Victoria was having none of her excuses. 'I am more than capable of looking after my children, so I suggest you go now, unless you want to find that you have no job to come back to.'

'But your husband said ...'

'I don't give a flying fuck what my husband says. Either you fetch me some pills or you're history here. You hear me?'

Despite her fears for the children, Chloe knew that she only had one choice if she wanted to keep her job and any hopes of potentially staying with Scott.

As soon as Chloe had gone, Victoria headed up to the play-room to see her children. They both appeared to recoil slightly as she entered the room.

Lexi was surrounded by her collection of dolls. A selection of plastic faces stared up at her from the floor, each of them framed in a sea of ringlets. Leo, his foot still bandaged, clutched an Action Man in his hands.

Victoria sat down on the floor with her children. Even though she was low on painkillers, she had enough for another day or two but she had wanted some alone time with her offspring. Scott had been guarding them like a Bullmastiff ever since the bath incident and even though the pain in her side was still agonising between pills, the thought of her children not even wanting to be in the same room as her pained her more. It was why she had orchestrated the necessity for Chloe to disappear for an hour or two. She wanted the children to herself.

They both stared at her, their sadness almost palpable. Victoria picked up one of Lexi's dolls and looked at the face. Innocent and cherubic, its spheroid eyes and rosebud lips gazed up at her. It reminded her of when Lexi was born, six years ago. Such a pretty girl.

Victoria's mind began to wander. Images soaked her mind. Of the moment she was handed her baby girl by the midwife in the delivery room, of the euphoria on Scott's face as he kissed his wife and new babies in rapid succession, unable to comprehend his own happiness and of the joy of learning that both of her beautiful new babies were healthy and glowing with vitality. It was every parent's dream. Nothing else compared to the moment when a family is born. Unadulterated happiness.

So why would Victoria risk it all? Why would she let herself succumb to the pain and chance everything she had? Because she had no choice. No control. She could no longer look at Scott without feeling a river of disgust running through her body and no longer hold Leo and Lexi in her arms without wondering what they might be thinking about her. Everything around her appeared to be slipping through her fingers.

She couldn't even bear to look at herself in the mirror anymore. How could someone still so relatively fresh in age have become such a diseased, putrid whirlpool of self-loathing and disgust at what she saw in herself and in the minds of those around her? How had she let herself fall so far from grace?

As images of her once beaming jubilation taunted her, the edges of Victoria's thoughts began to darken, as if someone was holding a lighted match to them and laughing at her as the edges started to curl and blacken into tiny, irreparable flakes. The earthy crack and splutter of the burning image filled her head, the noise growing louder and more drowning as the long-distant image of her smiling teenage youth disappeared from her mind and was replaced with an image of her face as she saw it now. Grey, infected, sick. Unloved. All happiness gone.

As the last trace of her old blithe self ebbed away in her mind, the new, rotten face that replaced it was a stranger to happiness, alien to love. Hadn't she once been told that the definition of love was when someone else's happiness became your own? She loved her family, idolised her children. They were her all. But they weren't happy. How could they be with a mother like her?

It was the sound of Lexi's crying that forced Victoria's thoughts back into the present. Her daughter was screaming. Confused, her brain fogged by her thoughts and the effects of her pills, Victoria just sat and stared at her daughter as she watched heavy tears flow down Lexi's face.

Why was she crying? Why? What was she supposed to do? Victoria's caring, motherly instinct to cradle, love and nurture had all but erased itself. A barbed coating of helplessness seemed to wrap around her as she stared at Lexi's misery. Leo too began to cry, distressed at seeing his sister so unhappy.

Victoria began to rock back and forth, a momentary madness taking hold. She could hear the voices begin to gather in her mind. Whispers telling her to silence the screams. To block them out. To stop them hurting her thoughts. But she didn't know how. Her own confusion and the constant shrieking of her children's dismay escalated inside Victoria's head.

The words boomed from Victoria's lips before she even had time to think about them. 'Shut up. Just shut up. Shut the fuck up.'

Lexi's crying became louder, the look of horror on her pure features showcasing her complete lack of understanding at her mother's reaction. Her tears endless, no words forming, all the child could do was point at her mother's hands.

Victoria looked down. She still held Lexi's favourite doll, but the head and body were no longer connected. Unknowingly, Victoria must have twisted it and snapped it off as black thoughts filled her head.

It stared up at her. Broken. Just like her family. Just like her own body. Just like her life. And Victoria wasn't sure if any of it was capable of repair.

Scott stood in the doorway, having finished work early for once. The broken family was complete. His face was red with rage. She had no idea how long he'd been there but his anger and disgust were clear. He raced over to his children and gathered them in his arms. He didn't even look at Victoria, as if she were a stranger to him. He left the room, the bawling children clinging to his body. It wasn't until a few minutes later that he returned to the playroom. Victoria was still staring down at the broken doll in her hands.

He delivered one sentence. It was all she needed for her own tears to flow. Heavier than they had ever flowed before.

'I want a divorce, we're through …'

CHAPTER 51

Georgia could feel the burning of her lungs inside her body as she and Charlie ran off across the car park in pursuit of Mitzi.

Her mind raced; she was ecstatic that finally she knew that her friend was alive, but equally confused by the fact that Mitzi was running away from her and Charlie. Why? Was it an admission of guilt? Georgia couldn't even bear to contemplate the thought.

She and Charlie watched as an obviously petrified Mitzi reached the camper van, opened the door and disappeared inside. A moment later the headlights illuminated, their signal obvious.

'Do you have the car keys, Charlie? She's going to drive off.' Georgia was determined not to lose the opportunity to finally talk to her friend, no matter what she might learn.

Charlie patted his jacket pocket as he ran alongside his girlfriend. 'They're here.'

They changed direction, heading towards their own vehicle. By the time they had both climbed inside and turned the key in the ignition, Mitzi and the RV were already screeching their way out of the car park exit, trailing dust in the dark night air.

Charlie drove.

'We can't lose her, Charlie. Not now, we're too close.'

'I have no intention of letting her slip away, don't worry.' Charlie did his best to sound as confident as possible despite the road vehicle having a good head start on them. It was already tearing down the open road heading out of Tijuana before Charlie and Georgia had even vacated the car park.

Had this been a car chase in a film, then no doubt every other vehicle on the road would have miraculously steered its way out of Charlie and Georgia's path, leaving them with free passage to catch up with Mitzi. But this wasn't some Vin Diesel *Fast and the Furious* flick, and as a result it seemed that every car, motorbike, bus and taxi seemed to be in their way. They could still see the road vehicle in front of them but as red lights and crossings turned against them and the roads leaving the city became darker, the tail lights of Mitzi's ride seemed to be moving further and further into the distance. It wasn't long until they were nothing more than virtual pinpricks on the horizon.

Neither Charlie or Georgia were giving up though, Charlie switching from lane to lane on the highway in the vain hope of saving a few seconds in order to gain on the vehicle they were chasing.

As they left Tijuana, there seemed to be fewer cars on the road and keeping tabs on their quarry became slightly easier. The roads inclined and narrowed, venturing upwards, the landscape becoming hillier as the madness of the city disappeared behind them.

It was clear though that the road vehicle had no intention of being caught and even though the roads were becoming narrower and more meandering, Mitzi was still keeping her foot to the floor and maintaining a good speed. Georgia had trouble keeping the vehicle in sight as it twisted from left to right as the road wound its way upwards.

They must have been in pursuit for about twenty minutes when finally it seemed that they were gaining on the road vehicle. Maybe it was the power of their own car or the heaviness of the RV slowing it down as they snaked the road, but they were definitely gaining.

Georgia could feel a list of questions clicking into place in her mind. There was so much she needed to say to Mitzi. The thought of finally being able to spend time with her, no matter what the circumstances, seemed somehow comforting to her. She needed answers that only Mitzi would be able to give.

Droplets of heavy rain started to fall onto the windscreen, unseasonal for the late summer and Charlie flicked on the windscreen wipers to push them away. The red lights of the RV in front of them blurred slightly with every pass of the blades.

The RV could have been no more than five hundred yards in front of them when it attempted to take a severe turn to the left as the road angled sharply. The combination of the extreme weight of the van and the acuteness of the angle were a far from perfect mix and in an instant the RV began to swerve as the driver behind the wheel attempted to keep control.

Georgia and Charlie could only watch on in horror as the RV swerved perilously across both lanes of the narrow road.

It was mere moments before the RV skidded its way across the wet road and crashed through a barrier on one side. What was on the other side was unclear in the dark and the rain but as the red lights of the RV disappeared from view it was obvious that there was an incline.

It was only when a terrified Georgia and Charlie stopped their own car and ran over to where the RV had vanished from view that they could actually see what had happened. The upturned road vehicle lay at the bottom of the deep drop, its wheels spinning.

Neither Georgia nor Charlie could see clearly. Or at least they couldn't until a ball of flames filled the air as the RV exploded.

Heavy drops of rain fell down on Georgia as she watched the fireball, the heat and suddenness of it causing her to fall to the floor. She felt her tears mingling with the rain on her skin. Had she chased her best friend to her own death? The thought horrified her. As Charlie placed his arms around her and pulled her close she felt the rain soaking her hair and her face, washing away any final hopes she'd had of seeing Mitzi alive and finally gaining some answers to her questions.

CHAPTER 52

The smell of hot dogs and fried onions wafted in the air. A backdrop of spinning lights and flashing bulbs lit up the sky as dusk settled itself over the theme park on the outskirts of Los Angeles.

Screams resonated from every direction. Those of thrill-seeking daredevils riding the array of rides spread across the park, their terror and delight merging into one big ball of adrenaline as they shot into the air, spun round at breakneck pace and plummeted into hidden tunnels. But tonight the screams of the people enjoying their rides were drowned out by those gathered to try and catch a glimpse of their TV hero in the big, bold, beautiful, buxom flesh.

Nova Chevalier was filming at the park. The story for *Super Nova* was that she and a group of her girlfriends wanted to spend some fun time together on a day out to 'chillax after another hard round of press launches, media bashes and the day-to-day grind of just having to look downright fabulous in LA'. She and her socialite friends were hardly industrious compared to the millions of real working Angelinos but the TV viewers would doubtless lap up the chance to see Nova and her pals with wet backsides from the log flume and hair out of place as they clung on for dear life to each other on a rollercoaster.

Not that there was any chance of a hair out of place for long with a team of hairdressers and make-up artists following Nova and her two 'besties' – an actress from US glam-soap *Peregrine*

Palace and one of the panelists from *The View* – as they tiptoed from ride to ride on completely inappropriate skyscraper high heels.

It would be must-see car-crash TV. The type for which *Champagne Super Nova* had become famed.

Sitting in her make-up chair and sipping a flat Diet Coca-Cola, Nova had one more ride to experience before the end of the filming. A fact that she was hugely glad about. The day's filming in the park had literally turned her stomach upside down, making her feel like she was bouncing off the ceiling, hence the need for flat coke to quell her nausea, but at least it had taken her mind off the middle-of the-night phone call she'd received from Charlie in Tijuana informing her about Mitzi's death.

It was news that had already spread throughout the crew of *Super Nova* faster than Hollywood tittle-tattle and various news stations had started to pick up on the story. It had saddened Nova enormously and Jacob had been incredibly upset when she'd told him the news. As had Addison, evidently full of compassion for her new friend, Georgia.

Addison and Sarah were standing alongside Nova now, Addison with production clipboard in hand, Sarah looking bored, as the make-up artist brushed on another final layer of Laura Mercier's Secret Finishing Powder onto Nova's already flawless skin.

'So when are Georgia and Charlie back from Tijuana?' Addison asked.

'They're on their way back now. They had to explain to the police about what they were doing in Tijuana and why they were chasing after poor Mitzi, but it seems the authorities have just said she lost control of the vehicle and careered to her death. I guess we'll never know why she killed that Foster chap now.'

Addison and Sarah were both visibly shocked at Nova's words. 'So you really think she killed her boyfriend?' said Sarah.

'Well until somebody tells me otherwise I really don't know what to think. She ran away to Mexico for some reason and as far as I can see, fleeing the scene of the crime to escape capture is probably the most likely explanation, don't you agree? It's all completely awful but can you think of any other explanation? The police seem to be happy with that theory according to Charlie.'

Neither Sarah nor Addison replied at first, lost in their own thoughts. It was only after a gap of about fifteen seconds that Addison finally murmured, 'Yes, no other explanation I suppose,' before losing herself in contemplation again as she considered the fragility of life.

It was Nova who broke the silence, this time speaking to the make-up artist.

'Now, could you reapply my lipstick, shape up these brows a little and I'm thinking I might like my hair given a touch more bouffe if you don't mind. It's been dreadfully flat since that god-forsaken trip on that water ride earlier. Chop chop.'

Addison checked her watch. 'We are behind schedule, Nova. You should have been on the ride forty minutes ago and the park actually closes in an hour. Unless you want to come back tomorrow to film again of course. But Jacob did say that this had to be a one day shoot due to location costs.'

Nova wasn't swayed. There were times when only playing the diva would do in Hollywood and now and again Nova enjoyed playing it, just for the sheer wicked enjoyment of it all. She was as savvy as any industry player. She had learnt from the best in Jacob. Even though the cameras were off, she was still the star.

'My adoring husband would not mind us coming back tomorrow if need be, ladies. When you are married to me then there is no question about cutting corners on cost.' She turned to the make-up artist as Addison looked at her watch yet again, sent Sarah off to phone Jacob to inform him of Nova's decision and frowned with worry.

'Now, let's start with the brows, shall we? A little shaping would be good. I need to outshine those two bitches I'm filming with today.' She was only half-jesting, enjoying her 'role'. 'And as for being late, Addison, well, my darling Jacob would also tell you that it's better to arrive late than to arrive ugly no matter what you're doing. Even if it's being thrown around on a sodding fairground ride.'

CHAPTER 53

The bedroom floor at Jack Christie's house was never a clean one. Between the pile of wank magazines in the corner, the dirty mugs quarter-filled with stone cold coffee and a varied selection of butt-filled ashtrays dotted across the carpet, his bedroom floor was student-worthy in its messiness.

Not that Jack cared, as the woman in his bed was far tidier than his bedroom floor would ever be. In all senses of the word.

It felt good to have Chloe back in his life. Not as a girlfriend, he didn't need that. He was a lone shark, someone who thrived better without the heavy albatross of emotional attachment around his neck. And besides, from what she'd told him, she was much more into the older professional type of man these days. The bankers, not the wankers. A DILF lover. And specifically, one, in the form of the husband of the rich family she was nannying for.

But he was loving her regular visits to the flat he shared with Andy North. Because while she wanted something from him, a never ending supply of painkillers, he was able to get what he wanted, and that was getting his leg over on a regular basis too. This jackdaw was a randy bird.

Jack had already fucked Chloe once that afternoon and as he buried his face deep within the fleshy wet folds of her pussy he was ready for round two, his cock stiff and the veins within it throbbing with lust.

Jack adored going down on a woman. There was something so deeply satisfying about it. In some ways he preferred it to getting his end away. Once you'd shot your load, the euphoric sensation of climax quickly ebbed away but even hours after lapping at a wet, willing pussy Jack adored the fact that the taste of his lover's stimulation was still ripe on his lips.

Chloe lay underneath him, her legs spread wide as he feasted on the succulent layers of her sex. She gave a slight moan as he found her clitoris and nibbled against it, the rough texture of his day-old stubble and the biting of his teeth causing her to thrash her hips upwards allowing him even deeper access into her pussy. He pushed back the outer lips and marveled at the glowing pinkness of the flesh hidden inside. It was warm and inviting. Jack extended his tongue as far as it would go and dipped it into her sexual darkness, moving it as fast as he could, causing Chloe to moan with excitement again. Her breathing became harder and faster. This was erogenous nirvana.

Jack was still flicking his tongue across the top of Chloe's clitoris when the bedroom door opened. The action made Chloe jump and she attempted to grab the bed sheet to cover herself. Jack looked up from between her legs to see Andy standing at the door.

'Fuck, sorry, man, I didn't know you were …' He left the sentence hanging for a moment, ' … busy.' He stared across at Chloe, the sheet covering her breasts but her pussy still exposed. A smile spread wide and clown-like across his face as he took the scene in.

Whether it was the provocative cocktail of fleshly juices still on Jack's lips or the copious lines of coke he'd taken during their sexual athletics, something in Jack's brain stirred. And if he wasn't mistaken there was something stirring in Andy's joggers too. The telltale tenting of the material as he looked at Chloe showed his evident and apparently rather huge interest.

'Come join us, man, there's plenty to go around.' Jack was more than happy to have a threesome and the gender combo was not important. He and Andy had shared most things in life, why not take it into the bedroom?

Chloe remained silent, her opinion equally unimportant and besides, if she wanted painkillers for Victoria, she knew the rules. This was Jack's circus and he was ringmaster.

As Jack returned to banqueting on Chloe's wetness, Andy tore off his T-shirt, sweatpants and boxers and moved towards the bed, his erection ready for action. As he climbed onto the bed and began to fondle Chloe's breasts, another three garments lay discarded on an already crowded bedroom floor.

A pair of mud stained jeans, the knees marked with round green patches of dirt, lay on the floor, in complete contrast to the ivory coloured pure wool velvet bedroom carpet underneath them. Little dry flecks of deep brown mud dotted across the ivory material where they had loosened themselves from the denim as they'd been thrown to the floor.

Tanya had been deeply eager to rip the jeans off Aaron as soon as she had the chance. After her experiences in Milan, she needed him. Both alongside her and inside her.

She'd been watching him all day, Aaron's first day back gardening for her and Devon since his return from the States. Devon had been there most of the day too, his presence deliberate, stopping them from having any kind of time alone. It pained Tanya greatly. She longed to feel the rough masculinity of Aaron's body against hers. But while Devon sat, staring wide-eyed out into the garden from his vantage point in the study as Aaron beavered away, Tanya knew that she had to keep her distance from the gardener.

She and her husband hadn't discussed her affair with Aaron since their return from Italy. The air between them had been frostier than Italian gelato. But Tanya knew that Devon had spoken to Aaron. She'd watched them from afar as the two men confronted each other. Aaron had been setting up his tools for his day's work at the bottom of the garden.

Aaron had been expecting the encounter and watched out of the corner of his eye, pretending not to notice as Devon marched towards him.

'You and I need to fucking talk.'

Aaron stopped what he was doing and looked up.

'I know about you and Tanya. You've been fucking her. She's confessed all.'

Aaron didn't let on that he'd already been told by Tanya that Devon had discovered their secret. He didn't say a word, powerfully still.

'She's my wife, and my property. You can just back off, or else …'

Aaron broke his silence.

'Or else what? Is that a threat?'

Devon shifted from foot to foot as he eyeballed Aaron. He was obviously a man who didn't thrive on confrontation.

'Or you'll be sorry … you don't mess with me.'

Aaron couldn't stop himself. 'Or what? You'll get heavy handed with me, like you did with Tanya in Milan? What kind of sick fuck are you?'

'You don't scare me, Mr Rose, with your big brute force. You need this job, don't you? You need the money. If you want paying then you don't touch my wife. If I see you within spitting distance of her then you don't see a penny. Let's not forget that right now I own you.'

The money will come from Tanya, so Devon could go fuck himself, mused Aaron.

Devon read his mind.

'And my wife won't be stealing from me again, so you can forget about any payouts from that department.'

It was true that until something better came along, hopefully wrapped up in a big Los Angeles sized bow, Aaron was in need of the gardening money. He was keen to draw the conversation to a close. 'Then I'll get on with my job, shall I?'

'Yes, if you would. I was thinking of asking you to plant some wolfsbane. I think a copious amount of it would look incredibly good around here, don't you? So pretty for Tanya to pick, too.'

As Devon turned and walked away from Aaron, it was clear that he was indeed threatening the gardener. His choice of flower proved that. Wolfsbane, one of the most innocent looking yet deadliest flowers a gardener could work with.

Aaron knew the plant well, as would any gardener worth their salt. Aconitum, also known as Devil's Helmet and Monkshood, could cause multiple organ failure for a human just by brushing against it. The toxins of the plant, that was simple to grow in the UK given the right soil and location, could easily enter the blood if protective clothing was not worn when handling the flower,. causing death to even the strongest of bodies.

Aaron had never worked with it and he never wanted to. But it was clear that Devon knew what he was talking about. There wasn't a more murderous yet pretty flower around. A killer in a gorgeous purple coat. One that grew wild and free and wouldn't be contained. A symbol that defied everything Devon stood for.

Aaron watched as Devon disappeared back into the house. A chill ran across his body, not just caused by the coldness of the breeze. Devon was obviously a very dangerous and calculating man.

It was hours later, at the end of a busy day's gardening, that Aaron finally found himself alone with Tanya, Devon having left the house for a meeting. She had come to see him as he was putting his tools away.

He had intended to tell Tanya about the threat that had been made against them both. He had intended to resist any advances that she made towards him. But both seeds of intention had landed on hard rocky ground with no chance of germination. Especially as Tanya wrapped her arms around him and pulled him towards her, her lips finding his and opening to allow their tongues to entwine together.

As they began to kiss, the rock hard bulge in Aaron's jeans proved that Tanya and her prurient advances were still able to wrap Aaron around her little finger. In just a few minutes they had returned to the house and Aaron's jeans were discarded on the bedroom floor as he slid his member deep into her, the scent of the day's toil still slicked across his skin. For a moment all thoughts of threats and marital nastiness subsided as the gardener and his rich Russian lover rocked their way to orgasm. Everything apart from their lust temporarily forgotten.

Everything. Including the cameras installed at various places around the house to spy on Tanya. She'd assumed there wasn't one in the bedroom they were using. Not in Georgia's room.

She assumed wrong.

Later that night Devon watched the footage of his wife and Aaron fucking on the bed. His daughter's bed. Devon had known it would happen. He could read Tanya like some smutty book. He knew how to pay her back. To hit her where it would hurt. This wasn't just about betrayal, this was about coming out on top. Even if it could hurt him as much as it would hurt her. And Devon was already hurting a hell of a lot.

Nova's orgasm juddered to a flourishing finale, the steely feel of Jacob's manhood still deep inside her as he too unleashed his love for her. Jacob adored sex and there were times when his demands for love-making were sometimes a little more frequent and unquestionable than her own desires actually wished for. But she worshipped him and even though she sometimes entered into a sexual bout of between-the-sheets activity with about as much enthusiasm as she did for a Botox injection, she had to admit that Jacob never disappointed. He was a skilled lover who would not allow his own orgasm to come before hers. And even if she wasn't in the mood there was something about Jacob's touch that ignited her.

'I love you Jacob.' Nova stared up into Jacob's eyes as a wash of climactic exultation spread across his face. They were the only words necessary to convey her complete adoration for her husband.

Jacob withdrew his cock from her and turned over onto his back. 'I love you too, darling.' He reached for a cigarette from the packet on the bedside table. It was one of the few habits he had that irked Nova greatly. Especially when he lit up after sex.

'Oh Jacob, if you're going to smoke then please do it outside by the pool. You know I can't bear the smell of it in the house. A filthy habit.'

'Which is why we employ Juanita to spray the air in here as much as possible and make everywhere smell of gardenias and apple blossom and heaven knows what as opposed to my, as you say, filthy habit. I have not slaved away my entire life to stop myself enjoying the occasional cigarette in my own home. Especially the ones after a good shag like that. It's one of the joys of life. So I suggest you drop it.' Jacob lit his cigarette.

Nova knew she couldn't argue. But as Jacob flicked his ash and missed the ashtray positioned alongside their bed, sending the sooty flakes onto the bedroom floor carpet, Nova couldn't stop herself.

'Not on the carpet, Jacob. Please take it outside. Charlie and Georgia will be back soon and I will not have cigarette burns on the floor.'

Sliding from underneath her silk sheets, Nova moved towards the bedroom door and wrapped the Ralph Lauren shawl-collar robe hanging on the back of the door around her.

She turned back to face Jacob, who was also out of the bed by now, naked, holding the marble ashtray in one hand as he held the cigarette in the other.

'Now, put some clothes on, for heaven's sake Jacob. I'm off to grab Juanita. This room will need spraying and this floor still needs cleaning, there are bits everywhere.' She let her eyes gaze longingly down Jacob's body as she spoke, taking in the form of his chest and the sizable cylinder of flesh between his legs. Jacob spied her as she did so and made it twitch slightly. 'Fancy a rematch?'

'I'm not sure what's dirtier, Jacob Chevalier, your filthy mind or this bedroom floor. Now get dressed, will you. I will not let Juanita see you like that. The poor girl will never pick up a vacuum hose again.'

Nova smiled to herself as she vacated the bedroom.

CHAPTER 54

Addison flicked off the television, the image of Jessica Lange in *American Horror Story* that she'd just been watching still drawn onto her mind. She loved that woman. Class, talent, a demonic streak at creating the most devilish of characters, and a sexiness that most women in LA could only dream of. Especially for a woman of Jessica's advancing years. She was definitely another of Addison's favourite females.

But not even an hour watching one of her top actresses in action could shift the funk that had fogged across Addison's mind.

It hadn't been the best of days. For once she wasn't working on *Super Nova* as there was no filming to be done. Scenes had wrapped for a few days and wouldn't resume until the following week.

For starters, she missed Aaron. He'd made quite a splash with her during his stay and she wasn't just thinking about their aquatic display of debauchery in the hotel shower. She was praying that he would bag the part on the pilot show as that would have him flying back to LA quicker than you could say 90210.

Then there was the phone call earlier on from her agent telling her that the part she'd auditioned for in *Clampires* didn't work out, so her hopes of spending some time at the mercy of a blood sucking mollusk were smashed like shellfish in the beak of a ravenous oystercatcher. And to rub extra salt into an already overly salty wound, it had been her flatmate Diana who had actually bagged the role and was currently slamming tequilas in some Hollywood backstreet bar to celebrate. It would probably be seventy-two hours before she returned back home. That girl had a Studio 54 mentality when it came to partying.

But even all of that Addison could have coped with if it wasn't for a nagging feeling that kept pulling at the back of her brain. It was something that had been playing on her mind for days. Something that she didn't really know how to deal with. What was for the best? It had already caused her a few sleepless nights and she needed to make a decision.

On a day where nothing had gone her way she decided to do the right thing. She picked up the phone and dialled.

It clicked onto answerphone after eight rings.

'Hello, Georgia. It's Addison, can we meet? There's something I need to tell you. Something important. It's about Mitzi Bidgood.'

Addison left her address and hung up. As she flicked the television back on she breathed a sigh of relief. She was definitely doing the right thing.

Victoria flicked the television off and felt yet another tear of misery run down her face. She'd been watching Evie discussing her latest film on *Rise and Shine*. Her interview with that lovely, dashing Charlie Cooper had aired.

Victoria loved having Evie in her life again. She couldn't wait to see her again at the forthcoming charity event. She needed her. Needed a close friend. When was the last time they had enjoyed a special night out together? The two women had a lot in common and Victoria rued the fact she had let their union break.

The jovial female host of *Rise and Shine* had mentioned the event after the interview. It somehow seemed even more fitting and poignant now that Mitzi was dead. Such a sad, mad, bad world. But had Mitzi been bad? Nobody knew. All explanations of what had happened to make Mitzi run off to Mexico for now remained unknown. The thought of Mitzi's demise, no matter what had gone before it, made Victoria incredibly sad and long even more for the carefree days of her friendship with Evie and the girls at the Zumba group.

Not that it was just the dancer's death that was causing Victoria's tears. No, the cause of her wretchedness was also the situation within the walls of her very own home. Scott was adamant that they were through. Seeing Lexi and Leo crying helplessly while their mother did nothing was the final straw for Scott.

What did he need her for now? She was a danger to the children, no use around the home and lifeless in the bedroom. She had become a stranger in her own home. An imposter in her own clothes.

Her only contact with those around her over the last few days had been to gain the painkillers from Chloe. Chloe – the woman who had replaced her. The woman who guarded her children and kept them away from the person who had brought them into the world. Victoria had tried for stolen moments with Leo and Lexi, but Chloe was unshakeable in her quest, obviously at Scott's demands, to keep the twins away from Victoria. If she hadn't needed the painkillers she would have jettisoned the young woman's backside out into the North London streets straight away but she knew that keeping Chloe didn't just alleviate her own pain. It also helped the children's too. What was the point of farming them off to some new nanny, a stranger that they didn't know or indeed want to know? At least they felt safe with Chloe, knowing that she was a familiar face in a home that had become a sea of raw bewilderment to them. Merely for Leo and Lexi's pain alone, she had to keep Chloe under the family roof.

What made it worse was that, clutched in Victoria's hands as she switched off the TV, were the hand-delivered divorce papers that had arrived on her doorstep that morning. Even though they still lived under the same roof, Scott wanted out and he wanted out as quickly as possible. And he wanted the children too. Full custody. No court in the land would rule with the father, would they? Not one that could spend sixteen hours a day at work. Not one who would never see his children or be able to spend time watching them flourish into young adults. Not one without a woman at his side.

But as Victoria popped a painkiller into her mouth and contemplated what her life had become and how Chloe had suddenly become mother to her own children, maybe even makeshift wife to her own husband, she realised that maybe it wasn't just Leo and Lexi who were living in a state of raw bewilderment. Maybe she was too.

CHAPTER 55

Column inches on the horror of Mitzi's Mexican mountainside demise were remarkably short lived. In a modern world where Instagram and Twitter allowed for an immediate fix of what had happened mere seconds before, the dancer's tragic end was soon yesterday's news. Tales of reality star 'kiss and tells', boy band gay confessions and red carpet romances soon pushed any visibility of Mitzi's death from all of the UK tabloid front pages. Speculation that Mitzi had been behind the death of her boyfriend, Foster, screamed out from under the red tops for a day but after that, a sea of sensationalist silence returned as far as Mitzi's story was concerned. It was old news, not instant enough to warrant anything more than a fleeting mention as the days rolled by.

It was a fact that pained Georgia greatly as she scrolled through the various news websites on her MacBook in the middle of the night sitting in the kitchen at Nova and Jacob's Bel-Air mansion. She couldn't sleep. She and Charlie had been back from Tijuana for less than forty-eight hours and already all thoughts of Mitzi were fading away from the beady glare of the media world. On American websites her death had hardly figured.

Charlie joined her in the kitchen, just back from one of the studios in LA where he'd been filing a live report back to *Rise and Shine*. With the time difference between LA and London any live reports were made during the wee small hours to cater for the UK breakfast newsmongers. He had told his bosses that the Mitzi story was the one celebrity piece of gossip he wouldn't comment about or report on. Despite his current LA location, it was too close to his UK home life with Georgia. And how the hell could he speculate about whether Mitzi was in fact a murderer?

His heart was breaking for his girlfriend. Every time he looked at her he had flashbacks to nights out alongside Georgia and Mitzi. Drunken happy evenings in bars watching the girls as they threw their bodies around the dance floor to the tunes of vintage Madonna.

Georgia had been inconsolable on the entire journey back from Mexico. She had come to the States with the intention of trying to find out what had happened to Mitzi, to hopefully reunite with her best friend. To see her and yet not be able to speak to her had crushed Georgia. Where was the closure? Where were the explanations?

Charlie wrapped his arms around Georgia as she sat at the granite kitchen breakfast bar and pulled her close, lifting her face towards him and kissing her forehead. He could tell she had been crying, her eyes both tired and glossy with tears.

For a second they remained entwined in each other's arms in silence, the mere touch of each other enough to share their love.

'It's so good to have you two back. Things will get better, I promise you.' It was Jacob, who had entered the kitchen to grab a glass of wine. He was suited, a sharp Tom Ford jacket hugging his frame. He'd spent the evening at an industry party, discussing ideas for the forthcoming pilot season and had only just returned, despite it nearing 2am. Nova had declined to accompany him, never keen to head to a party where her own show wasn't number one on the agenda. Jacob was glad that she wasn't there. It was something he needed to handle himself. Jacob had shaken the right hands and schmoozed the necessary money men but a fun time it was not. Jacob could never relax until the deal was done ... and it had to be the deal he wanted. He'd driven home stone cold sober, never good in Hollywood, and craving a glass of quality vino and a much needed cigarette.

Charlie and Georgia watched him as he opened the fridge door, pulled out a bottle and poured himself a glass. 'Care to join me? I'm heading out to the pool for a smoke. Tonight's party was as flat as a Kansas horizon. How come you're both up so late?'

'I couldn't sleep,' said Georgia. 'My mind won't switch off.'

'And I was doing a report for the TV back home,' stated Charlie. 'I'm just in.'

'I missed you,' said Georgia, pulling him even tighter towards her.

'I did ring to say I'd be home as quickly as possible. It should be the last report I have to do before we head home.'

'When did you ring?' asked Georgia.

'I left a message a few hours ago. I assumed you must have crashed for an early night.'

Georgia picked up her phone that was located on the breakfast bar. 'Ah, that explains it then, I've had it on silent and didn't hear it ring. I turned the ringer off. I didn't want to speak to anyone or be disturbed in bed. Not that that includes you of course,' she smiled at Charlie.

Georgia continued, 'It says I have two messages. One from you and one from Addison. What does she want?' She pressed the voicemail button on her phone and put the phone on loudspeaker so that both she and Charlie could hear.

Jacob waved to them both and opened the sliding doors that led from the kitchen out to the poolside area, his glass of wine and a cigarette in one hand as he slid the door open with the other. He mouthed 'goodnight'.

Addison's voice filled the air as Georgia and Charlie listened. Her words were intriguing to Georgia. 'Something important about Mitzi Bidgood? What can she mean? I need to phone her, or seeing as she's left her address maybe we should go round there now.'

Charlie was the voice of reason. He looked at his watch. 'It's gone 2am, Georgia. Let's get some shut eye and we can go and see Addison first thing tomorrow. Whatever she has to say is going to be exactly the same in a few hours' time, isn't it?'

Charlie was wrong. After a restless few hours trying to sleep, Georgia's mind racing with thoughts about what Addison might have to say, she was up, showered and dressed by 8am the following morning. A sleepy yet willing Charlie accompanied her as they drove to Addison's address.

The scene that greeted them outside her apartment was not what they were expecting. An ambulance, its light flashing, was parked there as were two police cars.

Georgia and Charlie ran from their car to where the ambulance was situated. An ambulance worker was just shutting one of the back doors to the vehicle.

'Excuse me, can you tell me what's going on, please?' asked Georgia. 'A friend of mine lives at this address.' A recent friend, but a friend nevertheless.

'It's a police matter now. We're too late. Apparently the girl over there came back after a night out and found her house mate with her head caved in and the apartment turned over. Seems she was murdered as somebody tried to burgle the place.'

Georgia and Charlie looked over towards the apartment. A young woman, dressed in the shortest of dresses and looking completely out of place given the early hour of the day was sitting on the steps at the front of the apartment. She was sobbing uncontrollably. Her hysteria heightened as two officials carrying a body bag walked past her out onto the street. She reached out to touch it in vain.

Georgia's fears were confirmed as the woman let out a pitiful scream as the body was taken away. 'Addison!'

One word. One conclusion. And for Georgia and Charlie their second brush with death in nearly as many days. Whatever Addison had to say about Mitzi they would never hear it from the woman herself.

CHAPTER 56

Georgia had told the police about Addison's phone call to her regarding Mitzi, but as far as the authorities were concerned there was no connection between that and her death. Addison had simply been the victim of a particularly brutal robbery attempt by some LA chancers. Money, jewellery and technology such as iPads and laptops had been stolen but it didn't amount to much. The place had been trashed and the police guessed that maybe Addison had disturbed the criminals in action and had sadly paid the ultimate price. Another young, beautiful life snuffed out.

Nova and Jacob had been deeply upset by the news and halted any further filming on *Super Nova* as a mark of respect. It seemed the least they could do for a woman who had become part of the *Super Nova* family over recent months. They sent flowers to her funeral a few days later but decided not to attend for fear their presence turning it into a media circus.

All filming on hold, the timing seemed right for Nova and Jacob to get away and with Georgia and Charlie having to return home to the UK, it was decided that they should all go together. Evie's charity event was merely a few days away now and maybe a stretch of time away from the glare of LA would be just what the group needed. Plus Georgia wanted to make a visit to see Mitzi's mother. They had spoken on the phone and the torture in her voice at the news of her daughter's death was something that Georgia would never forget. Mitzi's mother asked her if she would help arrange the funeral. She said she would consider it an honour.

'Ladies and gentlemen, we will be landing at London's Heathrow in just under fifteen minutes. We hope that you have enjoyed your flight with us today and that you'll be flying with us again in the future.'

The voice of the in flight attendant woke Georgia up from her slumber. She'd managed to sleep for most of the flight back to the UK. As she stretched her arms above her head and looked around the cabin of the airplane she felt grateful for the support she had around her. Nova and Jacob, both draining the final drops of champagne from their glasses as they prepared for landing, had become a real family to her. It was amazing to spend time with them again in America, despite the gravity of the situation. Having a woman like Nova to talk to, a real woman who knew after all that she lived in a plastic world, reminded Georgia just how much she missed her own mother. Nova and the late Sophia may have been poles apart but they both shared a common love for Georgia, which was clear. And Jacob, so different from her own father, Devon, was a solid pillar of strength to those around him and that now included Georgia too.

Nova raised her glass as she spied Georgia looking at her and smiled. Jacob followed suit. It felt good to have them around a little longer than she'd planned. The charity event organised by Evie Merchant would be the perfect opportunity to try and put all of the horrors of recent times behind them. Whatever Mitzi was, good or bad, just the mere fact that people were coming together to remember her felt right. Maybe it would provide her with the answers she needed, if not to questions, then at least to her own personal quest for closure and inner peace.

Even though they wouldn't be filming in the UK for Nova's show, the star had still insisted on bringing a team with her. There were four seats in premium economy occupied by Nova's make-up artist, Nova's favourite LA hair stylist, Sarah the production assistant – who was finding herself incredibly busy now that poor Addison was no more – and one of the senior producers on the show named Mike. Nova still needed to look her best as doubtless there would be papped photos in magazines and Jacob had thought that even though no TV filming would occur, it would be wise to have crew members to consider locations and potential future UK storylines for the show as well as having their loyal service should he or Nova require anything.

So it was a team of eight that taxied from Heathrow into London. Jacob and Nova went to his house in Kensington, Nova's stylist and make-up artist following them to set up camp in two of the many bedrooms at the palatial house. *Super Nova* crew members, Sarah and Mike, went to a Kensington hotel not far from the Chevalier London home. Nova was keen to have them near, but certainly not under the same roof as her and Jacob. And finally, Georgia and Charlie went to his flat in Old Street. Georgia was in no hurry to return to work and worry about early morning meetings concerning cloud striations or cold air funnels and if her bosses were gracious enough to give her extended leave then she intended to make the most of it and be close to Charlie as much as possible.

As she stared out of the cab window her thoughts turned to Devon and how she would have to go and see him. He had not been himself on her last visit and she needed to find out why. Hopefully that guttersnipe of a wife, Tanya, wouldn't be there when she visited.

Georgia still couldn't work out why a man like her father had married such an odious creature as Tanya.

CHAPTER 57

'It's simple. You get me and Andy an invitation to that charity event and I'll sort your fucking life out.' Jack wasn't joking.

Chloe cursed her own big mouth. Post-coital conversation with Jack Christie, especially after he'd just tipped a rather fat line of cocaine onto her pussy and then proceeded to rub it in with his own tongue, had made her loose-lipped. Both those on her face and those down below.

Chloe's sex life with Jack seemed to be becoming more and more unconventional. Since the threesome with him and Andy, which she had to admit she had found much hornier than she would have imagined, they had tried all sorts. He'd tied her up, used amyl nitrate, introduced a range of sex toys and even persuaded her to finger his ass. Plus he'd started to use drugs during their sexual adventures. She'd always been aware of his own narcotic habits but he had been insistent that she too should try it, starting with cocaine. She'd tried snorting it herself but didn't like the feel of it up her nostrils, so he'd suggested he rub it onto her gums and that had in turn travelled south to the fleshy folds of her pussy. It was another novel way for the drug to enter her blood stream.

When she became a little high, she became a lot talkative. And one of the things she'd talked about was the invitation to Evie's charity bash.

'I love that fucking actress,' spat Jack as soon as Chloe had mentioned it. 'I knocked one out thinking about her many a time when I was inside. How come you're going?'

'I'm not … as yet. The invitation is to Scott and his wife. She knows her really well, and Scott's work has helped out with Evie's finances on many an occasion so they both have their own reasons for going. But now there's talk of divorce, I assume they won't both go.'

Chloe had filled Jack in about the situation at the Palmer-Roberts household on one of her previous visits.

'So get your feet right under that table and get rid of the wife. Get her out of the picture, you bag banker man and everybody's happy. As long as I still get a shag on the side once in a while then all is good.'

'Is that what I am to you, a shag?'

'Yes. If you want more, you're barking up the wrong tree.'

This wasn't news to Chloe.

What was news to Chloe though was that maybe she would be much better off if Victoria was out of the picture once and for all. Maybe then she and Scott would stand a real chance. No wife, ex or otherwise, meant no chance of a reconciliation.

Scott held all the aces. He had money, he had the swanky home, he had the capability to put her out on the street should he become fed up of her. Then what would her future hold? Sure, their sex life was good, he seemed to like what Chloe had to offer between the sheets, but what was to stop him trading her in for another younger model in a few years' time? Shagging the hired help was one thing, letting it become mother to your kids was quite another. But that was what she wanted, wasn't it? She was falling for Scott and she had to make sure that Victoria didn't upset the apple cart. Chloe's imagination was piqued by Jack's words. Plus the feeling of the coke ribboning its way from between her legs was making her mind stray into many different heavenly scenarios.

'So, what are you suggesting?' asked Chloe.

'You leave that to me and Andy. Ask no questions and you'll receive no lies. But make sure you swing us an invitation to that charity event. When is it?'

Chloe cast her mind back to when she'd seen the invitation. 'Next week I think. But how the hell do I manage to blag you and Andy an invitation?'

'Just bring me an invitation and leave the rest to me, alright? You'll be pleased you do.'

It was true. Chloe was loving the idea. Whether it was the coke or the thought of being some kind of Bonnie to Jack's Clyde as he planned Victoria's downfall and secured her own future with Scott at the same time, the notion of it all was igniting her nerve endings and turning her on.

'So what are you going to do to her?' coaxed Chloe.

Jack wasn't really listening though. He was thinking about the charity event. One successful job like this and it would be easy street for a few years to come for him and Andy. And it was all Jack's idea. Major kudos.

And if sorting out this Victoria woman for Chloe so that she could be with this banker twat of a husband was what he had to promise to gain entry to this Aladdin's cave then so fucking be it. Mind you, if you asked Jack, this Scott bloke sounded a right tosser.

Jack grabbed his bag of coke, licked a line of moisture across one of Chloe's breasts and poured out the white powder. Let the Jackdaw play.

CHAPTER 58

'Nobody can ever say to me that contemplating buying a Zac Posen dress one size larger to cater for the delights of that dessert is not a totally valid option,' enthused Nova. 'That poached William pear, sticky toffee pudding and crème fraîche sorbet was just to die for.'

Georgia smiled as she watched Nova virtually bury her spoon into her plate in an effort to remove any last traces of the food from her crockery and into her mouth.

The two women had just finished their lunch at Galvin At Windows on the twenty-eighth floor of London's Hilton Hotel on Park Lane. Nova had wanted to dine and experience some of the best views of the city and their balcony table at the famous eaterie had allowed them to do just that. As they treated their palettes to a fare of gastronomic gems, Nova, a typically effusive American in the UK capital, had stared out across Green Park, Knightsbridge and her beloved Harrods, and of course the most British delight of all, Buckingham Palace. A sight that Nova was not going to let pass by without telling Georgia and indeed a few people not really within ear shot, just exactly what it meant to her.

'To think that Her Majesty is in that house right now while little old me, the queen of reality TV, is looking down at her from this great height is just something else. It only seems two minutes ago I was back in West Hills dreaming of a prince, and now look at me. There might be all sorts of princes running around down there. It's too much. I count my blessings. At least I have found a king in Jacob.' It could have been a script from one of her shows. There were moments when Nova couldn't resist ramping up the melodrama to infinity and beyond.

'So where is *King* Jacob today?' queried Georgia, sipping on a chilled glass of rosé wine.

'Business, darling. Same old nonsense. He's out with Mike and Sarah, looking for some potential storylines for future *Nova's*. Keeps them busy and it means you and I manage to spend more time together. Shame Charlie couldn't join us today.'

'He has some winner of a TV talent show to interview today, but I'm sure he'd much rather be here than speaking to a troupe of street dancers or a girl and her dog or whoever it is he's grilling,' grinned Georgia.

'Well, I'm hoping one of the future storylines on *Super Nova* might be Jacob and I heading to these shores for a wedding, soon. Namely yours and Charlie's.' It was now Nova's turn to grin.

That old chestnut. Georgia had last dodged this line of fire around the poolside in India. 'One day, Nova, one day …'

'Maybe we could have the wedding at Westminster Abbey,' cried Nova, riding the rollercoaster of her own enthusiasm. 'Prince Willy and Kate just looked amazing there and those children George and Charlotte are too adorable. Can I see it from here?' Nova returned to staring out of the window and at the magnificent view across London.

Georgia didn't want to pop Nova's effervescent bubble of frothiness even if the chances of her and Charlie ever getting married at Westminster Abbey were slimmer than a supermodel's waistline. They were much more likely to run off to Hawaii and get spliced in a private barefooted ceremony on the beach. Not that she could imagine Nova agreeing to that in a million light years. Maybe some things were best left undiscussed until the 'I do's' were done and dusted.

'I don't think you can.' Georgia wasn't really sure but had given up scanning the panorama. 'So, what would you like to do this afternoon? Are you feeling the urge to splurge?'

Nova looked confused.

'Splash out. Go shopping. Buy something fabulous?'

Nova obviously liked the notion. 'Well I did pack light this trip so maybe we could take in a few boutiques. I'm sure I could pick up a dress or two. Always good to have choices of what to wear at Evie's party, eh?'

Georgia nearly sprayed her rosé wine across the table. 'Packing light! I've seen less cases on the carousel after an entire flight to Ibiza have disembarked. It would take a pack of sniffer dogs several days to root their way through your luggage, Nova.'

Nova was unapologetic. 'I learnt the art of packing after hearing a quote from the designer, Diane Von Furstenberg. She said, "I get ideas about what's essential when packing my suitcase." So do I, and it's pretty much everything. You can never have too many clothes, shoes, handbags and jewellery with you. Besides, I want to have exactly the right outfit for Evie's gathering. What are you wearing?'

'I honestly haven't given it a moment's thought as yet,' half-lied Georgia. The truth was that whatever she was going to wear she wanted to outshine Tanya. She guessed that her father, a big supporter of Evie and her charities since her rise to fame in Hollywood, was on the guest list and that would mean that sadly, by default, so would her stepmother.

'You'll meet my father and stepmother at Evie's charity event, I suspect. That should be fun.'

'Yes, Charlie's mentioned her. The Russian oligarch's daughter. Apparently we're very big in the Baltic States. They adore me. Maybe she'll be a fan.'

'Somehow I'm not sure you will be,' deadpanned Georgia, choosing to gloss over the fact that, if her geography and history served her well, then the Baltic States were Lithuania, Estonia and Latvia, which had gained independence from the Russian Empire and Tanya's homeland many years before.

'Will I not like her, then? How glamorous is she?' Nova's suddenly panicked at the thought of potentially being outshone at Evie's charity event by the other 'mother of the bride' as it were. For Nova it was a fate not even worth contemplating. She would not let it happen.

'She's very glamorous, but let's just say that class and taste are not necessarily bedfellows of glamour. And she's young. Just a few months older than me.'

'Bitch.' The word had slipped out before Nova had a chance to stop it. She hadn't planned on her potential daughter-in-law's stepmother being glamorous and young. A flawless, unblemished young skin could disguise any lack of class.

Georgia found it hysterical. 'I believe she is!'

Georgia's giggling was interrupted by the ringing of her phone. 'Maybe this is her now. Perhaps she's phoning to tell me that she's disappearing back off to the dark and dingy alleyways of Moscow to leave my father alone.'

It wasn't Tanya. Georgia hadn't expected it to be. It was much more likely to be Charlie or somebody from work. It wasn't either. In fact she didn't recognise the number but she could see it was from abroad.

She considered letting it click through to her messaging service but curiosity took hold and mouthing 'sorry' to Nova, she pressed the answer button.

'Hello ...'

It was two minutes later that she pressed the end button. She'd hardly said another word. All colour had drained from her face.

'What is it, dear girl? You look like you've seen a ghost?'

Wide-eyed at what she'd just heard, Georgia took a swig of her wine before speaking.

'That was the authorities in Mexico. I gave them my number when we left Tijuana. They said they would ring me if there was anything to discuss.'

'And what did they say?'

'They rang about Mitzi's body. They've extracted it from the wreckage of the camper van and examined it. They are sure it can't be Mitzi.'

Nova looked confused. 'But how can they tell? One burnt body is going to look exactly like the next one, surely? They must be mistaken. You saw her go up in the explosion.'

Georgia's expression portrayed that there had been no mistake. 'They're sure. There's no way it could have been Mitzi. The body from the wreckage wasn't female ... it was the body of a man.'

CHAPTER 59

The warmth of the bath water felt good against Victoria's skin. As she lay back, allowing herself to be enveloped by the tendrils of steam that came up off the water she closed her eyes and let her mind drift, grateful that the cocooning of the bath, her ever-faithful anti-depressants and the swallowing of another painkiller were relieving her misery.

Her whole being seemed to be built upon a foundation of hurt. As she stared at the greyness inside her own eyelids, she felt the sadness of her life wash over her. What would it take to immerse her head completely under the surface, to feel the heat of the water over her cheeks, her nose and her mouth? To open her mouth and let the hot sensation flood in, down her throat and into her lungs? How long would it take? Would it be a pleasing sensation? Would it cause pain?

Doubtless it would cause a degree of pain to a few around her. Would Scott grieve? What about the children? Would they be young enough to forget their mother in a few years' time? Who would find her? Would her own body turn cold before the water did? A constant flow of questions poured into Victoria's mind.

She focused on moments in her life. Her first ever Mardi Gras back in New Orleans, the vibrant colours of the floats and the technicolour characters passing in front of her. The softness and the delicacy of her prom dress and the crystal clarity of the jewels as she was crowned Queen on the most magical night ever. The rosy cheeks of Leo and Lexi beaming up at her from their cribs. It all turned to grey, colours staining with misery and hopelessness. Indistinguishable.

No, maybe grey was the only escape. Like a blanket, one that she could be wrapped in for forever. One where hurt couldn't find her.

Victoria smiled to herself, the music of the radio playing from her bedroom the only sound as she felt the warmth rise up over her neck and across her face.

Chloe let herself out of the front door and let it click silently behind her. Scott was at work, the children at school and Victoria was upstairs taking a bath. If she timed it right, she could be back before her employer dressed and returned downstairs.

She had done what she needed to do. Located the invitation and placed it on the colour printer. Pressed the button for copy and thirty seconds later it was done. Printed out, identical but for the gold leaf around the outside of the original. She cut out the photocopy and placed it back in the drawer where she had found the original ticket. She'd seen Victoria stash it there. She put the original in her pocket and texted Jack to say that she was on her way.

Chloe pulled the gate behind her and walked away from the house. Time was of the essence. At least if Victoria was alone in the bath, nothing could go wrong, could it?

CHAPTER 60

She'd given up trying to shout. There was no point. There was no-one to hear her anymore. The binding in her mouth had been removed, as had the ropes around her ankles and wrists. Hands tearing at her. Were they the same as those that had pulled at her skin and bruised her tender flesh that night in the open air? When was that? How could she tell? There was no clock. There was no day and night. There was no hope. Maybe she would try one final cry. All she could manage was a short, barely audible whimper. Now there was no voice either.

CHAPTER 61

There was a celebratory chink of decadence as the three heavy crystal wine glasses bumped up against each other, but not even the noise of such normally jubilant conviviality could do anything to thaw the gelid air that glazed the atmosphere of Devon and Tanya's front room.

'Cheers, darling. It's wonderful to see you again and great to have you back home safely from America. I'm just so sorry to hear about your friend Mitzi.'

Devon was pleased to see his daughter again and of the three people toasting her return, there was only warmth between Devon and his offspring. Georgia and Tanya had hardly looked each other in the eye since her arrival and there was clearly a sub-arctic situation brewing between Devon and his wife as far as Georgia could make out. It would take more than a glass of Pinotage to liven up this party of three.

Georgia was worried about her father. There was a jitteriness about his demeanor that suggested that he was preoccupied with something deeply troubling. She would have asked him outright but with Tanya hovering like a designer-clad misery too, she suspected that the Russian may have been the reason for her father's chagrin. Maybe life with wife number two was not the bowl of Beluga caviar that her father had planned. She'd have to choose her moment.

Georgia took a mouthful of the wine and sat herself down on the chocolate leather sofa at the centre of the room. Tanya sat awkwardly beside her as Devon placed himself on a matching armchair facing his daughter and wife.

'Thank you, but I'm not really sure what to think about the whole Mitzi disappearance anymore. Charlie and I thought we'd seen her go up in smoke in Tijuana but now it appears that it wasn't her after all.'

Georgia explained the phone call that she'd received from the Mexican authorities. Their jaws dropped as she unfolded the tale.

'The body was male! So some man was pretending to be Mitzi. Now that is some fucked-up weird. Some macho Mexican running around in heels and a skirt.' It was a disbelieving Tanya who spoke, her seemingly mocking tone immediately annoying Georgia. The crease of anger scratched across Georgia's face did not go unnoticed by her father.

'That still doesn't make the tragedy of Mitzi's ongoing disappearance any easier for Georgia, does it Tanya? The two of them were very close. At least it means Mitzi could still be alive.' Devon wasn't sure he believed his own words. He looked at Georgia. 'Do you think?'

'I don't know what to think. The whole thing is definitely a bit, as *she* puts it, "*fucked-up*".' Her eyes snapped onto her stepmother as she spoke. 'Why would a man be dressed as Mitzi? Charlie and I were certain it was her. And how would the authorities know? The body would have been destroyed beyond recognition.'

'Speaking with my scientific head on, it's incredibly easy to see the differences between a male and a female skeleton, even one that has been through an explosion,' said Devon. 'For one, in general, a female skeleton would not be as large as a male's, it would be smoother and the hollows that serve as muscle insertion points would be less accentuated. The lumbar curve would be greater in a woman and the angle of the pelvic bone would be different too. Plus there are major differences in hip width and things like that.'

'So they can't have re-sexed it by mistake?' questioned Georgia, still desperate for a definite piece of closure about the dancer's disappearance.

'I'm afraid not, darling. Their findings will be very conclusive. If they say the body was a man, then it was indeed a man.'

'And therefore not Mitzi,' sighed Georgia.

'Unless she'd been a man underneath all of those sequins all along.' Tanya let out an inappropriate giggle. She wasn't sure whether it was the glass of Pinotage or the fact that she always became somewhat snippy when in the same room as her stepdaughter, the animosity between them causing her to lose any sense of tact or decorum, but either way she didn't really care.

Devon obviously did. 'For Christ's sake, Tanya, if you don't have anything useful to say then just shut the fuck up.'

It was unusual for Devon to swear in front of his daughter. Georgia could see that he was riled. As was she. Something inside her snapped as her father's lamentable appearance and her stepmother's tactless, uncaring ways smashed into each other at full pelt.

'Yes, that's not exactly helpful, Tanya. It's my best friend who is missing.' Georgia was becoming more fired up, her anger rising. She couldn't stop herself. 'You sit here with your barbed comments and your poker-faced iciness and you have no idea about what I've been going through. It's alright for you isn't it, sitting here without a care in the world other than which fashion house creation is next on your shopping list or which of my father's credit cards needs using next, but you haven't got a clue about anything.' Georgia placed her hand over her chest. 'I'm hurting in my heart. Something you'd never know about, being such a heartless bitch.'

Georgia's mind was red with rage. The confrontation with Tanya had been a long time brewing.

'You may be Dad's wife but I don't trust you and I don't like you. I don't know what you've been doing to him, but he looks a wreck.'

Georgia turned to face Devon, her entire body now shaking with anger. 'I'm sorry, Dad, but it's true. You look so tired. It's not like you. What's happened?'

Devon remained silent, a deep sadness spreading across his already melancholy features.

'You seem so miserable, Dad. You were never like this when Mum was here. Never. Those were happy times.'

'Enough!'

It was Devon who shouted. He banged his wine glass down on the table as he did so, causing the stem to crack. The glass collapsed to one side, spilling its deep red contents across the surface. 'Georgia, enough ... you do not bring your mother into this.' A tear fell from Devon's eye as he stared at his daughter.

He continued, 'I trusted your mother. And look where that got me. She left me for another man. You can put her on a pedestal all you like, but the fact is we didn't stay together because she left me. Your mother was not perfect. I was wrong to trust her. They say be careful who you trust as the devil was once an angel.'

It was now Georgia's turn to cry, the tears a woeful concoction of misery about Mitzi, the tainted reality of her late mother and her fears for her father.

Devon stood up and moved to his daughter, sitting on the arm of the sofa alongside her and placing his arms around her as she cried. He pulled her close to him. Silence was sufficient, the comfort of his embrace speaking volumes. He kissed her on the top of her head, his own tears falling onto her hair.

Tanya had remained silent and somewhat awkward throughout the conversation between her husband and stepdaughter.

'Your mother and I were very happy together while it lasted but don't now hate Tanya. You shouldn't have that kind of hatred within you, Georgia,' said Devon. 'Your mother and I didn't bring you up to hate. Tanya has made me a happy man, and that counts for something. I was alone after Sophia left and I was miserable, doubting myself and fearing the future. I needed something and I found that in Tanya. She helped me rebuild my life, regain control.'

She wiped her eyes and stared at her stepmother. She didn't hate Tanya. She just didn't like her but if she made her father happy then she would have to respect that. So why then did Devon look so God damned awful? Georgia looked up into her father's face. There was definitely a hurt etched across it.

It was Tanya who finally spoke, feeling that her turn had come. 'You see Georgia, I am here for a reason. Your father adores me.' There was still an air of smugness in Tanya's voice, insinuating that victory was indeed hers after all.

She refilled her glass of wine without offering any to the others and was just taking her first sip when Devon replied. He was about to put his plan into action. Was that a smile that escaped from his lips? Not even he was sure.

'Oh I did. I adored you. But then you let me down too. Just like Sophia. Into the arms of another man. But then I shouldn't have expected any different really, should I? When you're born in the gutter then you will always be a sewer rat, won't you?' Images of his wife and Aaron together swamped Devon's mind, the images he'd seen on the hidden camera. 'I should have left you where I found you, shouldn't I?'

Georgia felt her brow crease with confusion as she listened to her father's words. 'I think it's about time you discovered the truth about Tanya, Georgia.'

A few droplets of Pinotage splashed from her glass and landed on Tanya's magnolia Tory Burch silk blouse as the Russian began to shake with fear at what Devon was about to tell his daughter …

Devon Bellamy lay back naked on his Moscow hotel room bed and felt a stirring between his legs. It was the anticipation of what was to come. He was primed and ready for what the evening of fun in his five star hotel suite was about to offer.

He loved his time working in Russia. When Sophia had been alive he had often contemplated bringing his wife and daughter with him to make the trip into more of a holiday but it had never happened. Instead, he had furnished them both with souvenirs of his time in the Soviet Union, delighting Georgia with Matryoshka dolls that would fit snugly together and decorating Sophie with some of the finest diamonds in the world.

But that was then and this was now. Sophia was dead and Georgia was all grown up and beyond playing with dolls. And Devon was alone.

The days in Moscow kept him busy but the nights were when his solitude kicked in. More often than not, Devon would find himself alone in his hotel suite with nothing more than room service and an unintelligible Russian news channel to keep him company.

It was the room service attendant on one of his visits who had suggested that maybe he would like 'some company' to help pass the time. At first Devon had been reticent. He had never paid for sex and didn't really intend to start now, but after one too many lonely nights with nothing but his right hand for company, it didn't take a scientist of his calibre to realise that money could satisfy any amount of loneliness and the deep seated horny desire that he had been experiencing.

Devon was asked what he wanted by the hotel worker – everything from straight vanilla to bondage and fetish through to the more specialist kinks of watersports and erotic asphyxiation seemed to be on offer for those with the currency to pay.

With each Soviet visit Devon become more of a regular client, using the service to satisfy his desires. It wasn't love, but it was the love of a good shag, the relief of emptying his balls into a woman prepared to do whatever it took to make sure that she could continue to put food on her family's meal table in order to survive the hardships of Russian life. It was a win-win situation, both sides satisfied. And for Devon it took away the heartache of his solitary life back in the UK.

A knock sounded at the door. His latest 'takeout' had arrived. He had requested someone who would be happy to provide full penetrative sex but would be happy to maybe indulge in something a little kinkier if need be.

Nothing had prepared him for the vision that greeted him on the other side of the door. The long red hair, as straight as a number one, framing her face to perfection. There was an air of innocence about her, fused with a burning, volcanic lust bubbling away behind her eyes.

Devon smiled, and immediately it was reciprocated, a wide – dare he believe it, genuine? – smile, that seemed unlike any that he had experienced before during his nocturnal Russian adventures. The girl, in her mid-twenties he guessed, entered into the room and pushed a naked Devon onto the bed.

Within seconds she too was naked and working his erect cock with her mouth, allowing her expert tongue to flick over his shaft. There was a softness to her touch. Devon was euphoric and could feel the juices within his balls beginning to pulsate, ready to explode. As if possessing a sixth sense the girl stopped with her mouth and reached down into her bag to pull out a condom. She rolled it onto Devon's cock and lowered herself onto him. He found himself lost in her beauty.

She tipped her head back and closed her eyes as she rode his cock, allowing it to exit her pussy to the last tip before sucking in his whole length once more.

It was only when she had drained the last drop of excitement from him that the woman dismounted and lay alongside him, allowing her head to rest on his body. Devon could feel his heart beating within his core, the rhythmic pounding of it calming as he wrapped his arm around the woman. This was different to his other experiences. There was a gentleness to her, a vulnerability that he liked. Protectively he drew her close to him and stroked his hand along her upper arm. She kissed his chest as if showing her gratitude. Devon closed his eyes, enjoying the sensation. They fitted together. As if it were supposed to be. Two interlocking pieces of a jigsaw from different ends of Europe, the time zones and differences between their worlds erased.

His eyes still closed, Devon spoke.

'What is your name?'

'Tatiana,' replied the woman, her voice already sluggish yet rich with accent.

It was nearly an hour later that Devon awoke. For a few seconds he struggled to work out where he was, the ceiling of the Russian hotel room he was gazing at seemingly unknown to him. As clarity seeped its way across his brain his thoughts stopped on the woman he had 'ordered'. He'd fallen asleep, doubtless she would be gone and his wallet cleared of cash, anything of value stripped from the room. But no, she was still there, breathing softly into his chest as she had been before he had fallen asleep. Devon stared down at her face. She truly was beautiful.

As if aware she was being watched, Tatiana opened her eyes and looked at Devon. A second later they were kissing. Within minutes they were both locked together again, their intercourse urgent without aggression. It was only after they had both climaxed for a second time that they started to talk, Tatiana answering Devon's questions.

She had been working as a prostitute for five years, her good looks her only qualification for making any kind of decent money. She had been born to a single mother in the back streets of Moscow. Her father was a man she had never known. He had vanished the moment her mother had fallen pregnant. Her mother had done everything she could to cater for Tatiana, taking any job in order to try and bring money into the hovel of a family home. But new clothes and shoes and a square, balanced meal were all delights that Tatiana had never been able to enjoy.

It was her dream for a new life that had spurred her into prostitution. At the age of sixteen she was propositioned by a man on the street for sex. He offered her cash, she was wise enough to know what to do. It was the easiest cash she had ever scored and bringing money to her mother brought her such joy that the machinations of how she had earned it didn't matter to Tatiana. It made her mother happy and that was all. She told her mother that she had a secured a bar job.

Before long, Tatiana's client list had snowballed. She was young and in demand.

Some of her experiences were beyond horrendous; men not so much having sex with her, but raping her with their violence. As they bit at her skin, forcing their way into her, Tatiana just thought of the money and tried to disconnect herself from the brutal, physical acts. Sex was money, and money meant financial happiness and security for her mother.

But there was something about Devon that had immediately sparked a flame of romance within her. Just as he had anticipated from their first meeting as he opened the hotel bedroom door, there was something that had told Tatiana that Devon would be an important man in her life.

She hadn't realised just how important. They met on countless occasions, sometimes on the books and sometimes not, Tatiana needing money but also needing to see the man who made her feel good about herself. She missed him when he was back home in the UK. Devon would take his work to Russia as often as he could.

Tatiana still serviced other men, needing to earn cash, but nothing compared to the love-making she shared with Devon. He was soft, tender, caring yet with a devilish streak that satisfied her wilder side. Less than six months after their first meeting Devon asked her to marry him, a man once broken with grief now allowing himself to finally love again. Any reticence about giving his heart once more forgotten as he gazed deep into Tatiana's eyes. It was a leap of faith he was certain of taking. She said yes straight away. He was the prince, rich and handsome, who would allow her to fulfil her dreams. To live the life she had seen in the fashion and celebrity magazines.

Overnight her life changed. They were married in a ceremony in Moscow, her mother the only guest, and before the ink had dried on the marriage certificate, Tatiana, now Tanya, was living in the lap of luxury with Devon in the UK. It was beyond her wildest dreams. And with Devon providing regular payments for her mother back in Moscow, she was able to move her mum to a better house and provide her with decent food, clothes and hot water. Tanya was a success, her past life a secret that she had thought would always stay just that.

But not now. Now Georgia was hearing it told with relish by the man who had saved her from a life on her back underneath endless strangers. But hadn't that been Tanya's own fault? She had chosen to betray the prince who had rescued her. Chosen to fall under the spell of Aaron the gardener. She had allowed herself, quite freely, to cheat on her husband.

And as Tanya listened in horror to Devon telling both her and Georgia how he had caught his wife and Aaron red-handed even after Tanya's post-Milan promises of fidelity, Tanya realised that she had thrown it all away. Her own security, her mother's future comfort which was so important to her, and any chance of a happy ever after with Devon. This was Devon's revenge. To see her hurt, not with a physical pain, but with an emotional one that could signify a return to life before Devon. Both for her and for her mother.

Tanya's face crumpled as she listened to the story unfold. Georgia, her expression a mélange of told-you-so and horror at what she had heard, just sat and stared at Tanya. She'd suspected she was a liar but not even she had imagined that she was nothing more than a call girl.

Georgia turned to her father. 'So what are you going to do?'

'Do? Nothing. Nobody else needs to know. Unless she crosses me again, of course. She's not leaving me. She can't. She won't. I've told you, Georgia, because you're my daughter. You deserve the truth. Family comes first. Tanya will put her mother first. You might think I'm mad to keep her but I know Tanya better than anyone. I love her, despite everything. She can hurt me, but she must never forget that I know how to hurt her more. By sharing the truth.'

There was an eerie calmness and a warped sense of logic to Devon's words.

'The gardener will have to go,' he continued. 'We'll employ a seventy-year-old. At least she won't try to shag that one. But mind you, what do they say, once a whore, always a whore. Who knows? She'll stick with me. Besides, she has nobody else. The gardener doesn't have enough money to keep her in eyelash extensions, let alone designer clothes.'

'That isn't true.'

The voice came from the door. It was Aaron.

'And here he is, the man she's been shagging,' sneered Devon.

'Aaron, what the hell are you doing here?' Georgia was shocked to see the man that she'd met in LA. She had no idea that he was working for her father too. He was equally as astonished to see her.

Any momentary surprise was forgotten as a teary Tanya ran from the sofa and into Aaron's arms. 'I'm so sorry,' said Tanya. 'Forgive me.'

'For what?'

'For what he has been saying about me. It is all true.'

'And I couldn't give a shit,' said Aaron. 'Fuck you. I quit!'

As Aaron and a sobbing Tanya left the room, the four individuals involved in what had just occurred were all letting their minds race into overdrive. Aaron was thinking that he had just cut off his only decent means of money. Tanya was contemplating whether running off with Aaron was actually the shrewdest move to make, especially now that he'd quit. She had signed a pre-nup before marrying Devon, and worried that both she and her dear mother would be penniless once more. Georgia was wondering whether she had just witnessed the demise of her father's second marriage, and was still reeling at the thought of Tanya being a former hooker. And Devon? Well, he was shaking with rage at the thought of potentially losing his Russian bride, because despite what he had just announced, *she* was actually all that *he* had. Without her, he was alone once more.

'Another drink?' asked Devon his daughter. His words were cold and emotionless.

CHAPTER 62

There are moments in life where good fortune is obviously shining down on a certain individual. When for just one moment, the universe at large decides to intervene and turn what seemed like a forgone conclusion into quite the opposite.

As Victoria Palmer-Roberts let her head sink beneath the surface of her hot bath water the last thing she ever considered was that less than twenty-four hours later she would be feeling a heat of a different kind against her skin. In fact she truly believed that any future heat she would be experiencing would be courtesy of the fires of Hell as she roasted in eternal damnation for being a bad wife and mother.

But somebody somewhere had decided that it was not to be and that Victoria was indeed supposed to die another day. And her guardian angel had been in the shapely form of Evie Merchant, the woman currently lying out alongside Victoria on a sun lounger around the pool at Gran Canaria's five star Seaside Grand Hotel Residencia resort. And the woman keeping a close eye on Victoria's every move.

It had been a hectic day. One that Evie hoped she'd never have to experience again.

With filming wrapped on her latest movie, Evie had been keen to see her friend. Things weren't going well for her right now and if Evie had learned one thing in life it was that friends needed to stick together through thick and thin. She'd just pulled up outside the Bellamy family home when she'd seen Chloe leaving the house. There had been something sheepish about her as she'd raced off down the street. She had seemed distracted and in a hurry. Evie wasn't a fan of the girl after what Victoria had told her and was tempted at first to follow the nanny to see if she was meeting up with Scott behind his wife's back.

But at least if Chloe was out of the house she would be able to speak freely to Victoria about what had been going on. She walked to the front door and to her surprise, found it ajar. Chloe had obviously not shut it properly in her haste to leave the house. She knocked on the door. There was no answer.

She could hear the sound of the radio coming from upstairs. She recognised the singer as Sam Smith, one of her current favourites. She called out for Victoria. No reply.

Evie felt a tightening in her chest, her sixth sense telling her that something was wrong. Pushing the door open, she walked inside and followed the sound of the radio upstairs.

The door to Victoria's bedroom was open. Evie stuck her head around the door. The room was empty. Victoria's dressing gown lay across the bed. Maybe she was having a bath. Evie moved towards the bathroom, where the door was also open.

A bolt of panic fired through her body as she stared through the door. She could see a body immersed underneath the patchy suds. She knew straight away that it was Victoria.

Rushing towards the bath, she reached in and looped her hands under Victoria's head, pulling her up above the water-line. It was still fairly hot which filled her with hope that maybe her friend's body hadn't been under the water for too long. She pulled the plug out and let the water start to swirl away down the plughole.

Attempting to remember any rudimentary first aid that she had learned on any of her film sets, Evie tried not to panic.

She'd once made a film where some of the characters had been trapped on a sinking boat. What had she been taught about potential drowning victims? She racked her brain for answers. Check for a pulse, keep the person still, that was one thing to do and the other was the kiss of life. What did she remember – clear the mouth of any foreign objects, tilt head up and breath into mouth whilst holding nose. She prayed she had it right.

Less than thirty seconds later her prayers were answered as Victoria let out an almighty cough and spluttered a fountain of soapy bath water from her mouth. Evie's resuscitation technique, basic though it was, had worked.

'What the hell are you doing?' Evie let out her frustration and screamed at Victoria. 'You could have died.'

'That was the idea,' rasped Victoria. She looked into Evie's eyes and began to sob, seeing her own predicament reflected in the horror of Evie's face.

'What's happened to me? Evie, help me.' The tears began to flow down Victoria's cheeks as the last of the bath water circled away and disappeared down the plughole.

'So most people would have rushed me off to the hospital or had me locked up in a padded cell, not brought me somewhere where my toughest decision is whether to have a Pina Colada or a Mai Tai.' Victoria still wasn't completely sure that the sun warming her flesh under her loose-fitting clothes and the sound of lapping water patting the side of the saltwater pool wasn't just a euphoric hallucinogenic state caused by being pumped full of drugs. Was she in fact lying in a hospital bed wired up to a life support machine with hopefully a few worried onlookers by her bedside?

'I didn't think it was the best thing for you. You said you'd only been under the water a few seconds and you seemed to be making sense. Well, as much as you ever do. The one thing that was clear is that you wanted to get away from everything. You're dealing with a lot of shit right now and what kind of friend would I be if I took you straight back into a hospital? I figured a couple of days in the sun being pampered with me would be more beneficial to you than a sterile hospital ward. You've only just come out of one, I didn't want to send you straight back. You deserve better than that.'

Victoria was silent for a few seconds thinking about what had happened. 'I didn't really want to die, you know. I just wanted some kind of peace, some kind of ending to my pain. I'm so lucky you came along when you did and that Chloe obviously left the door open by mistake. Maybe I should give her a raise for saving my life.' The last sentence was suffocated with sarcasm.

Evie let out a sigh of incredulity. 'Why do you still employ her if you think she and Scott are at it like rabbits behind your back?'

Victoria shifted position on her sun lounger, a little awkward at the questioning. Could she tell Evie about the painkillers? She already knew about the anti-depressants. She wasn't sure just yet. 'The kids love her.' It was all she could say for now.

It had been a few crazy hours that had followed Evie finding Victoria in the bath. Victoria had cried for a long time, suddenly realising just what might have happened had she let the warm waters of the bathtub take hold for good. Leo and Lexi would have grown up without a mother. She would have never seen those landmark moments that every mother dreams of for her children. Hitting double figures, becoming a teen, first love, first job, seeing them betrothed to another. All of that would have been wiped out for a moment of madness as she sought a painless sanctuary beneath the surface of the water. But her sanctuary would have immediately become her children's prison – the bars to a cell marked 'motherless'. To a lifetime of others saying that Leo and Lexi were the twins with the 'crazy bitch of a mother who had drowned herself selfishly when they were just six'. How could she have been so stupid?

It was Evie who had made the decision. She had packed a few of Victoria's clothes into a suitcase, located her passport and before Victoria could even have time to contemplate whether it was the best course of action, Evie had phoned the film company she was working for and ordered a private jet to be ready and waiting at the nearest airport to take her and her friend to Gran Canaria. What was the point of being one of the most famous actresses on earth if you couldn't play the diva card now and again? She'd told them she was 'a little fatigued' and needed some downtime before the next round of filming. Eager to please their leading lady, the jet was revved up before Evie had even finished packing Victoria's case.

'Do Scott and the twins definitely know we're here?' asked Victoria.

'I've spoken to Scott. They know you're in safe hands. I didn't mention the suicide attempt but I did tell him that I know about him and Chloe. That knocked him for six.'

Victoria sat bolt upright, a spasm of pain leaping through her side as she did so. It caused her to wince. 'Oh my God, what did he say?'

'He was horribly unapologetic. He said the romance had gone from your marriage and that he was having to "re-evaluate the balance of his marriage and work out exactly what he was getting out of it". Once a banker, always a banker, eh? He said not to worry about the kids as "Chloe had everything in hand". I wanted to tear his head off to be honest, but it's not my place, is it?'

Victoria could feel her blood boil. 'Everything in hand? Yes, like his cock for one thing.' Victoria's words were inappropriately loud, causing a young woman lying on the next sun lounger to her to look up in shock. Victoria smiled at her awkwardly. She was sure she recognised her from somewhere, but couldn't quite place her.

Lowering her voice she continued. 'Did Scott mention *the D word*?' She mouthed the phrase in a whisper, aware that they could be overheard.

Evie sat up to face her friend. 'Divorce? Yes, he did. He seems pretty adamant to be honest. He told me about coming home to find the twins crying their eyes out and about when you burned Leo's foot. I don't know what's been going on, Vic, but you have to put the children before everything. You're so lucky to have them and nothing should stop you from putting their welfare first.'

Victoria knew it was true.

Evie's phone vibrated. 'Will you just excuse me, Vic? I need to get this. It's the film company. They're probably wondering when I need the jet to take us back. I'm thinking another couple of days at least, aren't you? I think my *fatigue* might be a little more crippling than I first thought!' winked Evie.

Evie walked off leaving Victoria to contemplate her life back home. The twins would always be her priority but as for Scott ... she really wasn't sure what emotions she housed for him anymore. Did she want to fight for his love in order to save their marriage? Could she trust him again? Could he really end their union just like that? Was their marriage as disposable as a burnt match? And did he want to be with Chloe? Too many questions and for now, in her blurred state, not enough answers. The thought of trying to seek the solutions made her brain ache, but this was one symptom that could not be relieved with a chalky white pill.

The pain in her side was still stabbing. She reached down into her bag and tried to locate her painkillers. In her hurry to leave the house the day before she had just remembered to grab a blister pack at the last moment. The pills weren't there.

'Shit, where the fuck are they?' Again her words were unnecessarily loud given the serenity of her surroundings and the woman alongside her glanced up inquisitively. Victoria curled her lips in an attempt to smile.

Unable to find the pills, she grabbed her room keys from her bag and walked back towards the hotel.

As she was walking through the lobby she heard a voice from the far side of the room. It was hugely familiar.

'If you're after the ultimate body pamper then you could try the Turkish soap brush massage for deep down cleansing, or maybe a diamond dust body peel. And for those who don't want to spend hours lounging around in the sun but still want that dazzling, dynamic healthy looking glow then why not give into the delicious temptation of the Bronceador DHA 100% natural bronzing system. If you'd like to win a weekend here thanks to *Rise and Shine* then all you have to do is answer the following question ...'

'And cut ...' Another voice rang out.

Not that Victoria was listening to the second voice, that of the man behind the camera. She was engrossed by the American twang of Charlie Cooper as he filmed his piece to camera. He was wearing an open-necked shirt and a pair of thigh-hugging shorts. Victoria's eyes were immediately drawn to his crotch again. God, he looked good.

All pain seemed to miraculously disappear from her side as Charlie spotted her and called her name across the lobby, a broad smile spreading across his tanned face. Victoria felt her knees wobble as he revealed a set of perfect white teeth and jogged over.

'Well, look who's here. How are you? We must stop meeting at hotels around the world. First India and now here. People will talk.' Charlie chuckled while Victoria heard her brain silently scream 'let them'.

He kissed her on both cheeks and Victoria was suddenly conscious of her own appearance. Did her hair look okay? Why did she have to bump into him when she was make-up free? Did her flouncy blouse/sarong combo show her off in a flattering light? Thankfully Charlie, ever the flirt, answered her question for her.

'You look great. Nice to see you on the mend. You had us all worried. How are you feeling?'

'Er, I'm f-fine,' stammered Victoria, suddenly strangely nervous and worried that her cheeks would colour at her lie. She figured that telling him she'd tried to commit suicide the day before wouldn't be the best poolside patter.

'So what are you doing here?' enquired Charlie. 'Treating yourself to a few days of QT? You here with your husband and kids?'

Scott was another subject she preferred to gloss over. 'Just a couple of days. I'm here with Evie Merchant. She thought the sun would do us both some good.'

Charlie's smile seemed to spread even further. 'You are kidding me. Evie's here? It was on her recommendation that I came here. She told me about this place when I interviewed her and I told the TV bosses that we should try and run a competition for the viewers to win a trip here. I'm filming a comp slot VT today and then interviewing some soap starlet tomorrow in the Salt Cave.'

Victoria suddenly placed the young woman she'd smiled at earlier. 'So, you're here till tomorrow, then?' Victoria's mind was strangely alive with images of herself and Charlie sipping a cocktail in the candlelit glow of a hidden poolside cabana or indeed of a shirtless Charlie sharing the delights of the resort's famed Salt Cave with her.

'Yes, so if you're around tonight for a drink, then maybe you, me and Evie can get together. Saves me hanging out with Darren the cameraman. Nice guy but I think he wants to hit one of the island's gay clubs anyway.' Charlie motioned to the muscled, tattooed man who had been pointing a camera at him moments earlier.

'That would be fabulous. I'll let Evie know. I was sorry to hear about all of the Mitzi business in Mexico by the way. Seeing the explosion and everything. It's heartbreaking.'

'But it wasn't Mitzi. The body in the wreck was a man. The authorities phoned Georgia. We're all completely stumped now as to what's been going on.'

'But, that makes no—'

Victoria's words were interrupted as Darren, the hulk on the *Rise and Shine* camera called across to Charlie. 'Charlie, love, we have a lot of things to get in the can today, so we'd better crack on.' His voice did not match his frame.

'Shit, I'd better go, but I'll see you both later, okay, and we can talk. Great to see you. Really.' He kissed her on the cheeks again and jogged back over to a waiting Darren, smiling at the knowledge that Victoria was doubtless checking him out.

His cockiness was justified. As Victoria watched Charlie move away, the firm mounds of his backside jiggling slightly within his shorts as he ran, the pain in her side seemed to creep back over. So did the girlish feeling that maybe Scott wasn't the man she wanted to spend her life with after all.

CHAPTER 63

The name of his agent hadn't popped up on his phone for a while, so to see the words *Rachel Jerome* actually appear on his mobile screen for what seemed like the first time in an eternity, took Aaron completely by surprise. What with all of the drama with Devon and Tanya and the fact that he had severed his only form of financial income by quitting his job, all thoughts of pestering his agent for work, sensible though it would have been, had become lost in a sea of wallowing discomfort and the constant tears of his Russian lover. Ever since he and Tanya had walked out of the Bellamy family home, Tanya had been inconsolable.

More by default than as the result of any real planning from either party, Tanya had more or less moved into Aaron's Chelsea apartment, which in theory should have been a dream for Aaron. None of the recent sordid revelations about her chequered past had done anything to dilute his feelings towards her. In fact, if anything, her newly witnessed vulnerability was beginning to make him feel that maybe she had a softer, more loving side nestled up against the sexual tiger. Not that they had really had a chance to discuss anything in any great detail. Tanya had spent days crying into her pillow, unable to cope with her recent fall from grace. Love-making between them had become non-existent, their once fiery passion extinguished by the tears. Aaron, still just a simple hapless bloke in so many ways, was unsure what to do. As so many men had probably reasoned before him, he decided he would have to let Tanya speak to him when she was good and ready. And her tear-stained cheeks and red-rimmed eyes suggested that it may be some time yet.

Which was why Rachel's phone call had come as a welcome relief, the phone sounding as he cradled a sleeping Tanya in his arms. Leaving her to doze, he prayed that Rachel might have good news about the pilot show in America, his thoughts immediately crossing the Atlantic to his glorious time in the Californian sunshine. Maybe that would be just what he and Tanya needed. A new start in a new time zone. Money would be flowing in the land of plenty, surely?

But to Aaron's disappointment, Rachel's news was not about a potential yellow brick road to Los Angeles. 'Still a big jar of silence on that one. Fear not, news will come.' Aaron immediately hated the way that Rachel could be so glib about something so potentially life-changing to him.

'Are you chasing them?' he asked, his tone heavy with setback.

'Darling, you cannot airbrush Hollywood. It does what it wants when it wants. Those telly execs will be phoning I am sure, but in the meantime you have the chance to impress one of them on this side of the pond. I hope you're looking good as I have a photo shoot for you.'

'Not another teeny-tiny hot pants one for some men-only magazine I hope?' said Aaron. 'Those shorts were so tight they were cutting off my circulation.'

'Don't knock it mister, being a gay icon is a very lucrative thing. Bag yourself a decent calendar shoot and we'll be doing mucho-moolah signings in every pink bar from here to Blackpool's Golden Mile. Look at Ben Cohen or that ridiculously handsome Mark Wright. They're hardly ever dressed in anything more than a snug-fit pair of underpants these days, darling. And the gays love it. There's a lot to be said for a heaving chest and a pair of ass cheeks so firm and pert you can rest your Margarita glass on them.'

Aaron had zoned out. 'So what is the photo shoot?'

'Well, I've had Jacob Chevalier on the phone. Lovely man, straight to the point. Reminds me of a male version of me. He's one of the people deciding your fate. Which is why it's super exciting that he called me. He and Nova are here for Evie Merchant's charity bash, which I know you're going to, you lucky man.'

'And?' Aaron was impatient for Rachel to cut to the chase.

'Jacob's organised a photoshoot for Nova at The Pavilion Fashion Rock 'N' Roll Hotel in Hyde Park. It's one of the funkiest hotels in London. Everybody has shot there. Mario Testino did the most marvellous shoot there for *British Vogue*.'

Mario who? thought Aaron. The only one he knew was that plumber bloke from the computer game.

Rachel was on a roll. 'The rooms are themed. It's the most amazing place. There's Casablanca Nights, Indian Summer, Honky Tonk Afro, Enter The Dragon, Cosmic Girl … they're all decorated to perfection and the names have queued up to be seen there – Naomi Campbell, Daft Punk, David Blaine, Leonardo DiCaprio, Kelly Brook …'

At last, names that even Aaron had heard of. Kelly Brook was hot.

'And now they want you, darling! Jacob has hired some of the rooms for a day's shoot, styling Nova in different ways. Like a Bollywood queen for the Indian Summer room, all metallic and spacy for the Cosmic Girl room, you get the drift, and she has requested you as her male model. Apparently you left quite an impression on her. Seems you have buns that leave a good impression on the ladies, too. I've confirmed and sent them your sizes. It's tomorrow, a 9am start and five grand for the day. I take it you have no plans to dig up weeds tomorrow or anything equally as ... er ... horticulturally tragic.'

Despite his annoyance at her condescending tone, at five thousand pounds for the day and the chance to work along-side reality TV goddess Nova Chevalier, Aaron could have been planning to win the Chelsea Flower Show the next day and he would have rearranged. This was too good an opportunity to miss. And the cash would come in very handy. He would need to look his best. He hung up the phone, scribbled a note for a still sleeping Tanya and headed to the gym.

'If you could just open the waistcoat a little further so that we can see your nipples, Aaron.'

As days went, the shoot at the hotel had been particularly surreal. Aaron had started the day stripped to the waist, smeared with silver paint and dressed in foil trousers. This had been for the Cosmic Girl shoot where Nova had been dressed as some sort of slutty Barbarella, her fulsome breasts barely contained under-neath the merest wisps of strategically placed silver ribbon. This had been followed by a turn as a 1970s hippy complete with flares, beads and Peace, Love and Understanding accessories as he writhed against a mini-skirted Nova along the vibrant lime green furry walls of the Honky Tonk Afro room, which came complete with its own glitter ball. And now, as he approached his eighth hour of shooting, Aaron was dressed Aladdin-style in voluminous harem pants, an open waistcoat and a genie's lamp clamped to his hand. Sharing the bed with him in the Indian Summer room was Nova dressed as a scantily-clad genie. It was the final of the three set-ups arranged by Jacob and production assistant, Sarah, who was watching from the corridor outside with Nova's stylist and make-up artist.

The hotel room was jewel-box bright and an exotic mix of crystal lanterns and coloured glass. The tiny bathroom's walls were an edge-to-edge mosaic of smashed mirror. It was a heady assault on the senses and an experience that Aaron was enjoying. There was something he found incredibly refreshing about the *Super Nova* team and he hoped that Jacob was impressed. Maybe it would help him bag the acting job. The more he thought about it, the more it seemed that maybe moving to LA could be the answer to everything. There was a happiness about the sunshine state that he found infectious.

It was a question that he couldn't resist raising as he sat in the hotel lobby area with Nova, Jacob and Sarah after the shoot.

'I've loved today, and I have to say thanks to you guys for making me feel so welcome in LA. I have everything crossed for the pilot show job. Any idea when a decision might be made?' Rachel may have told him that you can't airbrush Hollywood, but surely you could still give it a hint of a tint to hopefully shade it in your direction, given the opportunity.

It was clear though that Jacob was not yet prepared to comment. 'Not as yet.' It would take more than a gentle oiling from Aaron to lubricate this particular wheel into action.

'I hear you were fabulous though,' said Nova. 'I am sure Hollywood will be seeing more of you at some point soon, Aaron. You were the perfect model today and when the network see just how hot you look in the photos they'd be foolish to turn you down.'

Aaron could feel a smile spread across his face from ear to ear.

'Not that we can promise anything, of course,' followed up Jacob.

Aaron's smile disappeared. Even if the signs were good, Jacob was definitely trying to remain professionally tight-lipped.

'Well, you have my vote, Aaron,' said Nova, sipping on her gaudy coloured cocktail. 'That last shot with you as my dashing Indian prince will definitely persuade the bigwigs with the money that *Super Nova* should do a few shows over at the Taj Mahal.'

'For what it's worth, you have my vote too.' It was Sarah the production assistant who spoke, staring directly at Aaron as she did so. She took a mouthful of champagne with more than a hint of suggestion as she completed her sentence. It wasn't lost on Aaron who felt a stirring in his trousers. Thankfully it hadn't happened when he had been wearing the harem pants. At least his jeans could keep any unwanted erection from growing.

'Thank you. So how long have you been working for Mr and Mrs Chevalier, Sarah?'

'How hideously formal,' piped Nova. 'You make us sound like a couple of extras from *Mr Selfridge*.'

Ignoring Nova, Sarah answered the question. 'Er … just a few months. I worked with the previous production assistant …' There was another awkward moment's pause.

'Sarah worked with poor Addison,' stated Nova. 'I trust you heard the awful news about her, Aaron. Such a waste of such a young beautiful life.'

Aaron had indeed heard through Tanya, who had heard about it when Georgia had spoken to Devon. He had been upset as she was a great girl.

'Oh.' It was all he could say. As an afterthought he added, 'Have the police discovered who was behind the attack?'

'Some fucking chancer who preyed on an innocent young girl home alone. Personal belongings were stolen from Addison's flat but they've never been traced.' It was Jacob who gave the report.

'Language, Jacob. Walls have ears. You never know, there may be reporters around the corner.'

'Well, it fucks me off.' He whispered the F word in order to try and appease Nova.

It was up to Nova again to try and lighten the mood. 'Sarah is a marvellous asset to us. She'll be making sure that all of my pre-charity bash needs are catered for. I trust you're going? You had a connection to Mitzi after all? Now she is a mystery, what has happened to the poor girl?'

'I imagine she's dead too, Nova,' said Jacob matter of factly.

'She has been missing for a long time,' added Sarah.

'One must never give up hope, if only to keep the spirits of poor Georgia afloat,' remarked Nova. The thought of her son's girlfriend swayed her mind into another direction. 'Her step-mother is going to the party too. Apparently she's frightfully glamorous and as young as a newborn lamb. Another reason to make sure I look magnificent.'

'Oh, she's my date for the party. I'm going with her,' said Aaron just as Nova was adding, 'Apparently she's pretty frightful full stop, according to Georgia.' Both Aaron's and Nova's sentences were spoken simultaneously, but both loud enough for the other to hear.

'You're taking *that* woman to Evie's charity bash? How can she be your date when she is married to the man who could one day be my son's father in law?'

Aaron didn't know where to begin. 'Things have become a little complicated lately … Tanya and Devon aren't together anymore.'

'Complicated?' barked Nova. 'And you're obviously the reason why, Mr Rose.' It was the first time that Nova hadn't called him by his first name. It hurt to hear. 'Georgia's father must be distraught. Now if you'll excuse me, I think it's time for us to go, don't you Jacob? Sarah, have a driver meet us outside immediately.'

Nova turned to Aaron again. 'Complicated appears to be an understatement, does it not? Home wrecker seems more apt. Despite living in Bel-Air I am actually a huge believer in family values, Mr Rose. Till death do us part and all that.'

As the three Americans left the hotel Aaron couldn't work out exactly what had just happened. He could see the slight look of disappointment on Sarah's face that was maybe because he was dating another woman. He could definitely see the huge disappointment streaked across Nova's face that he was dating Georgia's stepmother. But the biggest disappointment of all was the knotted boulder that gripped his heart telling him that perhaps he had unwittingly just blown his chances with Team Chevalier of bagging his dream job under the gaze of the Hollywood sign.

CHAPTER 64

Victoria added a final light dusting of powder to her cheeks and stared at her reflection in her hotel room mirror. Eyelashes extended and curled to maximum flirtation potential? Check. Long blonde hair pulled back from face and tied into a flowing ponytail, affixed with a neon bright Paul Smith head scarf to compliment the rosy hue that had started to kiss her skin? Check. Loose-fitting blouse and push-up bra combo to demonstrate that her outfit for the evening ahead was one built for a carefree fluidity of movement yet spiced with a hint of exotic sexuality? Check. Well, should she happen to find herself strolling romantically at midnight around the Residencia pool she wanted to be sure that it didn't look like she'd tried too hard to impress, even if her breasts had strayed a little too far into the semi-pneumatic realms of *Dallas Cowboy Cheerleaders* for her own liking. Maybe the purchase of a boob-hoisting bra at the eleventh hour for the evening was a touch too far.

She had thought of nothing but Charlie since their chance meeting earlier. Her mind had been full of his winning smile, his healthy glow, that solid ass. Another fashionable combo.

Evie had been thrilled to hear that Charlie was staying at the hotel too and had booked the three of them a table for dinner at the restaurant terrace overlooking the island's famous sand dunes. It was a stunning view and as Victoria picked at the few final crumbs of her dessert, she watched the sky turn from a deep carmine into an enveloping black on the horizon, suddenly aware of just how impressive her situation was. Or at least how it seemed that way on the outside.

The evening had been joyful. Evie and Charlie were great company. It was only occasionally that Victoria would find herself feeling insecure, worrying, as she listened to her fellow diners' stories that maybe she had no right to be there. What did she have to contribute? How had she, someone who had been part of the amazing melting pot of talent and inspiration that was Farmington Grange ladies' college managed to feel so washed-up at twenty-eight?

As she listened to Charlie talking about his love of Georgia, his hopes for the future and his upcoming work projects she felt that pang of jealousy that had become far too familiar to her. The same occurred when Evie talked of movie offers coming her way and lucrative sponsorship deals.

What was Victoria's future? Her mind started to wander until she felt a hand on her shoulder. It was Evie's.

'Victoria, what's wrong?' Evie moved her hand from Victoria's shoulder and raised it to her friend's cheek. 'You're crying.'

Victoria hadn't been aware that she was, but as she moved her own hands to her cheeks she found that they were both damp with sadness, her inner thoughts of misery manifesting themselves. More pill mood swings perhaps. Or was it genuine sadness? She knew the answer.

'Are you okay? Was it something we said? Is it the stuff with Mitzi?' It was now Charlie's turn to show concern and he placed his hand on her knee. A frisson of excitement shot from her leg and through her nerve endings. Even in her misery, his touch felt good.

Victoria knew that she had to explain.

'I'm sorry, the last thing I want to do is put a dampener on what has been such a lovely evening. I'd like to say it's Mitzi's disappearance making me cry ... but it's not.' She motioned to her tear-stained cheeks. 'This is about me. About what I've become.'

'What do you mean?' asked Charlie.

As Evie gave Victoria a supportive squeeze under the table, Victoria opened the dam that had been keeping the flow of thoughts stemmed inside her head. She began to tell Charlie about everything that had been happening in the Palmer-Roberts household. About Scott, about Chloe, about her reliance on the painkillers, which horrified Evie, and about the possibility of her entire family falling apart. The only thing she kept from her friends was the fact that she had developed feelings for Charlie that she really didn't know how to deal with.

About an hour later, Victoria found herself wandering around the hotel pool with Charlie by her side. They were alone in the moonlight, Evie having had to head back to her room to give a phone interview with an American newspaper about her latest movie. Seeing as she had claimed fatigue in order to spend a few days away with Victoria, she had felt obliged to say she would do an interview for the film company even if it meant that, given the time difference between Gran Canaria and America, it would be midnight when they rang.

Evie had been shocked by Victoria's confession that she was addicted to painkillers and was determined that she would do everything to help wean her friend off them. Money would be no object in finding Victoria the best help possible.

It felt good for Victoria to finally talk about all that had been going on. Like a cleansing of her soul. It hurt to hear the words, the admission of just how screwed up her life currently was, but maybe it was necessary to share in the present in order to fully try and move on with her future. As Evie unwillingly left the table for her interview, she promised Victoria that she would make things better. When a determined Evie Merchant decided to do something, Victoria knew there would be no stopping her. Maybe the actress would be the one to bring Victoria back from the brink of despair. Maybe her next role would indeed be that of Victoria's saviour. The thought gave her hope. Was there light at the end of the painful tunnel that Victoria was currently travelling through?

The pain in Victoria's side made her wince as she walked around the pool with Charlie. He noticed the wave of discomfort spread across her face, causing her to sway slightly.

'Are you okay?' He held out his hands to steady her. Again the frisson returned. Victoria cursed herself inwardly at its appearance.

Victoria tried to toughen herself against the pain. Despite wanting to scream in agony, neither the situation nor the company were right. 'Not really, no,' she said through gritted teeth. Again it felt good to be honest. And controlled. At least having shared her story to Evie and Charlie she felt much more free to be truthful.

'But I'll manage,' she continued, making a mental note to swallow another painkiller as soon as she returned to her room. Going cold turkey in the heat of the Canarian night was not an option just yet.

'That's the spirit,' said Charlie, unsure how to react.

'I think it's the spirit that might be a problem too,' said Victoria. 'I'm not sure Spanish alcohol and tablets are a good mix.' It was true. Her brain still felt somewhat fuzzy from the wine and cocktails that had kept free-flowing during their evening meal.

'Maybe not, but you are going through a lot right now, so you can be forgiven for wanting a drink or two,' reassured Charlie. 'I am really sorry to hear about the divorce. I'm hoping that you guys sort it out, especially for the sake of the kids. You still love him, don't you, despite everything ...' He left the words hanging.

The question stopped Victoria in her tracks. Did she?

Charlie continued. 'After all, you have so much to lose. Those kids of yours need a mother. I grew up well, Nova always looked after me, but the one thing I never had was a solid family unit. You know, the classic mum/dad scenario. And I missed out on it, I reckon. I never knew my real dad. He didn't even know I existed. Then my grandfather, who acted as my dad, died in front of my eyes when I was fifteen and it hurt like hell. That was like losing a limb. Then a few years later, Mum's first husband, Goldman, died too. Again it was like losing a father. It sucked big time and I sometimes think that if it wasn't for the family unit I have now with Nova and Jacob that I could have gone off the rails. Every boy needs a father figure, no matter what their age. And the same for a girl. Lexi will always need a mother figure and that's you. You adore your kids don't you?'

'Of course I do.' Victoria almost snapped the answer, affronted that the idea could even be questioned.

'And Scott?'

'Oh, he adores the twins too. No doubt.'

'That's not what I meant. I meant do you adore him?'

Again that question. This time, Charlie waited for an answer.

'I did. I loved him with all of my heart when we got married. I chose him above everything else. I had plans, dreams, places I wanted to go and work, but they didn't matter. I gave him everything I could.'

'You don't walk into love, you fall in,' said Charlie. 'That's why it's so hard to get out. That's if you really want to.'

'Aren't you the regular Maury Povich?' deadpanned Victoria.

'Or Jeremy Kyle, depending on which side of the Atlantic you are,' replied Charlie.

'Hopefully I have a better orthodontist than half the people who appear on that show,' smiled Victoria.

'That is a given,' said Charlie, placing his hand under her chin and raising Victoria's face to mock-check her teeth. Did Victoria imagine it or was his hand pressed against her flesh a little longer than was actually necessary? She pushed the thought aside.

'Do you love each other now?' asked Charlie, releasing her chin.

'He loves the nanny, it seems.'

'Does he? He's thinking with his pants, not with his head. He's cheating on you with her for sex. Do you really believe there is more to it than that?'

'But he can have sex with me.' Victoria felt her cheeks blush as she said it.

'And have you been?' It was a blunt question from Charlie, but one that hit home straight away.

'No.' It was all that she needed to say out loud. She thought of the times that Scott had tried to instigate sex between them. The number of times that she had refused because of a lack of confidence in her own body. Or because of how spaced out she was from the anti-depressants. Had she pushed Scott into Chloe's arms? Deep down, she reckoned that perhaps she had.

'I don't think either you or Scott want this divorce. Maybe it's time to start fighting back.'

'But he has betrayed me. His infidelity had destroyed me.'

'Love is giving someone the power to destroy you but trusting them not to. Scott has hurt you. But if you really want to keep your marriage alive you have to push his infidelity to one side. To win him back and make him see you as the beautiful wife and mother you are. Holding a grudge is letting someone live rent free inside your head. Nobody benefits.'

'But how stupid will I look trying to win him back now that people know what he's done to me?'

'I'm not condoning his actions, but there are two sides to every story and you and Scott need to sit down and work out what you actually want to say to each other. And don't do it through a solicitor. You need to work out if you both think there is something worth fighting for. And as for friends judging you … who gives a flying fuck what they think? Fake friends believe in rumours, whereas real friends believe in you. Now, I think it's time we turned in, don't you? I have a rendezvous with a soap starlet at the crack of dawn and a flight back to the UK to catch mid-morning. It's been fantastic to talk and I hope that things work out for you, Victoria, I really do. You deserve it. And so do your kids.'

Charlie took her hand and bent to kiss her goodnight on the cheek. Whether it was the fact that he had called her beautiful, or the sympathy she felt about his childhood, his wise words of comfort and wisdom or just the fact that she found him incredibly gorgeous, something idiotic snapped within Victoria. As his lips brushed against her cheek, she swiftly maneuvered her head so that his lips came into contact with hers. Without thinking about what she was doing, she let her lips open and wrapped her other hand around the back of his head, pulling him urgently towards her. Her intent was clear.

But her advances were rejected, Charlie dropping her hand and pushing himself away from her as quickly as he could.

'Whoa … what are you doing?' Even for a serial flirt like Charlie this was not as planned. He'd not been leading her on tonight, he knew he hadn't.

Victoria regretted her actions immediately. 'I am so sorry, I didn't mean to …' She floundered over her words, unsure what to say.

Charlie was visibly taken aback but understanding in his reply. 'It's the drink, and your pain … and your confusion.'

'I am so sorry.' As she stared at Charlie she suddenly realised just how idiotic she had been to think that there could be any chance of a hint of romance between them.

'It's forgotten,' said Charlie. 'You know I love Georgia. And deep down I reckon you know that you love Scott still too.'

'But, after everything …' stumbled Victoria.

'As I said before, Victoria, there are two sides to every story. We've all done stupid things that we regret later.' There was a moment of silence between them before he added. 'Haven't you just proved that?'

Victoria knew that he was right.

CHAPTER 65

Victoria's return to the UK was just as quick as her departure had been. Before Charlie had even finished asking a series of innocuous questions to the soap starlet lying poolside in the skimpiest of bikinis live on *Rise and Shine* the next morning, Victoria and Evie had touched down on British soil and been chauffeured directly to The Abbey Rehabilitation Centre, set within two hundred acres of lush English countryside.

But this was to be no rural picnic. Evie had dealt with the centre in the past and knew of many celebrity colleagues who had booked themselves into the palatial splendour of The Abbey in an attempt to unhook themselves from an addiction that was ruining their life. It was the number one rehab centre in the land for a reason. It worked. And results cost thousands. But luckily for Evie, and more so for Victoria, money wasn't a problem. Evie was determined to nurse her friend back to full health, no matter what the price tag.

Having found Victoria crying into her pillow with pain in her hotel room during the night, an empty blister packet of painkillers staring up at her, Evie knew that she had to do something. And that she had to do it fast. If Victoria was out of painkillers – her wretched cries to Evie to find her some more on the island immediately proved that she was – then there wasn't a moment to waste. Evie had seen it before. People desperate for their next fix, no matter what the drug. Immediately

The Abbey came to mind. If she took Victoria home, Chloe would be furnishing her with painkillers straight away. And a continued addiction was the last thing Victoria needed to try and save her marriage.

Despite Victoria's protests, the pair of them left for the airport and travelled home. It was only once back on UK soil that Evie told Victoria about her plan to take her to The Abbey.

By the time the sun rose fully over the British countryside, Victoria was booked in and ready to begin the slow road to recovery. As Charlie's sun-soaked interview went to air, both Victoria and Evie were crying. Victoria was in tears of pain as she contemplated the hardship of tearing herself away from the medicinal crutch that was her painkillers and Evie shed a solitary tear at the heartache her friend was set to endure, as she was driven away from The Abbey. Before leaving, she had given strict instructions that no-one was to contact or visit Victoria. And that included Scott and the children. She would let Scott know exactly what had been going on, including Chloe's narcotic handouts. She was determined to save Victoria's marriage, whatever it took. After all, that was what friends were for.

'It's a good job I trust your son implicitly,' grinned Georgia as she watched Charlie wrapping up his interview with the soap star. 'I'm sure every virile heterosexual man in the land will be leching like crazy looking at her in that bikini.'

'A girl has to do what a girl has to do,' said Nova, staring at the TV screen affixed to the wall in front of both her and Georgia as they sat in the *Rise and Shine* green room. Nova had already been interviewed on the show that morning. It was her only TV appearance since arriving in the UK, her allegiance being to the show which had made her son a star.

Georgia had accompanied her to the studios as she had some work emails to catch up on and needed to see her boss about extending her time off until the mystery of Mitzi had been solved. Georgia wasn't stupid and knew that having her potential mother-in-law with her when she begged for more time off would stand her in good stead with her bosses. Nothing upped your brownie points like having the biggest TV star in the world alongside you as you went on bended knees asking for more time away from the weatherboards of the land. They had no choice but to agree or look spitefully mean.

'We've all worn next to nothing in our time,' said Nova, trying to work out just which designer name was behind the bikini. If they made one a little larger she would be featuring that in the next season of *Super Nova*. 'And you have nothing to worry about with Charlie, my dear, he worships you and rightly so.'

'And I him,' sighed Georgia. Maybe the wedding that Nova longed for wouldn't be that far into the future. Charlie had only been gone for about thirty-six hours but already she was missing her fiancé like crazy. Her longing for him grew stronger every time they were apart.

'Right then, darling girl, shall I order the car to pick us up? This early morning TV stuff has given me a hunger. How about breakfast at The Dorchester?' mused Nova. 'We need to discuss that dreadful Tanya woman shacking up with Aaron Rose. He may be hugely attractive but I am regretting using him for my photo shoot now that I find out that he's taken her from your poor father. Families, eh? Mind you, he did look divine.'

The idea pleased Georgia. Not the thought of Aaron's perfect body, and certainly not the thought of her father's wife – she still hadn't told Nova about the revelations about Tanya's past, maybe over eggs at The Dorchester would be the ideal opportunity.

They were just leaving the green room when Georgia's phone pinged, signaling an incoming email. 'I'll just check that, it could be work and if it is then I might as well deal with it while I'm in the building,' said Georgia.

It wasn't work. It was from her father, Devon. 'Georgia, the maid just turned up and showed me this. It's on some celebrity website today. Her daughter saw it and thought I should know. I trust you've seen it. What the hell ...? Does nobody have any morals these days? Love Dad.'

'What are you on about, Dad?' she mused to herself. As she scrolled down the email she realised what he was talking about. As she saw it, her legs turned to jelly and she fell weakly to the green room floor, as if she had been punched in the stomach. The action caused Nova to scream and the other guests in the green room, a *Real Housewife Of Cheshire* and a glamour model turned bodybuilder to come running to her aid.

'Oh my goodness, Georgia, are you okay?' squealed Nova, not sure what to do. With the help of the other two guests they lifted a silent Georgia to the green room sofa. 'What is it, what's the matter?'

Without saying a word, Georgia showed the phone to Nova. The picture on the screen was instantly recognisable as the pool they'd just been watching on the television minutes before, except it was a nighttime shot. At the centre of the shot, clearly visible in the moonlight and in the glow of the bulbs around the pool were Charlie and Victoria. Her hand was behind his head, pulling him close as their lips touched.

Underneath the photo was the caption 'CHEEKY CHARLIE WILL BE HEADING FOR STORMY WEATHER WITH GIRLFRIEND GEORGIA.'

Nova's scowl as she surveyed the photo was dark enough to equal the heaviest of rainclouds.

'We've leaving now, Georgia, come on,' she barked, aware of prying eyes and flapping ears within the room. 'And I suggest you get that son of mine on the phone right now, don't you?'

CHAPTER 66

Scott made a fourth attempt at trying to tie his bow tie using the smallest of mirrors balanced on his office desk.

'Shit, why can't I get this fucking thing to tie properly?' he asked his reflection. 'Where is Victoria when I need her?'

She had always been the one who secured his tie neatly into place when they had an important function to go to. She was always the one who had done a lot of things for him over the course of their marriage. Only she could manage to make his flyaway curls sit right on his head, only she could charm the stuffy suits he needed to schmooze so that they were financial putty in his hands, only she would belly laugh at his sometimes rather puerile jokes. Only Victoria.

But she wasn't there. He'd not seen her since her admittance into The Abbey over a week ago. And if he carried on with the divorce proceedings then he wouldn't be seeing a lot of her at all, especially if his request for full custody of Lexi and Leo was granted. She'd be all but out of their lives. And even though her behaviour lately had been nigh on life-threatening to the children with her wild rants and blank space moments, he had to admit that the simple fact that he was unable to see her and have her in his life had made him long for the normality they had once shared.

Scott stared down at the professional family portrait on his office desk and cast his mind back to the day it was taken. When

was it? Two years ago, maybe three? They had all been so happy. Lexi had insisted on combing her mother's hair into place
a hundred times before the photographer had been allowed
to even snap the first frame. His daughter had also insisted on
wearing a puffy, bright red, frilled dress for the photo, despite
her mum wanting her to wear something 'a little less *Gypsy Wedding*' but Lexi loved it and beamed with delight in the photo.
Leo too looked a picture of happiness as he smiled out from
the photograph, his ruddy cheeks, butterscotch blonde hair
and gap-toothed grin a winning combination. Scott smiled as
he remembered how proud Leo had been that one of his front
teeth had been knocked out when he'd fallen off his tricycle the
day before the shoot. Victoria had been horribly upset, but Leo
loved it, showing off his ejected gnasher to all of his friends.

Scott felt his eyes mist over as he looked at how beautiful
and proud his wife was in the grouping. She really was the glue
that held them together. When had that glue lost its hold? How
could he have let such a wonderful unit of strength and love fall
apart so easily? When had he started to take it all for granted and
let it slip away? And let Victoria slip away from him?

The last week had been a tortuous one for Scott, unable to
see his wife. There were so many things he needed to say to her.
Evie had read him the riot act over the phone and he had to admit that for the first time in a long while the words had actually
hit home as intended. His dalliance with Chloe may have been a
satisfactory one between the sheets but even he knew that there
was no depth or longevity to it. He didn't love her. He'd never
given her any indication otherwise. He liked fucking her that
was for sure, but was his marriage and the break-up of the family
worth risking for the minutes of satisfaction he would achieve
from emptying his seed into the hired help?

The rage he'd seen in Victoria had shocked him but he was able to understand a bit more about the reasons for it now that he knew his wife was addicted to the painkillers on top of anti-depressants. Painkillers that were supplied to her illegally by the woman he'd been having an affair with. A stupid, silly, idiotic, pathetic affair. That's all it was.

Scott had confronted Chloe about the pills. She had cried and admitted that she had been blackmailed into supplying them by Victoria. It was them or lose her job. Scott could understand why she had done what she had, but he didn't like it. A part of him blamed Chloe for aiding his wife's erratic behaviour. If she had said no, not offered in the first place, then maybe things wouldn't have become so out of control and snowballed to their current state. Hindsight was always such a wonderful thing.

So why was Scott taking Chloe to Evie Merchant's black-tie charity bash that evening? Victoria would be there. It would be her first outing since her admittance to The Abbey. Not that he'd been told that, but he knew his wife well enough to know that she would not want to let Evie down if it was at all possible. And seeing as his wife's photograph had been plastered over several newspapers over the last week in a clinch with her supposed new beau, Charlie Cooper, her appearance would doubtless fill a few column inches which would help keep the ongoing disappearance of Mitzi Bidgood in the public eye. Scott could feel his heckles rise at the thought of Charlie. He didn't even know him and he disliked him. There was nothing like a serving of masculine competition to make you realise what you'd been missing.

Scott gave up on his fifth attempt to fix his bow tie and let it dangle around his neck. Chloe would have to tie it for him when he arrived at the event. He'd told her he'd meet her there as he needed to finish some work at the office. It felt wrong taking Chloe, but if he was to believe the papers that Victoria and Charlie were indeed wrapped up in each other, then he was buggered if he was turning up without a woman on his arm. Now that would be stupid, silly, idiotic and pathetic. Even if he was rapidly realising that Chloe was not the woman he'd really like to be there with.

Scott ran his hand through his mass of curls on his head and gave one last check in the mirror before leaving the office. 'Shit, even my hair doesn't look right without Victoria,' he tutted as he closed his office door behind him.

Charlie and Jacob stood alongside each other at the double sink in one of the huge bathrooms at the Kensington mansion Jacob shared with Nova in London. They too were making unnecessary last minute touches to their outfits before heading off to Evie's event. The two men had been ready for the best part of an hour already but seeing as Nova and Georgia were still busy mid lipstick, powder and paint in one of the mansion bedrooms with Nova's personal make-up artist, the men were trying to fill their time by slight repositioning of pocket handkerchiefs and yet another spritz of cologne.

'Christ knows what time Nova will be ready,' joked Jacob as he wet his fingers and ran them along his eyebrows in the mirror. 'But she has insisted that the make-up has to be spot-on tonight for this event. It is the reason we're here after all, and doubtless she'll be working those paparazzi like a playful kitten with a ball of wool. Your mother is a very skilled woman, Charlie, and one not to be messed with.'

'Tell me about it, Jacob, I thought she was going to tear my head off when I flew back from Gran Canaria. That was not a kitten with a ball of wool; that was a rampaging lioness with the most weakened of antelopes. I've never seen such disappointment in her eyes. Thank Christ it wasn't true.'

'You wouldn't be the first man to stray into the arms of another woman, Charlie. In LA infidelity is a badge dished out at summer camp. It's what most people expect, sad though I am to admit it,' laughed Jacob. 'So Nova gave it to you with both barrels, then?'

'And rightly so, given what she saw in that photo of Victoria and me. I can't believe the sodding camera guy I was working with took it on his phone and then sold it to his mate on some website. Stupid prick. People will do anything for a fast buck. The photo did look pretty incriminating, but I flirt for a living. I can't help it. Both Mum and more importantly, Georgia, have my word that an innocent kiss was all it was. At least from me anyway. I've told Georgia the whole story about what's been going on with Victoria and her husband and how things have been spiralling out of control for her and how she simply misread my friendship for something else. Victoria was mortified. I am sure she'll be even more so now that photos have been plastered across websites and papers. It's hardly going to help her divorce, is it?'

'If it turns nasty in court you could be dragged into it all, Charlie. Hubby shagging the nanny, her kissing famous TV man in some sun-soaked destination. It's all very *Revenge* isn't it?'

'That won't happen. I know the truth, as does Victoria and thankfully both Georgia and Mum believe me. I have too much to lose and I adore Georgia with every bone in my body. I wouldn't jeopardise that for anything.'

'I knew my ears were burning, especially under the weight of these rocks ...' Georgia appeared in the doorway of the bathroom, her body covered in the most gorgeous satin two-piece.

The white of her top, teamed with the red of her three quarter length skirt was a flirty, hypnotic joy. The mere sight of her
caused both Charlie and Jacob to open their mouths in unison.

'Wow! You look incredible,' said Charlie.

'Seconded,' piped Jacob.

'Thirded,' grinned Georgia, a smile coated across her face.
'Even if I say so myself. Well, I was thinking, I do have the pages
of every newspaper in the land to appear in, with my delicious
boyfriend at my side, just to prove all of those silly rumours
wrong, don't I? So, a satin two-piece from Sachin & Babi, a top
Hollywood make-up and enough bling on my ears to tempt every ex-crim on the Costa Del Crime to come out of retirement
seemed to be the best combination. Plus I have the ultimate
accessory in you in that dinner jacket, Charlie Cooper. You look
seriously sexy.'

Georgia walked across the bathroom floor in her heels and
planted a kiss firmly on Charlie's lips. 'You are mine, all mine.
All night long. For a lifetime … despite what the papers may
think.'

'Okay, too much information, feeling a little bit awkward
standing here,' joked Jacob. 'I think I may need to find my accessory. Is she ready yet?'

Georgia let out a laugh.

'Well, let's just say that she may be a little longer. When I
left her she was just contemplating a third attempt at her make-
up. Apparently tonight is all important for Nova and she was
wasn't quite satisfied with the first two attempts, so she's asking,
or rather *forcing* the make-up lady to start again. I'm not sure
what's redder right now, Nova's lipstick or the poor girl's angry
face. I'd give her another thirty minutes … at least.'

'What Nova wants, Nova gets,' said Jacob. 'Thank God I
love that woman. As long as she's happy at the end of it, then

we'll wait as long as it takes. Now, I'll go and pour some fizz for us all.'

Charlie smiled as Jacob left the bathroom. He pulled Georgia close to him.

'We're happy, aren't we? I couldn't imagine a life without you.'

'Me neither,' said Georgia, her voice soft and layered with joy. 'Despite that bloody photograph. I can't believe your flaming camera guy stitching you up like that. And as for that woman … I am trying to understand, but it will be hard to see her face to face if she's there tonight.' The joy in her voice was replaced by dislike.

Charlie glossed over the mention of Victoria and returned to the subject of the disloyal colleague. 'His loss in the end. Now, talking of stitches, how does this little satin number come off? We could have a little fun if my mother is still not going to be ready for another thirty minutes.' Charlie looped his hand around Georgia's back and reached for the satin skirt's zip. His hand was flicked away by a smiling Georgia.

'Woah, handsome. At ease. This skirt is going nowhere. And you are not messing up this make-up for any kind of deep, depraved pleasure, despite how appetising that might be. I think the make-up lady redoing one person from scratch is enough for her, don't you, poor woman?'

Charlie could feel his erection pressing urgently against the inside of his trousers. He didn't subside as Georgia led him from the bathroom by his bow tie.

'Now, let's grab that fizz,' grinned Georgia. 'And that …' she said, spotting his erection through his trousers, 'can come see me at the end of the night when we make sure every paper and mag in the land has a photo of you and me for the morning. In *Heat* first, on heat later.'

Aaron pushed his middle finger down behind the winged collar of his shirt and the bow tie nestled there and pulled it away
from his neck in an attempt to breathe. He felt awkward. Suits
were not his thing and bow ties certainly weren't. He was more
of an open-necked polo shirt kind of guy so having to dress up
like some kind of posh office Johnny was not sitting easy with
him.

'This bloody thing is too tight. It's strangling me.'

'Then loosen it off a hole or two,' remarked Tanya, watching
Aaron's reflection in the mirror as he became increasingly exas-
perated by his neckwear.

'How do these things even work? You're lucky I didn't buy a
clip-on for tonight. At least I can pop that on and off with ease.'

Aaron yanked at the tie, unhooking it on one side. He sighed
through gritted teeth as he did so, happy that his thick neck
could relax a little and feel less choked.

Tanya couldn't help but stare. What a difference between the
man stood before her and the man she was married to. Two
opposite ends of the style ballroom and as she stared at Aaron,
despite his deep, masculine, sexual appearance, she couldn't help
but find her mind waltzing to the other end of the imaginary
dance floor and wondering what Devon was doing right at that
moment.

As it happened, Devon was thinking of her too as he stared
into their bedroom mirror. He had just finished expertly fixing his bow tie into place. It was one of those things that every
man should have. Especially in this day and age where bow ties
seemed to be popping up everywhere. He'd turned on the TV

the other day and seen some juvenile from a boy band wearing one. It had obviously been Tanya who had last been watching the television. She loved the music channels. Devon actually had to admit he missed the noise, not any particular song or group, just the mere presence of his wife watching some kind of loud, anarchic, beat-laden sound. It gave the house a sense of life, breathed a youthful heartbeat into what had become a pretty empty shell since she had left with Aaron.

That man. No class. Would he be there tonight? He suspected he would be. Christ, he'd be in a bow tie too, no doubt. The irony. Devon was of the school of thought that a bow tie hinted at intellectualism and technical acumen, not the ability to surf and spot a nettle at twenty paces. Bow ties were for lawyers, professors, country doctors, not grubby gardeners. Devon hated that man. He should hate his young wife for being with him, but he didn't. She'd learn, she'd know what was best for her. He'd make her see.

Checking his reflection one final time, Devon was pleased with his innate sense of style and flair. He looked good. No-one could compete. No-one.

Scott let the early evening air caress his face and the slight breeze run through his hair as he headed across the car park to his vehicle at the back of his office block. He'd drive to Evie's event. He needed to be at work early in the morning and to be honest, he thought it would be best if he kept a clear head if both Chloe and Victoria were in the same room together. Now that the truth was out, there was a lot to discuss and countless flutes of champagne would not help the situation. He needed to be sure about what he was saying, because deep down he knew what it needed to be.

Scott's mind wandered to what he planned to say. He was only a couple of sentences in when he felt the weight of a fist connecting with his face. He could hear the crunch of his nose as it gave way under the weight of the heavy object smashing against his skin.

His legs buckled underneath him and he made a vain attempt to look up at his assailant as the coldness of the concrete swept across his body. The last thing he saw was a foot swinging towards him and smashing into his face. As the metallic flavour of blood flowed across his taste buds and everything wrapped in black, Scott was vaguely aware of thinking what a very smart shoe it was for a mugger.

CHAPTER 67

Every inch of the tomb she was in was becoming familiar to her. The blackness had turned to the darkest of greys. She could see the four walls, the steps, the bareness of everything else. The food she had been left was virtually gone. The water jug she had been supplied with was nearing empty. The one thing that wasn't was the bucket that shared her cell. The squalid mixture of urine and feces was nearing the top. Why wasn't someone coming to empty it like before? The stranger who she had grown to hate, the person stopping her once vibrant life from having any light, any joy, any hope. It was clear she was alone.

The only stitch of colour in the throw of darkness came from the small rectangular outline of light around the outside of the door at the top of the steps. With what little strength she still possessed, she had managed to pull herself up the steps and rest her body against the door. Walking was no longer an option, her legs hollow with fatigue.

She pressed her ear up against the crack of light and listened to see if any noise was coming from the other side. It wasn't. The crack was too small to see through but she knew that whatever was on the other side was light. Escape. Freedom. It may as well have been another galaxy as there was no way she could get there.

Pressing her nails, or what was left of them, into the hairline of light, she attempted to scrape away at the wall. Miniscule pieces of it gave way and fell across her fingers and onto the floor. For a few short seconds there was hope. A sliver of something to live for at the end of the end of the tunnel. But then the pieces stopped. She carried on scraping, her nails and fingers starting to bleed as she dug them as far as she could into the crack around the door. Nails that used to be so pristine, so beautifully painted.

Any force she had left within her was zapped within seconds. Her focus on the crack seem to fade. Was this it? Was this death creeping towards her? After the shortest, brightest of lives, was this how it was to end? She prayed not, willing thoughts of herself at school, kissing her first boyfriend, euphoric nights out with friends into her mind. That was another lifetime. One to which she could no longer relate. Images of happier times were replaced with the horror of the night that had passed just a while before. The heat of the night air, the heat of her burning core, the heat of a stranger's breath as she was manhandled away.

But her prayers stopped as her eyes closed and she rolled back down the stairs and across the stone floor. Only the bucket slowed her momentum as she crashed into it unaware. The dark toxic liquid inside sloshed from side to side and then emptied itself across the floor as the bucket fell on its side. She was mercifully oblivious as the contents splashed up against the wall and then ran back towards her soaking her already filthy clothes.

CHAPTER 68

Evie Merchant had never intended for her charity party to be a media frenzy. That had not been the idea at all. It was to raise money for charity and to raise awareness about the ongoing disappearance of Mitzi Bidgood.

But as Evie's car pulled up in front of the event, even she, as an award ceremony veteran who had seen many a crowd, was amazed by the sea of flashing lights and inquisitive reporters standing outside the venue flanking the red carpet.

As she stepped out of her car and a barrage of questions fired at her, Evie took stock in her head. Normally red carpets meant questions about her latest film, lovers both on-screen and off and her predictions for Oscar season. She would just talk about Mitzi. Let the press report on that in the morning. She knew how to work them. Every ceremony from the BAFTAs to the Brits had taught her well.

Little did Evie know that as the first question about the event fired her way and she gave a clear, concise, controlled answer, that reports in the next day's press would hardly mention Mitzi at all. The night was set to be remembered for a completely different reason altogether. One over which the actress would have no control whatsoever.

CHAPTER 69

Jack Christie had always been told that one of the major secrets of being a good criminal was the art of timing. Picking the right moment to get the job done. Nothing was impossible in his mind, and it was an opinion he shared with Andy North as they perched behind the wheelie bins at the back of the event venue.

As Jack would say, 'We just need to bide our time.'

The two men had been staking the venue ever since Chloe had delivered the invitation to them several days before. Despite being dressed in head-to-toe Savile Row and certainly looking the part, there was no way the two of them were risking entering into the building along the red carpet. Too many cameras and too many chances of being discovered afterwards. It would only take one pap shot of a frocked-up reality TV star with a couple of dodgy looking crims skulking around in the background to put two and two together and make a connection that could see both of them back behind bars. And the only bars they intended to be seen near in the future were the boozer dives near their beloved flat.

Mind you, if tonight went well, then maybe they'd be trading the flat in for something a little swankier. Jack had been watching a lot of those *A Place In The Sun* type shows and maybe a villa in the sunshine of Ibiza or a bolt hole in Majorca would be the perfect place to get smashed, trashed and gashed. The women would love it and flock to them like bees around a honey pot.

Plus it was pretty much party season all year round. And that was win-win in Jack's eyes.

But tonight needed to be a success first, and for that to happen both he and Andy needed to work out how to gain entry to the venue.

Which is why they had been hovering together behind the wheelie bins for about twenty minutes waiting for their moment. The pair of them had seen caterers and event organisers coming and going all week, using the back entrance to prep the venue. Andy had been watching and waiting for a good thirty minutes before Jack had even arrived and had already seen ice sculptures, floral arrangements and crates of booze being delivered. It promised to be a brilliant party in more ways than one.

The men had also seen various members of the waiting and catering crew standing outside every now and again for a crafty cigarette. It was this that picked at both Jack and Andy's criminal minds.

They had watched one young woman in particular. Slightly overweight, her hair was tied back into a bun in a style not overly flattering to her moon-shaped face and a pair of horn-rimmed glasses perched on her nose. She couldn't have been more than about twenty in age and she kept popping outside for a sneaky puff with almost synchronised timing. Just by herself, not really speaking to anyone, it seemed, and somewhat glum at the thought of having to work. 'Dowdy' would be the word on most people's lips. But every twenty minutes, there she was. As she made her latest appearance, Jack and Andy swooped into action.

Moving towards the back door, they both lit up a cigarette and joined the woman. Their arrival didn't appear to shock her and she summoned up a one-word greeting. 'Alright?'

'Hello there, gorgeous,' opened Jack, his proclamation bringing a smile to the girl's face and a smudge of red to her cheeks.

'You're a dirty smoker like us too? That's why we crept round the back, we can't be seen having a ciggie on the red carpet. Not good for the career. One pap shot in the papers and we'll be strung up and never touched in Hollywood again.'

'Why? What do you do?'

'You don't recognise us, darling?'

The girl shrugged as she took a long drag on her cigarette. 'No, should I?'

'Only if you've seen any of our films. We're both action stars in Hollywood. We've been working with Evie Merchant.'

'Who?'

Jack and Andy smiled at each other. If she didn't even know the name of the award-winning party host then getting her to believe that they were Hollywood royalty would be a breeze. They'd picked her as she didn't look clued up and their instincts had been right. This was going to be like taking candy from a baby.

'Yeah, we've just finished working on *Expendables 5*, or was it *4*, I don't know?' joked Jack. 'Could have been number *12* for all I know. We just turn up, blow a few shooters and get paid a fortune. Stallone, The Rock, all the muscle greats. You a fan?'

'No, I like sci-fi, that's it.'

'We're supposed to epitomise health and fitness so we can't be seen with these.' Both Andy and Jack consciously stubbed out their cigarettes as the girl did the same to hers. 'Right, we'd better get into the party. Here's our invitation.' Jack reached into his pocket and pulled out the piece of card.

'Can we crash through here, sexy? It'll save us working our way down the red carpet answering shedloads of as-dull-as-bat-shit questions.'

'Please yourselves. Are you famous then? What are your names so I can tell my mum?'

'You tell her you met Jack Daw and Tommy Thrush, alright.'

Andy let out a cough of hilarity at his made-up name. Surely the girl would realise they were taking the piss?

She didn't. As the two men walked through the corridors at the back of the building and made their way into the main arena of the venue where A-list guests were already gathering, nobody questioned why they were there. They looked the part and their timing had been perfect. The girl was back stacking plates in the kitchen trying to remember the names of the actors who had called her sexy by the time Jack and Andy picked up their first flute of champagne.

It was only as Jack raised his glass to his mouth that Andy commented on the appearance of his bloodied knuckles and the bruised skin around his jackdaw ring. 'You might want to clean that up, mate, looks a bit sore, what you been up to?'

'Just had a little something I needed to do on the way here. Hold that, I'll just go and clean up.' He handed Andy his drink.

'And you might want to clean your shoes up and all,' stated Andy. 'They look scuffed to hell. This is supposed to be a posh do.'

Jack looked down at his shoes. Andy was right. 'Fuck, kicking the crap out of someone ruins your frigging leather,' he moaned to himself as he headed to the toilet. Still, with the money coming his way after tonight, The Jackdaw could buy as many pairs of designer shoes as he flaming well pleased.

CHAPTER 70

Victoria was feeling mixed emotions. On one side she was feeling elated that, thanks to her treatment at The Abbey Rehabilitation Centre over the past week, she was feeling both brighter and more in control of her own body than she had in a long while. The past few days had been hideous and hard, but worth every agonising moment as she had been taught about coping with the pain in her side and dealing with it without reaching for another of her little white tablets. Or at least *those* little white tablets. According to the experts at The Abbey it had been those that had sent her brain into meltdown and made her emotions so erratic. For a while Victoria's life would have to be withdrawal assistance drugs and incremental dosage reduction but if that was what it would take to put her life back on the straight and narrow and maybe bring her family back together, then so be it. She would do everything required to keep herself away from her former drug-addled state. There were too many people that she didn't want to disappoint. She'd spent too much time doing that recently and it was time for it to stop.

That was why she had come to the party. It would be a challenge but one that she wanted to face full on. Evie had believed in her and given her the help she required. If it hadn't been for her famous friend, she would have ended her life as a corpse in a bathtub full of tepid water. Her children would have only been able to be close to her at her graveside. At least while she had life, she still had hope.

The red carpet was an obstacle course for Victoria. A few days ago she was unknown, and would have been able to glide down it with ease, ignored by the scavenging reporters and click-happy photographers. But after that photo of her and Charlie in Gran Canaria had been posted across the media she was somebody who could give their hungry minds answers. Was there something between her and Charlie? Was she competition for Georgia? Had it gone beyond kissing? What did her husband think of it all?

Victoria knew that tonight was the night when she would have to face so many of those she had hurt, and indeed those who had hurt her. Charlie, Georgia, Nova, Jacob, Scott, Chloe, Evie. All in one place. Her brain told her not to attend, the sensible side of her mind saying that she was entering the gates of Hell, and that given her somewhat fragile state, she risked more than simply having her fingers burned.

But this was a new Victoria. One who was indeed determined to take pole position once again and have some pride in her existence. As she walked down the red carpet, her Erdem print dress framing her inwardly-weakened body to perfection, to the outside world she seemed strong and sure of herself. She ignored every question that was fired at her, knowing that if she did start to talk her voice would wobble with nerves. Hadn't she always longed for some kind of notoriety? When she'd left Farmington Grange hadn't she wanted to succeed? To one day be in the spotlight like her friend Evie, like Mitzi, like Georgia? Well, now, for all the wrong reasons, she was. She was the centre of attention and as she moved off the red carpet and into the warmth of the event, the cries of the reporters still baying like cattle behind her, Victoria would have swapped all of that attention for a lifetime cuddled up on the sofa watching *Bake Off* or *Sewing Bee* with Scott and the children by her side.

And she knew that the warmth of the venue was about to turn icy cold as she faced so many people that she needed to say sorry to. How ironic that a harpist in the venue lobby was playing 'Sorry Seems To Be The Hardest Word' as she spotted Nova, Georgia, Jacob and Charlie ahead of her. Mixed emotions indeed.

CHAPTER 71

Jack's evening was running like clockwork. In fact it was running better than he had even dared hoped.

He and Andy had already managed to dip their fingers into a variety of coat pockets at the venue cloakroom. The original plan had been to try and sneak in there when the attendant on duty wasn't looking but when their dowdy cigarette loving friend from the back door had appeared as the night's chosen cloakroom worker – a surprising choice given the grandeur of the occasion but a welcome one nevertheless – Andy and Jack could pretty much come and go as they pleased as long as they gave her a cheery 'hello gorgeous' or winked at her as they went in. In her delirious state of adulation about having met 'Jack Daw' and 'Tommy Thrush' she seemed oblivious to the fact that neither man had arrived with a coat or that they seemed incredibly forgetful when it came to 'just fetching my glasses/ciggies/raffle tickets/lighter' or whatever excuse they managed to concoct next. Seeing as they were the only people that had actually noticed her existence all night she was more than overjoyed for them and their cheery compliments to come and go as they pleased, oblivious to their thieving hands in coat pockets and handbags that were laden down with wallets and purses, unneeded thanks to the free bar in operation. A mere two hours into the evening they had already amassed an illegal cash total of nearly ten thousand pounds. And the night was still young.

Jack was fuelling himself between sessions in the cloakroom by dipping his fingers into a sizable bag of coke that he'd brought with him. Andy had shared a few lines, but there was something about the euphoria of the evening's event and the ease with which they were reaping their ill-gotten gains that spurred Jack's greedy side into action. The constant buzz of the coke in his system mixed with a never-ending flow of expensive fizz was a cocktail he was loving.

It was as he was coming out of the gents that he bumped into two people. The first was someone he recognised as the showbiz reporter from the breakfast TV show. He'd sometimes seen him when he and Andy were still snorting a cheeky line in the early hours back at the flat after a night out on the rob, their brains too wired for sleep. 'Good looking chap, better in the flesh than on TV,' thought Jack as he held the toilet door open to let him pass.

The second person was Chloe, who had been waiting patiently for him to come out.

'Alright, bird.' Jack went to kiss her, his eyes wide and jittery as he did so. She pushed him away before he could make contact. He didn't appreciate that and glared at her accordingly.

'Okay, calm yourself, sister. You need to chill. Care for a line?' He patted his pocket.

'No I don't. Christ, Jack, you're wired. What the fuck are you doing? Just do whatever you've come to do and get out of here.'

'And what have I come to do, Chloe?'

'Steal stuff. What you always do. I'm not aware of you having any other function in life.'

Something was obviously eating Chloe and Jack didn't appreciate her tone. He didn't want anything to spoil the high from his coke, certainly not Chloe.

'Who rattled your fucking cage? Just get back in there and enjoy yourself and if you change your mind about a line or fancy a quick bunk-up in the toilets let me know.'

'How can I enjoy myself? I've been stood up. Scott's not turned up and I'm running around in there trying to avoid Victoria who suddenly seems to have forgotten that she's a psycho bitch and is being sweetness and sugary nice to everyone. Plus our gracious hostess, Evie, has made it clear that Scott and I are going nowhere and that he only wants me for ...' Her words faded away as she found herself unable to finish the sentence. She didn't need to.

Jack grinned, Joker-like. 'Yeah, about Scott, he won't be coming tonight. He had a little run-in with my fist. And my foot too. In fact both. If I haven't killed him, which I'm pretty sure I haven't, then he may be coming around about now in the car park behind his office.' Jack looked at his watch as if to check the time.

Chloe's mouth fell open. 'You what? What have you done? You're not supposed to hurt Scott. If anything it's Victoria who needs not to be here.'

'That's just it, isn't it, Chloe? Don't you get it? If something happens to Victoria then you're prime suspect number one because you're the one noshing off her husband behind her back. All fingers point at the horny nanny. But this way nobody suspects. You love Scott, so why on earth would you be connected to anyone beating the crap out of him? And anyway, I thought he needed teaching a lesson for poking my shag. He doesn't even fucking compare!'

The buzz of the coke rushed through Jack's veins as he continued his confession. He was definitely riding some kind of narcotic madness high and he was loving the power. Loving every crest. 'I'm a bit worried there may be an imprint of my jack-daw on his face though.' He lifted up his hand to show Chloe the bruising and the dried specks of blood on his knuckles.

Chloe placed her hand to her mouth in shock. 'You're fuck-ing mad, Jack. Scott will know it's you!'

'How? Only if you tell him and that's unlikely as you're the one who told me where he works, you're the one who told me he was coming straight here from his office, you're the one who wants rid of his wife. Which may well have happened by the time you track down your cashpoint lover boy.'

Jack patted his pocket again.

'What do you mean?'

Jack held out his jacket and opened one of the pockets wide for Chloe to peer inside. She could see a small pistol housed in his pocket alongside the bag of coke. The sight of it caused her to inhale sharply.

'What? You're going to shoot her? Here? You'd never get away with it.'

'Well, if I don't, then you'll be going down with me too, won't you? You want her gone. You've hinted at it a million times. It wouldn't take much to convict you, would it? Here you go, take the gun and do it yourself if you like.'

Jack reached into his pocket, pulled out the gun and forced it into Chloe's hands. In a panic she shoved it back into his jacket.

'Just leave me alone,' she pleaded.

'And now your fingerprints are on it too.'

Chloe could feel a prick of misery stab at her eyes as tears began to form.

'You're evil, Jack. Pure evil.'

'And you love it, Chloe. You always have done. Now, let me carry on with my evening, I have lots to do and standing here talking to you isn't getting any of it sorted.'

Chloe ran into the ladies before Jack could see the first flow of bitter tears cascading down her cheeks. At that moment any feelings of nostalgic love or bad boy respect that she'd ever housed for him disappeared.

Jack smiled to himself and walked back towards the main hall where he could hear Katy Perry's 'Roar' pumping out of the huge speakers either side of the dance floor. He was just about to enter when Andy came storming out, a look of horror written across his face.

Not that Jack noticed. 'Let's go dance, man. I love this song. Remember the time we sat up all night watching her perform this during half-time at the Superbowl. She was seriously fucking hot, Andy. Let's go.'

Andy wasn't in the mood for dancing and grabbed Jack by the collar of his dinner jacket. Not taking no for an answer he dragged his friend away from the main hall and into a little alcove at the bottom of the stairs beyond the toilet. It was as hidden a place as he could find.

'What the fuck, Andy? C'mon, dude, this evening is going like a dream.'

'Well it's just become a nightmare. One I don't want to relive or go anywhere near. Two of the guests here are Georgia and Devon Bellamy. Names ring any bells?'

'Nope, should they?'

'Her mother, his ex-wife, found dead with a slit throat and a bullet ripped through her chest and the new boyfriend with his brains blown out and the gun in his hand?'

Jack's face suddenly went as white as the cocaine housed in his pocket, his mind suddenly registering what he knew Andy was about to say.

'Jack, we should get out of here now, this is too close for comfort. The police may have decided that her new fella topped himself after killing her but we both know what a crock of shit that is. We know that we butchered them both.'

The sound of Katy Perry singing was blanked out by the sound of the almighty roar of horror flashing across Jack's brain. Despite not wanting to reflect on the past, Jack suddenly found himself back at the darkest day of his life ...

CHAPTER 72

Several years before …

Andy and Jack had been in the house a little longer than they had planned. Normally they worked to their rule of in and out as quickly as possible. No searching for money under the mattress or scanning the paintings hanging on the wall to see if any were genuine Monet's, Manet's or Matisse's, not that either Jack or Andy would have been able to recognise one anyway. The closest either of them had come to art was probably watching *The Da Vinci Code*.

But something about the house they'd broken into that night had sparked their interest. And surprisingly for two non-art-lovers, it was the array of interesting paintings decorating every room.

They'd had no idea that the two people living there were of an artistic persuasion when they'd broken in. They'd been watching the couple, a stunning woman with an air of days-gone-by chic and beauty about her which oozed class and a man whose taste in clothes and waxed moustache were eccentric to say the least, for weeks. As ever with their criminal activities, Jack and Andy wanted to make sure that they knew occupiers' habits. What time they left and how long the house was usually empty for. Most nights the couple would leave the house around

8pm and not return until after midnight. Where they went, Jack and Andy neither knew nor cared. All they knew was that the house was worth a mint and that there would more than likely be prize pickings inside.

They weren't wrong. After days of observation they watched Sophia Bellamy and Nicolas Belvoir leave their plush home just after eight one evening and drive off out of sight. Within five minutes the two men had expertly picked the lock, worked their way inside and smashed the alarm.

As per usual, the two men split up and scanned every room, grabbing anything they deemed of value. Jewellery, money, fancy objects … if it shone, they stole it.

They could have been in and out in fifteen minutes. If they had have been, then what followed would never have occurred. But things don't always go to plan.

Both Jack and Andy found themselves drawn to the artwork on the walls. It was bright and vibrant and attracted them like moths to a flame. The colours were rich and nothing quite made sense, making it more enticing. Splats of electrifying paint mixed with strips of neon-bright colour. Every one of them was random in its form yet they all possessed the mark and style of the same artist.

Both Andy and Jack couldn't resist commenting on it as they regrouped in the sitting room.

'The paintings everywhere are awesome. I love the colours,' said Andy.

'If they were smaller I'd nick one,' remarked Jack. 'They're much better than a picture of a vase of bloody sunflowers, that's for sure.' All of the paintings were massive and had obviously been painted on a huge canvasses.

It was then that they saw it. It was Andy who spotted it first. On the table in the sitting room was a scrapbook, about twelve by twelve inches in size with a photo of one of the paintings they'd seen around the house featured on the open page. Alongside it were some words describing how the creation was painted and another photo. It was of the stunning looking woman they'd seen leaving the house earlier than night. She was naked but instead of feasting on the curves of her breasts and the small neat triangle of hair between her legs, both Jack and Andy were immediately captivated by the fact that she was covered in paint. Her hair was coated and tangled, her breasts a collage of shades and her legs possessed more colours than a rainbow. Yet even in this state of camouflage her happiness at her artistry shone through, her smile almost as broad as the page itself.

Andy flicked through the pages. On every one there was a similar set of photos and words. The image of a painting, the description of how it was created and a joyous paint-covered nude of the lady of the house. Running a gloved finger down the writing he began to read.

'This is amazing,' said Andy. 'She paints them herself using her own body. She covers her tits and ass and literally rolls around on the canvas. Beats a brush any day I guess. Smart.'

'I wouldn't mind dipping into her paint pot,' joked Jack, looking at the beauty of the woman's body. She may have been old enough to be his mother but she was one seductive lady.

The two men spent an extra five minutes flicking through the scrapbook admiring the contents. It was time that they couldn't afford.

They were snapped out of their appreciation by the sound of the front door slamming and the voices of a man and woman laughing.

'I can't believe I've forgotten that book. I promised Frida I would show her how I created the paintings. I'll just fetch it from the sitting room, darling, wait two ticks.'

Andy and Jack immediately began to panic. They needed to escape and they needed to do it now, before being caught. Jail was not an option.

But before they had a chance to run they heard the voice of the man crying out that the alarm had been smashed. He had obviously seen it hanging off the wall. He called to the lady but it was too late. She had already walked into the sitting room and come face to face with Jack and Andy.

For a moment she was dumbstruck, unsure what to do. After a split second she went to scream. Without thinking about anything but the need to escape and in blind fear that they had been caught in the act, Jack picked up a small craft knife that was sitting alongside the scrapbook. The woman had evidently been using it to trim her photos. As the first mini-notes of sound started to erupt from her throat, Jack rushed towards her and swung the knife in her direction. To this day he still didn't know if he really meant to do what he did. The sharp blade sliced through the soft skin of the woman's throat and all noise ceased as she fell to the floor, blood gushing from her neck.

'What the fuck?' Andy could say no more. He tried but words failed him at what he had just witnessed. It was as if his own throat had been cut too.

Any air of tragic silence was shattered as Nicolas Belvoir, a look of layered terror matted across his face, came into the room. In his hand, shaking with horror at the sight of Sophia dead upon the floor and terror at his own potential fate, he carried a gun. It was one that he always kept in the hallway drawer. It went with the territory of being a millionaire business owner in a rich part of town. If you were a potential target then you needed to be prepared and Nicolas was.

Not that he had ever been called upon to use it before, and in his head he wasn't sure if he could.

As he walked into the room he could see Andy directly opposite him. He pointed the gun in his direction. Jack, still in shock at what he had done, was standing to one side, partly hidden from Nicolas's direct line of vision.

Images of jail flashed across Jack's mind. He'd go down for life for sure. He was still young, still had so many plans ahead of him. He couldn't risk going to prison. A lifetime behind bars was no life at all. He hadn't meant to kill the woman, had he? He'd just panicked. He wasn't a cold-blooded killer, was he? The body on the floor said otherwise. There was no way he was throwing his life away on a stupid mistake. He and Andy would have to come out of this alive and blameless. They were a team. He couldn't let his own cretinous moment of idiocy send them both behind bars.

Before Nicolas had a chance to see him, Jack charged full pelt into him, knocking him to the floor and causing the weapon to fall from his hands. Nicolas was a big man but his build and age were no competition for the young, sinewy prowess of Jack.

Jack grabbed the gun and in the time it took for Nicolas to let out a whimper of pain and fear as he looked up at Jack, the young villain had placed the barrel of the gun to the side of the millionaire's head and pulled the trigger. A red spray of death jetted across the floor. It was the life of the man or his own life lost to decades at Her Majesty's pleasure. To Jack, there was no contest, despite the pandemonium raging through his own head.

Andy placed his hands to his head, his breathing heavy and fast at the shock of Jack's actions. 'This is not good, Jack.' The words were unnecessary given the scene that lay in front of him.

Jack tried to take control of the situation. 'We need to make it look like a suicide. He went crazy, slit her throat and then shot himself. He used his own gun, man, that's our get-out clause.'

'Are you fucking mental?' Andy's voice trembled with fear as he spoke.

'We can do this, Andy, come on. We are not going to prison. They'll bang us up for life. Is that what you want? No parties, no women, no nights out. I am not going down for this and neither are you.'

It was left to Jack to try and cover up the fact that they had ever been at the house. The mansion was large enough for none of the neighbours to have heard the shots.

He set to work, telling Andy what to do as well. They replaced everything they had intended to steal, leaving it exactly where they had found it. Objects back on tables, jewellery back on the dressing table, cash left in drawers. They were both wearing gloves so there were no telltale fingerprints.

Jack found a baseball bat near the front door. Maybe another preventative against unwanted intruders. They'd smashed the alarm. How could they make it look like Nicolas Belvoir had done that himself? Jack's only thought was to destroy a few other things as well, to make it look like they'd struggled. Grabbing the bat, he marched into the sitting room and smashed one of the tables.

He threw the vase that was sitting upon it across the room in the direction of Sophia's dead body. It shattered into a dozen pieces.

Andy came back into the sitting room, having replaced all of the items they'd intended to steal. 'Let's get out of here now, Jack.'

'Not yet, something's not right. They would have struggled. If he wanted her dead they would have struggled.'

An idea flashed through his mind. 'Help me.'

Jack explained what they needed to do. It seemed barbaric but a part of it made sense to Andy. Grabbing Nicolas's body, they moved it towards Sophia's and, careful not to let the blood that was still hot and sticky on the side of Nicolas's head drip in meaty blobs onto the floor, they pressed Nicolas's hands against her skin. They pressed his fingertips as hard as they could. On her arms, on her face, anywhere. The pool of blood underneath her neck undulated slightly as her body moved. Most of it had now sunk into the deep carpet of the sitting room.

Satisfied that his prints would now be more than evident, they carefully moved Nicolas's body back to where he'd died, matching the positioning of the spray of blood with the cavernous bullet wound on the side of his head.

'Now, let's leave, Jack. We've done all we can.'

'Okay. Let's split.'

Just as they were leaving the house, Jack turned on his heels. 'You get out of here, Andy. I'll see you back at the flat. There's one last thing I need to do.'

'What?'

'Just go.' Jack's voice was stern. 'It's best if we leave separately.'

As Andy disappeared out of sight, Jack walked back into the house. He picked up the gun from alongside Nicolas's body and walked over to Sophia. He fired another shot into her chest.

It was that particular shot that had haunted him every day since. Something had told him to do it, that it would make the whole suicide scenario more believable. Make Nicolas more crazed. He'd slit his girlfriend's throat and then fired a shot into her chest to make sure she was dead. To make sure that he had achieved what he wanted before turning the gun on himself.

Even though he had already killed twice that evening, it was that final shot into the corpse of Sophia Bellamy that still replayed in his mind for years to come. He could still see the jolt of her lifeless body as the bullet tore into her.

He placed the gun back beside Nicolas and ran, closing the door behind him. He ran as fast as his legs could take him. Andy had taken the car as instructed. Jack just needed to run. To run away from the scene, run away from his own actions, to run away from the possibility of his life being wasted inside a cold, dark prison cell.

Somehow they managed to get away with it. Somehow the police believed that Nicolas Belvoir had decided to kill his girlfriend and then himself. Friends testified that Nicolas was of an artistic temperament. His temper was fiery and famed among his inner circle. His actions surprised nobody. Shocked, yes, but didn't surprise. Maybe they should have seen it coming. Exes testified that indeed he had a violent streak and had raised his hands to them before.

The gods had smiled on Jack and Andy. Had Nicolas Belvoir been meek and mild then maybe nobody, police included, would have believed that he had turned on Sophia.

The two young criminals had escaped, got away with murder. Until now, that is. As they stood in the alcove underneath the stairs, a horrified Andy instructing a coked-up Jack that they should leave right now, what they didn't know was that someone was listening to their every word. Having heard his name mentioned as he searched for the toilet, he'd listened to the conversation unfold.

Devon Bellamy had stood on the stairs and listened to it all, hatred polluting his veins once again. And as he watched the two men rush back into the main hall of the event, he knew what he had to do. There was punishment to dish out. An equation to balance.

CHAPTER 73

A gathered hush descended as Evie took to the stage erected at the top end of the main hall. The evening was in full flow and, as far as she could gather, everyone was digging deep into their pockets for a good cause. It felt great to be doing something worthwhile. In her cinematic world it was often easy to become lost in a labyrinth of vanity, congratulatory backslapping and narcissism. For every Angelina with her humanitarian ways and mother to a brood of six – it was no wonder she was cited as the most admired woman in the world – there was a sea of actors who seemed to thrive on who wore what, who won what and who outshone whom. Evie was determined not to become like that. Another grinning bimbo, no more than a clothes horse for an army of fame-hungry fashion designers. She would always try to use her stardom for good. And tonight that 'good' was as in 'Bidgood'. She needed to remind people about poor Mitzi.

'Ladies and gentleman, my name is Evie Merchant and I'd like to thank you for all coming here tonight. I can see many familiar faces here this evening and for many of us, we have a friend in common who cannot be here unfortunately. That person is Mitzi Bidgood.'

A ripple of applause snaked around the crowd as a photo of Mitzi was projected onto the wall behind Evie.

'Mitzi and her boyfriend Foster Hampton went missing on a road trip across America and as we all know, Foster's body was tragically found dead. Nobody knows why or how this happened. As yet, there has been no sighting of Mitzi. What has happened to her is unknown. Despite the best efforts of the police both here, in America and in Mexico all paths of enquiry have so far led to a dead end. There are people here tonight who I understand have done their own investigating …' Evie glanced over to Georgia and Charlie as she spoke, a gesture acknowledged by a tearful Nova, who had started crying at the first photo of Mitzi, even though she didn't even know the poor girl. Nova squeezed her son and his girlfriend together with pride at what they had tried to achieve with their actions.

'They have discovered things about what has happened to Mitzi that are as yet unexplained,' continued Evie. 'I am sure that given time the truth will out and we will discover poor Mitzi's fate. I don't know what happened, as yet nobody does, but I am willing to say, between us here tonight, and this is something that I also said to the press on the red carpet, that I refuse to believe that Mitzi had anything to do with Foster's death. I don't have a crystal ball but I am sure that when the truth comes out we will find that Mitzi is a victim too. I just hope that she has not suffered the same tragic end as poor Foster and that whoever is responsible for Foster's death is brought to justice.'

Another burst of applause covered the hall as the crowd echoed Evie's words.

'I knew Mitzi when she was my Zumba teacher, way before she become famous as the TV dancer we all know and love today. It was a few years ago and in some ways it seems like a lifetime ago but I remember those days with fond memories.' A photo of a group of young women appeared behind Evie, and a flutter of squeals and giggles came from the audience. The photo was obviously taken at the end of a class and each of the ladies, dressed in a wealth of Vegas-bright stretch fabrics, looked sweaty yet euphoric at the workout they had just endured.

'You may recognise a few faces in this photo,' smiled Evie. 'In fact a few of them are here tonight. My good, sweet friend, Victoria is here, as is TV weather girl Georgia Bellamy. Mitzi, of course. And yes, that is me, pre-styling.'

Victoria and Georgia glanced at each other and smiled. They had already talked, Victoria determined to explain her actions and her regret at what had happened with Charlie and the poolside photo. Georgia wasn't convinced that she trusted Victoria just yet – would any woman who had been delivered a photo of her boyfriend being pounced upon by another woman not be inclined to put said woman on a par with a praying mantis? She had to admit though that having talked to Victoria, she was more inclined to believe her apology. And she was obviously very fond of Mitzi too, and wasn't that what tonight was all about?

'Mitzi was a good person.' Evie stopped, paused and corrected herself. '*Is* a good person. I believe she is alive. I have to as I can't imagine for one second that her effervescent burning flame of enthusiasm has been put out. What I would like every one of you here tonight to take away is the joy and delight that Mitzi brings to our lives, whether you know her in person or have simply seen her shimmying her sequins on the television. We must keep striving to find out the truth, because whatever has happened to Mitzi, I refuse to believe that she has given her last dance. She must never be forgotten. Thank you very much.'

The photo behind Evie was replaced by the opening titles of the TV show Mitzi worked on. The lights dimmed. It was followed by a montage of some of her most famous dances, many of them with Foster. American Smooth pirouetted into Foxtrot, segued into Viennese Waltz and then boogied into a Rumba. It was Mitzi at her best and the audience was captivated.

CHAPTER 74

The photographer employed by Evie that evening had taken many magazine-worthy snaps of those there to show their support for the hopeful quest to find Mitzi Bidgood, but if he had taken some photos as people watched the montage of Mitzi in action, not even the sharpest of lenses would have been able to capture the range of emotions of those gathered. As it was, he was entranced by Mitzi's moves too.

Nova Chevalier watched on through misty, tear-stained eyes. For her it was the thought that Mitzi may be dead that she found so upsetting, such a young life taken too early. Nova had grown up in a world where not everything turned out to have a perfect ending. People died. Hadn't she already lost many of those dear to her? Yet death at a certain age was a natural progression. Her tears were for Georgia, for Evie, even for that dreadful Victoria who may have lost a friend at such a tender age. As she watched Mitzi in action, her arm linked with Jacob's, sadness and despair also etched across his face as he watched the screen, horrified at the thought of her fate. Nova pulled him close to her, grateful that she had him in her life. Things could be taken away so quickly.

Victoria was bandaged in a cloak of insecurity as she watched Mitzi and Foster in action. The thought that she may be dead made her reflect on her own life. Yes, this evening had been hard for Victoria but at least she still had breath in her body, and while there is breath, there is always a hope for change and that is what she intended to do. She had confronted Chloe, telling her that she intended to fight to save her marriage. Chloe has been surprisingly pleasant. Maybe she'd lost her fighting edge, perhaps less confident since Scott had failed to turn up this evening. Victoria didn't know. She'd questioned Chloe about Scott's whereabouts. Was it her imagination or had she been remarkably skittish? He was probably stuck at work. Same old story. She'd deal with Scott tomorrow. Tonight was about building bridges. She'd tried with Georgia and their shared smile over the Zumba photo made her think that maybe, even though they would never be bosom buddies, just maybe Georgia could understand her and believe in her regret. As for apologising to Nova for her actions, well, she had just had to suck up Nova's words of 'wisdom' about her kiss with her son and move on. What had she said? 'You were abroad and drunk. Common sense goes out of the window as soon as you open your suitcase. But you will never be with my son, so never take advantage of him again or I will track you down.' A mother's words of protection, but words she could understand. She would always fight to the death for Leo and Lexi. Yes, Victoria was insecure about the future but she knew that she had to try and build one that put her family first.

Chloe was desperate to leave but knew that if she did so before Evie's speech it would look incredibly rude. If someone had said to her years ago as she stood outside the fish and chip shop meeting Jack for the first time that one day they would be in the same room, at a swanky party surrounded by some of the biggest names in showbusiness, she would never have believed it. And if she had, she would have assumed that the evening would be sheer perfection. It had been horrific. A no-show from Scott, the man she thought loved her, and then finding out from Jack the reason for his absence. How had she become so deeply

involved again with Jack? Was she that shallow to fall for the
bad boy image yet again? Well, not any more. And what was he
planning to do to Victoria? Chloe was almost scared to leave, in
case she logged onto the internet the next morning to read that
Victoria had been gunned down. Should she warn her? Something was stopping her. As she watched Mitzi spin around on
the screen she wished that her own life was no more complicated than working out which choreographed step came next.
But then, perhaps Mitzi didn't have a life at all anymore.

A wired Jack and a jittery Andy had returned to the hall just
as Evie had begun her speech. Jack had stashed away a huge wad
of stolen notes under one of the tables and wanted to grab it
before leaving. Andy was right, having Devon and Georgia there
was too close for comfort so they needed to quit and run. As Evie
began to speak, Jack and Andy found themselves stood directly
behind Nova and Jacob. For a split second Jack thought about
how funny he found Nova when he watched her on the TV.
He'd tuned in many times. He looked at her ginormous chest
in appreciation. His mind snapped back to the here and now
as he realised that Georgia Bellamy was standing next to them,
her boyfriend Charlie with his hand draped over her shoulder.
Now that was too close, but at least she'd never know the truth
about her mother. 'Listen to the speech, and then we're out of
here,' whispered Jack to Andy. Andy's face was full of horror as
he realised who was directly behind them. Devon Bellamy had
followed them in and the look on his face was one that Andy
would never forget. It was as dark as the dead of night. Something was poisoning him from within, that was for sure. Andy
just hoped he was wrong about what it might be.

Aaron Rose assumed that the look on Devon's face was aimed
at him. Why wouldn't it be? He was the man who had stolen his
wife away from him, fucked her behind his back. But as Aaron

watched Mitzi on the screen he was struck with a sense of loss. The loss of a woman he had never known. Someone who would have been part of his life, for whatever length of time he was not sure. She would have partnered him, taught him new skills and shown him something else in life. As he watched her expertly work the dance floor on the screen, he was amazed at the fluid sway of her body. She was like the finest athlete using her body to its full potential. He looked down at Tanya, who was standing alongside him, and smiled. It was a smile of reflection. She was another woman that he knew he had now lost. Their love, not that you could have ever called it that, was based on the illicit bedroom activity of the mansion she had shared with Devon. Her husband. Her master. Tanya would always be someone who thrived on affairs. But also someone who needed money, who needed thrills and who needed a man who needed her. Maybe depended upon her. She needed a man to be her protector, not just for her, but for her mother too. Aaron would never be that man. Why had he tried to convince himself otherwise? Since she had moved in with him, their romance could not have been flatter had it been steamrollered. Tanya's lust for life and sexual adventure had appeared to dry up the moment she was away from the financial comfort of Devon's home. She had hardly looked at Aaron all night, he'd had more attention from Sarah, Nova and Jacob's production assistant, who had been flirting with him since she arrived. Nova had even commented to him that Tanya didn't exactly look happy to be in his company, a fact which seemed to thrill her. Nova was right. He had seen Tanya staring at Devon all night. And if he wasn't mistaken, he was staring right back at her. Perhaps they were two well-suited peas from completely different pods. After all they'd been through, the highs and the plummeting lows, maybe there was an understanding of how each other worked. No, Aaron was sure that his time with Tanya was over. It was up to her to decide what she wanted to do next, but he knew it wouldn't be with him.

Georgia and Charlie watched Mitzi's Catherine Wheel of sequins spinning around on the screen. It was delightful. How could something so beautiful potentially not be there anymore? Georgia reflected on the activities of the past few weeks – her trip to Hell's Canyon, to Tijuana and to her times in India and LA. She thought of poor Foster, dead in a cave; of Addison, her head smashed in during an attempted burglary; of the body that had perished in the road vehicle in Mexico. Why was life so cruel? So short for some who have still so much to give. Watching Mitzi, she refused to believe that Mitzi's light had been snuffed out too. That would be the cruellest blow of all.

As everyone stood in awe, watching Mitzi light up the dance floor on the screen, nobody saw one of those gathered reaching into their outfit and pulling out a small gun. Nobody saw it take aim and fire. Was it one or two bullets? But what they did see as soon as the sound of the gun exploded, was two people fall to the floor.

As screams shredded the atmosphere in the dim light of the hall, three minds went into action. One mind realising that the blood on their arm was their own, one realising that their life was ebbing away for good and one realising that they had seen the person pulling the trigger.

CHAPTER 75

Scott Palmer-Roberts had been admitted into hospital suffering from a severely broken nose and three broken ribs earlier that evening. He'd been found unconscious in the car park at his place of work by one of the nightly cleaners. She'd phoned an ambulance and prayed that he was okay.

His first visitor arrived after midnight on the very same evening. It was beyond visiting hours but Scott was in a private room and she was determined to see him, insisting to the nurse on duty that she would only be a few minutes. The visitor was Chloe Alexander. She had wanted to leave after the shooting at Evie's and come to him straight away but after the police had been called to the event she had been forced to stay there until she, like everyone else, had been questioned. It was only then, when she was allowed to go, that she'd phoned the nearest hospital to Scott's place of work to see if he had been admitted. He had. Her first thought was that at least he wasn't dead. She'd never have forgiven herself if he had been. She may not have been the one putting the boot in but after what Jack had said to her that evening she might as well have been. And besides, one death in an evening was quite enough, thank you.

Everything had changed for Chloe in a few short hours. For the first time in what seemed like years she felt that she had to take control of her own destiny. She was still young, soon to be

twenty-three, and if the last year had taught her anything it was
that she was not as grown up as she had thought she was. What
had she achieved over the past few months? Nothing, unless you
counted an affair with a married man and using what was left
of the money she'd accrued from the sale of her father's house to
buy illegal painkillers for somebody as achievements. And she
knew that they never would be.

She assumed Scott had been pleased to see her. It was hard to
tell underneath all of the bruising. His face was a patchwork of
dark blotches ranging in colour from plum through to scarlet.
His nose had been bandaged to hide the damage hidden beneath.

It was also difficult for Scott to talk, given the severe nature of his facial injuries. This suited Chloe. She didn't want to
be interrupted. Now that everything was out in the open, Evie
having informed Scott about her supplying the painkillers, she
knew that what she had with Scott, whatever it was, was no
more than a childish fantasy.

'You should drop the divorce proceedings. You need to keep
your family together, Scott. Leo and Lexi need their mother. I
love those children but I can never love them like Victoria does.
You have to forgive her for everything that has been going on.
It was the painkillers and the anti-depressants doing that to her.
Sending her brain into complete havoc.'

'But …' Scott attempted to talk but his swollen lips and the
tightness of the stitches that had been applied around his mouth
hindered him from doing so.

Chloe was quick to cut him off, placing a finger to her own
lips to indicate that he should be quiet. 'I spoke to Victoria tonight. She's doing well. Her time away has done her good. She
wants you. I can tell. Call it a woman's intuition. Even a young
naïve woman like me. She always has done. You just need to
love her a little more. Show her why you married her in the first

place. I will not be a home wrecker. I don't think you want me to be. You love her, not me. I know that now. I'm not sure why I ever thought otherwise.' A single tear rolled down her cheek as she spoke. She wiped it away with the back of her hand. 'I thought she might die tonight. The man who supplied me with the painkillers was at the party. He told me that he'd get rid of her for me, so that I could be with you. How could I do that? How could I even wish it? It was him that did this to you.'

Chloe could see the disappointment in Scott's eyes beyond the bruising. Nothing could disguise that. His eyes lost any semblance of shine as he listened to what Chloe had to tell him.

'I didn't know he'd do this to you. I didn't know he was capable. I should have guessed. But I loved him. You never get over your first love, do you?' The tears were free flowing now. 'Victoria is yours and you are hers. Why would you even contemplate throwing that away? You are so lucky to have each other. Don't let someone like me ruin it for you.'

'But who?' His words were muffled but she could tell what he was saying.

'Jack Christie's his name. Not that it matters. You don't need to worry any more. Just concentrate on regaining your strength. For you, for your children ... for your wife.'

Scott's eyes narrowed. Chloe couldn't tell if it was confusion, sympathy or hatred that he was showing her. It didn't matter.

'I'm quitting. I'll be gone by the time you arrive back home. I'll speak to the nannying agency and they can arrange for a new person to start until you decide on who you want to employ permanently. I'll tell Victoria you're here. I didn't even tell her you'd been beaten up. How cowardly is that? But I wanted to see you first, to tell you what I needed to say. She'll be at the house now. It all kicked off at the event tonight. But you didn't miss much,' she lied. 'You can read all about it in the papers.'

'But where will you go?' His words were rasped and weary with tiredness.

'I'll stay with friends and maybe contact my mum again. I've not seen her for the best part of a decade. I think every child needs their mother, don't you? Bye Scott, thank you for everything. I mean it.' It was true, she did.

Chloe turned to walk away. As she did so, she caught sight of her own reflection in the mirror on Scott's bedside table. It had been a long evening and her skin was drained of colour. She looked at Scott and then back at herself again. How could a young, beautiful girl like her feel uglier than a man who had been beaten up to within an inch of his life? Someone covered with scars, bruises and dried blood. She didn't know, but she did.

She waved her hand at Scott as she left the ward. The action was weak and she was unable to complete it, allowing her hand to drop in mid-air.

As she hailed a cab and gave the driver the address of the Palmer-Roberts residence she sank into the bank seat and cried. She cried for the loss of Scott, she cried for the loss of her job, for the joy she soaked up from Lexi and Leo. But she didn't cry for Jack Christie. She didn't cry for the man who had taken her virginity and been her first love, the man who had supported her through hard times. She didn't cry for the man who had been shot dead in front of her very eyes earlier that evening. If she had wasted tears over his death, then surely that would make her even uglier. Hadn't he finally received what he really deserved, whoever had pulled the trigger?

Chloe returned home, not that it ever really had been her home, and packed her belongings. The children were staying elsewhere for the night. She was glad they weren't there to see her go. Neither was Victoria. Maybe she'd stayed on at the event to be with Evie.

Taking a sheet of paper from the printer, the same one she'd photocopied the invitation on to give to Jack for Evie's event, she wrote out a note to Victoria explaining why she was going and that Scott was in hospital. She also explained why. They could all blame Jack but he'd now paid the ultimate price anyway. With that, she left the Palmer-Roberts household.

She would have been long gone by the time Victoria read the note in the early hours of dawn the following morning had she not accidentally left one of her hurriedly packed bags on the kitchen floor by mistake. Chloe would have left it for good but her passport and driving licence were in there and if she managed to secure a nannying job abroad she would need them. She had to return for it. Her timing was lousy; Victoria had come home just a few minutes before. As Chloe grabbed the bag and went to leave, Victoria stepped out from the living room where she'd taken Chloe's note to read.

'I'm going …' said Chloe.

'Consider this a reference,' said Victoria and with all of the might she could muster, she slapped Chloe across the face. It hurt her hand but was worth it.

Chloe raised her hand to her cheek and said nothing. She knew she deserved it. Tears washed her eyes.

'Oh don't worry, I'm sure nothing's broken,' said Victoria. 'I think you'll find there are some things that can't be broken, no matter what's been hurled at them. My marriage for one.'

Victoria held out her hand which was still smarting. 'Now, the keys if you please.' Chloe handed them over. 'Now get out of my sight. I need to go and see my husband. Just as it should be.'

CHAPTER 76

The other person admitted to hospital that night was Charlie Cooper. Not that he felt he needed to be.

'It's just a graze,' he said to the male nurse wrapping the upper part of his right arm in protective white binding.

'You were incredibly lucky,' said the nurse. 'It's not everybody that comes in here with gunshot wounds and can go home smiling. The bullet must have just skimmed the outer part of your arm.'

'Enough to make you bleed though,' said Georgia who was stood, chewing at her fingernails, at the end of Charlie's bed with Jacob and Nova. 'I seriously thought you were dead when you fell to the floor.'

'It would take more than some random bullet to cut me down in my prime,' remarked Charlie, trying to make light of the fact that he could have died. 'Not like that other poor bugger who copped it. Who was he?'

'Apparently he's a known criminal, Jack Christie,' Jacob answered. 'The police found a gun in his pocket, but it wasn't the one that shot you. He won't be using that again.'

'When I think I could have lost my baby boy. It doesn't bear thinking about!' wailed Nova. She had been inconsolable ever since she had seen Charlie fall. 'We will obtain you the best treatment possible, Charlie, and the person who fired that gun will be brought to justice. I will hire the whole of LAPD to find out who tried to kill you, or whatever the police are called over here.'

'I think I'm in good hands, Mum.' Charlie was trying to be as upbeat as he could in front of Nova. A hysterical Hollywood mother was the last thing he needed right now.

'No offence, my dear boy.' Nova was talking to the nurse. 'But this is hardly Cedars-Sinai is it? We need to fly you back to LA, Charlie. I know a few plastic surgeons who could skin graft that arm so that it doesn't scar. Nothing can spoil your beauty. I won't have it.'

'But it is only a surface wound. The bullet all but missed me. It's hardly worthy of an episode of *Botched*, Mother.'

'Mr Cooper is right,' offered the nurse. 'It's unlikely that there will be any major scarring. I don't think a plastic surgeon will be necessary, to be honest.'

'Well, I'd like a second opinion and that will be given in Los Angeles, young man,' stated Nova. 'And I'll have you know, Charlie, I am on good terms with all of the surgeons on that show and they are masters of their craft.'

Surprisingly it was Georgia who backed Charlie's mother's idea. 'I think you should, Charlie. What harm can it do? It will put Nova's mind at rest, and mine too, to be honest. You can't go back to work for a few days, so why not?' Thoughts of LA filled Georgia's mind. Not all of them strictly recuperative.

Charlie looked at Georgia agog. 'Really?'

She nodded, apparently not prepared to take no for an answer. 'It'll be good for us to have a few days together as a family while you recuperate.'

Charlie looked to Jacob for support. 'But won't the police want us to stay here for questioning?'

'Well, I spoke to the officers at the event when you were coming here in the ambulance. They have no reason to believe that the bullet was meant for you. Given Jack Christie's background they think it will probably have been some man he's ripped off or done over along the way who was out for revenge. I've left the police my number so if they have any further enquiries and want to speak to any of us I am sure they can do, no matter what time zone we're in.'

'That is it, then,' barked Nova. 'It's settled. We are leaving first thing in the morning. Can you arrange the plane tickets, Jacob? Eight first class seats.' Nova paused for a second to reconsider. 'Actually forget that, make it four first class – you, me, Charlie and Georgia and four premium economy for the others. I want no added distractions for Charlie. He'll need his rest.'

'I'll get Sarah onto it right away,' said Jacob. 'I'll just pop outside and make the call. You don't need to hear me talking business. Not tonight.'

'I'm just going to fetch a coffee,' said Georgia. 'Anyone want one?' She followed Jacob out of the room.

'I think Nova's right. Charlie should get a second opinion on his arm. There's no harm in getting it checked over. And nobody is going to know plastic surgeons better than Nova if he does need one, are they?'

'Good point, dear girl. Now I must go and sort these tickets.' Jacob seemed in a hurry to leave. Georgia noticed his urgency.

'Are you okay, Jacob? You seem a little flustered?'

Jacob smiled and held his hands up. 'You got me. I hate hospitals. Always have. They put me on edge. It's the thought of all those *life and death* situations. It's been quite a night and I need to sort these tickets so I'll take the chance to get some air outside.'

'Good job Charlie's only suffering with a scratch then, eh? Just life, no death.'

'Quite, now if you'll excuse me …'

'Just one thing, Jacob, can't we all go first class? Seems a bit elitist shoving the others into premium economy, don't you think?'

Jacob smiled. 'Georgia, if you think that for one minute I do everything Nova tells me then you're sadly mistaken. It will be first class for all and my wife will have forgotten she even requested otherwise in the morning.'

'Thank you.' Georgia winked at Jacob. 'Now how does Nova like her coffee?'

'Strong and rich, how do you think?' It was Jacob's turn to wink back before he rushed off.

CHAPTER 77

As Nova and her party headed skywards the next morning, all eight of them seated in first class, Aaron Rose was just opening his eyes for the first time that day back at his Chelsea flat.

'Jesus, I've slept like the dead.' As his brain came into focus he realised what he had said. 'Oh, maybe not the best turn of phrase given what happened last night, eh? That was quite a night, wasn't it?'

He waited for an answer. He was greeted by silence. Turning to face the other side of the bed he expected to see Tanya lying there. But the bed was empty. He reached out his hand and rubbed it along the sheets. They were cold. Either she had been out of the bed for a long while already or she hadn't even climbed in there in the first place.

Aaron cast his mind back to his actions prior to getting into bed. He'd poured them both a brandy when they'd returned to his flat and Tanya had flicked on the television. It was late, as they'd been among the last to be questioned by the police as to whether they had seen anything at Evie's event or indeed knew the dead man. It was a double negative from them both.

Tanya had been flicking through the channels and had come across a programme about Russia. Aaron had feigned interest for five minutes and then gone to bed. He didn't remember Tanya joining him.

Climbing out of bed, Aaron stretched and ran his fingers through his hair and beard. He walked into the front room of his apartment. There was no sign of Tanya. Instead, he saw a folded piece of paper with his name on it. He recognised the writing as Tanya's. He picked up the paper and began to read.

Tanya had been up most of the night packing her things into a small case. She hadn't taken many things to Aaron's in the first place. Looking back now she wondered if she had ever had any intention of doing so. Aaron was a wonderful man, but for Tanya the attraction only went as far as the biggest pound sign.

She'd come from nothing. And with Devon she was used to having everything. To excess. Aaron could have been the richest gardener in the UK or the biggest action hero Hollywood had ever pumped steroids into but he would never compare to Devon. Devon was the one who had saved her. He had protected her from all of the harm and the hurt she'd experienced in her homeland and had made sure that her mother was looked after too. She couldn't repay him by running off into the arms of another. Devon would always be her number one, even if she was tempted to stray from the path now and again. And even if their love was a strange one. A dangerous one. Maybe that was part of the attraction.

They had an understanding. She knew that. She'd seen it in his eyes at the event. He was missing her just as much as she was him. She needed to return home.

She hoped she was right.

When Devon opened the door to her and held her in his arms, pulling her tight without saying a word, she knew that she was.

There was an understanding between Victoria and Scott too. She hadn't been married to the man for several years without knowing that they were indeed meant to be together.

The sight of him lying there, all battered and bruised in his hospital bed, had shocked Victoria to her very heart. Just the thought of him being hurt sliced at Victoria's senses. The thought of losing Scott, of not having him in her life, was too hard to even consider. She knew that now.

As Chloe had done a few hours earlier, Victoria opened up to Scott about all that she had been feeling and going through; her thoughts about her own body, her resentment of those around her, the pill taking, her jealousy of her husband's relationship with their now ex-nanny. It wasn't the sexual relationship; that was something she could forgive (although not forget), but the way that they seemed happy when in each other's company. She wanted to scream. She wanted to shout, to bang her hands on his chest and tell him that he should never put her through heartache like this again. Perhaps she would do. But right now it felt ill-timed.

Victoria was determined to let her husband know that she could not envisage a future without him and that she hoped he would reconsider the divorce. His smile told him that he would.

'I love you, Scott, you know that, don't you?' Victoria placed her hand in his. 'Despite everything. I still do.' He squeezed it tight.

'I love you too.' The words were slurred but the meaning was clear.

CHAPTER 78

The flight to LAX had been a routine one, which after recent events was just what was needed. Charlie slept most of the way, only stirring from his painkiller-induced slumber for meals. Georgia had spent her time talking to Sarah and *Super Nova* producer Mike, as they were all of a similar age. Meanwhile Nova and Jacob worked their way through the urgent emails that had mounted up during their time in the UK. Nova's make-up artist and stylist were beside themselves with excitement that Lydia Hearst, star of *The Face*, actress, fashion model, blogger and heiress to a publishing fortune, happened to be on the same flight and seated only two spaces away from them in first class. They spent the entire time critiquing in great detail everything from Lydia's fashionista choice in designer flight wear through to jewellery, hair style and shade and even nail polish.

They had touched down in Los Angeles before any of them had really had a chance to think about the length of the actual journey.

'Home sweet home,' remarked Nova as she, Jacob, Georgia and Charlie pulled up in front of Chez Chevalier in her chauffeur driven Rolls Royce. 'That was quite some trip, but after last night I am looking forward to some pure and golden Hollywood peace and quiet.'

'Yes, because that happens all the time, doesn't it?' dead-panned Charlie, smirking at his mother. 'The inhabitants of LA are famed for their love of peace and quiet.'

'Well, you will be taking it easy for the rest of the day, Charlie Cooper, that's for sure. And then first thing tomorrow we are taking you to the hospital to see about the need for a skin graft.'

'I think I'll be fine with a tube of antiseptic cream,' said Charlie cheekily, but he knew it wasn't worth arguing.

For a Bel-Air household, especially one belonging to one of the biggest names in reality TV, life at the Chevalier household was incredibly normal that evening. Charlie was dozing in front of the television, Georgia by his side, while Jacob was in the kitchen making work phone calls. Nova was taking the cleaner, Juanita, to task about the state of one of the spare bedroom floors again. 'Why do I pay you to clean up when at least one of the rooms is always littered with mess? If I had friends round to stay I'd be ashamed to bring them in here. I'd be the laughing stock of Hollywood. They'd be calling me dirty in the bedroom for all of the wrong reasons!'

Georgia looked over at Charlie. He was fast asleep, evidently unable to keep his eyes open despite the delights of the flick they were watching. Georgia, not exactly gripped either, decided to vacate the sofa and consider the next angle to take to pursue the mystery of Mitzi. She needed to think carefully about her best friend and if the events of the night before had taught her one thing, it was that none of them could give up. She needed to believe that her friend was alive, or at least find out what had truly happened if an ending was ever to be achieved.

Did Georgia have any clues left to explore? She wasn't sure, but she had to try something.

Georgia went to her bedroom and retrieved her MacBook Air. It was virtually out of battery. She grabbed her charger and walked through to the kitchen. She was certain her adaptor was still there from her previous visit. She waited by the door for a few minutes, allowing Jacob to finish his work calls. Far be it for her to interrupt when he was setting up the next potential guest slot on *Champagne Super Nova*. She wondered who it would be and listened in on his conversation.

It was maybe two or three minutes later that Jacob finished his conversation. She walked in as he hung up the phone.

'Making the wheels of TV industry work again, Jacob?' she asked.

'You know it,' he answered, a little taken aback.

'So who's guesting next season, then? Anyone I'd know?'

'We're trying for Caitlyn Jenner and Bruno Mars, but you never know. Watch this space.'

'Sounds promising. I just need to charge my MacBook. I think my adaptor is out here.' She scanned the kitchen and located it on one of the granite breakfast bars.

'And I shall see what Nova is saying to Juanita. She puts that poor cleaner though hell,' said Jacob, leaving the kitchen.

Georgia plugged in her machine and clicked on her email icon. She opened a blank email, typed an address into the bar at the top of the page and then composed her message.

'Mind if I pop round tomorrow morning? Have something to discuss. Gx'

She pressed the send button. As she did so, Charlie's sleepy voice came from the TV room. 'Georgia, you there?'

'I'm in the kitchen,' she shouted back.

'Can I have a glass of water? I'm thirsty.'

Georgia smiled to herself. Charlie may have been one of the most masculine men she had ever met but there were times when he reverted to being a child. And when he had just woken up was normally one of them.

'Sure.'

Georgia went to the fridge and filled a glass with ice cold water. She took it through to Charlie, who was still bleary-eyed on the sofa. 'Why don't you go to bed? It's been a long day and you have to be up pretty early for your mother to take you to hospital. You would think you've been fighting on the front line the way she carries on. But it's only because she cares.'

She watched Charlie stumble sleepily from the sofa, kiss her fully on the lips and toddle out of the room.

'I'll be with you in a moment,' she called after him. 'I'm just going to check something on the computer.'

Georgia wandered back to the kitchen and opened a new page on her computer. Firstly, she checked the weather, a habit that came with the territory of her job. Secondly, she typed the words 'Evie Merchant charity shooting' into the search bar. Hundreds of news reports from around the world popped up on her screen. She knew they would. A death at a charity event organised by a worldwide star like Evie did not happen every day. She scanned down the reports. Nova's attendance was noted in many of them. That would please her. The name of the deceased, Jack Christie, featured on most of them too. Maybe it was the early editions that hadn't known his name. A few of the later reports mentioned a friend of Jack's, Andy North, who had handed himself into the police to aid their enquiries into the death of his friend. The suggestion was that the two of them were there to steal as much as possible. Enquiries were also being made as to why Jack was carrying a gun. There was definitely more to the evening than had first appeared. She knew it.

Charlie's injury featured on a lot of the reports too, as did mention of Georgia's own attendance in a lot of the UK papers. The one thing that seemed to be missing from nearly all of them though was any mention of Mitzi. Occasionally the reason for the event was cursorily touched upon, but all talk of Mitzi's on-going disappearance was lost in a maelstrom of new page-filling headlines.

The thought upset her. Georgia closed the internet pages and her email account and left the machine to charge overnight. She let out a yawn. She needed to sleep. She suspected she might need all of her energy when the sun came up over the Hollywood hills in the morning. As she snuggled up next to an already lightly snoring Charlie, she definitely felt that the peace spreading itself across the Chevalier Hollywood home that evening was merely the calm before the storm.

CHAPTER 79

'Will you shift that carcass of yours out of bed now, Charlie Cooper? We have a meeting with my surgeon in ninety minutes. He's kindly fitting you into his busy schedule before he sets to work fixing the face of a talent show judge whose chins seems to be drooping a little more towards her décolletage than they did last season.'

Charlie slowly opened his eyes, and then rapidly closed them again at the sight of his mother standing in the open bedroom doorway. 'You are kidding me, mother. It's only …' Charlie opened one eye again to glance at the LCD clock on his bedside table. '… just before 8.30am.'

Actually it was later than he'd imagined. He'd obviously been sleeping for almost ten hours. Back in the UK he would have already gone live to the nation with his showbiz updates and a few frothy interviews with heaven knows who by this time. Maybe it was the fact that for once he hadn't had to set six alarms before going to bed, or maybe it was the fact that the combination of painkillers and jet lag had sent him into slumber cloud nine. Or maybe it was simply the warmth he was enjoying from Georgia wrapped around him, her soft feminine curves and alabaster smooth skin doing more to take his mind off his gunshot injury than any team of doctors could ever do.

'There is no point in your mother knowing the best specialists in town if she can't pull in a few favours now and again.

The man is booked for months ahead, so out of that bed now Charlie Cooper and don't make your mother tell you again.' Nova was adamant.

Charlie knew there was no point trying to disobey Nova's wishes when she started talking about herself in the third person. It was a sign that she was on a mission that even Bear Grylls would find hard to trek his way out of.

'Now, get showered, shampooed and shaved and I'll meet you in the kitchen in fifteen minutes. We can't be late.'

Charlie looked down at his arm. Having removed the bandage the night before to let the wound breathe, he surveyed the damage. As he'd known all along, thanks to good fortune and a dodgy aim, the bullet had merely grazed his flesh.

'It does not need a plastic surgeon, mother. The man will laugh us out of the hospital. It's embarrassing,' shouted Charlie as Nova disappeared out of sight, banging the door behind her.

She shouted back through the door, determined to have the last word. 'Embarrassing? I think not. He's dealing with a baseball star who wants his ding-a-ling lengthened straight after you as apparently he's not giving his wife much satisfaction in the slam dunk department, if you get my drift. Now that's embarrassing, so move it! The doc's fitting you in as a major favour to me.'

Nova smiled to herself as she walked back to the kitchen. It was one of the things she loved about Hollywood. Money talked. She'd had to bribe the surgeon to see Charlie at such short notice. But when you're on very good terms with all of the best plastic surgeons in the state, it was amazing what the promise of highlighting one in particular on the next series of *Super Nova* and booking herself in for a procedure could do. He'd have his own reality TV show before you could say 'implants'. Maybe she could persuade Jacob's team to produce it. Mind you, Jacob always made his own decisions, she knew that.

'I suppose you heard all that,' said Charlie, turning to face Georgia. Her eyes were still closed.

'Every last word.' Her eyes stayed shut.

'Looks like I'd better move. Don't want to keep doctor waiting.'

'Hang on, cowboy,' said Georgia finally opening her huge, inviting eyes. She never grew tired of Charlie's face being the first thing she saw in the morning. She wished it were every day. He had that wonderful knack of being able to wake up looking just as deliciously sexy as he had when he'd climbed into bed the night before. Dishevelled was not in his repertoire.

'Yes, ma'am. What can I do for you?' Charlie grinned expectantly.

'Did your mother just say that some basketball player had something wrong with his dick?'

'She did.'

'Well, there's nothing wrong with yours.' Georgia reached her hand under the sheets and placed them around the thick girth of Charlie's erect member. It wasn't just matinee idol looks that Charlie woke up with every morning.

'No, that seems to be in mighty fine order,' he remarked, raising his eyebrows as he spoke. 'It must be the company.'

'So how about a little *slam dunk* of our own? I don't think Nova will mind, do you?'

Georgia guided his throbbing rod of flesh into her, the sexual dew between her legs revealing her eagerness to accept. As Charlie began to thrust into her, she let out a gasp of excitement. She needed to feel him close to her, as close as they could physically be. Even though her mind was racing with thoughts of what the day ahead would bring, she needed to savour this moment, to feel the warmth of Charlie against her. To momentarily let go of all fear and dread and just immerse in a sea of pleasure with the man she loved.

The love-making was urgent and silent, the thought of Nova and Jacob being potentially within earshot adding an extra wave of hypnotic frenzy to their carnal thrill-seeking.

They came together, their bodies working in unison.

As Charlie exited the bed to head to the en-suite, he turned to face Georgia.

'I love you so much, you know that don't you?' he smiled.

'I do,' said Georgia. She let out a snigger. 'But if you ever call *that* a ding-a-ling.' She pointed to his cock which was still twitching with post-coital delight between his legs. 'I swear I may have to reconsider. Who calls it that in this day and age?'

'Charlie, are you dressed yet? The car will be ready in five minutes. We will not be late.' Nova's voice boomed through the house at a volume a squadron leader would envy.

'She does,' laughed Charlie.

CHAPTER 80

'Bit showy for a trip to the hospital, isn't it?' laughed Georgia as she watched the Rolls Royce through the kitchen window. She kept looking until its splendour had pulled out onto the road via the open gates at the front of the Chevalier estate and disappeared out of view.

'Another little insight into Nova's world,' smirked Jacob, 'This is not just a trip to the hospital for her and Charlie. This is a pap opportunity to show that she is looking after her dear son in the …' He paused to think. 'How will the magazines play it? I imagine they will call it the *post-traumatic stress* she must be feeling after *the utter horror of seeing her only son gunned down in front of her at the biggest showbiz event London has ever seen.* Something along those lines. She cares passionately about Charlie as her only son, but she wants the papers to know that too. Hence the Rolls and the fact she's dressed up as if she were going out to be interviewed by someone on *Fashion Police.*'

'But Charlie hates being in the papers, especially if he's off duty.'

'Charlie is all Nova has to play doting mother to. It's not like she has a big brood like Kris Jenner. So I think we can forgive her, don't you?'

'Of course. I just can't imagine me ever popping down to St George's Hospital in Tooting in the same manner. I'm more of a black cab or bus kinda girl.'

'Nova on a bus? There's more chance of Nova being voted next year's Miss Natural Beauty than there is of that happening. And where the hell is Tooting?'

'Never mind,' said Georgia, not really that keen to start unravelling the geography of south west London with Jacob. Besides she had urgent plans, which is why she hadn't accompanied Nova and Charlie to the hospital. 'Right, I'm off, I'll see you later. Nova said it was okay for me to borrow one of the cars.'

'Going anywhere nice?' asked Jacob.

'I'll tell you when I come back.' Georgia let out a sigh of relief as she left the room.

Georgia knocked on the apartment door. Actually this was more of a house, much bigger than she'd expected. Maybe it was separate flats but the one door and solitary bell suggested that the three story house was a single property.

It had taken her the best part of an hour to drive to the upscale suburb of Los Angeles she found herself in, the place where she hoped to find some answers to the questions that had been pulling at her brain ever since Evie's event. She rang the bell.

Georgia looked at her watch. 10.30am. As arranged in a reply to her email. She could feel her heart pounding within her chest as she knocked, thinking that maybe the bell was out of action. The beat of her heart and the loud crack of her knuckles against the wooden door seem to synchronise together. She could feel her lips becoming dry as she waited for another thirty seconds or so. She prayed that this wasn't a wasted journey. It was too important. Just how important she wasn't sure, but it was definitely something she needed to do.

She knocked again. After what seemed like an eternity, finally the door opened.

The person who answered spoke. 'Hey girlfriend, great to see you. I was thinking we could head out for brunch. There's a fabulous little diner not far from here that serves up the most exquisite pancakes. And the mall just beyond that is fabulous for shopping. We can take my car.'

Georgia turned to look at the car she'd parked next to on the driveway. It was a sporty little Audi TT Coupé. It looked brand new and must have been of similar value to the car she herself had borrowed from Nova and Jacob that morning.

'Nice car,' remarked Georgia. 'Nice house too. You live here alone?'

'Right now I sure do. I've had a few roommates but at the moment it's just me. I'll get my bag.'

'Can I just come in and use your bathroom? And I could really do with some water if that's possible. I'm a bit hoarse. I've been singing my lungs out to 'Uptown Funk' on the way over. Great tune.'

'Banging! Sure, come on in. I'll grab you some water.'

As Georgia walked into the house and was pointed in the direction of the nearest bathroom she could feel goose bumps forming on her skin.

'I'll go fetch that water, Georgia.'

'Thanks, Sarah, I appreciate it.' She smiled weakly, her mind ablaze with questions about how a production assistant working on a show like *Super Nova* could afford such a fabulous house and car.

Georgia spent a few minutes in the bathroom. She hadn't needed to use it. It had merely been an excuse to come inside the house, but a tower of newspapers and magazines piled up in the corner of the room grabbed her attention. Her mind racing, she flicked through them. They were all different and none of them that current, but they all seemed to feature stories about the disappearance of Foster and Mitzi and the subsequent discovery of Foster's dead body. The goose bumps that Georgia was already experiencing seemed to grow as she gazed at the stories. A cold chill lapped across her body, like a wave breaking on the shore.

She let out a deep breath, checked herself in the mirror, looked at her phone and vacated the bathroom. It was time for action. She found Sarah in a large sitting area, decorated in the height of expensive taste. She was sitting on one of two large leather sofas that dominated the room.

'You took your time,' half-joked Sarah, seemingly a little perturbed that she'd had to wait longer than she'd expected. 'Those pancakes are waiting.'

'Do you mind if we skip the food? I'm feeling a touch nauseous,' lied Georgia. 'It must have been something I ate this morning. That's why I was a little longer just now.'

'You need some Dramamine? I have some in the kitchen if you want?'

Georgia neither knew nor cared what Dramamine was and declined the offer.

She sat down on the opposite sofa. 'Sarah, I need to speak to you.'

'Sure, what's up? After that mighty fine chat we had on the plane coming back here, you know you can ask me whatever you like.'

It was true, the two women had discussed everything on the flight back to the States; Georgia had been keen to learn more about Sarah. That was why she'd deliberately seated herself next to her and requested that Jacob move the entire party of eight to first class. She needed to find out about her. Boyfriends, ambitions, background, her take on Mitzi's disappearance, it had all come up in conversation. Hadn't Sarah said that her folks were poor farming folk from one of the southern states of America? Unless one year's harvest had been particularly resplendent and bagged a fortune, Georgia wasn't aware that the offspring of poor farming folk could afford such luxuries as the house they were seated in.

But there were two sides to every story. Staring across at Sarah, Georgia thought to herself, *I have to bite the bullet and do this*. The word *bullet* bounced around her head, overly apt for what she was about to say.

'Why did you kill that man at Evie's party, Sarah? I saw you shoot him. And fire at Charlie.' All moisture drained from her mouth as she spoke, the fear within her absorbing her ability to talk.

Any friendliness that Sarah had portrayed at seeing her supposed new pal wiped from her face at Georgia's words.

It wasn't just bullets that could kill, it was looks too, and the one that Sarah was giving Georgia meant that the weather girl was in the deepest trouble.

CHAPTER 81

'You don't know what you're talking about. You're mistaken.' But the look on Sarah's face told her that she was not.

Trying to keep her cool, Georgia continued. 'I saw you. It was a dim light in that hall but I know what I saw. I was watching Mitzi on the screen, just like everybody else, and it hurt to watch, to see her in action, so alive and beautiful when she could already be dead. She could have died weeks ago just like Foster. It hurt so much that I turned away from the screen just for a split second. And I saw you, trying to hide yourself behind a pillar, trying to be discreet, but I know what I saw. You took your gun and fired two shots. One that murdered that man, Jack Christie, and one that nearly killed Charlie.' Georgia could hear the trembling coat of fear that cocooned her voice as she unlaced the tale of what she'd seen.

'So why didn't you say anything? Tell the police what you saw. Why the secrecy?' Sarah's southern drawl wasn't coated with fear, it was coated with an iciness that nothing could chip at. Hard and calculated. If she was scared then she wasn't showing it.

'Because there's more to it than meets the eye. Why would you, somebody who doesn't appear to know the man you killed, risk everything you have to shoot him in front of a crowd of people?' She circled her finger at the house they were sitting in and added, 'risk all this?

'Did you know Jack Christie? He's nothing to do with *Super Nova*, is he? What's the connection between a London criminal and an LA-based production assistant from a deep south farming family?'

'You tell me,' sneered Sarah, almost appearing to enjoy Georgia's confusion. 'You're the one playing Jessica Fletcher.'

'So then I thought that maybe the bullet wasn't meant for him, which is why you fired a second. The one that hit Charlie. I started thinking that maybe you and Charlie knew each other. That maybe there was some connection there. You work on his mother's show, after all. Your paths may have crossed. But then you said you'd only been on the show for a few months and that started me thinking. Did you know Charlie? Was there … is there something between you two that I don't know about? I'm fully aware my fiancé can flirt like Casanova.'

'Go on. You're quite the storyteller aren't you?' Georgia could feel the sweat running down her back and on the palms of her hands. 'I trust Charlie. I know him. He wouldn't cheat on me. That's why I didn't ask him here with me. A woman knows. There's no way. Besides, you're not his type.' Georgia couldn't resist the dig. Sarah was beautiful but their two looks were poles apart. 'So I guessed that maybe Charlie wasn't the person you were aiming for either. There was a big crowd and people were moving around, shifting position to watch the screen.'

'So if it wasn't this Jack man, and it wasn't your oh-so-perfect Charlie then who the hell was I aiming at? Have you worked that one out?'

'It could have been Nova, it could have been Jacob. I thought it might have been Evie. What a way to gain your notoriety – killing off one of the most famous actresses on earth. But then it occurred to me. It could have been me. I was in front of Jack Christie and Charlie was right beside me. You could have been aiming at me. That's why I didn't say anything. I wanted to know if it was. I needed to ask you face to face. It was, wasn't it? It was me you were aiming at?'

Sarah shifted uneasily on the sofa, taking her stare off Georgia for the first time since they had started the conversation. Her face was stony and severe in its expression as she looked back at Georgia to speak.

'And there we have it. Finally the Brit girl gets it. I was aiming for you. That other poor stupid fucker moved himself in the way just as I shot and then your poor boyfriend copped an injury too. I should have tried a third and finished the job.'

'But why me?' It was the only answer she needed to hear. She moved her hands nervously behind her back, her palms still clammy with dread and fear.

'Because of your incessant meddling. Why couldn't you just leave things be, Georgia?'

The voice speaking was not Sarah's. Georgia turned her head to the doorway leading out into the hall where a figure stood, gun in hand. It was pointed at Georgia.

'I think it's time we finish this, Sarah, don't you?' said Jacob Chevalier.

CHAPTER 82

Jacob Chevalier marched over to the sofa and grabbed Georgia by the arm, pulling her to her feet. In an instant he roughly twisted her arm behind her back and pressed the cold barrel of his gun against her cheek. Nothing had ever felt icier to Georgia. Sarah grabbed her by the other arm and the two of them escorted her from the room and out into the hallway.

'It wasn't supposed to be like this, Georgia. But you just couldn't stop yourself, could you? Interfering all of the time. Determined to try and find out more and more.'

Georgia was confused, despite the fact that she'd been having suspicions about Jacob. He'd been acting shiftily for days in her opinion. 'Stop it, you're hurting me,' she cried, a blade of pain running up her arm. 'To find out more about what?'

'About what happened to Mitzi. All of this is because of Mitzi, don't you understand?' spat Jacob, his voice barking the words into Georgia's face.

Sarah let go of Georgia to open a wooden door that led off the hallway of the house. Beyond it were a set of stone steps leading downwards. It was dark but the outline of the steps was clearly visible. Sarah disappeared into the dark while Jacob still gripped on tightly to Georgia, causing another thunderbolt of pain to shoot its way through her body.

A shallow light illuminated from within the room and as Jacob and Georgia reached the top of the steps, she tried to focus on what lay ahead. She could make out shapes but nothing more.

'This is all Mitzi's fault. Everything. So many people affected because of Mitzi. Mitzi and her stupid boyfriend. It's a pity she didn't die too. It would have made everything so much easier.' Jacob was marching Georgia down the steps as he spoke. A stench hit Georgia's nostrils as they descended. Jacob noticed it too.

'Christ, Sarah, I told you to keep this place as clean as possible. What's the point of me letting you live here rent free and paying for everything if you don't do as I say?'

'Sorry Jacob, I cleaned up last night. There was crap everywhere.'

Georgia tried to focus on what was around her as they reached the bottom of the stairs. The smell was getting stronger, almost like a sewer in its pungency. 'Why is it Mitzi's fault? What has she got to do with any of this?'

'Why don't you ask her?' snapped Jacob. He pushed Georgia away from himself and onto the floor. It was only when she fell that Georgia spotted the body in the corner of the gloomy basement, curled up in a ball, roped at the wrists and ankles. It was animalistic. Alongside the body was a bucket, the contents of which were obviously the source of the smell.

Georgia could feel the vomit rising up from her stomach. She swallowed in an attempt to keep it down. Even in the body's dirty state, Georgia knew exactly who it was. The blonde hair, although matted with dirt from the floor of the basement, gave it away. It was Mitzi.

Georgia moved to the body and spoke Mitzi's name as she lifted her friend's face from the floor. Mitzi opened her eyes slightly in recognition. She was alive. Her body, one that a few weeks before had been bursting with pure energy and dynamic power, now looked angular and disjointed where she had lost muscle mass. Her fingers were bloody and her skin branded with scorch lines from the ropes. Georgia could feel the tears begin to run down her own face as Mitzi, still with the tiniest sequin of sparkle in her eye, looked up at her and attempted a smile at her recognition of Georgia. Relief flooded through Georgia's body, her quest to find her best friend had been finally achieved. But her relief was tinged with the toxic taste of what was now to happen.

'What have you done to her, you bastards? How long has she been here?' Georgia held Mitzi in her arms, as tightly as she dared, given her condition, and attempted to undo the restraints.

'Too fucking long, I swear. She shouldn't be here. I didn't want this, none of us did,' said Jacob, his hand shaking as he held the gun which was still pointed in Georgia's direction. 'This should all have been so fucking easy, just a bit of fun. But no. It turned into this sorry fucking stinking mess.' His voice was maniacal. It scared Georgia even more. Jacob could be harsh, she knew that, but she'd never heard him shouting like this before.

'They made me do it.' Jacob glared at Georgia, the gun still pointed towards her and Mitzi. 'They all did.'

'All of you? Who are you talking about? Who else is involved? Not Nova?' said Georgia.

'Oh for God's sake, no. She's one of the last few remaining good things in Hollywood. She may play fake for the TV, but Nova couldn't be more genuine if she tried. She doesn't have a clue about any of this. She's not been tainted by it. And I suggest you stop trying to untie those ropes if I were you. There is no point.'

Georgia did as ordered, still holding Mitzi in her arms, unable to let go now that she had finally found her. 'Tainted by what?' If Georgia was going to die at the hands of this madman then she needed to know why.

Jacob continued to rant, the gun shaking in his hand. 'The club. My club. A secret society. Hollywood's biggest. I run it. There are big names from all over Hollywood in it. Actors, producers, casting agents, film backers. It started as a kind of old boys' joke a few years ago, back before I met Nova. Some boring old suits with too much money, including me, looking for the next kick. We have more money and power than we know what to do with, so what else was there? We needed more. We needed thrills. All those dollars can become boring when there's no challenge to anything anymore. One night at an industry party a few of us were talking about how bored we were and that it would be good to spice things up. I suggested a sex club. Everyone in Hollywood loves something a bit kinky. Especially ever since *50 Shades* became all the fucking rage. But everyone talks in this town. You could guarantee that someone would let slip that they'd seen me or some Oscar-winner all strapped up and being whipped at some club and I can't have that getting back to the wrong people, especially now I'm with Nova. So we started our own club, behind closed doors.'

Georgia listened on as Jacob explained, her mind trying to deal with the situation around her, her hands stroking Mitzi's hair and rocking her in her arms as he spoke. She glanced around the room, her eyes now accustomed to the dark, wondering if this was to be the place that she would die. And if it would be at the hands of a man that she had come to trust.

'But we needed to find some women. What is the good of a group of dirty old men wanting to get their rocks off in interesting ways if you can't find the women to satisfy you? But it's amazing what ambition can do to a girl. The answer was out there under our eyes all along. Young actresses come to

Hollywood every day looking to become the next big thing. Waitresses, secretaries, dental clerks, nail technicians ... all the same, with a headful of hopes and one big dream. To make it big in Hollywood. To be the next Evie Merchant or Jennifer Lawrence. And dreamers will do anything to achieve their lucky break, even if it means pleasing somebody who can give them a helping hand up the Tinseltown career ladder. Pay them for their silence, offer them bit parts in films to bump up their CVs, even get them on the payroll like Addison and Sarah here and they'll do whatever you want. Prostitution is a time-honoured tradition, it's been feeding media players like me for years. This town is built on corruption.'

'You're not saying that Mitzi was one of your ...' Georgia left the sentence open.

'No. She was just in the wrong place at the wrong time. I keep telling you I didn't mean for this to happen, none of the club members did. It was supposed to be harmless.' Was Jacob's voice beginning to crack as he spoke? Was there regret forming in the words of the madman?

'Then how?'

'Just having sex parties wasn't enough. We wanted more. More power, more thrills, more kinks. The club was getting bigger, we were selecting members from all over California. Even further afield. It's like any secret society, invitation only. For the chosen few. But for those invited, it's a case of everyone wins. The money men get to play away from home, behind their wives' backs, maybe regaining a bit of that playboy nature we used to have when we were younger. Pumping our egos with something more than just the ability to fund whatever our society wives want. Where's the excitement in that? They say you can never have too much money. Well, let me tell you, you can. It becomes boring. So we created our performance nights.'

'What are they?'

'They're what Mitzi and Foster stumbled across. Every few weeks the group will go somewhere and we perform a 'ritual'. Call it mock devil worship if you like. It's just an excuse for us all to dress up in hessian robes, dance around a camp fire and mock up a sacrifice before indulging in an outdoor orgy. I'd seen it on a film and thought it seemed erotic and exciting. All very *Wicker Man*. Of course we have to be very careful where we do it, so our locations have to be remote and known to someone in that area. They're handpicked. We went to Hell's Canyon as one of the group members owns a hotel there. He owns a chain of them in fact, and he knew somewhere remote in the Canyon where we could act out our fantasies. Mitzi and her boyfriend were there and sadly saw us. We couldn't risk them spilling the beans. They might have taken photos or anything. There are too many big names involved. The scandal would destroy this town like a disaster movie earthquake. I can't risk losing what I have, Georgia, not for anything. I've spent years achieving what I have today.'

'So you killed Foster?' Georgia was horrified at what she was hearing.

'No, not at all. Are you not listening, you stupid, stupid girl? It's all supposed to be harmless. Sex is harmless. We saw your friends in the Canyon just after we had performed our mock sacrifice. Fake knife and a bit of comedy blood. Like something out of one of those third rate horror flicks and as an alternative kind of foreplay it worked for the group. A thrill that no amount of money can buy. But we saw the reflection of your friends' binoculars watching us and we couldn't risk them telling. So we chased them. I guess the plan was to bribe them with money for their silence. But the guy, Foster, he fell in the panic of running away and hit his head. Must have hit it bloody hard, too. He was dead when we reached him. We were suddenly left with a body on our hands. Who'd believe it was an accident? And we could hardly offer Mitzi enough money to silence her about her boyfriend's death, could we? It wasn't our fault, but we can't have any kind of scandal linked to us. Hollywood would fall apart. So the group panicked and blamed me. I was stupid, let Mitzi see me. We hid Foster's body in a remote cave in the Canyon and we kidnapped Mitzi and brought her here. We didn't know she was famous in your godforsaken country. We even filmed a ransom message from her. We were going to use it. Try and push the blame onto somebody else. Some local criminals. But what was the point? As long as Mitzi could talk about her ordeal she might be able to say who she had seen. I was careless, she saw my face. That's why I had to sort this. The others in the group said I had to. Gave me no choice. Even at Nova's party they were telling me over and over that I had to finish it, get rid of any loose ends. Making their demands to me. That's not the way I work, but I couldn't risk losing everything. They said that if fingers were pointed then I was to be the fall guy. Their word against mine. Not even I could take them on. I've too much to lose. I can't spend the rest of my years in prison. Mitzi saw me, so she couldn't be allowed to live. If she does, then I'm damned. She's been here ever since.'

More and more vulnerability was creeping into Jacob's words. 'I thought if we stole the road vehicle and made it look like poor Mitzi had done a runner then maybe the spotlight of blame would fall onto her, even though she was totally innocent.'

Georgia was relieved to finally know that Mitzi had had nothing to do with Foster's death. She had never doubted her friend but it felt good, albeit for just a split second, to have it confirmed. 'How long were you going to leave her here?'

'We'd not thought that through. The others wanted her dead; to dispose of the one women who could potentially crumble an empire. Bring them down. They kept telling me, ordering me, but I couldn't do it. But now I'll have to.' Sarah, who had been smiling throughout Jacob's confession, moved behind him as he spoke, as if ready for action. 'This has all gone too far and loose ends need to be tied up. You leave us no choice. Another stupid death. Addison and now you.'

'Addison?'

'Poor Addison had to go. She was one of our girls, she was the faux-sacrifice Mitzi saw, but it seems she couldn't handle the guilt of what happened. I promised that I would wangle a few roles for her and her flatmate, Diana, not that she was involved, but Addison bottled it. I had her phone bugged, I do it with all of the girls. If we're paying for their houses and providing them with flashy cars and jobs then I hardly think they can complain if we invade their privacy a bit. I think we're entitled to, don't you? She left you a message, I guessed she was about to open up a little too much so sadly she had to go. A shame, as she was a great worker and a dirty little bitch at the parties.'

'You killed her?'

'Not me. I couldn't do it. I may be ruthless in business, Georgia, but to have blood on my own hands is not part of my make-up. She did it for me. It's so much easier to order others.' He pointed to Sarah standing behind him. 'She's an ambitious one, is Sarah. She's been waiting in the wings for a while. I set her up here to keep watch on Mitzi while we decided what to do. She was always keen to grab Addison's glory. Second assistants always feel just that though, second best. And as I like to sometimes take my carnal desires beyond the club, shall we say, and both Addison and Sarah were more than happy to fulfil my every fantasy it was easy to play them off against each other. I kept suggesting they were up for the same roles outside of the bedroom too so there was always an unhealthy rivalry between them that Sarah here was happy to end once and for all when I needed her to.'

Sarah was happy to confess. 'Caving her head was easy – I've done it countless times before to disease-riddled animals back on the farm at home. It's where I learnt to shoot, too. I was state champion for two years running. I could have shot Addison, but I think bashing her head in kind of fitted the whole interrupted burglary theme I was going for. Nice girl, but with her gone there are more acting parts for me and a tidy little promotion with Jacob. Plus it made me number one on the bedroom front as well. Opportunities like this don't always come the way of a girl with my kind of upbringing. I'd have killed off Mitzi ages ago too if it wasn't for Jacob pussyfooting around and letting her linger on.'

Sarah squeezed Jacob's shoulder in an attempt to show her allegiance to him. He ignored her.

'But I spoke to people who saw Mitzi after the disappearance. That girl, Alice, at Hell's Canyon who told me about Tijuana.' Confusion blazoned itself across Georgia's face.

'Worked at the hotel owned by one of our club members. He said she could be bought easily. We gave her some cash and told her what to do. Her entire story was false. As for Tijuana, another unfortunate incident, but it took you out of my hair and away from Nova and me. One of the club members had driven the road vehicle directly from Hell's Canyon to Tijuana the night of Foster's death. It seemed as good a place as any and given Tijuana's size we thought it might be easy to make it disappear. We needed to make it look like Mitzi had done a runner. That's why I had somebody pretend to be her and accidently happen to be at the same hotel I booked you and Charlie into in Mexico. Didn't you think it was rather coincidental that both you and the road vehicle should happen to be at the same hotel in such an immense city?'

'But that person died. We saw them die in the van? We thought it was Mitzi. We thought she was gone.'

'An unfortunate casualty. Another of the club had been involved in the fetish scene in Mexico before so it was easy to hire a female impersonator to dress up as Mitzi. Again the power of money. I should have employed a woman but the sense of it being a man actually rather tickled me to be honest. I found it particularly dramatic. I also thought he'd be a better driver. Sadly he wasn't. He was supposed to lose you, not lose his own life. Having to explain how a female death actually turns up a male corpse is something not even money can buy a suitable explanation for.'

'But the police didn't seem to take it any further. Every clue seemed to reach a dead end.'

'Georgia, the society is very far reaching. We have members who can manage to see important papers and documents buried in the in-trays of even the busiest of police stations. Corruption is the foundation Hollywood was built on. And that corruption runs far and wide.'

There was silence, a moment of contemplation for Jacob as he looked back on what he had revealed to Georgia. At the role he had been forced to play by those around him. 'Jack Christie wasn't supposed to die, but I don't give a shit about him, that was just Sarah here being a little less Calamity Jane with her aim than she should have been. Shame really, as her skilled shooting was one of the reasons I thought she'd make such a perfect addition to the club. Thank God she missed Charlie, Nova would never have forgiven me if anything had happened

to him. It was supposed to be you on the receiving end, it had
to be to save my own skin. And now it's your turn, I'm afraid. I
truly am sorry, but it's you or me and I can't afford to lose this
battle.'

'How did you know I was here?' asked Georgia. If Jacob was
going to dispose of her then she needed to keep him talking. At
that moment in time it looked her only chance of survival.

'I knew you were coming here because I read your email to
Sarah last night. You should always close your mailbox before
leaving a room.'

'And *you* should always check who's listening to your conversations when you're talking on the phone. I heard you talking to
Sarah. I knew you were involved, I've suspected for while. Your
little chat confirmed it. But I just didn't know that everything
linked back to poor Mitzi too.'

'Well, now you do and it's all too late. Time for a drive, don't
you think? You and Mitzi in a car. Maybe you fall asleep at the
wheel, we can help with that with a little bang on the head, and
sadly you and the car disappear over the edge into a fireball of
oblivion. Just like in Tijuana except this time it really will be
Mitzi. And when the autopsy is done, two female bodies will be
identified, putting you two together. Maybe they'll think you
and Mitzi were in cahoots all along. I don't care what people
believe to be honest, because finally I can put this whole sorry
mess behind me. I'll have to lie to Nova, but this whole industry
is built on scandalous lies, so what's new? It'll break Nova and
Charlie's hearts for a while but they'll get over it. He'll just think
he picked a bad one in you after all, and Nova will be there to
pick up the pieces.'

'But it seems it's me who's picked a bad one.' The tearful
voice came from the top of the stairs where Nova and Charlie
were standing. Georgia wasn't even sure how long they'd been

standing there but it was obviously long enough for both of them to have caught wind of what was going on.

Relief washed over Georgia as she realised that at last her plan to alert Charlie had worked. She'd typed out a text message to her fiancé giving Sarah's address when she had been in the toilet. The text had told Charlie that he should come to the house immediately, that it had been Sarah who had fired the gun at Evie's event and that Georgia was now in grave danger. She had set it up so that all she had to do was press the send button on the phone at the moment when Sarah confessed to the shooting. She had placed the phone behind her back on the sofa when she had been sitting opposite Sarah. Thankfully the message had successfully sent when she had pressed the send button while wiping her sweaty hands and Charlie had reacted to it, obviously driving like the wind given the swiftness of his arrival. What Georgia hadn't planned on was that Nova might accompany him. Or that the tale of Sarah and the shooting would be linked back to Mitzi.

It was Nova who had just spoken at the top of the stairs. And it was she who continued to speak, horrified at what she and Charlie had heard. 'Not you, Jacob. I thought you were a good guy. I thought you and I ... we were forever. A true family.'

Jacob turned to stare at his wife and stepson in the doorway. The two people who he had hoped would never learn the truth. Or learn of his failure. His failure to stay top dog. He automatically pointed the gun at Nova as she spoke. Just the mere thought of what he was doing and the heartache he was causing her forced tears to fall, all former bravado evaporating as they flowed silently down his cheeks. She was the beautiful rose that he had never wanted to blacken with his actions.

'You weren't supposed to hear this, Nova. Never. I am a good man. I was, before all of this. I can be again. I should have given it all up when I met you, but I couldn't. How would that have looked? I started it all. This is bigger than just you and me.' He knew that his words were empty and useless. Regret raged through him, but it was too late to save his soul.

Nova shook her head as she stared down at her husband. There were many things she could forgive but putting her son in danger was not one of them. 'For me, nothing is bigger than you and me. Except this.' She reached out and held Charlie's hand. 'How could you? It's too late.'

'Don't say that, Nova, please.'

'But it is, Jacob, it is. There's no turning back. There's blood on your hands and that's something I won't ever be a part of.'

'But I had no choice, don't you understand?' His words were pathetic. Beyond hope. Beyond turning back.

'There's always a choice.' Nova's weren't.

For the second time in less than forty-eight hours, two shots sounded out in quick succession and two bodies once again fell to the floor. The woman, later identified as Sarah Ellison, Production Assistant on *Champagne Super Nova*, had died from a bullet shot directly into her chest. The second body, identified as media millionaire Jacob Chevalier, husband of the show's main star, had died from a bullet wound to the side of his head. Witnesses testified that Jacob had fired both bullets.

EPILOGUE

Georgia Bellamy sat herself down, let her head tilt back and the crisp freshness of the Chevalier sitting room leather sofa caress the back of her neck. She closed her eyes and let a cloud of fatigue wrap itself around her. Even months after her ordeal finding Mitzi had come to an end, there were still moments when a fear of what could have been gripped her soul, making her realise just how lucky she was to be alive. Both she and her friend, Mitzi.

Georgia had decided to stay on in Hollywood with Charlie and Nova at the Bel-Air home. She had grown increasingly fond of the kooky reality star and a bond of understanding had developed between them during the course of her quest to find Mitzi. Nova had always been there for her, protective and willing to help in any way possible. So when Charlie decided to give up his job on *Rise and Shine* to be with his mother, Georgia quit hers too. Nova was the closest thing Georgia now had to a caring mother of her own and she wanted to be there for her. Despite the nature of Jacob's demise, Georgia could see that Charlie had lost another father figure from his life, an occurrence that had happened far too many times for any one man. The thought of being without Charlie on a day-to-day basis was simply one she wouldn't even consider. He was hers for eternity, her constant sunshine no matter what storms life decided to throw at her.

The news of Jacob's death rocked Hollywood. Images of Nova filled virtually every front magazine cover that Georgia chose to read, no-one quite believing that such a big player as Jacob Chevalier, husband and producer behind the ultimate TV reality star could have been involved in something so seedy. The founding member of a secret sex society, a cult, one that seduced young actresses into believing that opening their legs would open their careers. A new kind of casting couch and one that had taken a fatal unexpected twist.

Georgia, Charlie and Nova would often sit and discuss how varied quarters of Hollywood media high life were reacting in different ways. For those with money it seemed to be a story which no-one wished to acknowledge. Maybe they were too close to the truth. Perhaps they feared that loose lips could still cost someone their million dollar job or embroil them in a scandal which they wanted to keep not just at arm's length, but in a different stratosphere altogether. It was a story wrapped up in barbed wire with the potential to damage many. Georgia would scan the credits of virtually every film or TV show and stare at the names of actors, producers, directors, execs who were potentially linked to the scandal. But with the gossip mongers of Hollywood obviously on shutdown as to who could potentially be involved in the secret society sex cult, even the most venomous of mags and websites seemed to treat the real reason behind Jacob Chevalier's suicide as a no trespassing area. Had they been paid for their silence? Lips were locked tight. Young aspiring actresses coming into town seemed to become suspicious about everything and any established actress giving TV interviews to promote her latest movie was quick to drop into conversation that they'd earned everything they had through sheer talent, hard work and determination. Some were telling the truth, some weren't. It was left for the public and for viewers like Georgia to decide.

For weeks after Jacob's death, Georgia had often heard Nova sobbing alone in her bedroom at night. It was a sound that would live with her forever. Such sorrow. The one thing that Nova desired was now gone for good and no money could ever buy it back. Her love for Jacob. Despite all that he had done they had been perfect together. She would never forgive him for what had passed, for the soiled legacy he had left her, but she was determined that she would look back on their happy times together as joyously as she could. All future episodes of *Champagne Super Nova* were cancelled at her request. Who could she trust? Nova's star would rise again, of that Georgia for sure, but for now she chose a life of privacy, of family, behind the gated façade of her estate. This was one story she would not be milking for publicity.

Georgia invited Devon and Tanya to come to Los Angeles to stay with them. Only for a vacation, as both Devon and his Russian bride preferred their climes a little cooler. Plus she knew LA would be a little too haphazard for her structured father's liking. Tanya seemed happy to be by Devon's side, and his happiness meant Georgia felt a new-found respect for the Russian that hadn't existed before. A mutual happiness causing a thawing between them. Hadn't they all suffered enough? Maybe now was the time for a white flag to be flown permanently. Tanya's mother sadly passed away due to a brief illness shortly after Devon and Tanya reunited. Tanya shared with Georgia how she took comfort in the fact that she had been able to make her mother's life as happy as possible in her final years, thanks to Devon. With the loss of her own mother came an understanding that the two women shared.

Devon chose never to tell Georgia what he had discovered about the truth behind the death of Sophia and Nicolas Belvoir.

Who would it profit? Jack Christie was dead and Andy North was serving time for his part in the events at Evie's charity night. Didn't Georgia have enough people to hate now that she had discovered the truth about Jacob and how the bullet that night at Evie's event had been meant for her?

Georgia had become closer to Evie after Mitzi's ordeal. The actress located to Los Angeles for her next movie, a rom-com casting her as the undecided, ditzy love interest stuck between falling head over heels in lust with her boss, played by Eddie Redmayne and settling down with her childhood sweetheart, played by Jamie Dornan. The two women often lunched, discussing Mitzi's recovery and reminiscing about the cards that life had dealt them. Evie explained to her what Victoria had been through with her addiction and over time, Georgia came to understand just what had made Victoria so vulnerable and insecure. After everything, she forgave.

Evie had donated the entire fee for her latest movie to funding the ongoing treatment of Mitzi Bidgood who was attempting to get over her ordeal with the best aid available. On a week's break midway through shooting the new movie, Evie was visited by Scott and Victoria and the twins. She had rented a huge secluded villa with a pool and play area as she knew that the children would be coming to stay. Georgia and Charlie had joined them for days around the pool, all thoughts of rivalry between Georgia and Victoria erased. Victoria and her husband seemed solid and even though Scott's injuries were still evident in the form of a crooked nose and a slight limp, neither of them were popping painkillers or pills of any kind. They brought their new nanny with them, a gay man called Jasper. It seemed that both Victoria and Scott adored him, as did the children.

Opening her eyes from her slumber, Georgia focussed on the huge plasma screen on the other side of the Chevalier sitting room. A familiar face filled it. Aaron Rose. Aaron had arrived in Hollywood at the start of pilot shooting season. Despite Jacob's death, those bigwigs who had survived the Mitzi scandal had decided that the rugged slab of prime British beefcake was exactly what was needed for their new show. It was news that his agent, Rachel Jerome, was overjoyed to relate to Aaron who had all but given up on securing the job. The pilot was badly written and Aaron's acting even worse, but somehow the public loved it and an entire series was commissioned. Before he knew it, Aaron's handsome, bearded face was staring down from billboards from Times Square to Tampa. His love interest in the show was played by Diana, the actress last seen in *Clampires*, the girl whom Charlie and Georgia had found crying her eyes out outside poor Addison's flat the day of her death. The role turned Diana into the star that she had always wanted to be. Despite initial bad reviews – and Georgia had to admit that the episodes she and Charlie had watched curled up on the sofa were beyond ridiculous with their farcical storylines – the show cleaned up come awards season, with Aaron bagging best TV newcomer. His award was presented by a beaming Nova, fighting fit and back to prove that there was life after loss. In her introduction she claimed that it was she who had discovered Aaron in the first place.

Georgia could hear the sound of the vacuum coming from upstairs. Juanita was doing her job. Nova had never had to reprimand the maid again about the state of her carpets. After Jacob's death, she had instructed Juanita to clean out the cupboards in order to donate all of Jacob's designer outfits to charity. Perhaps something good could come from his death. One of the cupboards was locked. When Juanita managed to find the key they found that it was full of hessian robes, the same ones used for the club 'performances'. The same hessian that had kept flaking all over the floor, much to Nova's annoyance and poor Juanita's perplexity. It never happened again.

Georgia looked around at the expensive trappings surrounding her. She may have been in the glamorous heights of Bel-Air, thousands of miles away from where she grew up and a million miles away from the home life she had shared with Devon and Sophia, but this was home now. And despite the madness of everything she had experienced it was one that was filled with the important things in life. Love and friendship. Two things she would never take for granted.

It was months later when Mitzi Bidgood finally returned to the UK, her recovery in Los Angeles complete. Thanks to funding by both Evie and Nova, Mitzi had been able to recover from her hideous ordeal in the quickest time possible and thanks to Evie organising a private jet, Mitzi's mother could be by her side throughout. She was frail but there was a newfound strength since discovering her only child was alive that allowed the elderly lady to feel up to travelling. For Mitzi the nightmare of losing Foster, of what she had seen in the Canyon, even when she discovered it to be fake, and the weeks of degradation locked away in the basement were things that she would never totally recover from. They would always be there as dark, haunting shadows in her mind. But as she stepped into the limelight of the London TV studios to give her first interview since her ordeal, she knew that she would be okay. She felt stronger, her body almost as it had been before that fateful night in the Canyon.

As she walked onto set to rapturous applause from those gathered in the audience, which included the newly-married Georgia and Charlie who had flown in especially to support her, the music that introduced the Saturday night TV show she used to dance on was played to accompany her entrance. It took her by surprise. She hadn't heard it for the longest time. She thought that it would freak her out, make her realise what she had lost. But somehow it didn't, because deep inside her once broken frame, she knew that one day soon she would dance again. If anything could banish those shadows for good it would be the lure of the dance floor. As Georgia watched on, she had never been prouder of her friend.

LETTER FROM NIGEL

Hi there everyone!

It's a scandal! I totally hope that you loved *Scandalous Lies* and that you became engrossed in every page-turning moment. Did you guess what had happened to Foster and Mitzi? Were you rooting for Georgia and Charlie? Did you fall under the spell of the madcap Nova? I hope that you enjoyed *Scandalous Lies* as much as I loved writing it. It was a blast!

One of the things that I loved doing with *Scandalous Lies* was relating back to things that you may have recognised from my previous books *Trinity* and *Addicted*. Evie Merchant was (and still is of course!) one of the three *Trinity* girls and if you'd like to see her play the leading role in one of my books then check out *Trinity*. Also The Abbey Rehabilitation Centre (where Victoria went) is the place featured in my thrilling romp *Addicted*. I love including things from other books as it makes everything so much more real for me in creating our own dynamic booky world!

If you enjoyed *Scandalous Lies* I would LOVE you to leave me a review on Amazon. Hearing what readers think is one of the many great pleasures of being an author. We spend months giving birth to these characters and crafting a tale for each of them so it's wonderful to hear what you think. Did devious Devon give you goosebumps? Did frosty Tanya send chills down your spine? Were you screaming at conniving Chloe? Would you like Aaron to be your gorgeous gardener? Let me know.

If you liked this book, perhaps you'd like to read some more of my sun-soaked blockbusters! And feel free to tell your friends. Let's all catch up on Twitter, Facebook and Goodreads too. I'm never happier than when I'm talking about my stories, especially if people love the characters as much as I do.

To keep right up-to-date with the latest news on my hot new releases just sign up at:

www.bookouture.com/nigel-may

I'll see you poolside in some glamorous exotic location soon with more fabulous adventures!

Stay scandalous!

Nigel x

 @Nigel_May

www.nigelmay.net

TRINITY

When friends become enemies there are no rules…

Ambitious gossip queen **Anoushka Silvers** is the daughter her abusive father never wanted. Determined to prove herself to her family, she'll stop at nothing to get what she wants. But when her bitchy tongue gains her death threats and the unwanted attention of a stalker, it could be Anoushka who is making the headlines.

For actress **Evie Merchant**, her childhood dreams of becoming the world's hottest movie star are just about to come true. But a string of hurtful liaisons with lovers out to use her fame, has made Evie uncertain about her future. And with Oscar day looming, Evie's biggest prize of all could be cruelly snatched from her.

A loveless upbringing has made wild child **Regan Phoenix** search for quick-fix highs from drink, drugs and meaningless sex. But when the opportunity of starring in her own reality show comes along, Regan grabs it with both hands, hoping to put her trashy past behind her.

From fashionable London to stunning Venice and glitzy LA, Trinity takes you into a glamorous and thrilling world you won't want to leave.

'**An addictive plot that is packed with twists and turns.** Prepare for larger than life characters, fabulous locations and plenty of humour.' *The Sun*

'Trinity is so much fun. **A great summer bonkbuster.**' Tasmina Perry

ADDICTED

Fame, fortune and five-star luxury. Meet four fabulous women – all of them hold a dark secret… one of them won't live to tell the tale.

Nancy Arlow – the fading entertainer determined to gamble and charm her way out of a mountain of debt.

Laura Everett– behind the façade of the perfect politician's wife lies a woman with an outrageous past and a spiraling drug habit.

Portia Safari– the world famous opera diva, adored by millions, has it all, but could her secret drinking problem cost her everything?

Martha Éclair– The millionaire wine heiress whose appetite for kinky sex could bring down her father's business empire.

Each woman must face their own addiction before they pay the ultimate price…

Switch off your phone, grab a glass of bubbly and escape into an outrageous word of thrills, glamour and passion. You'll be addicted…

'Packed full of sauciness, darkness and intrigue, this lively romp of a story takes you on a colourful journey through the world of showbiz, from the ultra-highs to the face-planting lows. **If you're**

looking for a sexy, racy, riotous read for your sun lounger this summer, this is the perfect choice.' *Heat* Magazine

'ADDICTED is **a sexy, dark, thrilling celebrity whirlwind** that lifts the curtain on some blistering superstar scandal. It's the most fun you can have between two covers. I need more!' Victoria Fox